S0-BMW-150

Dear Reader,

With decadent desserts and darling doggies, Duets has a double dose of delights for your reading pleasure!

Weddings mean one thing to caterer Delilah James: wedding cake, something she is far too intimate with, at least as evidenced by the inches on her hips. Zach Tanner, the hero of Kimberly Raye's *How Sweet It Is,* however, finds every inch of her absolutely delectable. In *Second-Chance Groom* by Eugenia Riley, the bride-to-be never gets a chance to cut into her wedding cake as she runs off with the best man! But he's not the marrying kind.... Both of these delicious stories are found in Duets #11.

Duets #12 meanwhile goes to the animals! In Sandra Paul's *Head Over Heels,* Prudence McClure, dressed as a cat at a Halloween party, casts her feline spell over handsome Nicholas Ware—but what happens the morning after? Then Godzilla the matchmaking dog takes control of his errant humans' love lives in *Puppy Love* by Cheryl Anne Porter.

Enjoy the laughter and the romance.

*Malle Vallik*

Malle Vallik
Senior Editor

## How Sweet It Is

### *"Luuuceee! I'm home!"*

Delilah's jaw dropped. She knew that voice...

"Honeybunch," the voice drawled. Suddenly, she was hauled up from the chair. "Sorry I'm late, but the guys and I stopped off for a couple of brewskies."

Delilah gulped, turning to find herself face-to-face with Zach Tanner. His firm mouth touched hers, making her lips tingle. Worse, other places were doing some major tingling of their own.

"Delilah? What in the world is going on?" her mother asked.

"I'm sorry, ma'am. I just couldn't wait to say hello to my little woman," Zach said.

Zach smiled and Delilah barely resisted the urge to land a well-deserved kick to Zach's backside. He was laying it on pretty thick.

"My, my, you're the charmer, aren't you?" Gladys giggled.

Delilah looked away as heat rose in her cheeks. Unfortunately, she knew all too well just how *charming* Zach could be....

*For more, turn to page 9*

## Second-Chance Groom

## *What was happening to her?*

Cassie couldn't be standing at her own wedding and feeling attracted to the best man, someone she'd never met before! Yet, she was thoroughly intrigued by Brian Drake, his touching gift of the flowers for her bouquet, and especially the passion for life she glimpsed in his eyes.

The minister's voice jerked Cassie back to reality. The reverend paused for dramatic effect and then continued, "For who can predict that magical moment when one looks across a room, sees a certain face and falls in love?"

These last words electrified her. Again she found her face riveted to Brian's. Again she glimpsed that sexy, devilish smile, and her insides melted.

This couldn't be happening to her! Surely it was impossible for a handful of blue columbine to change a person's life, or for a stranger's smile to steal her heart.

But Brian Drake was doing it....

*For more, turn to page 197*

HARLEQUIN DUETS

ISBN 0-373-44077-4

HOW SWEET IT IS
Copyright © 1999 by Kimberly Raye Rangel

SECOND-CHANCE GROOM
Copyright © 1999 by Eugenia Riley Essenmacher

# KIMBERLY RAYE

## How Sweet It Is

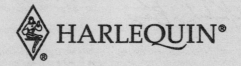

# HARLEQUIN®

TORONTO • NEW YORK • LONDON
AMSTERDAM • PARIS • SYDNEY • HAMBURG
STOCKHOLM • ATHENS • TOKYO • MILAN • MADRID
PRAGUE • WARSAW • BUDAPEST • AUCKLAND

Dear Reader,

I've always loved bad boys! So when Zach Tanner, the hero of *How Sweet It Is,* strode onto the stage, I was hooked. He's sinfully handsome with a wicked smile, a naughty sense of humor and enough charm to make even the strongest woman melt. And he proves it when he sets his sights on gourmet cheesecake caterer Delilah James. The *last* thing Delilah wants in her life is a marriage-minded alpha male like Zach. At least, that's what she's telling herself and her matchmaking mother, and anyone else who'll listen. It's a classic case of denial that ends in true love, with a little help from Momma Gladys, of course!

I'm so happy to be writing for Duets. I love romantic comedy, and this story is one of my favorites since it contains two of life's finest offerings—a sexy man and cheesecake! And you can enjoy both right here without gaining an ounce.

I hope you enjoy reading *How Sweet It Is*. I'd love to hear from you. You can drop me a note at P.O. Box 1584, Pasadena, TX 77501-1584.

Wishing you lots of love and laughter,

Kimberly Raye

For Joe.
I'll love you always.

# 1

DELILAH JAMES CLUTCHED the back of her skirt, fled down the crowded hallway of the youth center and shoved open the first door she found. A storage closet. An *empty* storage closet. There was a God!

She slammed the door, flipped on the light and plopped her purse between a roll of paper towels and an industrial-size bottle of Mr. Clean. Taking a deep breath, she tried to calm her pounding heart.

She was *not* going to cry!

So what if she'd busted the zipper on her new skirt? So what if she'd been about to get her picture taken with the mayor of Dallas? So what if that picture would have been a sure shot to a load of free advertising for her gourmet cheesecake business? And so what if a dozen six-year-olds had started chanting, "Yessirree, I declare, I see someone's underwear?"

So *what?*

She blinked, sniffled and squared her shoulders. "Stop it. You own a company, employ seven people and you're up for Dallas's entrepreneur of the year. You're a calm, controlled professional." She *was*. Usually. Then a quick bend to pick up a napkin she'd dropped and *ripppp!*

She twisted and stared at her backside. The rip ran from her waist, down the middle of her derriere. The edges gaped, revealing a pair of lace undies. Undies that an entire group of carnival-goers—kids, counselors, not to mention sponsors—had seen. Several of them male sponsors. Good-looking, successful, *eligible* males.

Jeez, her mother was probably having a heart attack at this very moment. Mothers could sense these things even across vast distances such as the three hundred miles that separated Dallas from Houston. Gladys James knew instinctively when her only daughter was hurt, in danger or ruining possible marriage prospects.

She opened her purse and started hunting for safety pins. Not that she, Delilah Belle James, was in the market for a man. With her cheesecake business on the rise, she was too busy with short, sweet and delicious to have much time for tall, dark and handsome. But did her mother understand that? Of course not. Mom wouldn't be happy until Delilah was married and making babies instead of cheesecakes.

Delilah retrieved a safety pin.

It wasn't that she didn't want kids. She loved kids, otherwise she wouldn't be spending her Saturday at a local orphanage, sponsoring the Spring Carnival's cake walk. Kids were great and she certainly wanted some of her own, but not *now*. There was no way she could take care of a husband and family *and* manage her business. Delilah had learned by watching her own mother that such a thing was impossible.

Years from now, after How Sweet It Is hit its peak, after her cheesecakes became a staple in every household and she fulfilled her ten-year business plan—she was only on year four—she could put aside her career and focus on domestic bliss. A husband to love and a baby on each hip. Apparently, right now, her hips were big enough on their own.

She wiped at another tear and searched frantically for another safety pin. *Stop crying. It's your own fault anyway. You should've bought a larger size.*

*Larger?* But she'd been the same size for years. Even as a teenager, she'd been a voluptuous—her mother's nice way of saying chubby—size twelve. She glanced down at the ripped seam and her eyes burned with renewed vigor. Heavens, she was larger—

Reality check! Accept it and get on with life. There were worse things that could happen. She could accidentally mistake the salt for sugar in a batch of her cheesecakes. Her mother could set her up on *another* blind date. Her fifty-gallon mixer could blow up. Her mother could sign her up for another one of those dating services. Her two delivery drivers could call in sick on the same day. Her mother could write her phone number on the men's room wall at the Astrodome *again*. Her present moment of misery could be interrupted by a half-dressed Batman— *Wait a second.*

Her hand stalled in the bottom of her purse as she stared over her shoulder at the figure who'd just burst into the closet behind her.

Batman? All those fad diets were finally getting to her. She was light-headed from lack of solid food. She blinked, but he was still there. The famous Caped Crusader—tall, powerful, *male*. Black and gray body-clinging spandex accented a well-muscled torso and sculpted arms. Black tights hugged his powerful legs, muscular thighs, his, um, you know... *Wow*.

"Is there anyone else in here?" His voice drew her attention upward.

The top half of his face was hidden beneath his mask. He had a strong jaw shadowed with dark stubble, firm lips, high cheekbones. A pair of blue eyes—like twin blue laser beams—stared back at her through the eyeholes of the mask. Intense. Assessing. Suddenly she felt like a deer caught in a blaze of neon-blue headlights.

"I…" She cleared her throat. "If you mean Bat Girl or Cat Woman, I'm afraid they've already left."

He grinned. "Actually I was talking about kids." He shoved his cape over one shoulder and stared down at his side. "I just need a little elbow room to get this suit zipped all the way. The men's room is packed with six-year-olds screaming about some lady's panties—" His voice broke off as his gaze fixed on her torn skirt.

*Could the earth just open wide and suck me down now?*

"I figured they'd be through chanting by now." She faced him, effectively killing his view. "It's been at least ten minutes."

He smiled, a flash of white brilliance in the dimly lit closet and the air stalled in Delilah's lungs. "Black," he said. "I like black panties."

"Um, me, too." *Me, too?* She was standing in a storage closet discussing panties with Batman. What next? Spin the bottle with Spider Man?

"Yeah, I sort of figured that." His gaze took a leisurely trek down the front of her skirt, to her legs encased in sheer black stockings—everyone knew black was slimming and Delilah needed all the help she could get—clear down to her feet stuffed into matching pumps. "Do you always wear black panties or is this a special-occasion thing?"

"I have other colors, but black went with the suit and I had to wear this suit. This is—was—my favorite suit and I always wear it for publicity pictures, not that I'll be posing for any now, but that's for the best anyway. I'm not really photogenic and when I found out there would be press here to cover the carnival, I almost said no—I donated the cheesecakes for the cake walk—but then how could I say no to all of those kids?" She laughed. "I mean, I promised, and just because I hate getting my picture taken is no reason to deny a bunch of little kids." She grimaced. "I'm rambling, huh?'' She rubbed her hands together. ''I always ramble when I'm nervous, not that I'm usually nervous. I'm never nervous so I never ramble, but today hasn't been my typical day. First my skirt rips in front of at least a dozen sponsors, then I meet you in here and, uh, not that you make me nervous.'' She swallowed. *Jeez, did he have to stare at her like that?* She tried for a smile. ''It's not every day you run into Batman.''

He grinned. ''The carnival theme is superheroes. I'm the photo booth attraction.'' He twisted and tugged at his side zipper. ''That's why I need to get this thing up. The booth opened five minutes ago. I'm late and the line is already twenty kids strong.''

''Here.'' She scooted around him, careful to keep her partially exposed backside well out of his viewing range. ''Let me see if I can help.'' Her hand paused and her heart kick-started. The zipper had stopped midthigh. From there on up, the fabric gaped open to reveal a hard, tanned body and a pair of black briefs. *Zowie.*

While she wasn't exactly a virgin when it came to seeing men's bodies—she had three older brothers—this was different. He was different.

*Well, of course he is. He's Batman, for heaven's sake.* On the surface. But she'd always prided herself on not taking people at face value. *It's what's underneath that counts, and boy, does he have it underneath!*

She took a deep breath and gripped the zipper, careful not to touch any bare skin. Touching was a bad idea because then she was liable to unzip and that wouldn't do at all. He was expected in the photo booth and she made it a habit never to molest superheroes in storage closets.

Closing her eyes, she tugged. Out of sight, out of mind. ''I think some of the material's stuck. Let me see if I can...'' Okay, so he was out of sight, but he was still right there. Warm and strong against her fingertips, her knuckles—everywhere she happened to touch while fighting with the zipper. "It doesn't seem to want to cooperate."

"Tell me about it. So you're into cheesecakes, huh?"

"The best in Texas." *If only the darned thing would zip.*

"I love cheesecake. So how big is your business?" *Not nearly as big as your...*

She cleared her throat. "Well, I, um, produce about eighty dozen cheesecakes a week, but I'm expanding. It's still a small operation. I give it a lot of hands-on."

"Hands-on? Now that sounds interesting."

Her fingers slipped and she wiped her hands on her feeble excuse for a skirt. She could feel him staring down at her, smiling, and she fought for a breath. *Don't look at him. Don't look at his body. Just don't.*

"Is this your first time as a volunteer?" he asked.

"Uh, yes, but I plan on doing it again." Her hand worked at the material and zipper. Push, pull. Push, pull... Definitely the wrong verbs to be thinking of with a half-dressed man at her fingertips. "The kids—" she cleared her throat "—they're, um, really great. How about you?"

"I think they're great, too."

"I meant, what's your story? Is this your first time here?"

"No, I'm a regular. I come out once or twice a week, do what I can. I don't think most people realize how much an hour here and there means to these kids." The words, so heartfelt and sincere, rang through her head, thrummed through her body and zapped something deep inside her.

No. Nothing deep. She didn't have time for deep. She struggled, muttered, then gave one hard tug. Her eyes opened just in time to say adios to all that great tanned skin. "There. All done."

"Hey, thanks." He smiled and her heart kick-started. "Now your turn."

"No, that's really not necessar—oh!" Strong fingers gripped her waist and swung her around. "Look, you don't have to do that. I can manage on my own."

"Fair's fair." He tugged at the edges of her skirt. His fingers burned through the thin protection of her panties and Delilah swallowed. They were so close and he was so warm and he smelled so good.

"Do you have a safety pin?" His deep voice slid into her ears and prickled her skin.

"Uh, sure." She dropped the one she'd unearthed into his open palm and tried not to think about him. Behind her. His hands on her—

"You have any more?"

"More?" *More* was a nice word. More of him surrounding her. More warm touches on certain parts of her body. Yeah, more was really good.

"More safety pins," he said, shattering her thoughts. "I don't think one's going to do it."

*A dozen wouldn't do it,* not with the size of the rip and the size of her...assets. The realization brought a wave of tears to her eyes and she sniffled.

"You're not crying, are you?"

"No," she choked, wiping at her face.

He eased her around to stare down at her. One strong finger tilted her chin up. "You're crying."

"Okay, I am, but I usually never cry. Ever. Except when my mother comes to visit." She swiped at her cheeks. "Not that I don't love my mother. I do. She's great, but last time she came, she set me up with this guy at the corner gas station. Not that I have anything against gas station attendants. He was sort of cute and really nice. He brought me a few handfuls of green stamps—at first I thought they were

shamrocks—he was Irish, you know, and I thought it was
an Irish gesture. But no, they were green stamps. Not that
I don't like green stamps. It's really the thought that counts
and I even got a free coffeemaker, which I sent to my mom
as a bribe to please, *please* butt out of my personal life.
But you know mothers—"

He touched a fingertip to her lips. "Can't say that I do.
Mine died when I was just a kid. That's why I volunteer
here. I grew up in an orphanage just like this."

"Oh." Her eyes teared up again. "I'm sorry. I had no
idea. You must think I'm a complete dimwit."

"I wouldn't say complete. Maybe a quarter." He gave
her a teasing grin, wiped a trickle of wetness from her
cheek, and Delilah all but melted into a puddle at his feet.
A guy who didn't freak when a woman turned on the wa-
terworks? *Take me to the Batcave, baby!*

"I've got an idea." He unhooked his cape, folded it over,
then wrapped and belted it around her waist. "There. It's
the same color as your suit. Nobody will ever notice."

She sniffled again. "But you can't give up your cape.
What's Batman without his cape?"

"I've still got the rest of the outfit. What's the use of
being a superhero if I can't help a lady in distress?"

Handsome, nice, chivalrous and he wasn't afraid of a
crying, tactless woman… Oh my God, it was him. *Him!*

No, no, no. She'd barely met this guy. No way could she
know this stranger was *him*. Mr. Right. The One. A Big
Three man—sweet, sensitive and sincere. A man who
would stand by her. Who would make babies and change
diapers and get up for feedings in the middle of the night.
Who would love her until his last breath and never leave
his socks on the floor and happily eat take-out when she
was too tired to cook, or who would even cook himself.

No way. Besides, she wasn't ready. *Him* would come

later, in six or so years when her business wasn't so demanding, after she'd won the Sara Lee award for best dessert and finished her ten-year plan. Not a day sooner. Not *now*.

"Cheer up, okay?" He wiped a tear at the corner of her eye and a tingle of warmth shot through her. *A tingle. Oh, no.*

"You—you're touching me," she blurted.

"Is that what I'm doing?" He grinned while his fingertip blazed a tantalizing trail down her cheek. *Tantalizing?*

Was her mother playing with that voodoo doll again? What the woman wouldn't do to see her only daughter married.

"You really shouldn't do that. I mean, we don't even know each other."

"Sure we do. I'm Batman and you're…"

"Delilah."

"Batman and Delilah. So there. We know each other." He stopped just shy of brushing her lips. "You've got really soft skin, Delilah."

"You've got really great hands, Batman." *Batman?* Was she insane? Yes, she was. Batman was touching—no, caressing her—and she was convinced he was *him*. No, not him. This was way too soon. Way too fast.

"Really soft skin," he said again. His finger lingered, and then he surprised them both. He leaned down and kissed her, his lips firm and warm against hers…. Oh, no.

*"Her."* The word was no more than a murmured sigh against her mouth, or maybe it was her imagination. Yeah, her imagination. That had to be it, because he wasn't her *him* and she wasn't his *her*. Delilah James didn't believe in love at first sight. Not between real people in the real world.

He deepened the kiss and her thoughts disintegrated.

Mouths moved, tongues tangled, bodies arched, and it was the Fourth of July in March. Fireworks exploded in her head. Her hormones sang "America."

And then it was over.

"I... You—you kissed me." She held a hand to her trembling lips and tried to figure out what had just happened. He'd kissed her. She'd kissed him. They'd kissed each other and it had been unlike anything she'd ever experienced before. *Him. Her. Them...*

"Sorry. I didn't mean to get carried away." He looked as surprised as she felt. "It's just that you have such soft skin and...it's crazy, but it just seemed right." He shook his head, as if amazed at the realization. "Yeah, it seemed *really* right. Here. Now. You and me." The shrill ring of her cellular phone punctuated his sentence.

*Saved by the bell.* Unfortunately.

She pulled out her phone. "This is Delilah."

"Delilah!" screeched a woman on the other end.

"You've got great timing, Lisa."

"The mixer's on the blink, I've got four dozen cakes to make this morning and—sweet Jesus! I think I saw a spark! Ohmigod, it's on fire!"

"It's not on fire," Harold, Delilah's delivery boy, shouted in the background. "Keep cool, boss. It just sparked."

"Okay, Lisa. Just calm down. You and Harold cut off the electricity to the mixer and I'll call a repairman."

"Trouble at home?" he asked once she'd dialed Abe's Appliances, reported the problem and hung up.

"My business." She tucked her phone away. "I really have to go." *Move,* her brain screamed, but her feet refused to cooperate. He was this close to kissing her again. She could feel the warm rush of his breath, the heat from his body. *Lay one on me, baby.*

Her eyes closed and he leaned down. She felt his breath fan her lips. His mouth brushed her cheek and disappointment jerked through her. *Her cheek? Hey, no fair.*

Then he stared down at her, into her and she did the impossible. She tingled again. But, this time, all over, from her head to the tips of her toes. *Oh, no.*

"Maybe we could get together later?" he asked.

Yes! No! It couldn't be *him,* but she was tingling and she never tingled. The past year, since her father's death, had been filled with her mother's matchmaking schemes, and Delilah hadn't once tingled. No sweaty palms or hot flashes or unconscious panting. Nothing, but now... Yep, her mother was definitely doing the voodoo thing again. Maybe even a love potion.

*No!* "I *really* have to go." As if on cue, her cellular phone started ringing again, accompanied by pounding on the door. "Batman? Are you in there? This is Joy. I'm the photographer at the photo booth. We've got a mile of kids waiting for you and I need you front and center."

Their eyes caught for one long moment before the ringing and the pounding finally spurred them into action. Delilah dived for her phone and he opened the door.

"Later," he promised.

Then he disappeared, leaving Delilah stunned, and oddly disappointed. *Him.*

"IT STILL SMELLS like smoke in here." Lisa, Delilah's right hand and one of the best pastry chefs in Texas, walked through Delilah's office, a can of air freshener in her hand. "Lucky for you the fire didn't spread to all these records and computer equipment."

"For the last time, there wasn't a fire. Just some major sparks when you didn't shut the electricity off like I told you to." Delilah stared at the open doorway that connected her office to a commercial kitchen where she produced her cheesecakes.

The "sweet" wing as she liked to call it, had been added to the two-story Colonial she called home more than four years ago. While she liked the freedom of being near her work—she could crawl out of bed, walk downstairs, and she was there—she still had fantasies of big factories and corporate offices.

"There were flames shooting up to here." Lisa, a petite brunette with pixie-short hair and sparkling green eyes, raised her arms dramatically and shot off more air freshener. "I could've been toast!"

*"There was no fire."* Delilah examined the ticket the appliance repairman had left. "It was a faulty plug. That's what Abe said, and the firemen confirmed it."

"What do those stuffy firefighters know? They got here after the worst was over."

"The station's three blocks away. The truck made it in one minute and twenty-two seconds, and Harold said they were pretty upset to find a false alarm."

"So there wasn't an actual fire. There could have been. I was just being cautious."

"You were overreacting, as usual."

"I couldn't help myself. I saw those sparks and, I swear, my life flashed before my eyes. You know, I've never been to the Caribbean, or gone ice skating or climbed a mountain." She blew out a deep breath. "You know what? I'm going to turn over a new leaf. No more boring Friday nights perfecting my baklava recipe. I'm gonna go out and live it up, starting tonight." She turned an expectant gaze on Delilah. "So what do you say? You want to join me?"

Delilah shook her head. "I've got work to do. I lost three hours doing that charity carnival."

"How'd you make out?"

*In a storage closet with Batman.* She smiled. "The cheesecakes were a huge success. Mitzi, the orphanage's administrator, called an hour ago and said the cake walk made more money for the kids than any other booth."

"Great. We should definitely go out and celebrate. Your charitable contributions and my escape from near-death. Let's check out one of those retro clubs. What do you say?"

Delilah stared at the stack of ledgers on her desk. "Friday night is invoice night."

"And Saturday night is inventory," Lisa chimed in. "Boring. You need to get out and meet some men. How are you ever going to find Mr. Right with a nonexistent social life?"

"Have you been talking to my mother?" At Lisa's guilty expression, Delilah sighed. "You have been talking to my mother."

"She called today while you were at the charity thing. She said her hairdresser's sister's son is coming into town next week on business. He's a dentist with his own practice. She said he's perfect for you and she already told him you were dying to show him around."

"Oh, no." Delilah buried her head in her hands. *Mom strikes again.*

"Cheer up. He sounds kind of nice."

She lifted her head and squared her shoulders. Crying wouldn't do a bit of good. If her mom set it up, it was going to happen whether she liked it or not. Better to face the music. "Okay, what does he look like?"

"Your mother's exact words?"

*No.* "Yes."

"About a hundred thousand a year. Two-story house near the lake, and a nice four-door BMW perfect for her two future grandchildren." Delilah groaned, and Lisa added, "It's not that bad. A dentist and a cheesecake caterer. It does sort of go together. You rot their teeth, he fixes them."

"Bye, Lisa."

"See you Monday, boss."

Delilah took a deep breath and switched on her computer. A stack of invoices later, the clock struck midnight and the phone rang.

"Aha! I caught you."

Delilah's usually efficient fingers slipped on the keys. A row of zeros appeared, sending the cumulative total of cheesecakes off the screen.

"Mom?" She punched the delete key.

"It's Friday night and where are you? Sitting in your office, huddled in front of your computer."

Her fingers slid again and she added a string of nines to her numerical display. "Mom, you didn't bug the place the last time you were here, did you?"

"A mother knows these things, dear. Why, I bet you haven't even changed your clothes, or eaten a sensible dinner."

Delilah gave up on the frenzied screen to stare down at her wrinkled jacket and torn skirt, the Batman cape still tied around her waist. A half-full glass of Aunt Shirley's Shake-Away, the fat-burning chocolate drink Delilah was trying this week, sat on her desk next to an empty can of diet soda. Who needed Big Brother when Gladys James was within a three-hundred-mile radius?

"Work, work, work," her mother clucked. "Dear, you'll never meet a man as wonderful as your dear departed father if you keep this up."

Her computer launched into overdrive, staging a riot against Delilah's capable hands. Numbers blinked. Scrolled.

She shut her eyes. "Mom, I don't need a man, period. I'm really busy right now. What is it? Are you crying?"

"Of course not," her mother said, the sentence punctuated with a huge sniffle. "Don't mind me. I'm just fine. I don't care what that stuffy old Dr. Harris says."

"Dr. Harris? Wasn't he the cardiologist who attended Dad?"

"The day your father—bless his soul—keeled over. Anyhow, I told that man I didn't need to take a stress test, but he insisted and—"

"A stress test? What for?"

"Just a few little chest pains. It's nothing, dear. Really. And I still can't believe that Dr. Harris had enough nerve to insinuate that my heart is under duress. Why, I haven't felt this good since I ate your Aunt Bertha's cheese casserole—"

"Duress?"

"My heart is pumping double time, at least according to Dr. Harris. Take it easy, he says. Let the kids fend for themselves. If your daughter winds up old and lonely, at least you tried."

"Wait a second. You're telling me you're under stress because of me? Did the doctor say that?"

"Of course not, dear. And it's nothing. You can't help it if you can't meet Mr. Right, and I can't help but worry over you. A mother can sense when one of her own flesh and blood is unhappy, and how can I not be concerned? My own daughter, alone and miserable and—"

"I'm not alone." *Don't say any more. Take it back. Just take it back and keep your mouth shut before you say something you'll really regret.* "I—I've got company, Mom." *Big mouth.*

"Company?"

"I've got someone here. A man." *A man? What the*

heck was she doing? Having a nervous breakdown. A big one. "Yeah, a man. A good-looking, single man. We—we were just going over my accounts."

"Is he your accountant?"

"Accountant? Uh, yes, no. I mean, yes he's *an* accountant, but not *my* accountant. I mean, I guess he's *my* accountant, so to speak, considering he's my man." My man? "We talk shop once in a while and he offered to look over my business records and help me find ways to cut costs." Rambling again. Twice in one day. Definitely a breakdown. "Once we finish here, we're headed out for a midnight snack or a moonlit walk or something romantic."

"What's his name?" Breathless excitement laced the question and killed any hope Delilah had of retracting her string of statements. Her mother was suffering chest pains because she worried too much over her only daughter. Yours truly. Talk about guilt.

"Name? Uh, it's..." Her gaze shot around for something. *Anything.* "Well, you see it's..." She fingered the cape still wrapped around her waist and blurted out, "Batman." *Batman? Great, Delilah. Get ready for the straitjacket.*

"What, dear? We must have a bad connection. It sounded like you said—"

"That man," she cut in. "That man's name—er, I mean this man's name is..." Her gaze darted to a nearby bookshelf and she blurted the first word she saw. "Percy." Percy? "Yeah, Percy. He's here and we're going out." Her hands gripped the cape and she closed her eyes, feeling as if she'd just jumped overboard. Nothing to do now but try to swim. "You should see him, Ma. George Clooney's got nothing on him. He's a dream. An absolute dream..."

*Funny farm, here I come.*

# 2

*Six months later*

"OKAY, WE'RE HERE. So now what?"

Delilah stared at the attractive dark-haired man standing in the cookie aisle of the local Food Mart and steeled herself. "Now I put on my sexiest smile, strut over there and bang him."

"*Bang* him?" came the shocked voice of Delilah's best friend, Melanie. "You've lost it, Dee. That, or you're light-headed from lack of nourishment. I told you to give up that grapefruit diet."

"His *cart*, Melanie. Bang his cart. And the grapefruits were last month. I'm doing the Banana Fat Basher this week."

"Just bananas?" At Delilah's nod, Mel added, "Well, that explains why you look ready to faint."

"No, it doesn't." Delilah turned determined eyes on her best friend. "My mom's coming to visit day after tomorrow."

"You poor thing."

"She called and sprang the news on me this morning." Delilah turned her gaze back to her prospective target. "I've got seventy-two hours to find a man."

"But here? This whole idea is ridiculous."

"With a great build," Delilah went on. "And dark hair."

"Get real, Dee. The man's a *stranger*."

"Not for long. Besides, *Cosmo* says the grocery store is a prime place to meet eligible bachelors."

"For *desperate* women."

"That's me." Otherwise Delilah would never be caught dead standing in the middle of a crowded supermarket on a Monday morning, scoping out every male who fell into the category of over eighteen, but not quite ready for the motorized grocery cart.

Then again, she thought when a cute little elderly man zoomed past her and winked. Maybe...

She shook away the notion. She had criteria to meet, and the cookie guy was the closest she'd come so far. Brunette, nice body, great tush, just a little over six feet... Now to get a front look.

Seconds later, Delilah was apologizing to a very handsome green-eyed babe for banging her cart into his, crushing two packs of Oreos and sending his six-pack of beer flying across the aisle. "Tall enough, but the wrong eye color," she told Melanie when she rolled back.

"I'm telling you, Dee. That's where you made your mistake." Melanie grabbed an Oreo bag and fished for a cookie. "You were too specific with your mom."

"Tell me something I don't know, Sherlock." She gripped the cart with renewed determination. "But there's no use crying over it now. What's done is done. I just have to find someone."

"As your accountant, I have to advise you to give this up for the good of your business. It's nearly ten o'clock on a Monday morning. You have today's production to think of."

"Big Tex Bistros," Delilah cut in. "Two dozen Raspberry Rumbas, three dozen Tangerine Tangos and four dozen Chocolate Cherry Cha-Chas—noon delivery, check. Daphne's Tea Room—six dozen Hazlenut Hustles, five dozen Pecan Praline Polkas, and two dozen Macadamian

Mambos—one p.m. delivery, check. Wild Man Ribs—four dozen Chocolate Cherry Cha-Chas for three different test locations—five p.m. delivery, check.''

"Okay, so daily production is covered. What about staff supervision? What if Lisa dumps oranges into your Luscious Lemon Lambada or chocolate chips into the Cappuccino Charleston? What if Marge pulls everything out of the oven too soon, or Fritz decides to alter the temperature in the cooling room?''

"I sorted supplies and left specific instructions before I left, and this trip is not a waste of time. I'm buying spices for product development.'' She held up a bottle. "Until I get my new Tutti-Frutti Twist perfected, I can't buy bulk. I had to shop, so I might as well kill two birds with one stone.''

"Okay, forget staff supervision. What about the presentation for Wild Man Ribs? You've been working to get this account for the past two months.''

"It's covered. I've got a full proposal that gives them top-of-the-line cheesecakes at a great price. Jeff Black— he's the manager—will be falling over himself to give me their entire account.'' She glanced at her watch. "If only my personal life were going half as well. I've got one hour and forty-five minutes before I have to get back to the kitchen, so let's hurry this up.''

Melanie shook her head. "This is crazy. Call your mother and come clean. Just tell her you don't want to get married, that your business comes first and you don't need a man to validate you.''

"And risk her having a full-blown heart attack like my dad? There were never any warning signs with him. One day he just keeled over. At least Ma is forewarning everyone. I have to think of her health.'' Delilah watched Mel eat two cookies. Her tastebuds watered, her stomach grumbled, and she mentally calculated how many bananas she would have to forgo if she ate half a cookie.

"Didn't you think when you made up this guy that she might want to meet him? I mean, he is supposed to be her prospective son-in-law."

"I was desperate and she was crying and..." She reached for a cookie. "I opened my mouth and out it came. I figured that later, when she started to feel better, I could say we broke up. That he was a rotten snake and she wouldn't want him in the family anyway."

"So use the rotten snake story now. You said yourself she passed the stress test with flying colors."

Delilah shook her head. "I can't. You know my mother. She's the queen of guilt trips, and it's gotten even worse since my dad died. She's used to taking care of someone and now that he's gone, I'm the someone."

"What about your brothers?"

"It's not the same. I'm her only daughter, her only chance to live out her unfulfilled wedding fantasies." Delilah snatched a cookie out of Mel's hand, popped it into her mouth and ignored a rush of guilt. "I have to find someone. Otherwise, she's likely to have a relapse, or bury me in guilt, or both." They rounded a corner and started up the next aisle. A timid man with a cart saw them and rushed the other way. "I figured I could just show up with a guy, one who meets the description, and say we're planning on a long engagement."

"You're just prolonging the inevitable."

"I know. But it's too soon after her recent heart problems. Once I'm sure she's completely healthy, I'll come up with a way to fade Mr. Perfect out of the picture."

"Hey!" Mel's eyes lit with a smile, "I bet Ralph's cousin, the one we introduced you to last month, would probably jump at the chance to help you out."

"Get real, Mel. The guy is the current belching champion of Texas."

"He's accomplished," Melanie said defensively.

"He belches the Cotton-Eyed Joe."

"So he's musically inclined."

"I'm desperate, not deranged. This guy is supposed to be my dream man—tall, dark hair and blue eyes—and Ralph's cousin has a beer belly."

"He always has a beer belly around competition time. He has to eat a lot of gassy foods while he's practicing, namely chili-cheese dogs. He dropped ten pounds right after the finals."

"But he *belches* competitively." Delilah blinked back a sudden surge of tears. "No way would Mom think he's the guy I've been describing." Delilah ate two more cookies before Mel snatched the bag away from her.

"Jeez, you are upset." Mel tossed the cookies into the grocery cart and gave Delilah her best don't-worry-I'll-fix-everything look. "You need a man, so we'll find a man, one who doesn't belch. Simple."

But two dented grocery carts later, they still hadn't found anyone to fit the description, and Delilah had exactly ten minutes to get back to her kitchen. Where the hell was Batman when you needed him?

"There he is," Mel said, snatching up a copy of a local newspaper while they were in the checkout lane. Delilah's cart held the Tutti-Frutti supplies and a nearly empty bag of Oreo cookies, a dozen eggs, three bruised grapefruit and a crushed box of condoms—all banging casualties.

Melanie pointed to a picture in the lifestyle section. "The man of your dreams."

"Wild Man Tanner? The rib king of Dallas?" Delilah smiled for the first time since the phone call from her mother that morning. "Jeez, I've always wanted a man who could drink beer out of a double D bra."

"It says right here he was doing it for charity."

"He did it to show off, his primary activity when he isn't pushing ribs and dodging paternity suits."

"That's just his media image. I know a reporter for the *Dallas Star* who interviewed him last year. She said he spends a great deal of his time fund-raising for different charities." Melanie glanced at her. "Have you ever met him?"

Delilah shook her head. "To my knowledge, Jeff Black manages all the Wild Man joints. Other than the weekly pregame parties Zach Tanner hosts during football season, he never even sets foot inside his rib joints. He's just the money behind the place and the face out front. A showpiece."

"A sexy showpiece," Mel added with a smile. "And he certainly fits the description you gave your mother."

Delilah studied the picture. He was cute and he did look a little like her Caped Crusader. She held her hand over the upper half of his face. Yeah, sort of… Fat chance she could get Zach Tanner to fill in for Mr. Perfect. She'd stand a better chance of tracking down Batman himself, which she'd been desperately trying to do all morning. But it seemed that her superhero wasn't the original man—Bernie Calhoun—who'd signed up as the photo booth volunteer. Bernie had gotten sick and had called in a replacement, identity unknown. After getting Bernie's phone number from Mitzi, who coordinated all the volunteers, Delilah had put in two calls to the man. But Bernie, a travel agent by profession, was off on expedition in the Amazon routing his latest tour package. Just her luck.

She eyed the picture again. Okay, so Tanner sort of looked like her guy, but personality wise he was about as close to being Batman as Beavis or Butthead. Tanner was as rough and tough and crude as they came. Hardly Mr.

Perfect. "Forget it," Delilah said. "I don't even know him, and I don't do macho jocks."

"Dee, you don't *do* anyone. That's the trouble. If you were a regular *doer*, you'd have someone to con into playing this little charade. Instead, you're cruising Food Mart. For someone desperate to find a man, you sure are being picky. Time to lower your standards, girlfriend."

"My standards are low," Delilah said defensively. "Okay, if a macho jock jumped in front of me right now, I might consider doing him." At Mel's cryptic stare, she added, "I would do—ask—him. It's just that for a dream man, I've always envisioned the nice, comforting type. You know, strong, but not macho. Sensitive, but not wimpy. Someone eager to help a lady in distress or fight evil for the better of mankind."

"You're hot for Superman."

"Batman."

"Who?"

"Never mind." Delilah took a deep breath. "These are desperate times. I don't really have to marry this guy. Just pretend, and that means, as of this moment, Batman is history. I have zero standards. If they're oozing machismo, I don't care. I'm propositioning them." Delilah tossed the newspaper back on the shelf and squared her shoulders. "I'm psyched. Okay, what do we have so far? Zilch for the grocery store. What about your office?"

"Wally Pemberton, but he's barely five feet and he's bald."

"I guess that leaves only one solution then." Dread churned in Delilah's stomach and she forced a smile. "Well, I always did want to learn the Cotton-Eyed Joe."

ZACH TANNER BARELY had time to swallow the last of his beer before he saw the giant fist flex in front of his face. So much for a nice friendly pregame commentary.

"Come on, Wild Man. Put your money where your mouth is. A little one on one, you and me. I win, you admit Terry Bradshaw was the best damned quarterback to ever throw a ball."

If Zach had been smart, he would have kept his mouth shut and his right arm free and clear of Pete Mackey. Pete was a bruiser with tree trunks for biceps. Zach, retired for eight years with a bum shoulder, didn't stand a chance.

Zach positioned his elbow on the bar and flexed his fingers. "Nobody could beat Montana. He was in a class way above your boy. Younger, stronger, he pinpointed his passes."

Mackey's face blazed red, then purple. His meaty fingers clamped around Zach's. Cameras clicked as every paper in the city, as well as a local TV station, witnessed this major arm wrestling event.

"And the debate continues." Dan Smith, the sports anchor who hosted the live pregame show, stood near a wide-screen TV, microphone in hand. "Pete Mackey was the best right tackle to ever play defense for the Cowboys, and he certainly knows his football. But Wild Man Zach Tanner, ex-Cowboys quarterback and a legend in his own right, seems to have a different opinion. Let's see if these two can settle the question."

The waitress behind the bar blew a whistle and the struggle was on—all of five seconds. Zach's shoulder wrenched, his arm went down just an inch shy of the bar and Mackey gloated.

"Uh, oh, folks. Looks like Tanner might be losing his edge."

*Losing his edge?* He might be tired—hell, he'd had a busy day shooting his new Wild Man commercial as well as a public service announcement for the local Say No to Drugs program. But losing his edge?

Zach Tanner losing at anything was about as likely as a

blizzard hitting Dallas. It just didn't happen. Not since he was fourteen. He'd learned the hard way that people love a winner, and so Zach had spent his life winning. First as a hotshot quarterback straight out of the University of Texas, then as a retired hotshot quarterback and owner of the largest chain of rib joints in Texas. *Losing?* Like hell. He was taking it easy on Mackey. After all, they'd been teammates.

"Sorry, old buddy." Zach gathered his strength and put everything he had into lifting his arm.

Mackey's smile turned to a frown. "Bradshaw's the best," he ground out.

More cameras clicked and Zach summoned his voice. "*Was* the best. Montana put him out to pasture." Zach punctuated the sentence with a quick shove to Mackey's hand. The man went down, the crowd went wild, and Zach wished like hell he had an ice pack. His shoulder was screaming.

"There you have it, folks. Zach Tanner proves he's still got what it takes."

The only thing he had at the moment was thirty seconds to get some ice. Otherwise, his shoulder would be killing him all week. He could forget about coaching the softball team at the orphanage tomorrow afternoon. And fishing with Travis, the boy he sponsored in the Big Brothers program, would be completely out. Like hell, he thought, speeding up his steps. Travis was counting on Saturday.

Zach picked his way through the crowd and headed for the kitchen that brought up the rear of the restaurant, but the hallway was jam-packed. Outside, he thought. He'd slip outside. Then he could walk around to the kitchen's rear door without dozens of hands clapping his shoulder. It was damned hard to keep smiling with so much pain beating at him.

He shoved open the side exit, strode outside and headed

for the rear of the building. Fresh air, empty pavement and ten seconds to go—

He rounded the corner and walked straight into something warm and soft and very female. He grunted. She shrieked. And a half-dozen bakery boxes scattered across the pavement.

"I'm sorry," he said, panting once the pain had subsided enough to allow speech. "I didn't see you—" The words stalled in his throat as his gaze collided with a pair of pale, smoky gray eyes, framed by dark lashes.

It was *her*. Here. Now!

His throbbing shoulder faded into a dull ache as he took a good look at the woman he'd nearly trampled. None other than the five feet or so of curved female who'd haunted his thoughts for the past six months.

A tangle of wild strawberry-blond hair framed her face, a few wayward tendrils tucked behind one delicate ear. She had a peaches-and-cream complexion with a dust of freckles on her nose, her mouth full, pink and thoroughly kissable. He knew that firsthand.

Her gaze fixed on him and his stomach went hollow the same way it had that day in the closet. There was just something about the way she looked at him, into him, as if she wanted to see more than the outside.

No woman had ever looked at him that way, and plenty had looked. But they'd all stopped at the surface, more interested in his appearance, his success, his bad-boy reputation, than the man beneath. Hell, Zach had started to wonder if that man even existed anymore. Then he'd met her, and she'd stared up at him, and he'd seen himself—his dreams of marriage and family, hell, his *kids*—reflected in her eyes.

He shook his head. Yeah, right. Turning thirty-five was short-circuiting his brain. He was too busy being the Wild Man to settle down as Domestic Daddy.

If only he could remember that when she looked at him.

"Say that again," she said.

"Say what?" he asked.

"I thought I recognized your voice and your chin and your mouth and… It's you!" she blurted, her incredulous words echoing his thoughts. "I thought I'd never see you again! I've been on the phone trying to find out your name all morning."

"You wanted to know my name?" A dangerous warmth spread through him.

"Your name, your phone number. I need you."

"Need me?" He smiled.

"More than you can imagine." She laughed and stared down at the ruined cheesecakes. "A dozen phone calls and nothing. Then I have the morning from hell—my driver calls in sick, I have to fight rush hour traffic to make this delivery—and here you are." She reached out, her fingertips trailing down his jaw. "Jeez, it really is you."

He caught her hand, his fingers closing over hers, the contact startling. She was so warm and soft, and she was *here*. "I'm really glad to see you again."

She shook her head. "I just can't get over this. It's you. Me. Us. Here." She smiled. He smiled.

And Pete Mackey shoved open the back door behind him.

"Two out of three," Mackey pressed. "Come on, Tanner. You got lucky and you know it."

"Tanner?" she asked. "As in Zach Tanner? *The* Zach Tanner?"

Her questions faded into the buzz of voices as the crowd spilled out of Wild Man's and into the back parking lot.

"…and the great quarterback debate continues, folks. Will Tanner agree to a rematch? Will youth and agility prevail over experience and brute force? Montana or Bradshaw?'' The sports announcer's voice carried from the open doorway where Dan Smith posed for the television camera.

Delilah's gaze shot to the commentator, then back to Zach. Her eyes widened as if she were seeing him for the first time.

"You *are* Zach Tanner." She withdrew her hand from his. *"You."* There was no wonder or pleasure in the word now. Only cold accusation as if he'd just kicked her favorite puppy.

*Puppy kicker!* her gaze screamed and Zach reached out. He didn't kick puppies. Hell, he liked puppies, and cats and birds and even goldfish—

*Click, click, click…* The cameras sounded behind him, accompanied by the murmur of the crowd and he felt the usual tightening in his chest, the eyes watching his every move. He stopped just shy of touching her.

"I can't believe you're him," she went on, oblivious to everyone and everything around them. "He's you. *Zach Tanner.*"

"In the flesh." He smiled—a slow, sexy smile that still landed him on magazine covers even though his football career had died eight years ago. A smile guaranteed to charm any woman and he had bags of fan mail to prove it.

She glared.

Almost any woman. He should have known she wouldn't be affected. She was different. That was the trouble. She reacted to him differently, looked at him differently, and he liked it. *That* was the real trouble.

"I can't believe this." Delilah resisted the urge to pinch herself. It was like watching a Dr. Jekyll and Mr. Hyde movie. Her beloved, kind, considerate superhero transformed into the obnoxious, outrageous, macho jock right before her eyes. She blinked. But he was still there. Still *him.* Oh, no. This wasn't *him.* This was Zach Tanner, as far removed from *him* as she could ever get.

"Believe it, honey." He smiled again and her frown deepened.

"Come on, Tanner. Rematch inside or I'm telling the whole damned town what a pansy you are."

"Sorry to run, sugar, but I'm being paged." His south Texas drawl seemed more pronounced, deeper, the words sliding into her ears like warm Jamaican rum sauce over a piece of her Luscious Lemon Lambada cheesecake. Sweet, intoxicating, irresistible.

Despite the rage boiling inside her, her body responded. The dreaded tingles sizzled from head to toe, stopping at every pertinent point in between…her knees trembled, her abdomen quivered, her nipples tightened, her cheeks blazed. *Stop it! No trembling or quivering or tightening or blazing—nothing.*

"Later, darlin'." He flashed a smile at the crowd and Delilah tried to gather her wits. Just walk away, she told herself. Turn. Put one foot in front of the other and start eating pavement—

"Not so fast, honey. Don't you want a little something to remember me by?" Before she could take a breath, he swung her into his arms, bent her over backward and kissed her.

"Go get 'em, Wild Man!"

"That a boy!"

"Lay one on her!"

The crowd hooted and cheered and Delilah did the only thing a woman in her position could do. She bit him.

"Ouch," he growled, breaking the kiss to glare at her. They were nose to nose, Delilah still draped over his arm, still looking like the starstruck fan to everyone but the man holding her. "What'd you do that for?" he whispered.

"Because you're Zach Tanner, damn you. Now let go of me right now or you'll regret it."

"You liked it the first time."

"You weren't Neanderthal Man the first time, and you weren't doing it in front of a crowd of people."

"But you did like it?"

"Maybe I did." She frowned. "And maybe I didn't. It doesn't matter. All that matters is that I don't like it now." She positioned her knee. "So move it or you'll be singing soprano for the next two weeks."

He stared at her long and hard and Delilah knew he was going to kiss her again. Or maybe she just wanted him to.

"I mean it," she warned. "I've got three older brothers so I know how to fight dirty. I can have you flat on your back before you can let loose a Tarzan yell."

"*Flat on my back*, huh?" His voice sizzled across her nerves endings. "Does that mean you'll be on top?"

His words sent a wave of heat through her and her courage faltered. Just for a second. Then he smiled, that insolent, lazy grin he'd turned on the cameras and she stiffened.

What a chauvinistic, egotistical, full-of-himself…*man*. Just let him try to kiss her again… *Please let him try*.

"You through playing lip-lock, Tanner?"

"What can I say? I'm a lover first, a fighter second." He hauled Delilah up against him, the action snapping her out of her trance. She blinked. Her vision cleared and she had an up-close and personal view of Zach's profile, and that damned smile that made her insides fumble around.

Before she could think about what she was doing, she stomped on his foot in front of a blaze of cameras, whirled on her heel, pushed past several reporters and football fans and marched off toward her van. If only she had a gun. She'd never been a violent person, but what she wouldn't do with a shotgun right now. Or an Uzi. *Come on, Zach Tanner. Make my day.*

Yards away, she climbed into her van and sat for several long seconds. Relax. Breathe. Think. She tried desperately to do all three while the crowd in the parking lot thinned and the camera crew retreated inside.

Her heartbeat finally slowed and she focused on the clipboard sitting on her dash. Regardless of the past few shocking minutes, she still had to finish her deliveries. A quick glance at her watch and she blew out a disgusted breath. She'd lost a half hour and all because of that loud, obnoxious, rude, overbearing, ham-it-up-for-the-crowd Zach Tanner—

"Now don't go away with your feathers all ruffled, sweetheart." The clipboard fell from her hands and her head snapped around at whiplash speed. He leaned in her window, a brilliant sunset blazing his outline, and her heart shifted into overdrive.

Anger, she told herself. Because no way in hell, heaven or the in-between was she having any kind of *reaction* to Zach Tanner.

"Let me give you a peace offering."

"An autographed picture?"

"Whatever you want."

"Good, I've been meaning to do a little target practice." She glared. "You just humiliated me in front of dozens of people—the whole damned town." She shook her head. "I can't believe this. My Batman is a ridiculous caveman and my mother is coming in sixty hours and forty-seven minutes and I'm going to be on the ten o'clock news looking miserable and ten pounds heavier when I'm heavy enough on my own, and there I was on TV and I didn't even plug my cheesecakes and—"

"Ssshhh." He touched two fingertips to her lips. His expression went from lazy and insolent to intense and compassionate and she felt herself sucked back in time, to the storage closet. *Dr. Jekyll strikes again.* "You're rambling." His fingertip traced her bottom lip. "I must be making you nervous."

"Not nervous. Mad," she snapped. She shoved his hand away and made the sign of the cross to ward him off. "Just stand back."

"That's for vampires."

"I'm not taking any chances. Just stay away from me." She revved the engine and grabbed an invoice off her dash. Work. Just think about work. Not about him—how he's so close you can smell his aftershave and the sweet scent of his breath.

"What's this for?" he asked when she slapped the paper into his palm.

"You ruined a half-dozen cheesecakes when you slammed into me, and I don't work for free. Here's the bill, and you can clean up the crushed boxes yourself." She shoved the van into Drive. "And for your information, Bradshaw is the first and only quarterback to take the same NFL team to four Super Bowls." Then she roared out of the parking lot, leaving Zach Tanner staring after her.

She was miles away when her own words came back to haunt her. *Okay, if some macho jock jumps in front of me right now, I'll ask him.*

No way was she asking Zach Tanner to play her fiancé. She would tell her mother the truth first. She'd call a male escort service or cruise every grocery store in Dallas or beg Ralph's cousin for help.

Zach Tanner was out of the question. If only she didn't have the insane urge to whip the van around and head back to Wild Man's.

Only to run over him, she assured herself. That was the only thing that would make her feel remotely better. A few tire tracks across his smirking face. That, or maybe another kiss.

_____

"MOM, WE REALLY NEED to talk."

Too casual, Delilah decided as she sat at her desk the next day, signed employee paychecks and practiced approaches to break the no-fiancé news. Maybe she should try being a bit more formal, just so her mom would know she meant business.

"Mother, I feel it imperative that we speak." Uh-uh.

"Mommie, I hate to bother you but…"

"Yo, Gladys, can we talk here—" The ring of the phone cut her off.

"Good morning. How Sweet It Is."

"Delilah Belle James. What on earth took you so long?"

She jumped. Her hand slid, leaving a streak of blue across Lisa's paycheck. *Mom strikes again.*

"Delilah? Are you all right, dear? You aren't sick, are you? Because Myrtle's granddaughter just came down with a horrible case of laryngitis—"

"I'm fine, Ma. I was just doing payroll. Then I have a business meeting, so I'm sort of busy right now—"

"I was calling to make sure you had a VCR. I couldn't remember from my last visit. My memory isn't what it used to be, you know. I hope that's not a bad sign. Dolores Whittington, her daughter is Emma—green velvet and carnations—" her mother had a habit of referring to everyone near Delilah's age by their wedding color and flower "—started having these spells where she would forget where she parked her car every time she went to the Wal-Mart. She ended up riding home on the back of a Harley motorcycle with some long-haired hippie named Duke.''

"I don't think they call them hippies anymore, Ma. And I'm sure you don't have what Dolores has. It's natural to forget things sometimes. I'm forgetful, too. Would you believe that silly me forgot to tell you that—"

"Anyhow Myrtle lent me the videos from each of her six daughters' weddings. I thought we'd get a jump on the wedding plans and the video could give us some ideas of what not to do. I mean, Myrtle's a dear, but that oldest one of hers, Maribel—navy blue and pansies—is a fruitcake. Why, she had her bridesmaids wear sailor hats, of all things. The food was a different story. Absolutely wonderful. Lobster with butter sauce, and shrimp scampi. I could practically hear my arteries clogging right there at the buffet. It was divine.''

"Ma, aren't you supposed to be on a low-cholesterol diet?''

"Nonsense. I eat an entire bulb of garlic every morning. That cures anything that ails you. Why, Estelle Butterworth had double-bypass surgery last year. Doctors said she could kiss decent food goodbye, but you know how much Estelle loves butter cookies. She heard about the garlic from Margie's sister, Esther, and she's been as healthy as a hog all year long.''

"Ma, I've been thinking about this garlic thing. Did you ask Dr. Harris about it, because I know foods can be medicinal, but there's a limit to their benefit and with your condition—"

"Old Harris is still living in the Dark Ages.''

Delilah wanted to ask what was so modern about eating a bulb of garlic, especially since desperate Transylvanian women had been doing it for centuries. But Gladys James wasn't a very good listener. Now talking she had down to an art.

"...before Estelle's surgery, she was doing the lambada at her daughter Kelly's wedding—pink chiffon and white tulips—and she started having these funny pains. She made it to the appetizers, then passed out at the cold buffet and nearly toppled the ice sculpture."

"How terrible—"

"You're telling me. Kelly's fiancé was a diver and he wanted a sculpture shaped like an octopus, of all things. There were these long iciclelike things dripping all over the cocktail shrimp and smoked oysters. It was repulsive."

"Ma, I really need you to listen to me. It's about Percy. He..." She could hear her mother's paused breath and she closed her eyes. She could do this. She could tell her the truth. *There is no Percy. I made him up in a moment of desperate stupidity. I'm twenty-eight and single, and I like it. I want a career first, before I have a family. Please, please, please understand.* "Percy and I aren't exactly eng—"

"Listen, dear, if your Percy wants an octopus, don't worry. I'm sure he'll change his mind once I speak to him. Oh, did I tell you Janie Wilmot—mint-green and daisies—is getting married next month at the Maroby Club? Her parents are both members, and they pressured the poor dear into using that awful red velvet room. The daisies are going to look like they're bleeding to death...."

Delilah got an earful about bleeding daisies and Janie's mother's hernia surgery before the second line finally beeped.

"Sorry, Ma. Gotta go. Wish Mrs. Wilmot a speedy recovery. Bye." Delilah clicked over to the other line. "Thank God you called," she told Melanie. "I was this

close to wrapping the phone cord around my neck and
stringing myself to the nearest curtain rod.''

"Forget your mom. You've got the Wild Man meeting
in one hour. Good luck and go get 'im.''

"Good luck? In case you've forgotten, I bit Zach Tanner
last night. *Wild Man* Zach Tanner. *Wild Man* as in Wild
Man Ribs. I doubt he's waiting with bated breath to give
me his account.''

"You said yourself he was just a figurehead. I'm sure
he won't hold it against you even if you did do it on the
eleven o'clock news. Not that anyone could actually see
you bite him. The camera got you two from the back, him
leaning over you, his head blocking yours, his hands on
your—''

"Enough. I was there, remember?'' Unfortunately.
Thankfully. *Hey, make up your mind.*

"So was half of Dallas. And from the way he was leaning into you and you were practically swooning in his arms,
I'd say you were enjoying it. So would half the newspapers.''

"The newspapers, too?''

"Uh-huh. Pretty hot stuff for the lifestyle section. Two
of Dallas's food gurus—Mr. Ribs and Ms. Cheesecake—
teaming up. It's a match made in cholesterol heaven.''

"We did not team up. Kissing Zach Tanner was pure
hell and I did not enjoy it, and I certainly didn't come
anywhere close to swooning.''

Mel didn't seem the least bit put off by Delilah's fierce
denial. "So you kissed him? Before or after you bit him?''

"Before.'' Way before. Six months before…when he
was *him* and she'd yet to blab about a fiancé to her mother.

"Was it great? Semigreat? Really great? Give me all the
juicy details.''

"Great is hardly the word I'd use.'' Spectacular. Earth-shattering. Mind-blowing. She shook away the thoughts and glanced at her watch. "I've really got to go or I'm going to be late. Though I don't even know why I'm going. I've got about an ice cube's chance in a Texas heat wave of landing this account now. I *bit* him, Mel."

"You're going, Dee, because you don't give up that easily, and this is business. *Maybe,* just maybe, Zach Tanner liked a beautiful woman taking a bite out of him. They don't call him the Wild Man for nothing."

And maybe some genius doctor would invent an eat-all-you-want-and-still-lose-weight miracle pill. *Dream on.*

"I HAVE TO TELL YOU, your cakes have done extremely well in our three trial restaurants," Jeff Black, the manager of Wild Man's, told her an hour later as she sat in his office. "We've been very pleased."

"Thank you." She smiled at the small man with carrot-colored hair. He gave her an easy grin and the nervous twinges in her stomach subsided. Maybe all was not lost. Surely if he was going to tell her to take a hike, he would have done it by now. She'd been here all of fifteen minutes, and he'd been nothing but friendly and accommodating, despite her having bitten his boss. And—and this was a big plus in Delilah's book—he hadn't freaked when her cell phone had bleeped three times with frantic phone calls from Lisa—uh, make that four. She smiled apologetically and reached for her phone.

"This is Delilah."

"I can't find the batch of tangerines for the Tangerine Tango," Lisa squealed. "I looked in the fresh fruit closet. There were crates of apples and mangoes and lemons, but zero tangerines. What are we going to do—"

"They're on the third pantry shelf. Second crate, next to the pineapples."

"Gotcha, boss."

She'd barely slid the phone back into her purse when it rang again. "Yes?"

"Dee, we're out of sugar! I opened the storage closet after I found the crate of tangerines and there it was, an empty shelf—"

"I ordered an extra ten pounds. It's being delivered at noon in plenty of time to finish today's orders. Relax, Lisa."

"Relax?" Several quick pants punctuated the word. "I don't work well under pressure, Dee. You know that."

"You've been in charge all of thirty-three minutes."

"That's exactly my point. I'm not a supervisor. I'm an artist. You coordinate this kitchen stuff, and I help create masterpiece cheesecakes. It's my element. My space." She gasped for air. "I can't breathe. I'm out of my comfort zone."

"I'll be back in one hour. Just stay calm until then.

"I'm really sorry," Delilah told Jeff after she ended the call. "I normally oversee daily production and my assistant's a little frazzled in my absence. One of the pitfalls of being a sole proprietor."

"No problem. It's understandable they can't get along without you. I'd say your personal touch is what makes your cakes so good."

She smiled. What a nice guy. Considerate, soft-spoken, albeit a little nervous, like Winnie-the-Pooh on a caffeine high. If only Jeff fit the description, she thought wistfully, she'd be sitting pretty right now. He was the perfect non-threatening man. No glittering blue eyes to steal her breath away. No sly grins to send her heart into overdrive. No rumbling caveman baritone to glide up and down her spine and echo deep in her quivering stomach.

Unfortunately, Jeff not only talked like Winnie, he

looked like him, as well. As far removed from Zach Tanner as she could get, darn it. Not that she wanted Zach Tanner, mind you. She most certainly didn't, even if she had been thinking about him all night. About the way it felt with his arms around her, his face so close to hers. The way his scent made her dizzy, his smile pumped her blood faster, and his kiss knocked her panty hose clear to her ankles—

"Miss James?"

"Uh, yes?" She shook away her thoughts and focused on Jeff.

"I said that we've been very pleased with how well your cheesecakes have been doing, particularly the chocolate cherry flavor. It's a big hit."

"Thank you." She smiled. "Chocolate Cherry Cha-Cha is my top seller." While he perused her proposal, she took the opportunity to glance around the room. A big mistake, she realized, when Neanderthal Man himself stared back at her, and her heart pounded faster. She was surrounded by him. Pictures lined every inch of the walls—posters, newspaper clippings—the guy was a media hound.

She saw him wearing a bib and eating ribs, his face flanked by T-shirt-covered breasts sporting the logo Get 'em Big and Hot at Wild Man's. She saw him bare-chested, muscles gleaming, wearing nothing but a pair of boxers and a smile—an underwear ad she remembered from a few years back. She saw him sweaty and tired, standing on the sidelines at a game, drinking a well-known sports drink—another ad. She saw him with a bra draped over his head, another in his hand—it was the photo from the lifestyle section of yesterday's newspaper.

Some of the pictures coaxed a smile, others a shake of her head. But only one stopped her heart for several long seconds.

It was an earlier picture—a black-and-white eight-by-ten

taken of him several years back when he still played for the Cowboys. He was walking off a rain-drenched football field, his uniform plastered to him, a strange expression on his face.

He wasn't hamming it up for the camera. No sexy smiles or flexing muscles or big-breasted blondes on either arm. It was just him, his face so serious and unguarded. He was Batman all over again. He was *him. Oh, no!*

Forget him, she told herself. She meant to, so why did the sight of him, a mere one-dimensional picture, tie her stomach into knots? Desperation, she finally decided. She needed a Mr. Perfect so badly, even Zach Tanner was starting to look good.

"…really impressed with your numbers."

"I'm sorry. What did you say?"

"Your sales record. All of your flavors did well, but that cha-cha one, in particular, went over big with our customers, and that's the one we would like to feature in all of our restaurants."

"You mean you're giving me the Wild Man account?"

"That's exactly what I mean."

The smile spread across her face, only to die a quick death. "But…? There's a but, right? Because you have that 'but' look on your face."

He held his fingers up. "A small one."

Here it was, she thought. The repercussion from last night's biting fest. "Look, I'm sorry. I know I bit him, but he caught me off guard."

"Who did you bite?"

"You don't know?"

"I'm afraid not. You really bit someone?"

"Um, yes, but it was nothing. Really. Small, inconsequential. I didn't even break the skin." She waved her hands and leaned forward. "So I've got the account?"

"If you'll sign an exclusive contract with Wild Man Ribs for your Chocolate Cherry Cha-Cha..." His words faded into the buzz of her cell phone.

"Excuse me." She whipped out the phone and stabbed the button. "Lisa, I'm busy right now."

"Don't use that tone with me, young lady."

"Mom?"

"Of course it's your mother. Your only mother. The woman who spent fourteen hours and thirty-five minutes in hard labor, sweating and gritting her teeth so that the fruit of my womb could sit there twenty-eight years later and sass me."

"I'm sorry, Mom. What's wrong?"

"I forgot to ask what size your young man wears. Grandma Rose asked me to take her shopping today. She thought she'd buy him something nice. A sort of welcome to the family present. I'll bring it with me tomorrow."

"I..." Her throat closed around the words. Dread churned fast and deep in her stomach, spreading through her like liquid concrete. Shopping? This was serious. Her Grandma Rose hated shopping. The last time she'd braved a mall had been more than six years ago for Delilah's cousin's wedding.

*Grandma Rose. Shopping. Presents. Welcome to the family.*

"Oh, no."

"Are you all right, Miss James?" Jeff asked her once she'd managed to mumble "Extra large" to her mother and pry her fingers loose from the phone. "Here." He pushed a cup of coffee at her, but the last thing Delilah needed was caffeine. A noose would have been nice.

Her mother was coming tomorrow. In twenty-six hours and thirty-seven minutes and forty-nine seconds...

"As I was saying," Jeff went on, "if you'll sign an exclusive, we're ready to make you a sweet deal."

And she expected to meet her future son-in-law.

"I have the contracts right here."

*And* she was bringing a present from Grandma Rose.

"We're prepared to pay you the amount indicated in paragraph three of your proposal, along with a bonus for any orders over the weekly quantity agreed upon."

Through the fog of dread hanging over her, her brain registered the news. *Yes!* rushed to the tip of her tongue. This was what she'd been waiting for. A major account with a major chain of restaurants. This could give exposure to her other flavors, gain her a lot of free promotion. Make her as famous as the Wild Man himself. A regular Wild Woman of the cheesecake biz. *Betty Crocker, move over. Sara Lee, eat my dust. Julia Child, you're out of here!*

*I accept.*

"I don't know if I can accept."

"Excuse me?" Jeff Black gave her a puzzled glance. "But of course. You want more. Quite the savvy businesswoman." He scribbled a figure.

She stared at the amount, let her hopes chant for a millisecond before shaking her head.

"Still not enough?" He jotted down another amount and she shook her head again. "You drive a hard bargain, Miss James, but we want exclusives on that flavor—"

"It's not the money."

"I'm afraid I don't understand."

"The money's great. Fabulous, particularly that last offer, and I would love to say yes. Normally, I would say yes, but my life hasn't been exactly normal since yesterday. I mean, I was cruising grocery stores and banging unsuspecting men less than twenty-four hours ago, and then last night I bit someone for the very first time and my mother's coming tomorrow, but first she's taking my Grandma Rose shopping.'' She swallowed. ''Shopping, of all things.''

Shock etched his expression. ''Pardon me?''

She shook her head. ''Never mind. Anyhow, I appreciate your offer, I've been waiting for this kind of offer for a long time, but I can't accept. Not under these terms.''

''Then tell me what you want and I'll see what I can do.''

She glanced around the room, her gaze sweeping the collection of Wild Man pictures, before coming to rest on one in particular. ''I want him.''

''SHE WANTS *WHAT?*'' Zach listened to Jeff recite the terms of Delilah James's proposition and tried to slow the pounding of his heart.

''So?'' Jeff asked once he'd finished. ''What do you think?''

Zach burst out laughing. So Delilah James wasn't half as offended by the Wild Man as she'd pretended to be. He'd thought for a second last night that he really was getting old, losing his edge—hardly. She'd fallen hook, line and sinker for that big show of good ol' boy charm. Just like every other woman Zach had ever met.

That last thought sobered him completely. Why, he wasn't sure. But it had something to do with storage closets and deep, knowing looks and the fact that he'd been so certain she'd seen past the surface when she'd looked at him. Past the Wild Man.

''I'm glad you're taking this seriously,'' Jeff said as he slid a stack of ledger sheets across the desk. ''Because her Chocolate Cherry Cha-Cha is really popular. We can make a killing with exclusive rights to this flavor. Right now, several restaurants around town are serving it. If we're the only one, it'll up our revenues considerably. A five-to-one profit ratio. So what do you say?''

''I'd say you're a genius at numbers, partner. This is a sweet deal, but under no circumstances am I going to saddle myself with Delilah James, even if it is only temporary. She's lethal to my image, not to mention my health.''

''She really bit you?'' At Zach's nod, Jeff grinned. ''Now that I would like to have seen.''

''Thanks a lot.''

''You know I love you, Zach. You're like a brother to me. *You.* The real you. But Wild Man's another story. He deserves to have a bite taken out of him every now and then.'' Jeff tapped the ledger sheets. ''Please think about this arrangement.''

''Just offer her more money.''

''She doesn't want money. She wants you.''

''Walk around playing fiancé for two weeks? With Dracula's daughter? Forget it.''

''What's the big deal? She's a pretty lady, she's got the hots for Wild Man Tanner, enough to want to parade him around as her fiancé. And you want her cheesecakes. You can both make each other very happy. And me,'' Jeff added, then downed half a cup of coffee and rubbed his red hair. ''You know what I found in my hairbrush this morning?''

Zach raised an eyebrow. ''Hair?''

Jeff cradled his head in his hands. ''I think I'm losing it.''

''You're only thirty-four.''

''About to be thirty-five. Middle-aged.''

''Like hell. Thirty-four is young. Damn young.'' And Zach should know. He'd been thirty-four for ten months, three weeks and two days now, and he felt the youngest he'd ever felt. He was pumped. In the prime of his life. Middle age was eons away.

"So I'm not ready for a walker yet," Jeff said. "There's more to it than age. It's genetics. You have a bald parent, you're liable to get a bald kid."

"You don't know if your dad was bald," Zach told him.

"Maybe it was my mom." Jeff downed more coffee. "I can't remember that far back before they died, and the two pictures I have aren't enough to say one way or the other. But the point is, it's happening to me. I can feel it, and stress only intensifies the situation. Ease my mind, Zach. No negotiating. Just do this."

"I can't." Zach rubbed his mouth, still feeling the nip of her teeth. Not that it had hurt. Far from it. That was the trouble. He'd liked it and he didn't want to like it. Not with her. *A woman like all the others.* "She bit me in front of a crowd of people *and* a television crew."

"She bit Wild Man."

"We're one and the same, Jeff."

"Hardly. You're water and he's fire. You're a nice guy, Zach, someone who cares about people. But Wild Man, he's out of control, domineering, he does what he wants, when he wants, with little regard for the consequences."

"And people love him for it."

"They admire him for having the balls to shuck convention. There's a big difference."

If only there was. But for Zach, orphaned at age five when his mother died in a car accident, the line between admiration and love had blurred long ago.

"Fire's powerful," Jeff went on, "but water can douse it to dust every time, buddy."

"You've been reading too much Keats."

Jeff smiled. "That's what marrying a librarian will do to you."

"How's Trudy?"

"More concerned about my hair than you are. She insisted I get some Rogaine and a new Mozart tape. Now if I could get my business partner to cooperate, then I could close this deal, head back home, give myself a hair treatment and relax." At Zach's stubborn expression, he threw up his hands. "Or I could offer Delilah James more money and see if she bites." He grinned. *"Again."*

# 4

"I'M INSANE." Delilah slumped against the kitchen counter later that evening and stared at Melanie.

"You are not. This is probably the smartest thing you've ever done. Black's upped the original offer three times. We're going to make a killing."

"I don't want to make a killing. I mean, I do, but... Oh jeez, what am I saying?" Delilah buried her face in her hands. "What happened to my priorities? My pride, for heaven's sake? I still can't believe it. One minute I was sitting there, envisioning myself on the cover of *Fortune,* then my mom called and, the next thing I know, I'm shaking my head and telling Black to throw in Zach Tanner as part of the deal, or no deal. I'm losing my business edge. I'm pathetic."

"Bargaining for a hunky jock isn't pathetic. It's Darwin's theory. Females are always attracted to the most virile males."

"I'm not attracted to him, not like that. He fits the description, that's it." He *was* the description. Her Batman. She shook her head. She still couldn't believe it. Someone upstairs was definitely out to get her. *Her* Batman was testosterone poster-boy Zach Tanner. How unfair could life be? "The whole meeting was like a bad episode of Geraldo. Sally Jesse will be calling first thing tomorrow."

"Regardless, Wild Man's still wants your Chocolate Cherry Cha-Cha."

"But Zach Tanner, of all people. The man's a cretin. I must have been out of my mind to ask him to pose as my fiancé." Delilah shook her head. "And I'm still out of my mind. As of five o'clock this afternoon, I was still praying he would agree."

"Maybe he will. Your mom doesn't get here until tomorrow afternoon."

Delilah shook her head. "I'm not holding my breath. There's no way he'll ever say yes to my proposition, even if he does take me seriously. I'm not exactly his type—big boobs, no brain and a face straight off the cover of *Cosmo*."

"Your boobs are big enough."

"But my brain is too big."

"Well, maybe he needs some incentive." Mel looked thoughtful.

"What do you mean?"

"Nothing. Just proceed with plan B, in case all else fails."

"Ralph's cousin," Delilah said.

The doorbell rang and she took a deep breath. She would march over, open the door, butter up Ralph's cousin for a few hours, then lay out her plan, complete with a nice bonus if he kept his belching occupation a secret from her mother.

This could work.

*Yeah,* a small voice whispered as she pulled open the front door and tried to smile. *And you could be the next cover model for* Spandex World.

"She's not biting," Jeff told Zach the next afternoon when he strode into the office of Wild Man's restaurant number one. "And restaurant number ten needs a new stove, and the building inspector is due at number thirty-five in the Dallas Galleria and—'' Jeff ran his fingers through his hair and held up several orange strands for Zach's inspection. ''I'm falling apart.''

''It's only a few hairs.''

''A few today, a few tomorrow. The next thing you know I'm a Telly Savalas look-alike.''

''Relax, Jeff.'' Zach sprawled in a chair. ''Give Delilah James some time to think about it. She's not a fool. I've done some checking. The woman's got a good head for business. She's doubled her revenues since last year and not only supplies her cakes to area restaurants, but also through a mail-order catalog that ships anywhere in the U.S.''

''So she doesn't need our business.''

''Forty-two restaurants? Are you kidding? She'll take our offer. It's more than generous and it'll be a big boost for her business.'' He plopped a day planner on the desk. ''I'll meet with the building inspector after lunch and then see about a new stove. You head home and relax.'' He watched Jeff down his third cup of coffee, way too much for a man who got nervous when the television was a little too loud. ''There's more. I haven't seen you this wired since the IRS did that audit on us the year before last.''

''As of three o'clock today, I've made four offers, and she's turned down every one. And,'' he said when Zach started to protest, ''this morning her business adviser—'' he glanced at some scribbled notes in front of him ''—a Miss Melanie Ragolli, told me that if you don't agree to play this little charade, How Sweet It Is will sign over exclusive rights to Bob's Barbecue.''

''*What?*'' Zach bolted from the chair. It was one thing to play hard to get with her cheesecakes, but to blackmail him and worry his best friend into a hair-loss frenzy? And to think he'd actually liked her when they'd first met in

that storage closet. Hell, he'd more than liked her. He'd...
He wasn't sure what he'd felt but it went way beyond *like*.

Pissed, however, summed up the way he felt right now.
He didn't like being backed into a corner, even if it was
by one very soft and sweet-smelling Delilah James. *Especially* since it was her. "She's crazy," he muttered. "Bob
only has twenty restaurants, half what we have. He can't
begin to match our offer."

"I told you, she doesn't want money. She wants you."

*"Bob,"* Zach muttered. "Why, the man dresses in a pig
suit to greet his customers."

"Two weeks of your time," Jeff went on while visions
of fat pink pigs ran through Zach's mind. "That's all she
wants and she'll sign over exclusives to her Chocolate
Cherry Cha-Cha for our original offer. Come on, Zach. You
can play things really low-key. I'll leak word to the press
that you're on vacation. You won't have to worry about
keeping up appearances."

Jeff's last words effectively killed the pig images. Instead
Zach saw himself face-to-face with one Delilah James. She
looked into his eyes, he looked into hers. She smiled, he
smiled. She leaned into him and he slid his arms around
her, pulled her close and... "Vacation, huh?"

"Someplace far away. You could be on safari in Africa,
hiking in Switzerland, fighting your way through the jungles of South America—something real Wild Man-ish. The
press'll eat it up, we'll get the cheesecakes, I'll have one
less thing to worry about, Delilah James will have you as
her pretend fiancé and everybody's happy."

Except Zach. He was the sacrificial lamb. It was his image that stood to suffer if he agreed to the arrangement and
the press got wind of it. *Wild Man Takes the Plunge*. No
way. The Wild Man thumbed his nose at convention. He
would never settle for something as tame, as docile, as mar-

riage, even if he was hitting the big three-five in less than two months.

But if he didn't? His business would take a hit. Wild Man's would lose to Bob's Barbecue, and if there was one thing Zach Tanner didn't like, it was losing. And Jeff—his nearest and dearest friend since the third grade—would lose another handful of hair, maybe two, and Zach would be responsible.

"Have our lawyer draw up the papers. If she wants the Wild Man, she's about to get him."

"Thank God." Jeff looked relieved for about an eighth of a second, until he saw the look in Zach's eyes.

"You're not going to do anything...*funny,* are you? I mean, I know she sort of blackmailed you and it's really not fair, but she's really a nice woman and she sounded so desperate. I really don't think she's your typical groupie."

Zach hadn't thought so either, but what other reason could she have for propositioning him? For *blackmailing* him? He stiffened, an evil grin playing at his lips. "Don't worry. I'm just going to grant the lady's request, is all. If Delilah James wants the Wild Man, she's about to get him." *In spades.*

"You LOOK REALLY wonderful tonight."

Delilah turned to see the attractive, if a tad too short, man standing next to her. Melanie had been right. Ralph's cousin, Oliver, didn't have an inch of belly overhang in sight. If Delilah hadn't known about his belching claim to fame, she never would have guessed in a million years.

"Thanks," she said, returning his smile.

"Don't be nervous."

She wasn't. Not anymore. Dressed in a navy suit, Oliver looked every bit the nice, conservative accountant she'd told her mother about for the past six months. So he had watery blue eyes instead of deep blue? And, of course, he didn't come anywhere close to filling out a Batman costume. But otherwise, he fit the description. Sort of.

Your average female wouldn't exactly go orgasmic at one glance, but hey, she hadn't once heard him make any bodily noises. It seemed when he wasn't in "training" for a belching competition, Oliver was actually very health conscious, and nice and quiet and reserved. For once, it seemed that things might actually turn out all right.

That alone should have clued in Delilah that disaster waited on the horizon. Oliver was too much of a godsend. Too nice. Too polite. Too *healthy.*

Gladys James hated him on sight.

Oh, she didn't say it. But Delilah knew. The moment her mother walked in, flustered from two hours stuck in airport traffic, Delilah had this terrible sinking feeling.

Her mother shrugged off her coat, collapsed on the sofa next to Melanie, who'd shown up for moral support, and stared across a tray of cheese puffs at Oliver, who hadn't even offered to put away her luggage.

*Strike one.*

Introductions were made and Delilah fetched a tray of lemonade from the kitchen.

"Oh, thank you, dear." Gladys took a cold glass dripping with condensation. She gulped half of it, then reached for a cheese puff. "Dreadful flight."

"Too bumpy?" Melanie sat on the other side of Gladys and sipped her own glass of lemonade.

"No, dear. The food."

"Too tasteless?" Oliver asked from an armchair on the opposite side of the coffee table.

"Too little." Gladys popped a cheese puff into her mouth. "How in the world is a person supposed to get full on a cupful of lasagna? Speaking of lasagna—" she reached for another cheese puff ''—Delilah, dear, did I tell you that Marjorie Braxton had a heart attack? Right in the middle of layering in the ricotta for her eight-cheese lasagna, she just collapsed.''

''That's terrible,'' Delilah said, perched on the arm of the couch. She nibbled on a cheese puff, all the while ignoring the urge to pop the whole thing into her mouth.

''*Eight* cheeses?'' Oliver flicked a piece of lint from his already lint-free suit. ''Cheese is terrible for your arteries.''

Gladys paused, hand halfway to the cheese puff tray. ''You don't like cheese?''

He flicked at another invisible piece of lint. ''I eat it once in a while, but I usually try to stay away from it. Too much fat.''

*Strike two.*

''Eat up, Ma,'' Delilah said, handing her mother two more cheese puffs. ''I made these especially for you.'' She snatched the half-empty glass of lemonade from her mother's hands, retreated to the kitchen and seriously considered bolting out the back door. Why the hell hadn't she warned Oliver about the food?

The guy belched competitively, for heaven's sake. She certainly hadn't expected him to be a cheese bigot, of all things.

Calm, she told herself. All was not lost. Lots of people didn't like cheese. Her oldest brother, Cole, hated cheese and her mother still loved him.

Then again, it wasn't as if she had a choice. She'd gone through sixteen hours of hard labor before squeezing out an eleven-pound screaming boy. That was commitment. Cole could declare war on Kraft and her mother would be right there smiling, saying, ''That's my baby,'' between bites of a grilled cheese on rye.

Boys had all the rotten luck. They could pee on the side

of a wall, belch in public and drink beer while wearing a bra on their head, and no one thought any worse of them.

It wasn't fair.

"...don't like pot roast?" Her mother's voice rose above the whir of kitchen appliances a second before Melanie ducked her head in the door.

"You'd better get out here."

"Not just pot roast," Oliver was saying as Delilah rushed into the living room with a tray of little smoky sausages. "I don't eat any kind of red meat."

*Strike three...*

Delilah came to a dead stop and nearly dropped the tray. Her gaze riveted on her mother's face.

Gladys James had turned a vivid cranberry and looked ready to explode.

*You'rrre...out!*

"But you eat chili dogs?" Delilah turned on Oliver.

"Vegetarian wieners and, of course, the chili is meat-free with extra beans when I'm in training."

"Of course." Her stomach did a flip-flop.

"He—he doesn't like meat." Gladys collapsed back against the sofa, completely oblivious to the training comment. "I don't think I feel so good."

"Did you have any meat on the plane?" Oliver asked, despite the warning look that Delilah shot him. "Because red meat is poisonous to the digestive system, not to mention the heart. Sometimes the system has difficulty breaking down the animal flesh and you start to feel these gaslike cramps—"

"Ma, have a sausage," Delilah thrust the tray at her mother.

"Those are pork and pork is just as bad as red meat—"

The doorbell sounded, effectively drowning Oliver's

words. Delilah and Melanie jumped up at the same time, but Melanie was quicker.

"I'll get it. It's probably Ralph. I told him to stop by and meet your mother."

Delilah sank down on the sofa next to Gladys. She stuffed two cheese puffs into her mouth while her mother looked ready to faint and Oliver entertained them with more health-conscious facts.

"...meat isn't nearly the protein source it's cracked up to be. Most people don't know, but good old-fashioned nuts and juice can give the body plenty of protein—"

"Luuuceee! I'm home!" The Ricky Ricardo imitation echoed through the house and Delilah's jaws clamped around her fourth cheese puff.

She knew that voice. It couldn't be. It just couldn't be—

"Honey bunch," the voice drawled somewhere to her left. Seconds later, strong hands gripped her upper arms and hauled her from the chair. "Sorry I'm late, but the guys and I stopped off for a couple of brewskies."

She gulped down the rest of her cheese puff and found herself face-to-face with Zach Tanner. Two vivid laser-blue eyes twinkled back at her and the air stalled in her lungs. And then he kissed her.

*Oh, no!*

# 5

FIRM LIPS TOUCHED hers in the loudest smooch Delilah had ever heard. The sound echoed in her ears, drowning out the frantic beat of her heart. Then it was over, but not soon enough. Her lips tingled. Worse, other more important places were doing some major tingling of their own.

"Delilah?" Her mother's voice drew her around to see the woman paused mid-chew. "What in the world is going on?"

"Yeah," Oliver chimed in, staring pointedly at Zach. "Who are you and what are you doing with my fiancée?"

"*Your* fiancée?" Zach anchored an arm around her waist and hauled a dazed Delilah up against his side. "He's such a kidder," he told her mother. "Delilah's my little woman. Thanks, man," he said as he turned to Oliver, "for keeping the old ball and chain here company for me. Sorry I'm late."

"*This* is Percy?" Gladys pointed an accusing sausage at Zach. "But I thought the other one was Percy."

"It's a popular name—" Delilah choked on the rest of her explanation when Zach's arm dropped to pinch her bottom.

"Our mothers were old high school friends," Zach said. "And they loved the name. So Percy here got it, and so did I. Lucky me." He punctuated the sentence with another butt pinch.

"Ahhh—uh, that's right." Delilah nodded vigorously.

"Ma, you really thought this was *the* Percy?" A hysterical laugh bubbled on her lips as she motioned to Oliver. "He's just a friend."

"That's right," Zach added. "I'm the Percy who's marrying honey bunch here. *Percy* Zach Tanner." Zach planted another loud kiss on Delilah's gaping mouth before turning to Gladys. "I've been waiting for this day much too long, ma'am, just dying for the chance to thank you in person for giving birth to my little sugar cookie here."

Gladys giggled, Zach smiled and the sugar cookie in question barely resisted the urge to land a well-deserved kick to the source of all that Wild Man charm.

She would have, if her mother hadn't been smiling from ear to ear. That, and the frantic thud of Delilah's heart, served as a constant reminder of her mother's failing health. Heart attacks were serious business. Her father had died of one. Who knew what would happen if Gladys got wind of the truth?

*No fiancé. No future son-in-law. No wedding. No reception. No buffet.*

No way.

She suppressed the impulse to deliver any attacks on Zach's...*charm,* and concentrated on not concentrating so much on all that heat and muscle standing next to her.

"You're that Wild Man person, the football guy," her mother said.

"You follow sports?" He dazzled her with a ten-carat smile.

"I have three boys. I can name every Super Bowl team complete with MVP players, Mr., uh, Percy."

"Why don't you call me Zach? Percy's so formal." He took her mother's hand and kissed it.

"I must say, it's such a pleasure to finally meet you,"

her mother gushed. "But I thought Delilah said you were an accountant."

"Among other things."

"A jack-of-all-trades. How handy." She turned a glare on Oliver. "I knew this man couldn't be the one who swept my baby off her feet. He doesn't even like pot roast."

"The communist," Zach declared and Gladys smiled before glaring at Oliver again.

Poor Oliver. Then again, a guy who belched competitively probably wasn't that easily insulted.

"I—I guess I'll get going." Oliver grabbed his jacket.

"You could stay and join us for dinner," Delilah offered. Guilt swamped her, along with relief, and a strange tingling in her spine. And on her lips. *Oh, no.*

Anger, she told herself. The tingling had to be anger, because Zach Tanner's hand had pinched her rear end, twice, and his hand still rested there. A sign of intimacy. Possession. She stiffened. Yep, it was anger, all right.

"I don't want to impose," Oliver said.

Delilah leaned forward, just a fraction away from Zach's fingers. "It's no imposition."

"That's right," Gladys chimed in, her old southern hospitality kicking back in now that the pot roast communist wasn't her potential son-in-law. "But if you really have something pressing, don't worry about us. You feel free to go on about your business, Percy. It was…interesting to meet you."

"Yeah," Oliver said, a glazed look on his face.

"Thanks again." Zach abandoned Delilah's butt to snake an arm around her shoulders and clamp her to his side.

Her gaze went to Melanie and she saw her friend's triumphant smile, accompanied by a thumbs-up.

"I think I'll duck out too, Mrs. James," Mel said once

Oliver had made a beeline for the front door. "Nice to see you again."

"Lovely, Melanie." Gladys tilted her head so Melanie could kiss her cheek. "I do wish you would come out to see me. Has Delilah mentioned her brother Jesse? Why, he's just about your age, single and so attractive—"

"I just might take you up on that when I get some free time. Bye."

Before Delilah could take another breath, not an easy thing to do with an iron arm locked around her shoulders and so much male body heat swamping her senses, Melanie was gone.

"Every team, huh?" Zach said once the front door had slammed shut. "That's mighty impressive, Mrs. James."

"It's nothing, and please call me Gladys. Delilah can name them all, too. Every NBA playoff team, as well."

"Ma," Delilah warned.

"Now, now, don't be so modest. You know, Zach, her expertise isn't limited to sports. She can also cook better than anyone I know—"

"Ma," Delilah cut in.

"—yours truly excluded, of course, and I'm not just talking desserts. And have you ever seen such a beautiful face?"

"Ma, please."

"And that figure, so soft and round and just perfect for bearing children."

"*Ma!*"

"That's exactly what I was thinking." Zach's gaze dropped, traveling clear to her toes and lingering at all the soft and round spots in between. Her cheeks caught fire and she barely resisted the urge to elbow him. "It's no wonder she's so accomplished with you as a mother."

"My, my, you're the charmer."

"Yes, he just oozes the stuff," Delilah ground out, her mouth fixed in a smile.

He turned an accusing stare on her. "But you never told me you knew so much about football, honey bun."

"Delilah tends to be a little shy. Takes after her father."

"Maybe on the inside, but outside, she's definitely got your good looks."

Gladys blushed while Zach grabbed a handful of cheese puffs and popped one into his mouth. "These are good," he said in between bites.

"Delilah made them." Her mother sank onto the couch and reached for the sausages. "I told you she's quite the gourmet. I can't wait to see what's for dinner."

"Me either." Zach let go of Delilah to plop down next to her mother. "This stuff is good." He grabbed another cheese puff. "But I'm more a meat and potatoes man."

"Really?" Her mother practically glowed and anger rippled through Delilah.

Funny how the knowledge that he'd saved her in the nick of time paled in comparison to the fact that he'd pinched her butt twice, called her "honey bunch" and a dozen other things that made her want to punch him in the nose on behalf of all womankind, *and* he'd kissed her—all in the course of three minutes, without warning, as if he had every right. Now he was sitting next to her mother, eating the cheese puffs and sausages she'd slaved over, and not even sparing her a glance.

The…the *cretin*. And she'd actually mistaken him for Batman?

"Could I speak to you for a second?" she hissed.

"Can't it wait, bunny bear? I'm starved—"

*"Now."* She grabbed his ear and pinched hard enough to pull him up off the couch. "We'll be right back, Ma."

"You two take your time. I was young once, too, you

know." Gladys waved them off before reaching for another sausage.

"Percy?" he ground out the minute they reached the kitchen and she turned on him. "Couldn't you have picked something that sounds like a guy instead of a geek?"

"Excuse me, but it's not every day I lie to my mother."

"Sure, sweetheart."

"I'm new at this, and uncomfortable and trying to make the best of a really bad situation. And for your information, Percy isn't a geek name. Percy Bysshe Shelley is one of my favorite poets, and he was man enough for Mary, so that's good enough for me. Besides, I wasn't going for a macho name."

"Obviously."

"Otherwise I would have picked one of those steroid names like Dirk or Brick or Kurk or *Zach*—something with a good strong consonant and a grunt."

"Damn, but you're good. That little frown thing you're doing, with your nose all wrinkled up and your lips pursed. You really don't look very happy to see me."

"I'm not."

"Come on, honey." The easy drawl of his voice didn't quite match the hard glint in his eyes. "The jig is up. Obviously you're hard up for the Wild Man, so I was just obliging."

"I'm sorry about that, it's just…I had to do something."

"Like blackmail."

"Blackmail? Sure, I attached a few conditions to the sale, but that's hardly blackmail. Just good business sense."

"I'm talking about Bob's Barbecue."

"Bob? That guy who wears the pig suit in all those commercials?"

"The one and only and my biggest competitor in the rib

business. Tell me you didn't threaten to sell exclusives to Bob if I didn't agree to be your fiancé.''

''*Pretend* fiancé, and I threatened no such thing.''

He shook his head. ''I have to tell you, this tactic is a first. Usually women sneak into my house, hide under my bed, in my shower, the back seat of my car. One even parachuted into my backyard to get close to me, but no one's ever resorted to blackmail. Poor Jeff's dialing the Hair Club for Men as we speak.''

''I'm not interested in you.''

''My business manager doesn't handle stress very well, which includes threats from your business manager.''

''I don't have a business manager.''

''She said she was your business manager. A Mitsy Ravioli or something like that. You must want me really bad to play so dirty.''

''Ragolli. Melanie Ragolli, and she was the one who answered the door. She's my accountant, and I never told her to…'' A vision of Melanie giving her a thumbs-up flashed in her mind and suddenly the pieces fell into place. ''I mean, I, er, never told her to actually threaten you, just lay out the conditions.''

''Blackmail being the biggest condition.''

''Well, um, yes.''

''So you do want me.''

''Only in a professional capacity.'' Right. And that would explain why she tingled every time he was around. She stiffened. ''This is all your fault anyway.''

''And how is that?''

''If you hadn't been parading around as Batman, I wouldn't even be in this mess. You were so nice and I liked you so much, and then I was trying to work and my mother was riding me about finding Mr. Right and there you were—he was—in my head and the words just came out.''

''You told your mother you were engaged to Batman to get her off your back about finding a man?''

''But I wouldn't have if I hadn't been kissed senseless—''

''Delilah, dear, do you have any more of these wonderful sausages?''

''Just a minute, Ma,'' she called over her shoulder, before turning back to Zach. ''Where was I?''

''Senseless.''

''Yeah, well, I normally have oodles of common sense, but after that kiss, I got all kinds of crazy thoughts about you and me and us and—''

''And some more cheese puffs, too, dear.''

''Right away, Ma!''

''What thoughts?'' Zach prodded while Delilah tried to find her train of thought. Unfortunately, that train had left the station way back when Zach had put his hand on her caboose.

''Not even thoughts, really. Just what-ifs. Like what if you were Mr. Right and I was looking for Mr. Right, but I wasn't, and you're obviously not and—oh, never mind. The point is, I wasn't thinking and it was your fault.'' She blew out an exasperated breath. ''And my mother's.''

''I'm waiting, dear,'' Gladys called out.

''In a second, Ma!'' She shook her head. ''She makes me crazy. One minute I'm focused and ambitious, the next, I'm so desperate, I'm condoning blackmail. I've sunk to an all-time low.''

He grinned. ''Once you put it in writing, it'll be an official all-time low.'' He pulled some folded legal documents from his pocket. ''My lawyer drew up these papers. Sign on the dotted line and it's official. We get exclusives, and you get the Wild Man for two weeks. Not all the time, mind you. I do have a business to run.''

''And bras full of beer to drink and men to arm wrestle.''

''That bra thing was for charity. It raised two thousand dollars for the Greater Dallas Boys' Home.''

''Congratulations,'' she said with stiff lips, but she felt a strange softening inside her. Maybe it was the way he spoke about the boys' home. He had the same look in his eyes she'd seen in that picture in his office. Thoughtful, contemplative.

Contemplative? Right. The only thing Zach Tanner contemplated was what color bra to wear on his head. His big, egotistical head.

''I'll need you some days. A few lunches, some dinners,'' she told him. ''Until my mom hops a plane for Miami in exactly ten days, six hours and twenty-eight minutes.'' She took the pen and noticed her trembling hand. ''I still can't believe I'm doing this.''

''You could always go back and tell your mother the truth.''

She scribbled her name and handed the papers back to him. ''I can't disappoint her like that.''

''Won't she be disappointed when there's no wedding?''

''That's not your concern. It's mine.'' Her biggest, as a matter of fact, but she couldn't worry over that now. One day at a time. She needed to make it through dinner. ''Just act normal, and no more butt pinching.''

''Honey, your mother expects us to pretend to like each other and I'm a toucher.'' To emphasize his point, his hand trailed down her arm.

Heat shimmied to her breasts and her mouth went dry.

''And I'm a biter.'' She snapped her teeth together to emphasize her point and he winced. ''So keep your hands and lips and any other wandering body parts to yourself.''

"You know, I'm almost inclined to think you aren't crazy about me."

"I'm not." She shrugged away from him. There, that was better. No touching and she could keep her hormones in check. Otherwise, she might have a rebellion on her hands.

Nix that. This was a dictatorship, with reason in complete control.

"If you want my attention, just clear your throat or something."

"Whatever you say."

"And try to act civilized."

"Dear?" Gladys's voice carried from the other room. "Is everything all right? There isn't trouble in paradise, is there? Because you two have been in there an awful long time, and I keep hearing voices."

"Paradise is fine, Ma," she called over her shoulder. "We'll be out in a flash." She shifted her attention back to Zach. "And don't call me any more stupid names—"

"Because you sound so...tense, dear," Gladys went on.

"You look tense, too." Zach grinned and Delilah frowned.

"I am not tense," she ground out and Zach's grin widened.

"You and your young man aren't having a disagreement, are you?"

"Yes!" Zach called out at the same time Delilah shouted "No!"

"Shut up," she muttered to Zach before she called out, "We're fine, Ma."

But it was too late. Delilah heard the footsteps a moment before the kitchen door swung open.

Before she could stop to think about what she was doing,

much less regret it, she threw herself into Zach's arms and clamped her mouth onto his.

"Stealing kisses." Gladys sighed. "How sweet..."

Anything more her mother might have said faded into the sound of blood rushing, hearts pounding, as her attention quickly shifted to the man in front of her, surrounding her.

Delilah wasn't sure when things changed. When the desperate press of her lips against his became a seductive stroke and glide. When the hands clutching his arms eased to slide around his neck and pull him closer. She only knew she was kissing Zach Tanner, and he was kissing her.

Boy, was he ever.

His tongue tangled with hers, exploring and tasting, his mouth eating at hers. The trembling started in her fingertips and worked its way through her body until every nerve vibrated.

From far away, Delilah heard her mother's soft voice singing the theme from *Love Boat*.

"Love, exciting and new..."

*Love?*

*No!*

Delilah tore her mouth from Zach's and stumbled backward just as the kitchen door rocked shut and her mother disappeared into the other room.

She gasped for air as her gaze collided with his. Blue eyes glittered back at her, hot and needy and...*him*. Oh, no!

*Get a grip. It isn't him. It's hormones.* Zach Tanner oozed sex appeal. No red-blooded female was safe around him, including Delilah, even though she'd always prided herself on being immune to such barbaric charm.

She was, or rather she would be. From this moment on. Now that she knew what the problem was—too much sex appeal on his part, not enough sex on her part—she could deal with it.

"Delilah, dear!" her mother called out. "You children save something for the honeymoon and come out here and join me."

"I...sure, Ma!" She turned to Zach. "You have to leave."

"Leave? But what about dinner?"

"I—I'll fix you a doggie bag." She whirled and grabbed a plate from the counter.

"That's not what I meant," he said as she started dishing up food from the pots lining the stove. "What's the matter?" His voice sounded right over her shoulder and she whirled.

"There." She thrust a full plate into his hands, putting some distance between them. "Take-out. Now take it out. Please."

"Won't your mom be expecting me at the dinner table?"

"Probably." When he didn't budge, she moved behind him, planted her hands on his back and started pushing him toward the back door.

"So how are you going to explain my leaving?"

"You've already put in an appearance. I'll tell her you had an emergency." She whipped open the door and started to shove him through.

"You're really serious."

"As a heart attack." A heart attack? "Forget I said that."

"What's wrong with you?" He stalled in the doorway.

"I need to think, all right? And I can't do that around you. Or my mother. And with the two of you, it's a double whammy. There's no telling what I'm liable to do. You have to go."

"You can stop playing hard to get."

"I'm not playing anything. I *am* hard to get, and you'll never get me. *Ever.*"

"I don't want to get you. You want to get *me.*"

"In your dreams, buddy." *Or in mine.* She forced the thought aside. "I don't like you."

"Right." He turned to face her. "I guess you go around kissing men you don't like all the time."

"That was strictly for my mother's benefit." *Liar.* "Whew, would you look at the time? You really should go. It's late."

"It's only seven-thirty."

"My point exactly. The evening is young and I still have tons of work to do."

"Tonight?" He looked suspicious.

"All night. I'm trying to land the Walter's Wings account and that Walter is a tough old guy."

"Delilah!" Her mother's voice echoed through the house.

"Coming, Ma!" she called over her shoulder. "I'll call you later," she told Zach. *Much later.* Then she slammed the back door on him. *Out of sight, out of mind.*

Unfortunately, his scent lingered in the air, on her, and followed her back to the refrigerator to retrieve more cheese puffs.

*Him.* No.

She was just suffering from a major case of sexual deprivation. Years of all work and no play had finally caught up with her.

At least that was what she told herself as she headed back into the living room to face her mother and make up some excuse for Zach's absence.

"He had an emergency call."

"What sort of an emergency forces him to run out on his fiancée, for heaven's sake?"

"Business. One of the restaurants was, um, out of barbecue sauce."

"Oh, my, that is an emergency. What a dedicated young man."

"I'm glad you think so, Ma, because Zach works a lot."

"A good provider."

"And we don't see each other as often as we'd like."

"Absence makes the heart grow fonder."

Or the hormones run wilder, Delilah thought later that night after three hours of tossing and turning. Yearning.

*No.* Yearning was not productive, and Delilah was already behind in her weekly production schedule from all the worrying over finding a fiancé.

She climbed out of bed, pulled on her robe and tiptoed downstairs to her office. Flicking on her computer screen, she settled herself and did her best to concentrate.

Funny how all the numbers started to swirl together and take on the extraordinary likeness of one dangerously handsome man with a sexy grin and—

*Work,* she told herself, because Delilah James didn't *do* macho jocks. No matter how good-looking, how great a kisser, how warm and strong. She would see Zach in a couple of days, when she couldn't put her mother off any longer and she'd finally caught up on her work, and she would play out the engagement charade with the same calm professionalism she used in running How Sweet It Is. The arrangement with Zach was business. Purely business, and no one would be *doing* anyone.

*A shame,* a small, traitorous voice whispered as she remembered the feel of his lips on hers and heat fluttered through her. *Definitely a shame.*

# 6

"WHAT ARE YOU DOING here?" Jeff Black glanced up from his ledger books as Zach walked through the doorway of Wild Man's later that evening.

"She kicked me out."

"Who kicked you?" Jeff pulled off his glasses and stared at Zach.

"Delilah James, and she didn't kick me, she kicked me *out,* right after she kissed me. I showed up for dinner at her place, as scheduled—" he set down Delilah's to-go plate on the desk and perched on the corner "—and gave her a dose of Wild Man charm."

"That's probably why she kicked you out. And why was she kissing you? I mean, I know you're supposed to be her fiancé and all, but she didn't say anything about kissing, and I doubt she was taken in by all that charm."

"Jeff, Jeff, Jeff. She's obviously crazy about the Wild Man. Can't keep her hands off him. You should have seen the look in her eyes." A look he wasn't likely to forget for one hell of a long time, which was why he'd opted to put in a few extra hours at the restaurant rather than go home to an empty bed. "She wanted me. Bad."

"So she kicked you out. Makes perfect sense."

Zach frowned. "It's a classic move. She thinks if she plays hard to get, the Wild Man will be interested."

"And is he?"

*Hell, yes.* "Hell, no."

"And what about Zach Tanner?"

"He doesn't go for blackmailing groupies, even one who's a hell of a looker, cooks a mean pot roast and kisses really good." *Great.* "Delilah James isn't wife material."

"Wife material? Since when does the Wild Man associate with women who are wife material?"

"Since I've been thinking that maybe it's time the Wild Man settled down." *Was that really his voice? Aw, hell, it was.*

"This upcoming birthday is really getting to you."

"Hell, no." He flexed and tried not to wince when his sore shoulder groaned. "It's just that I'd like to have a family and now seems like a good time." *Before my shoulder gives out completely.* "Look, I'm not in any hurry. I just thought I'd keep my eyes open for likely prospects."

"And it has nothing to do with the fact that you're about to turn thirty-five?"

"I can still run circles around you." *Just don't ask me to arm wrestle.*

Jeff didn't say anything, just stared at Zach with that contemplative look that made him want to confess every one of his sins. Not that he had to bother. Jeff knew Zach better than he knew himself.

"I don't like her," Zach said.

"Sure you don't."

"I want a woman who sees past the Wild Man image. A woman I can talk to, laugh with—"

"A woman who likes nice guy Zach Tanner?"

"Yes, and Delilah James is out of the running." Even if she had been the perfect candidate when he'd first met her in the storage closet.

That's what made him so damned mad. He'd been wrong, and he was never wrong. Then again, he'd never been this close to a major life change. The big three-five. Middle age.

It was just another year, didn't mean anything, he assured himself, despite the sudden urge to drop and do two hundred push-ups. He could, he told himself. Easy.

He eased down into a nearby chair, his shoulder ached, bones creaked. Okay, make that one hundred push-ups. Fifty minimum.

"If you're serious about finding a wife, I could have Trudy check around the library for any available women. I'm sure there are tons of women out there who hate the Wild Man."

"Thanks a lot."

"I meant that in a good way, and speaking of the Wild Man, did you at least get Delilah's name on the dotted line before she kicked you out?"

"Mission accomplished. Bob can serve Twinkies to his customers for all I care." Zach fished the documents from his pocket.

"Thank God." Jeff ran a hand through his hair and stared at his fingers, searching for any traitorous strands before breathing a sigh of relief. "Maybe it was just a temporary thing. That's what the psychic said."

"Psychic?"

"A friend of Trudy's. I had a consultation this afternoon, right after you left to play fiancé. Madame Soleil said if I could just get rid of my negative energy, my positive force will counter any more hair loss."

"You talked to a psychic? Don't you think you're going overboard just because of a few extra hairs in the hairbrush?"

"You wouldn't be saying that if it was your hair, and it's more than a few. It's fifty-nine. Anyhow, Madame Soleil is a personal consultant to some very influential people, including a lot of celebrities.'' He ran another hand through his hair just to make sure. "Look, she was right. Now that the cheesecake deal is squared away and last month's receivables are perfect, I'm completely worry-free and there isn't a loose strand on me.''

"You are not losing your hair.''

Jeff smiled. "That's good, Zach. I like your positive attitude. It feeds my energy.''

"While we're talking feeding, shouldn't you be home having dinner with Trudy instead of stressing out here?''

Jeff glanced at his watch. "Jeez, I got so caught up in the books, I completely forgot the time.'' He reached for his briefcase. "Oh, by the way, I'll be in a little later than usual tomorrow. Trudy and I are planning an all-nighter.''

Zach winked. "Working on Jeff Junior?''

"We're mixing up a batch of homemade hair tonic Trudy found in this old history book. Thank God I married a librarian. Anyhow, you can't add the final ingredient until the clock strikes midnight, then you have to stir for at least three hours.'' When Zach shook his head, Jeff added, "She found actual documentation that George Washington himself used the recipe.''

"I thought you were going with the positive energy thing.''

"The tonic is plan B. Just in case.''

"Doesn't a plan B count as negative energy?''

Jeff's smile faltered. Frantic, he ran both hands through his hair and came up with a single strand. "Oh, no! I blew it. I voiced my skepticism out loud and now look.''

"It's one hair, man.''

"Sixty hairs.'' He ran another hand through his hair and came up with a second strand. "Oh, God, make that sixty-one.''

"It's no wonder with you pulling on it like that. Keep your hands off and everything will be fine."

Jeff left and Zach leaned back in his chair and eyed the plate of pot roast. His mouth watered, but not for food.

He was hungry for something altogether different.

Closing his eyes, he remembered the feel of her lips, her body pressed to his as she'd kissed him and he'd kissed her—

That was what bothered him the most. Not that she'd kissed him. After the blackmail ploy, he would have been surprised if she hadn't kissed him. She was obviously eager to play out some football-hero fantasy with him. The real problem was that Zach had kissed her back. Worse, he'd liked it.

Too damned much.

*Her.*

His eyes snapped open. She wasn't The One, despite their initial attraction and the all-important fact that she'd thrown him out. That had been an act, just like her "I'll call you later" put-off. As if she didn't want to talk to him anytime soon. As if she really didn't like him. *As if.*

Sweet Delilah James was like every other woman he'd ever met. Drawn by his reputation. Eager to get close to him because he was the Wild Man. When he'd been a nobody Batman, she hadn't bothered to even find out his name. Six months later, once she'd discovered he was none other than Wild Man Tanner, she'd not only called, she'd blackmailed.

All the more reason to forget her kiss. To forget her.

Done.

He reached for a piece of pot roast. As his lips closed around the first bite, he couldn't help but groan. Her mother had been right. She was one hell of a cook.

A green-eyed, soft-skinned, lush-mouthed cook with the hots for a sports hero.

As angry as the truth made him, it also made him anxious. Restless. Desperate to see Delilah James again because, as good as the pot roast was, she'd tasted much, much better.

And despite his vow to keep his mind on potential marriage prospects, he was damned anxious for another taste.

"WHAT TIME IS IT?" Melanie's groggy voice floated over the line after several rings.

"It's six in the morning," Delilah told her, "and you're dead meat."

"Dee? Where are you?"

"At my computer."

"You should be in bed."

"I've been up for hours. I've got the presentation for Walter's Wings to do this morning."

"Oh, yeah. Good luck."

"I didn't call for moral support." Her voice took on an accusing note. "You blackmailed him, Mel."

"Who?"

"Zach Tanner. You told him we were selling exclusives to Bob's if he didn't agree."

"Beautiful move, wasn't it?"

"It's a lie."

"A teeny, tiny lie for a good cause. To make your mother happy and save your hide. It did make your mother happy, didn't it?"

"Yes."

"And it did save your hide?"

"That's debatable. Now Zach Tanner thinks I'm some groupie. Not that I really care what he thinks. It's just...a *groupie*. Me, of all people." She shook away an overwhelming feeling of disgust and took a deep breath. "Okay, so he thinks I'm a groupie. So what? I'm definitely worrying over this too much."

"It's no wonder when you get up so early. Speaking of which, I'm going back to sleep now. Bye."

"IT'S AMAZING to me you can even drag yourself out of bed so early in the morning, much less be so energetic with all this dieting." Gladys sat across the table from Delilah thirty minutes later and watched her daughter bypass pancakes for a cup of coffee.

"Caffeine," Delilah said, pouring her third cup. "It hasn't failed me in ten years." Up at the crack of dawn and go, go, go. That was Delilah. Always time conscious. Always early. "Speaking of which, I really have to get to my office and print out the day's schedule before my crew arrives."

"So eat something and make your old mother happy."

"You're not old." Delilah drank another sip of coffee and reached for a boiled egg. "And I am eating something."

"Something good."

"It's pure protein."

"Something that tastes good, dear. You're depriving your poor taste buds."

"This tastes just fine." At Gladys's frown, Delilah added, "I need to diet, Ma."

"Says who?"

"Every weight chart in the country, because by all counts I'm above average."

"Of course you are. You've always been an above-average woman. Highly intelligent, exceptionally beautiful."

"Generously rounded?"

"What's wrong with that? Men want a woman they can cozy up to, dear, hang on to when they're—"

"Have some juice, Ma."

"Thank you, dear." Gladys took the orange juice and sipped. "Take me, for instance." She stared down at her double Mexican omelet with extra cheese, jalapeños and side order of chili. "I never worry about what I eat and I've been the same weight for the past twenty years. I'm full-figured, dear, and proud of it. Your father appreciated a well-rounded woman and I'm sure your Zach does."

"Um, yeah." Delilah averted her gaze and downed the rest of her coffee.

"You're worried about something."

"Work. I've got a busy Friday planned and I've spent three extra minutes here when I should be in my office—"

"It's Zach, isn't it? Oh, a mother knows these things. You're worried I don't like him."

"I am? Oh, yes, I am."

"Rest assured, dear, he's wonderful. So like your father at that age. Handsome and outgoing. Strong and virile. Intelligent and keen enough to spot good breeding when he sees it. My baby." She beamed at Delilah. "What a face, a body, such perfect genes."

"Jeans that are too tight," Delilah muttered as she finished her third boiled egg.

"What did you say, dear?"

"I said…um, you're right. Absolutely right. I think I'll have a Danish."

"That's my girl."

"In my office."

"But I wanted you to tell me more about Zach."

"Later, Ma. I promise. I've got a busy day and I really have to get to work." Delilah escaped into her office, and sat down at her computer. Her hand paused over the trash as her mother's voice floated down the hallway.

"Don't even think about tossing that in the wastebasket. There are starving children in Guatemala, dear."

Delilah took a deep breath and tiptoed to the window. A few birds chirped from a nearby tree and she slid the pane up, placed the Danish on the windowsill and went back to her desk.

"Don't even think of feeding the birds, dear. Sugar is dangerous to such frail creatures. Why, I saw this special on TV where this robin ate a doughnut and internally combusted."

Delilah snatched the pastry from an aggravated blue jay, slammed the window shut and sank down at her desk.

The Danish called from the plate in front of her and she closed her eyes, praying for strength. It was only two weeks. Two tiny little weeks. She'd lived with the woman for eighteen years and lived to tell about it. What was ten days, four hours and twenty-two minutes more?

She shoved the Danish into a drawer, slammed it shut and turned her attention to the computer. Ah, work. Her savior. Her passion. Her fingers flew across the keys, the printer hummed and all was right with the world.

For the meantime.

Until Delilah faced her mother, gave in to the Danish's desperate call or kissed Zach Tanner again.

Her mother, food and *him*.

It was going to be a desperately long two weeks.

"Hey, sugar. How's it shaking?" Zach's deep voice rumbled in her ear Saturday morning when Delilah answered the phone.

"Didn't I say I'd call you?" she asked.

"It's been twenty-four hours," he pointed out. "Isn't your mother wondering where Mr. Right is?"

"I told her you had a crisis at work."

"Sure, and maybe you're just trying to psych me out? Make me anxious?"

"I'd like to make you dead, but that would really mess things up with my mother. She actually likes you— Wait a second." Her hand covered the mouthpiece and he heard a muffled "Yeah, Ma! It's Zach. He says he's sorry he has to work. He enjoyed meeting you, too." She moved her hand and her voice became loud and clear over the phone. "My mom says you were every bit as wonderful as she anticipated."

"Wonderful's my middle name."

"And here I thought it was obnoxious." Her hand covered the mouthpiece again. "Yeah, Ma. He says you were great, too. Yeah, he can't wait to see you." The hand moved and she muttered, "Did you call to torture me or did you need something? Because I'm trying to work."

"I'm on to you, so cut the act."

"Act?"

"Yeah, act. As in you pretending to hate me when you really don't."

"I do hate you."

"Right. I see right through you, but I have to admit, you put on one hell of a show."

"You want to talk show?" She bristled. "Watching you is like watching science fiction theater. Do you take pills to initiate the change? A potion? Or are you secretly possessed by the devil?"

"What are you talking about?"

"Your transformation into the Wild Man."

"Your dream man."

"More like my nightmares."

"You're good, sugar. In fact, I almost believe you, but no woman would go to such lengths to blackmail me if they didn't have a hidden agenda. You want the Wild Man. You blackmailed me to get close to me so you could live out some sports-hero fantasy you've probably had since you were a kid."

"That's the most ridiculous, egotistical, self-absorbed, outrageous..." A long pause followed, as if her mouth worked at words that refused to come. "I won't even waste my breath."

"On what?"

"Telling you how totally clueless you are."

"I'm clued in, honey. You think if you play hard to get, you'll get me."

"I don't want you. I mean, I do, but just for two weeks, while my mother's here." When he laughed, she growled, "This is strictly business and don't call me honey."

"Sure."

"Men!" She sputtered. "Okay, hot stuff, you found me out."

"I knew it."

"I've been lusting after you since high school."

"Get it all off your chest, sugar."

"Can I be honest?"

"Honesty's the best policy."

"I'm psychic. I know it sounds wild, but it's true. I have this gift and one day I had a vision of you."

"A vision?"

"A glimpse of perfection. I've spent the past ten years gearing my life toward this one moment, toward you. I went into the cheesecake business specifically because I knew you would hurt your shoulder, open a chain of he-man rib joints and someday beg me for exclusives on my Chocolate Cherry Cha-Cha." She gave a dramatic sigh. "I feel so relieved. Thank you, Zach. I've been crippled under the weight of my deception and you've set me free. Free at last, free at last, thank you Zach, I'm free at last!''

"Very funny."

"I'm dead serious."

"And I'm hanging up now."

"Good. You shouldn't have called in the first place. Some of us work for a living."

"You're awfully hostile for someone who needs me."

"I *do not* need you," she muttered.

The phone clicked and Zach found himself staring at the phone, a grin on his face. Maybe Delilah James wasn't out of the running, after all.

"I NEED YOU." Delilah's voice carried over the line that evening. "It's Saturday night and I *really* need you."

"Enough to say you're sorry?"

"You want me to say I'm sorry? For what?"

"For blackmailing me in the first place."

"Okay, I'm sorry."

"For kicking me out."

"Sorry."

"For hanging up on me."

"Ditto."

"And for lying about the fact that you want the Wild Man."

"I didn't lie. I don't want the Wild Man, no matter what warped fantasy your mind has cooked up."

"It's your warped fantasy."

"You *are not* my warped fantasy. Hold on." Her hand covered the phone and he heard a muffled "He just called, Mom."

"Liar, liar, pants on fire."

"I hate you."

"Don't I wish."

"So are you coming over or not?"

"Why should I?"

"It's Saturday night."

"So?"

"So engaged couples usually see each other on Saturday night, unless they have conflicting schedules or one of them is out of town, or they work shift work, or they have religious beliefs against weekend dating—you don't have any religious beliefs like that, do you?"

"None that I know of."

"And neither of us is out of town, and we don't work shifts, though I do have to finish invoices, which is why I need you because I can't do a thing with my mother breathing down my neck speculating on why you're not here breathing down my neck, or doing other things to me and my neck I won't mention because I can't believe she even suggested them, because I still have a very hard time seeing her as a real woman who's ever french-kissed a man, much less had sex with him, much less *enjoyed* it and—"

"You're rambling."

"I am not." Silence settled in. "Okay, I'm rambling, but I'm frustrated. I need you. Right now."

"Pretty please."

"I hate you."

"I must be hearing wrong, because I thought you said—"

"Pretty please," she ground out.

"With sugar on top?"

"I really hate you."

"Wrestling starts in five minutes. Gotta go—"

"Spoonfuls of sugar. Cups of the stuff. Now are you coming or not?"

"Maybe."

FIFTEEN MINUTES LATER, a worried Delilah opened the door to a breathless Zach.

"You're here." Relief washed through her.

"I was in the neighborhood." He gulped for air and moved past her. "You don't look glad to see me."

"I'm not." When he shrugged and started to turn, she grabbed his arm and yanked him inside the house. "I'm thrilled to see you." The moment of contact had every nerve in her body buzzing and she quickly snatched her hand away and made herself a promise not to touch him again.

Only under life-or-death circumstances.

"Zach!" Her mother floated from the living room, a bowl of buttered popcorn in her hands. "What a pleasure to see you again!"

"The pleasure's all mine, Gladys. You look lovely."

"I'm a mess." Gladys touched a hand to her head full of hot-pink rollers. "I just finished my nightly set."

"You're still the prettiest thing this side of the Rio Grande. Why, if I didn't have babycakes here, I'd be tempted to—"

"We'll be in the office if you need us, Ma," Delilah cut in. She grabbed his shirtsleeve and hauled him toward the sweet wing.

"I'm just going to watch some TV and I'm not coming out of my room," Gladys said, a suggestive light in her eyes. "No matter what I hear."

"Ma!"

"So you two have fun."

"If you want her to think we're really engaged, why don't we go out to dinner, make her think we're on a real date?" Zach asked as Delilah led him into her office.

"Because with my mother here—" *and you scrambling my common sense* "I'm behind on my paperwork. Besides,

I told my mom that you help me with my books, so this fits perfectly. She thinks we're getting romantic under the pretense of work, and I actually get to work. Now sit here.'' She steered him into a chair and slapped her delivery boy's latest copy of *Hot Rods and Hot Bods* into his hands.

Taking a deep breath, Delilah slid into her seat, flicked on her computer and reached for a stack of invoices.

"You really want to work?" He sounded suspicious.

"What else?"

"Well—"

"Forget I asked. Look, contrary to what you may think, I'm not hot for your body. I don't plan to molest you and live out any fantasy. I'm just a desperate woman who needs a few minutes of concentration.'' She took a deep breath and turned to her screen.

"You're fully automated.'' Zach's voice came from behind her and she realized he'd abandoned his chair to round the desk and lean over her shoulder.

"I had the software custom-designed for my business. All I have to do is key in orders, and in a matter of seconds, I've got a supply list, production schedule, delivery sheet, everything at my fingertips.''

"I'm impressed.''

The words slid into her ears and warmth unfurled inside her. She frowned. "Could you please be impressed from over there in the chair? You're crowding my work space.''

He rounded the desk and paused to stare at the pictures lining her walls.

"An ex-boyfriend?" He pointed to one in particular.

Delilah smiled. "My oldest brother, Cole.'' She indicated a nearby frame. "Those are my other two brothers. I'm the youngest of four children and the only girl.'' She pointed at another picture. "That's my dad. He died of a sudden heart attack last year.''

"I'm sorry."

"Thanks. Things were tough for a while there. It was so unexpected. One minute he was fine, and the next... My mom took it real hard. They'd been married for thirty-six years. She was so sad and then she started having her own chest pains, but she's doing much better now. She's taking her first singles' cruise next week."

"That's good." He stared at the first picture again. Her brother, dressed in his uniform, smiled back. "So Cole's a cop?"

"The youngest SWAT team commander in Houston. Then there's Billy, he's a professional bronc buster on the rodeo circuit. Then there's Jesse."

"Jesse *James?*"

She shrugged. "What can I say? My dad had a thing for old-West movies. Anyhow, Jesse owns JJ Construction back home in Houston."

"The cop, the cowboy and the construction worker." Zach grinned. "Where's the Indian and the biker?"

"My dad was one-eighth Cherokee and my mom has an exercise cycle."

The grin widened and her heart did a double thump. *Bad, girl. No double-thumping or pitter-pattering.*

"Any of your brothers married?"

"Don't I wish. Then they could have nice, distracting grandchildren to keep my mother occupied." She sighed and tried not to think about the way his eyes seemed so dark and thoughtful. The Wild Man? Thoughtful? Nah.

"So what about you?" she went on. "Any brothers and sisters?"

"It was just me and my mom until she was killed in a car accident when I was five. My dad was never in the picture. My mom was young when she got pregnant, unmarried. The guy didn't stick around."

"Do you ever wonder about him?"

"Once in a while, but there's no burning desire or anything like that. My mom always told me she loved me enough for two parents, and she did. She worked two jobs to make ends meet. That's what caused the accident. She fell asleep on her way home late one night and hit a median. After that I went to the West Dallas Home for Boys where I grew up."

"I'm really sorry."

His expression eased into a half smile as he spared her a glance. "Thanks, but don't be. I'm all right with the past. I grew up in a safe place, with a warm bed, food and Jeff. It wasn't perfect, but it wasn't half-bad."

"Jeff? Jeff Black? Your manager?"

"The one and only. We grew up together, now we work together. It's a good match. He's into numbers and I'm into people."

"Women, in particular, from what I hear."

Anger sparked in his eyes, before fading into a cool, remote blue. "That's me. Love 'em and love 'em some more Wild Man Tanner."

The look he gave her was pure wolf and Delilah felt like the last marinated meatball at a buffet table. "I, um, why don't you have a seat and I'll get to work?"

He sank back down into the chair, his long legs stretched out in front of him, booted ankles crossed. Dutifully, he opened the magazine and Delilah went back to her keyboard. Work was good. Work was distracting. Work was...quiet.

She made it through three invoices before the silence got the best of her and she glanced up.

Zach sat reading a magazine, only he'd traded the car and babe magazine for *Business Week,* and her heart paused. He looked so thoughtful, so serious, so...*un*wildmanish.

The minutes ticked by slowly, with Delilah painfully aware of the man sitting not more than two feet away from her, filling up her office, drinking in all her oxygen, making her think crazy thoughts about hopping over the desk and kissing him again.

*Kissing him?*

Yeah, kissing him. Again. And again. And—

The soft pad of footsteps shattered her thoughts. *Ma!* Before she could think about what she was doing, she bolted to her feet, flew around the desk and snatched the magazine from Zach's hands.

"What are you doing?" he asked as she plopped onto his lap and slid her arms around his neck.

"Convincing my mother there's no trouble in paradise."

And then she kissed him.

# 7

"CHILDREN." Her mother's voice rang out as the door creaked open. "I've brought a nice cheese log and crackers and some divine crab dip— Oh, my." Plates clinked and an excited whisper echoed through the room. "I'll just leave you two to your, um, work." The door creaked shut again, and they were alone.

And still kissing.

Zach's mouth ate at hers. His hands stroked the small of her back. Fingertips burned through the silk of her blouse. His lips left hers to nibble a path down her neck. He licked the tender skin where her pulse beat a frantic rhythm and she gasped.

"My mother's gone," she said in a breathless whisper.

"Ummm…"

"We can stop kissing now."

"Ummm…"

"I didn't mean to flop down on your lap. I—" She caught her bottom lip as his hands slid around her rib cage to the undersides of her breasts. "I should move. I'm too heavy."

"Light as a feather," he breathed against her neck. The words sang through her head, stroked her senses.

"I'm liable to crush you."

"I don't feel a thing."

She shifted and straddled him, her knees on either side

of his thighs. "I do." His hardness pressed between her legs and she rubbed against him.

He groaned, long and low and deep, and she reveled in the simple truth that she, Delilah James, an overabundance of womanhood with too many curves and way too much cushion, was turning on Wild Man Zach Tanner.

He wanted her. Regardless that she wasn't tall and leggy and model-thin. That knowledge temporarily overrode her common sense and the all-important fact that she should be working, her mother could walk in again at any given moment and she was kissing the Wild Man, of all people.

It didn't matter. With his hands working at the buttons of her blouse, his tongue licking her cleavage, she felt like one wild woman. Out of control. Aggressive. Hungry.

He lifted her, arms locked around her waist, her heat nestled against his hardness, and carried her the two feet to the desk. Sitting her on the edge, he turned and cursed when he didn't find a lock on the door. He settled for shoving a plant stand up against the wood before turning back to her.

"You don't have men over very often, do you?"

"Not since Eugene, but that was back in college and he wasn't actually *here,* he was in my dorm room when we...tried, but I didn't really want to, not like I want to now, and I guess he really didn't want to either, because he came out of the closet shortly after that, and I haven't seen him since."

"Good." He stepped toward her. "Now say it again."

"He came out of the closet—" He cut her off with another long, deep kiss.

"Not that," he gasped when the kiss ended. "Say you want to. Now."

"I want to. *Now.*"

He opened her blouse, pushed it down her shoulders, and her first instinct was to cover herself.

"Don't." His hand closed over hers, pulling her fingers away from the fabric and letting it slide to the floor.

"But the light is on and you can see me, *all* of me, and there's way too much—"

"Just enough," he said reverently. "Just perfect." Another kiss and her inhibitions slipped away. She pulled and grasped at his shirt while he worked frantically at her bra.

Buttons popped, his shirt opened. Lace ripped and her breasts spilled into his hands. He kneaded and caressed and thumbed her nipples and Delilah's eyes drifted shut at the exquisite pleasure.

Papers rustled, pens rolled to the floor and her back met the cool desktop. Strong fingertips teased her nipples as he licked and tasted his way down her throat. Warm breath rushed against her breast before he touched the pebbled tip with his tongue. The air whooshed from her lungs as she gasped, her chest lifting in silent invitation.

Zach quickly accepted. He suckled her breast, first one, then the other, long and deep as she clutched at his shoulders.

*More, more, more,* her hormones shouted, or maybe that was her mouth. She wasn't sure. She only knew that he quickly obliged. His mouth slid down, trailing kisses along the underside of her breast, down her rib cage, across sensitive skin to her navel. A lick here, a nip there. Delilah gasped and he turned his attention to unfastening the waistband of her skirt.

A button slid free, the zipper hissed, material fell away and his warm mouth touched the tender area above her panty line.

Electricity bolted through her and she arched off the desk. Her arm bumped plastic. The computer keyboard jumped. The screen scrolled a dozen colors and a loud *beeeep* yanked her back to reality. To the chaos of her desk and the half-naked man sprawled on top of her.

"I...we... *Stop!*" She drew in a gulp of air and tried to tune her ears to the computer going AWOL rather than to Zach's deep, heavy pants.

"Now?" Shock filled his expression.

*No.* "Yes."

"You're serious?" He looked stunned. And hungry. And very, very sexy.

"Don't be mad."

"Mad?"

"That I'm not putting out. I haven't put out in a long time and I would now, but I really do have to work and you and I really don't go together and..." She grappled for words while her hands scrambled for something, anything to put between them. Her hands nudged the platter her mother had brought and she smiled. "But we could share a cheese log instead."

"I ATE AN ENTIRE cheese log." Delilah stood downstairs in the kitchen, telephone hooked between her chin and shoulder, and wrestled the lid off a half-gallon of chocolate ice cream. "And it's all Zach Tanner's fault."

"You offered him cheese instead of sex." Melanie laughed. "I bet that was a first for him."

"I hate him." She yanked the lid free and grabbed her spoon. The ice cream was rock-hard. "He left. Can you believe that?"

"But you told him to."

"But I didn't mean it." She shook her head. "What's wrong with me? Of course I meant it. He never should have kissed me."

"But you kissed him first."

"You're not making me feel any better."

"I'm not trying to." Melanie stifled a yawn. "I'm your friend, so it's my job to be honest. You're sexually frustrated and it's making you crazy."

"My mother's making me crazy, and Zach Tanner, and this damned ice cream." She stabbed at the solid chocolate and barely made a dent. "All I need is one taste. One measly little taste."

"That's what I'm saying. You need a night of hot, passionate sex with a wild man who wants you really, really bad."

Delilah reached for a knife, dug it down deep. "You're right. I wanted him, he wanted me, things were perfect. Then I panicked." She wiggled the knife, the carton squeaked across the countertop and she growled.

"So call him up and tell him you've changed your mind."

"It's three a.m. and I have to work tomorrow—make that today." Delilah rummaged in a nearby utensil drawer. Her hand closed around a meat cleaver and she turned toward the ice cream with renewed determination.

"But it's Sunday."

"I'm a sole proprietor. I've got responsibilities."

"You're also a woman, and you've got needs."

A *desperate* woman, she conceded after she hung up. She slammed the cleaver into the knife, wiggled and managed to pull a hunk of rock-solid ice cream free.

Her needs? What she really needed was to push her business to the top, to have a life of her own, a career of her own, and finish out her ten-year plan before she turned her attention to hubbies and babies and domestic bliss. What she didn't need was Wild Man Zach Tanner hanging around, distracting her.

But her wants...? Her nipples tingled and her body

blazed and she fought back the urge to snatch up the telephone.

Now *want*... That was a different story altogether.

"YOU LOOK ALMOST as bad as this kitchen," Gladys said when Delilah walked to the table the next morning. The woman's gaze flicked from the counter streaked with ice cream to the now empty container. She smiled. "Looks like you and Zach were hungry last night."

"It was just me." Delilah slid into a chair opposite her mother.

"Worked up an appetite, did you?"

"Ma!"

"There's nothing to be embarrassed about, dear. I was young once, too, you know. Why, I remember when your father and I got engaged. We couldn't keep our hands off each other—"

"I don't want to hear this."

"We used to go to the drive-in and climb in the back seat of his Ford and—"

"Please stop."

"He would take me in his arms—"

"I'm already feeling sick."

"And touch me right here—" Gladys pointed and Delilah clamped her eyes shut "—and it drove me absolutely wild—"

"Have a Danish, Ma!" Delilah thrust the plate of pastries at her mother and tried frantically to kill the vision of her mother in the back seat of a car, going absolutely wild.... She shook away the thought. She definitely was going to be sick.

"Ah, cream cheese. My favorite." Gladys retrieved a pastry. "After an evening at the drive-in, I could down an entire tub of popcorn, extra butter and three bottles of Yoo-

Hoo, so I understand completely. Let's talk weddings, dear.''

"How's the Danish, Ma?"

"Fine, dear. Now I know you and Zach are planning on a long engagement. You haven't set a wedding date yet, have you?" At Delilah's frantic shake of her head, Gladys added, "I didn't think so. Mothers know these things, though you really should think about doing it soon, since you and Zach are practicing for a family. You are just practicing, aren't you, dear? Zach isn't driving the car into the garage without a car cover—"

"No!"

"Because I know the heat of the moment can get the best of you and make you forget your name, let alone protection—"

"Have another Danish, Ma!"

"Why, thank you." Gladys helped herself. "Now back to the wedding. I want to be a part of things, help you make preparations and pick out flowers and all that wonderful stuff. I've thought about canceling my cruise."

"You can't. It's already paid for. You're packed. Besides, you need to have some fun, to live a little."

"That's exactly what the doctor said, and, of course, he's right. But how am I supposed to enjoy that delicious all-you-can-eat seafood buffet and my daily Bloody Mary if I'm feeling guilty because I abandoned my baby in her time of need?"

"I'll be just fine on my own."

"Of course you will, once I help you get some of the wedding preparations out of the way, which is why we're going shopping tomorrow."

"Shopping?"

"For wedding invitations. You don't have to order them since you haven't set a wedding date, but you can at least pick out a style. And a color and flower scheme. I absolutely forbid hideous lime-green and daffodils like Tina Nixon. How her mother ever agreed to pay for neon-green dresses with black lace stockings is beyond me. Then again, Germaine hasn't been feeling well. Her heart, you know.''

''Mrs. Nixon has a heart problem? But she's your age.''

''Two months younger, dear.'' Gladys patted her daughter's hand and smiled. ''We'll look at dresses and music, too. Oh, and you should go ahead and choose your maid of honor and your bridesmaids.''

''But Ma—''

''You know, sweetheart, I've lived for this day.'' Her mother smiled and her eyes shone with pure joy.

*Joy.*

Delilah had to come clean. Before things went any further and she dug herself deeper. Before the joy turned to pure elation. The higher her mother's happiness, the harder the fall. ''Ma, there's something I should tell you.''

''Thankfully my health has held out for this blessed time. I had my doubts for a while there.'' Gladys touched her chest.

''Ma, what is it?''

''Just a little…'' She winced and Delilah stiffened.

''Ma?''

Gladys smiled. ''Ah, just a little burp. Nothing serious. This time. You were saying, dear?''

''Shopping would be great.''

''Good. We'll start tomorrow.''

''Tomorrow's Monday. My busiest workday of the week.''

''You'll take a few hours off. Lisa can handle things.''

''Now I do feel sick.''

''Nonsense.'' Gladys took her last bite of Danish and

wiped her hands. "You're tired, which is why I'll be glad to help out in the kitchen, just to ease your mind."

"You? In my kitchen?"

"An extra hand is sure to push you ahead of schedule, then you and I will have all the time we need to hit the bridal shops."

"You really don't have to—"

"And you don't even have to pay me, dear." Her mother smiled. "I have another surprise for you." She set the morning newspaper in front of Delilah. "Maybe this will cheer you up."

The lifestyle column glared up at her, along with a blazing headline that read, Say It Ain't So: Rib King Wild Man Tanner Set To Tie the Knot with Dallas's Own Cheesecake Queen.

"I sent in an engagement announcement." Gladys frowned. "Do you know the editor actually called me to verify the news? She said something about Zach being off on vacation, riding camels across the Sahara or some nonsense like that, so he couldn't possibly be here getting engaged. Let me tell you, I set her straight really quick."

Delilah stared down at one of the pictures snapped during her first meeting with Zach outside of Wild Man's, when he'd kissed her in front of the TV crew. He smiled. She scowled. And the camera added ten—ugh, twenty pounds.

Her stomach heaved and she bolted for the bathroom. "Now I *am* going to be sick."

"THIS REMINDS ME of old times." Gladys hummed as she sliced and diced mangoes bright and early Monday morning. She looked relaxed and content in a bright pink jogging suit and watermelon earrings, but her fingers moved with the practiced efficiency of a professional chef.

Delilah smiled and glanced at the list she'd penned onto

the production board. Her mother's kitchen duties. After a Sunday spent dreading her mother's help, she'd finally accepted the inevitable. Gladys James was bound and determined to lend a hand, so Delilah would simply treat her like any other employee and give her duties. Light duties, of course, because of her heart.

Surprisingly, other than the occasional mother-type comment, Gladys James had kept her mind on business.

Which was exactly what Delilah had to do. If it worked with her mother, it was bound to work with Zach Tanner.

After a busy Monday morning, she headed out to Wild Man's restaurant number one, determined to resist her hormones and get their relationship—their *business* relationship—back on track. She wanted him, but she didn't want to want him. She and Zach were like polka dots and stripes. Mixing the two was too scary to contemplate.

"Miss James!" Jeff Black met her in the hallway. "What brings you out to Wild Man's?"

"I need to discuss a few things with Zach. Is he in his office?"

"I'm afraid not. You two didn't have an appointment, did you? Because Zach never forgets an appointment."

"No, no. I just thought I'd drop in and discuss a few details about our arrangement. I should have called to make sure he'd be here. So where is he? Posing for publicity pictures? Doing a commercial?" *Swinging from the rafters?*

"He's out back in the kitchen. Kara, that's our sauce chef, is out having twins and Zach's been filling in for her. This is the biggest restaurant in the Wild Man chain and all the sauce is made here, bottled and shipped out to the other locations."

She smiled, then laughed. "Sorry. For a second I thought

you said Zach was out in the kitchen mixing up barbecue sauce.''

"The best in Texas. It's his recipe, you know. Well, not all his. I helped, but he was the one who kept at it after we'd added the honey—my idea—and it seemed to still be missing something. Zach was playing football back then and I was getting my CPA, but we'd get together on the weekends, grill up some burgers or ribs and try different things. Then one day Zach tries the secret ingredient.''

"Which is?"

"Secret" came the deep voice behind her.

She turned to find Zach not more than two feet away, a grin on his handsome face and a white sauce-streaked apron tied around his lean waist.

"Anyhow," Jeff went on, "everybody went crazy over the stuff. Our occasional weekend barbecues became every weekend and when Zach, here, hurt his shoulder, the sauce became our bread and butter, so to speak.''

Zach watched as she turned accusing gray eyes on him. "You cook."

"Yeah."

"B-but that's not fair," she sputtered. "You can't... I mean, cooking so a woman can go on maternity leave to have twins is sensitive and that's so unlike you, not to mention that's number one on the list and—''

"You're rambling again."

Her luscious mouth snapped shut and she gave him a suspicious glare. "You're really the one responsible for the sauce? How come I haven't read anything about that?"

"A well-kept secret," Jeff chimed in. "Cooking's not exactly good for his image. Too tame unless he's doing it in the bedroom and..." A blush stained Jeff's cheeks. "Well, you know what I mean. The Wild Man doesn't do anything as tame as mix up sauce.''

"But Zach Tanner does," Delilah pointed out.

"Perceptive." Jeff smiled. "That's good." He turned to Zach and indicated the clipboard. "I've got to run. I've got a meeting with the managers to go over the new quarterly budgets."

"Be sure to discuss the raises..." Zach's words trailed off as he sniffed. "What's that smell?" He leaned closer to Jeff and took another whiff. "It's you. It's your hair."

"Oh, that." Jeff beamed. "It's a vinegar and mayonnaise conditioning rinse. Trudy mixed it up for me."

"What happened to the midnight recipe stuff?"

"The lack of sleep only made me more stressed, which made me lose even more hair. I'm up to sixty-eight, but this new recipe should put a stop to it."

Zach grinned. "You smell like a Caesar salad."

"Very funny." Jeff cast Zach a sharp glance before turning back to Delilah. "It was nice to see you, Delilah. Really nice. Oh, by the way—" Jeff rummaged in his briefcase and pulled out the newspaper announcement "—great picture."

"Jeez, the whole world has seen it," Delilah said once Jeff Black had disappeared down the hallway.

"Thanks to you. This was supposed to be low-key."

She arched a blond brow at him. "As in riding a camel across the Sahara?"

"It's exciting and the Wild Man does exciting things. Not that it matters now."

"Look, it wasn't me. It was my mom and I'll make sure they print a retraction just as soon as this entire thing is over with."

"Is that why you're here? To explain the picture?"

"No, we need to talk. We've sort of gotten off on the wrong foot with this business arrangement, and I thought if I spelled everything out—"

"We already have a contract."

"I was talking about your duties. Exactly what I expect from you as a fiancé. That way we don't have any, um, misunderstandings like last night."

He touched a wayward strawberry-blond curl near her cheek. "*You* kissed *me*."

"I know. I shouldn't have, not like that, which is why I've made this list and included a column entitled 'Kissing.'" She handed him a sheet of paper.

"Kissing is allowed," she went on, "but only in front of my mother and lips only, no tongues, not to exceed fifteen seconds."

"You're serious." Zach stared at the neatly typed list and almost burst out laughing. He would have, except his blood was rushing so fast it was all he could do to keep from having a heart attack. "You really don't want me to kiss you?"

"Not a real kiss. This is pretend. Only pretend kisses."

"You're *really* serious?" As the knowledge solidified in his brain, a grin split his face. "You really don't like me?" He stared into her smoky-gray eyes and she swallowed.

"Well, of course, I like you. I mean, you're probably a nice person underneath all that machismo, which my mother happens to love, even though I, personally, like a more sweet, sensitive, sincere man, but for her sake, I'm willing to put up with you. But as far as *like* like you, no. Never. You see, I'd been dieting yesterday and I was light-headed and I really wasn't thinking...." Her voice trailed off as she took a deep breath. "This has to stay strictly business, especially now that I know about your cooking."

"Men who cook turn you on?" His grin widened.

"It's not the cooking itself. It's what it stands for." She shook her head. "Look, never mind. We have an agreement and this list will keep us on track. Any kissing will be strictly for show—''

"Thirty seconds and a tongue every now and then, and I do the machismo thing for your mom.''

"Twenty-five seconds, no tongues and you rave about her pot roast."

"Twenty seconds and we'll play it by ear on the tongue business, and I love pot roast.''

"Deal." She checked an item off her coveted list. "Now, about spending time together. I think dinner every night, followed by one hour of activity such as talking or watching TV, my mother included, of course, will work. Then you make an excuse and leave. Friday night, we'll make it two hours of after-dinner activity, and Saturday—''

"I'm busy Saturday.''

"Let me guess. You're drinking beer with a bra draped over your head?''

"I've got a fishing trip with a kid I sponsor in the Big Brothers program.''

"Someone upstairs is definitely out to get me," she grumbled.

"You don't like Big Brothers?''

"I love them. I, um—'' she swallowed ''—I have three, but that's irrelevant.'' She glanced at her watch and rushed on. "Okay, you're off the hook on Saturday. I'll save the wedding dress browsing for that day. You're not supposed to see me in the dress anyway. You can do Sunday dinner instead, no hour of activity afterward, then we'll start the same routine all over again for Monday, Tuesday and Wednesday.'' Another glance at her watch. "That covers it. We follow the schedule for the next nine days, then my mom catches a plane next Thursday for Miami and our business is finished, at least this part. We'll still have the cheesecake connection.''

"And the attraction thing." He started at her feet, treating his eyes to a slow, leisurely trek up shapely calves that disappeared too soon beneath her below-the-knee skirt, past rounded hips and a trim waist, to mouth-watering breasts hidden beneath a silk blouse. Her nipples pebbled and he grinned.

She stiffened and gave him a defensive look. "I am not attracted to you." At his raised eyebrow, her shoulders slumped and she sighed. "So I'm attracted to you, but it's just hormones. There is no future for us outside of a professional relationship." She stuffed the list into her briefcase and glanced at her watch again.

"Why are you in such a hurry?"

"I'm meeting my mother in fifteen minutes. We're picking out wedding invitations."

"Sounds like a future to me."

She made a face. "We're just looking."

"Don't go for all those goofy flowers. I like sailboats."

"On a wedding invitation?"

"Or maybe we could use the Wild Man logo. It would be good advertising. You should ask the printer about that."

"We are not getting married and I would dance naked at the Super Bowl before I let you put your stupid logo on my wedding invitation."

"*Our* invitation, and be careful what you promise, I'm tempted to call your bluff."

"Just be at my house for dinner tonight at six." She started to walk away.

"Ready, willing and able," he called after her.

"That's what I'm afraid of."

# 8

"HERE I AM. Ready, willing and—"

"Late," Delilah said as she grabbed Zach's arm and jerked him inside the house. "A half hour late. Do you know how worried I've been? You could have called. I thought you were lying in a ditch on the side of the road."

"I was at the florist." He pulled a dozen red roses from behind his back and handed them to her. "Then I was stuck in traffic."

"Flowers? You brought me flowers? *You* brought me flowers?" Her face fell. "How could you?"

"You don't like flowers?"

"I love flowers." She shook her head, inhaled the lush fragrance and glared at him. "This is a dirty trick."

"Delilah! Is that Zach?" Gladys James came around the corner, a fried mushroom in one hand and a stuffed shrimp in the other. "Why, Zach! How wonderful to see you. Hope you don't mind that I started dinner without you. But it looked so scrumptious that I couldn't wait—ah, roses."

"Zach brought them." Delilah thrust them at her mother. "They're for you, Ma."

"Me? How sweet! You know Cherry Wilhelm—roses and black taffeta—had her wedding flowers flown in from Connecticut, but they weren't nearly as lovely as this."

"I'll go check on dinner." Delilah left her mother ooh-ing and aahing and relaying wedding stories to Zach and beat a hasty retreat to the kitchen, an action that set the tone for the rest of the evening.

Advance, retreat, advance, retreat.

Every time Zach advanced, with his laser-blue eyes, an occasional brush of his hands, Delilah retreated to the kitchen, the bathroom, any place she could find to calm her pounding heart and remind herself of every reason why she shouldn't, couldn't be attracted to Zach Tanner.

Zach was a typical male. Dominant. Possessive. Sweet in his own cavemanish way.

Oh, no...sweet *and* sensitive.

So what? Zach still fell short in the sincere category, and that made him far from Big Three material. He was a classic Dr. Jekyll and Mr. Hyde. Always putting on a show. Sincere? Never.

She was a woman and the Wild Man treated all women the same. He hugged Delilah at every turn, kissed her on the cheek, and flashed sexy grins, all to the delight of Gladys James.

But that wasn't the problem. Gladys was happy, and happy was exactly what Delilah wanted. The problem was, Delilah actually found herself smiling at his actions.

Anticipating them.

Wanting them.

*Oh, no.*

She ignored the truth and concentrated on making it through a four-course dinner and a long, tension-packed hour spent looking at the wedding invitations she and her mother had picked out that day.

They reached an impasse. Zach liked the invitation with sailboats Delilah had chosen during a weak, lustful moment, while her mother liked the one with sunflowers. Delilah declared a draw, vowed to think about it and decide later, then she shoved Zach out the door, said goodbye and rushed upstairs to her office for a late night with her computer. But even typing invoices and planning the following day's production wasn't enough to wear her out. The minute her head hit the pillow and she closed her eyes, it wasn't sleep that came. It was him.

Handsome. Sexy. Wild.

He loomed over her, that devilish grin on his face. "You know you want me, Delilah. Just admit it."

"I do not want you."

"Your mouth says no, but your eyes say yes, sugar. Yes, yes, yes."

"No, no, *no!*"

Then he kissed her, touched her, teased her. Delilah closed her eyes as pleasure rolled over. Her heart thudded, keeping time to the rock song that surrounded them. His scent filled her nostrils, his voice filled her ears.

"I want you, Delilah. I want to…" The deep rumble of his voice went on and on in vivid descriptions that made her heart beat faster, the blood rush quicker, the music pound louder.

His hand stroked the inside of her thigh, closer, closer. "Do you like that, Delilah?"

"Yes."

"And this?" He touched her *there,* fingertips sliding over her moist heat, making her squirm and shiver.

"Yes."

"And this?" He slid a finger inside her and she arched up off the bed.

"Yes!" Delilah bolted upright, her eyes wide, the alarm clock screaming in the background, blending with the sound of her own breathless voice.

*Yes.*

She glanced down, saw the twisted sheets, her nightgown

riding her hips. A dream. Just a very vivid, very erotic dream.

She laughed, then frowned. This was far from her usual. No sitting by the river, listening to Percy recite poetry.

No classical music playing through her ears while some nice, sensitive hunk massaged her feet.

No soothing murmur of the ocean while some brooding intellectual artist brushed her hair.

This dream was red-hot, rock-and-roll, down-and-dirty S-E-X.

With Zach Tanner.

*Oh, no!*

Delilah bolted out of bed and hit the kitchen a half hour before her usual seven-thirty start time. So she'd had a dream? So what? Dreams were dreams. That didn't mean she was falling for Zach Tanner, and it certainly didn't mean she would consent to letting him…and liking it when he…and actually begging him to…

She forced the thoughts aside. Just a dream. She wouldn't be letting or liking or begging Zach Tanner for anything.

MONDAY SET THE PACE for the next few days. Zach brought balloons on Tuesday. Candy on Wednesday. Complimentary Wild Man T-shirts on Thursday. On Friday, he showed up with the ultimate gift, homemade Wild Man barbecue sauce, and Gladys wrote him into her will.

The woman was in mother heaven. Her future son-in-law was handsome, thoughtful and he'd finally seen the error of his ways and agreed to the sunflower invitations.

Delilah, on the other hand, was in hell. She wanted, needed to resist Zach, but each time she saw him, her heart pounded, her blood rushed and she actually looked forward to opening the door and seeing him standing there with his token gift. He'd wised up on the second day and showed up with two gifts. One for her mother and one for Delilah. She'd loved the T-shirt. She'd slept in it, reveling in the scent of him that lingered on the material, his screen-printed face stretched across her bosom.

Hormones, she told herself. He was good-looking, sexy, irresistible to most every female, and he tasted even better than any cheesecake flavor she'd come up with. She was sexually deprived, and he was a hot hunk. It was chemistry, nothing more, and she only had to make it through four more dinners, four more sleepless nights, then she'd be home free. No more mother, no more fiancé, no more chaste good-night kisses that were too long for her peace of mind and too short for her traitorous hormones.

Just work. Blessed, time-consuming work.

*Ugh.*

"ADD THE FIVE-POUND BAG of sugar to mixer number one, and three is just about ready for the fresh cream."

Delilah hustled around her kitchen, overseeing the daily mixing and baking, and feeling like her old self. Since it was Saturday, she worked with a skeleton crew that consisted of Lisa to help with the mixing, Harold to box and deliver, and Marge and Fritz who manned the ovens in the adjacent baking room. Her mother was at a local salon having a morning of beauty with Melanie, whom Gladys had roped in to driving her.

After watching a nervous Melanie leave with her mother, Delilah had taken a quick shower, downed three diet sodas and spent a half hour on her computer before tackling a busy Saturday morning in the kitchen.

Too busy to think. She'd gone a full half hour now without giving a thought to Zach or the dream.

And too busy to eat. She'd started her newest diet, the

Lemonade Lightener. Three glasses of lemonade, three times a day. Sugar for energy, lemon to burn the fat and plenty of water to keep her full.

All was right with the world.

Delilah finished slicing bananas, picked up the platter and walked toward the mixer at the far end. Stopping, she glanced at mixer number three. "This speed is too fast."

"That's Harold's fault," Lisa said from her spot near the chopping block. "I told him not to touch the equipment."

Harold paused from boxing cakes and held up his palms. "These hands were made for equipment."

"Save them for your own equipment." Delilah juggled the heavy platter to one hand while she leaned in to adjust the mixer's speed. "Go in the oven room and start boxing and labeling with Marge and Fritz. We've got six dozen cakes to get out today."

"So I guess that means you're too busy for a picnic." The deep voice sounded right in her ear.

Delilah jumped, the platter tilted and five dozen bananas plunged into the mixer. A tidal wave of batter rose up. Delilah clamped her eyes shut a second before the mixture splattered her.

"Ohmigod, an accident!" Lisa screeched somewhere to Delilah's left. "Help! She's fallen into the mixer!"

"My feet are firmly on the ground," Delilah sputtered as she leaned back and felt for the hem of her apron. "The batter's just in my eyes." And everywhere else, she thought, feeling the warm sensation oozing down her neck, dipping beneath the front of her blouse.

"Ohmigod, she's blind. Call 911."

"Don't you dare! It was just a minor accident. Everything is fine." Almost everything. She wasn't drowning, or blinded, but she was this close to having a heart attack. Not because she was wearing a face full of cheesecake, but because there was one very hunky, very lethal-to-her-sanity man standing behind her.

So close she could feel the warm rush of his breath prickling the hairs on the back of her neck. She wiped at her eyes and turned to find her worst nightmare realized.

Zach Tanner stood mere inches away, a grin on his handsome face. His brown hair had been combed back. Damp tendrils rested lazily against the collar of his shirt. A sprinkling of dark silk peeked at her where the shirt parted, the top two buttons left casually open. *Casual.* That's how he looked dressed in a faded denim shirt, worn jeans and scuffed brown boots.

Far from sexy.

*Sexy? Who said anything about sexy? We're talking casual. An afternoon at the ballpark, not a hot night in the bedroom. Big difference.*

She forced her gaze back to his face, to his strong, stubbled jaw, his sensuous mouth curved in that damnable grin. Aviator sunglasses hid his laser-blue eyes, but she didn't need to see them. She felt them. On her face, her neck, lower...

He reached out, one fingertip trailing down her neck, dipping dangerously in the valley between her breasts before he came up with a healthy scoop of batter and tasted it. "Good," he murmured, letting his finger linger on his lips a little too long for her peace of mind.

"I—it's not good," she sputtered, trying to recover from the touch she'd just felt clear to her toes. A touch she still felt. She focused on her anger and the empty banana platter. "You ruined my Fudge Fandango."

He shrugged and licked his finger again. "So call it Banana Fudge Fantasy."

"I already have a Banana Split Bump going in mixer number one, and I've got a huge order waiting to be filled with Chocolate Fudge *Fandango,* not Fantasy." She glared harder. "Aren't you supposed to be on a fishing trip?"

"Travis has a cold, so the trip was postponed." He scooped more batter from her neck. "This is really good. Want a taste?"

She shook her head and ignored the tempting scent of bananas and fudge. *Think lemonade, sugar, water.* "I'm dieting."

"Why?"

"You have to ask?"

"Yeah, I do. You look fine."

Not great or sexy or incredibly amazing. Just fine. "Certain parts of my anatomy could stand to lose a little baggage."

"Her hips," Lisa chimed from the corner where she wrestled with a sack of sugar. "She hates her hips."

"And her butt," Harold added. When Delilah glared, he shrugged. "Not that there's anything to hate, boss. Your butt is way bitchin'."

"Would you two mind giving us a few minutes alone, please?"

Lisa and Harold took a break and Delilah tried to regain her shattered control.

*Just breathe.*

"I'm trying to work, Zach. I really need to work now since I've ruined an entire mixer of batter, killed my favorite blouse—I'll never get this chocolate stain out—and now I'm five, make that six minutes," she added after glancing at her watch, "off schedule."

"You work too much. You need to take a break."

"I need you to stick to the list."

He grinned. "We can do the twenty seconds of kissing now if you want."

She blew out a frustrated breath. "I really hate you."

He grinned. "I know."

"If I had a gun, you'd be history."

His grin widened. "Music to my ears."

"One shot, right between the eyes. Then I'd mount you and hang you in my den."

"You swear?" He looked so hopeful that she had the insane urge to laugh when all she really wanted to do was inflict bodily harm. Or at least touch the body in question.

"Cross my heart," she muttered.

Rather than run for his life, he simply stood there and smiled. "Good."

"Good? I threaten you, and you say good?"

"Great."

"Men," she muttered. "Look, this has really been enlightening, but I need to get cleaned up and back to work and you need to take a hike." She sidestepped him and started for the door. "Consider it your day off—yikes." The swinging door jerked inward and sent her stumbling backward.

"Delilah, the salon was divine— Oh, my, I didn't see you. Whatever happened to you, dear?"

"A little food fight." Zach came up beside Delilah. A large, muscled arm clamped around her shoulder. "Honey bunch, here, is one wild woman, if you know what I mean."

"That's my baby you're talking about, young man." The woman's face softened and a giggle passed her lips. "But I know exactly what you mean. I was young once, too, you know. Why I remember one time Delilah's father and I—"

"Uh, Ma, where's Melanie?"

"She had to run, dear. I was just coming to invite you to lunch. Zach can join us."

"I don't think that's such a good idea—"

"We have plans," Zach cut in. "My fishing trip was

called off and I couldn't stay away from my little sugar pie, here.''

"Please don't call me that," Delilah growled.

"Why, it's sweet, dear." Her mother swallowed and touched a hand to her bosom.

"Ma, what's wrong? It's not a chest pain, is it?"

"Oh, no." Gladys sighed. "Hearing Zach reminds me of my dear, sweet Bob." She glanced heavenward. "Bob, honey, I'll be seeing you soon."

"Ma! Don't say things like that."

Gladys smiled. "But not until I see my baby and her young man happily married. So what are you two lovebirds doing today?"

"Working."

"A picnic."

Zach and Delilah both spoke at the same time, but Gladys James had selective hearing.

"A picnic? How romantic! You two just run along then."

"I can't go anywhere. I've got to redo the Chocolate Fudge Fandango. I can't just shuck everything to go on some picnic."

"Pooh, pooh, of course you can when your mother is right here to fill in for you." She steered Delilah around and pushed her from the kitchen. "Go and have a wonderful time. When you get back, I'll have a new mixer of Chocolate Fudge Fricasee."

"Fandango, Ma."

"Whatever, dear. Now run along." She shoved Delilah through the door, then Zach. Gladys's voice rose above the sudden whir of the mixer as she called Lisa and Harold back to work and started issuing orders.

"Does she know how to bake cheesecakes?"

Delilah turned distraught eyes on Zach—beautiful, smiling, good-looking-enough-to-eat Zach—and sighed. "She's been helping out in my kitchen, but she's never been in charge of it."

"She'll wing it. I'll meet you out front in five minutes. And by the way, your hips look fine, and so does your butt."

"How would you know? You've never even seen my hips, much less my butt."

"Yes, I have." He inched closer. "Through the tear in a tight-fitting black skirt."

"I keep forgetting that was you in that closet," she said as a wave of heat swept up her neck and her face caught fire.

He leaned forward until his mouth was inches from her ear. "It was me right behind you, *touching* you." The words whispered over her senses and the air stalled in her lungs. "And you looked and felt just fine." Her gaze collided with his. "More than fine."

"Funny," she said, gasping for breath. "Right now, I don't feel fine at all."

# 9

"THIS IS YOUR CAR?" Delilah came to a dead stop in the driveway, her gaze traveling over the silver Lexus, sophisticated and tasteful and so...*un*wildmanish.

"You were expecting something else?"

"A monster truck, with naked-lady mud flaps and a horn that plays 'Wild Thing.'"

He opened the passenger door and motioned her inside. "The truck's got a flat tire, the mud flaps are dirty and the horn's on the blink, so we're stuck with this."

She eyed him. "You don't really have a monster truck."

Blue eyes twinkled in the sunlight. "No, but if you'd be willing to pose for some customized mud flaps, I might consider slapping a pair onto this baby."

"Very funny."

"I'm serious."

*And I'm a size ten.* She slid into the passenger seat. The scent of leather and male wrapped around her and she quickly rolled down the window while he walked around and got behind the wheel. Having him next to her within the close confines of the car would be bad enough. She didn't need him filling her senses, making her think all kinds of crazy thoughts.

She shot a glance at him and her heart beat faster. If only he wasn't so handsome and sexy and...

Forcing her gaze away, she took a deep breath. She had

to look at the bright side. It could be much worse than a little physical attraction. She could actually like him.

SHE LIKED HIM.

The truth hit her an hour later as she sat at a picnic table at Bailey Park, after two rest-room stops and enough water loss to make her feel a few pounds lighter. She sipped lemonade and watched Zach lead a team of counselors against a pack of screaming ten-year-old boys from the Bailey Youth Center.

For an ex-pro, Zach was the worst player Delilah had ever seen. He fumbled and tripped, missed prime tackle opportunities and practically *let* the other team win.

He let them win.

It was so obvious, and so…*un*wildmanish, she wanted to hit him.

Or kiss him, particularly when she saw the half dozen smiling boys declare victory over the counselors and break for lunch. They bounded back to the picnic table and grabbed the burgers Zach and Delilah had picked up on the way over.

"Don't forget to wipe your hands." Delilah handed paper napkins to the boys as they took their burgers and spread out across the playground. "You, too." She shoved a handful at Zach.

"Yes, ma'am."

He gave her that slow, sexy grin and the air stalled in her chest. He'd slipped off his shirt during one of her rest-room breaks. It hadn't been so bad seeing him at a distance. Up close was an entirely different matter. A broad chest sprinkled with dark hair rippled with his every movement. Her mouth went dry and she forced herself to ignore the ridiculous urge to touch him.

She grabbed several sodas and rushed to distribute them

to the boys. "Everybody be sure to drink up. I don't want anyone dehydrating." Jeez, she sounded like a mother. Worse, she sounded like *her* mother. Gladys James, career domestic goddess.

"You like kids." Zach's grin widened as she walked back to the picnic table.

"I love them. I intend to have at least three later on."

"So do I, but I was thinking sooner instead of later. All I need is to find the right woman."

*Don't ask,* she told herself. *Just keep your mouth shut.* "And the right woman would be?"

"Someone who really likes kids and wants full-time motherhood. I bring home the bacon and she cooks it, bakes cookies, does the PTA thing. My mom always wanted to, but she never had the chance. She was too busy working to make ends meet, and then she died." He looked so thoughtful and sad, and something shifted inside her. He shook his head. "Not my wife. I've spent my life working hard so she won't have to."

Suddenly desperate to ease his sudden melancholy, she smiled. "With three kids, trust me, she'll be working hard. So tell me, have you taken out an ad for this model wife and mother? Wanted: a June Cleaver clone, no working women need apply."

He grinned. "That's a good idea. So far, I've been holding open auditions."

*Can I try?* She squelched the thought. "Any serious candidates?"

"Maybe. So what about you? What do you want in a man?"

"Nothing—I mean, at least right now. I'm too busy working to be a wife and mother, and I'm not giving up my career. My mother did that. She was a chef in Houston, one of the few female gourmet chefs in the business and she threw it all away at my father's urging, to clip coupons and change diapers. She never had a chance to live up to her full potential, but I intend to live up to mine. Then I'll settle down.''

''So you're not one of those women who believes a woman can have it all?''

''A woman can have it all with a Big Three man.''

''Big Three?''

''A man who doesn't mind sharing his wife. He's totally supportive and encouraging. He'll cook for her, do the dishes and the laundry and take care of the kids when she needs to work. Needless to say, my dad wasn't one of them. 'I'm your future, Gladys,' my dad used to say to my mom, 'and don't you forget it.' Anyhow, Big Three men are scarce, probably extinct with my luck, and so I intend to have my career first, then I'll do the family thing. Later. Much later.''

''You'll change your mind when you meet Mr. Right.''

''Any man who would make me change my mind about my dreams wouldn't be Mr. Right. I eat, sleep and breathe How Sweet It Is, and I'm proud of it.''

*Wrong,* at least on one count. She was proud, all right, but right now she was breathing Zach Tanner—a mixture of musky after-shave, sunshine and warm male that made her forget her name for a startling moment.

Zach reached around her and grabbed a burger off the table. She watched him sit down beneath a nearby tree, burger in hand, long, jeans-clad legs stretched out in front of him. She followed and sat down across from him.

He took a bite of hamburger and Delilah's mouth watered as she watched the way his lips moved around the mouthful.

The food, she told herself. She hadn't had a bite of real

food all day and she wanted a taste of the hamburger. No way did she want to taste Zach Tanner.

Her stomach grumbled and he grinned. "Want a bite?" *No. Yes. If you're on the menu.* She held up her lemonade. "Thanks, but no thanks."

"So tell me about yourself," he said in between bites.

"Why?" She eyed him suspiciously.

"How am I supposed to impress your mother as the perfect future son-in-law if I know next to nothing about you?"

She retrieved her purse, pulled out a piece of paper and a pen and jotted down a few numbers. "Here. If you really want to impress my mother, recite these to her."

He took his last bite of hamburger, wiped his hands and mouth and asked, "What are these?"

"Measurements."

"Yours?"

She glared. "My garage."

"That's what I meant," he said with enough wide-eyed innocence to cool her temper.

"My mom always thought the garage would convert perfectly into a family room. She's sure to bring up the subject and if you don't know the measurements, she's liable to think you don't know diddly about building things and that you haven't even thought about a family room, which means you haven't thought about a family, which means you aren't prime son-in-law material." *Rambling.* She busied her mouth swallowing the last of her lemonade.

"Your mom's a really nice lady." He stared across the grass at the counselors and kids who'd finished lunch and were taking the field for another game. "It must have been nice growing up with a big family. That's what I'd like. A big, traditional family."

For a split-second, he was Dr. Jekyll again—thoughtful,

contemplative, vulnerable—and Delilah couldn't help herself. She touched him. Soft fingertips met hard muscle and he looked at her, into her, and everything faded away for two heartbeats.

She summoned a grin and ignored the frantic pounding of her heart. "One Christmas at my house and you'll change your mind forever. Imagine five aunts, twelve female cousins and four female second cousins—all happily married, or so they say, and all trying to fix you up."

"How have you managed to stay single?"

"The question is, how have I managed to stay sane? And the answer is, I spend the whole day next to the punch bowl. My mom's eggnog is one hundred proof. Better than a tranquilizer." She smiled. "Now wow me with some Wild Man trivia."

"Well, I graduated from the University of Texas, played pro ball for three years, starting rookie quarterback for the Dallas Cowboys until a shoulder injury killed my playing days."

"Your favorite color is red," she added. "You like classic rock music, fast cars and faster women." At his incredulous expression, she shrugged. "You're a public figure."

"I'm surprised you don't know my measurements."

"Chest size 42, waist 32 and hips 35. Those tabloids are really detailed."

"I'm afraid to ask about my blood type."

"B positive."

"My social security number?"

She patted his hand. "The IRS isn't worrying, so why should you?"

"How comforting—" Zach's reply faded into a loud, "Heads up!" from the field.

Delilah's head snapped up to see a football sailing toward her. Instinct kicked in, her arms opened and she caught the ball, much to the surprise of Zach and the all-male group that quickly surrounded her.

"That was a great catch," Zach said.

"It was all right," one of the boys grumbled, "for a girl."

"A girl, huh?" She exchanged glances with Zach. "Those are fighting words." She twirled the football and smiled. "Anybody mind if I join the game?"

Denial murmured through the crowd. "No way. Forget it. She's a *girl*."

"And she's playing," Zach told the group of disgruntled boys as he dropped into position and hiked the ball. Soon, Delilah found herself clutching pigskin and running for her life. A dozen young boys trailed after her.

She felt the commotion behind her a split second before the weight hit her in the back and she slammed into the grass. The ball flew from her hands. She struggled onto her back, expecting to see a half dozen triumphant faces looming over her. She saw only one.

"The ball's free," a young voice cried. Small hands snatched up the football. Short legs pumped toward the opposite side of the field, and the rest of the players followed. All except for Delilah and the man sprawled on top of her.

"You tackled me." She stared up into the dark shadow of Zach's face, so close the rush of his breath warmed her lips.

"Yeah."

"But we're on the same team."

"Yeah."

"You're not supposed to tackle your own teammate."

"Yeah."

"But *you* tackled *me*." Hard muscles pressed against soft

curves and a shiver rippled through her. "You're still tackling me."

"Yeah."

"You're going to kiss me, aren't you?"

"Yeah." Then his mouth met hers and he was kissing her.

She didn't have to kiss him back, she told herself, despite the electricity zinging through her body. She wouldn't.

Her lips parted. Tongues tangled and heat swamped her senses. He shifted ever so slightly, one arm curving around her neck, drawing her closer, making the kiss deeper. Ahhh... He tasted like warm sunshine and picnics.

"Touchdown!" The word came from far off, pushing past the pounding of her heart, the rush of blood.

She opened her eyes just as the kiss ended and stared up into the deepest, the bluest, the most compelling gaze she'd ever seen. Her heart pounded, her blood raced and her body tingled in all the right places, and everywhere in between.

*Him.*

She shoved against his chest and scrambled backward.

"What's wrong?"

"You, me, us...*this.*" She gestured wildly between them and he frowned. "I... You can't... This isn't fair! Not you, not now. I don't need this in my life. I don't need a relationship or a man or kids or kisses or tingling or—"

"What *do* you need?" he cut in, gaze narrowed.

*Cheesecake fame. Fortune. A super-duper eat-all-you-want-and-still-be-thin diet pill.*

"A bathroom," she blurted as the lemonade caught up to her. "Now."

"ARE YOU ALL RIGHT in there?"

"Fine." Delilah stubbed her toe on the toilet, bit back the cry and concentrated on covering the rim with toilet paper. She pulled down her panties and let loose a sigh of relief.

Minutes later, she stared into the mirror and groaned.

"Are you sure you're all right in there?" Zach asked again, his deep voice carrying through the bathroom door.

"Yes. No." She picked grass from her hair. "My hair looks like a rat's nest, my dress is grass-stained, I'm wrinkled and I hate you right now."

"That's not what that kiss said. You want me."

"Fat chance." She grabbed a wet paper towel and rubbed at a grass stain. "You're nowhere near my type."

"And what is your type?"

"Sweet."

"Like a guy who helps a girl stand up and brush off her skirt?"

"After he's tackled her," she pointed out.

"True, but the tackle was for a good cause."

She wet another paper towel and rubbed at stain number two. "And what would that be?"

"I wanted to kiss you," came his deep rumbling reply and her hand faltered. "I *needed* to kiss you."

Her gaze riveted on her flushed cheeks, her kiss-swollen mouth and she couldn't help herself. Her tongue darted out and flicked her bottom lip. She could still taste him. She frowned.

"So what about your type?" he prodded.

"Sincere," she blurted, then shook her head. "Okay, I'll give you sincere."

"And good-looking?"

"Don't flatter yourself. Besides, looks aren't everything. I want a man with feelings. Someone sensitive."

Like an ex-pro ball player who spent his Saturdays letting a group of underprivileged kids beat him at football.

Three out of three.

Oh, God, he *was* her type.

"You're not crying are you?"

"I'm fine." She wiped frantically at a few stray tears.

"Because I could come in there—"

"*No!* I can use the bathroom just fine by myself, thank you very much," she snapped. Where did he get off being her type? He was the Wild Man. Lewd, crude, obnoxious. *Wild.*

"It was just an idea."

"A bad idea."

"This isn't that time of the month, is it?"

Her hand stalled. "What did you say?"

"I asked if it was your time of the month because you're acting really bent out of shape over a kiss. And grouchy."

Her face brightened. "You think I have PMS?"

"It makes sense. Most women would be ecstatic to find the man of their dreams, unless their hormones are raging—"

"For your information," she said, pushing through the bathroom door, a smile on her face, "I'm nowhere close to my time and to even insinuate such a thing is so typically male. Of all the chauvinistic, he-man comments..." She smiled.

Maybe her life wasn't totally screwed after all.

"MY LIFE IS TOTALLY screwed," Delilah said the moment they neared her house and she spotted the two fire trucks.

She jumped out before the car even rolled to a stop and started toward the door. Zach killed the engine and followed.

"She burned my house down."

"The house looks fine to me."

Her gaze scanned the structure for a spot of soot, a glimpse of smoldering wood. "Okay, so it wasn't the whole house. Just the back. Probably my kitchen.'' She came to a dead stop on the front porch and closed her eyes for a long moment. ''Okay, I can face this,'' she finally said, opening her eyes. ''I'll file an insurance claim, buy new equipment, set things up in my old kitchen temporarily until I can repair the sweet wing.''

She stiffened, pulled open the front door and walked into a smoke-free living room brimming with firemen happily gulping down cheesecake. Platter in hand, her mother floated through the group and refilled plates.

''What's this kind, Gladys?''

''That's my darling's Macadamian Mambo. Isn't it divine?''

''Damn good eating,'' another man chimed in.

''And how about this?'' asked another man.

''That's Raspberry Rumba. Then there's the Peanut Butter Bop and the Luscious Lemon Lambada, all my baby's recipes. She's brilliant. And beautiful. Why, she's got the face of an angel and the body of a—''

''Ma!''

''There she is now.'' Her mother waved. ''Come in and meet these lovely gentlemen, dear. We've been waiting for you.''

Horrified, Delilah stared at the assortment of cheesecakes. ''I spent all morning on these orders.''

''I had leftovers.''

''Leftovers? There shouldn't be leftovers. I have a very strict production schedule—''

''That I generously increased. Dear, it's better to have too much food than not enough. You never know who might stop by.'' At Delilah's frown, Gladys added, ''I had to give something to these fine men for all their trouble.''

''I knew it. There was a fire.''

''No fire, ma'am,'' one of the men said.

"Just a misunderstanding, dear. I was eating my lunch, a double sausage po'boy from this divine take-out deli, with a side order of stuffed jalapeños. Anyhow, I made the remark to Lisa that I was going up in flames, and before I could blink my eyes, what do you know? She'd called these nice boys."

Lisa rushed by Delilah with another platter of cheesecake. "Better safe than sorry."

Delilah faced her mother. "You didn't ruin my business?"

"Heck no, little lady," said one of the firemen. "Thanks to Gladys, we're ordering a few dozen for the monthly Firemen's Banquet over at the lodge."

Gladys beamed. "I've brought in a new client, dear."

"And cooked up a storm," Lisa added. "We're back on schedule with time to spare."

"So this is Delilah." One of the firemen grinned and eyed Delilah. "I hear you cook a mean pot roast, little lady."

"Now keep your hands to yourself, Dale. My baby's spoken for. Isn't that right, Zach?" All attention shifted to Zach and recognition lit a dozen pair of eyes.

"Wild Man Tanner trading in the women for a ball and chain?"

"Never thought I'd see the day."

"What's the world coming to?"

Zach's hold tightened on Delilah and his camera-ready grin slid into place. "A guy's gotta go sometime," he drawled and felt Delilah stiffen.

"Might be taking the plunge myself if I had a woman that cooked this good."

"Amen."

"Could I have some more cheesecake?"

"Me, too."

"And me."

The attention turned from the happy couple to a smiling Gladys. "My, my, you boys sure do love to eat. If only I were twenty years younger..."

The woman's words faded into a blinding stab of pain as Delilah grabbed Zach's upper arm and pinched.

"Could I speak to you?" she growled. "Outside?" Before he could answer, she shoved him out onto the front porch.

"A guy's gotta go sometime?" she bit out. "Couldn't you have thought of something a little more romantic?"

"How about you have really great eyes and lips and I lost myself the moment I looked at you."

"I..." She swallowed. "That's definitely more romantic." She shook her head. "What am I saying? It doesn't matter if it's romantic because my mother didn't hear it and—"

He touched a fingertip to her lips. "I really want to kiss you again."

Zack expected a protest, but all she said was a dreamy "Really?" when he slid his hand to the back of her neck.

"More than I've ever wanted anything."

He was this close to her mouth. Just a fraction away—

"Delilah!" came her mother's voice from inside. "I can't find the paper plates and Dale and Roger and Mario want to take a few pieces to the guys back at the station."

"Coming, Ma!" She took a deep breath, inched away from him and Zach barely resisted the urge to pull her back. "We'd better stick to the list."

"Thirty seconds."

"It was twenty and no tongues and only in front of my mother and she's inside...." Her words trailed off as she peered at his hairline. "I think you've got a piece of fuzz right here—'' Before he could blink, she plucked a hair and he screeched.

"Sorry. Oops. It wasn't fuzz. Just a gray hair."

"A *what*—"

"Delilahhhhhhhh! The plates!"

"I'm coming!" She handed him the strand of hair. "I really have to go." She stepped inside and started to shut the door. "I've still got work to do before dinner tonight and I bet you have a ton."

An understatement if he'd ever heard one, he thought as he slid behind the wheel and stared down at the gray hair. *Gray.* As in not brown. As in fading. Aging. Losing his edge and his youth and his livelihood. The clock was ticking.

He stuffed the gray hair into his pocket, gunned the engine and headed back to Wild Man's. He would just have to see how fast he could open her eyes and rearrange her priorities because Zach Tanner was Mr. Right, and he wanted Delilah James. *Now.*

# 10

"Thank God, you're here," Jeff declared when Zach walked into Wild Man's an hour and a half later at the start of a busy Saturday evening. "I was beginning to worry."

"You were already worrying, and have I ever not shown up for a business meeting?"

"It's after six. You're late."

"Only five minutes. The picnic lasted longer than expected. I had to shower and change, then stop off at the drugstore. Heads up." Zach tossed his friend a bottle.

"What's this?"

"High-powered Hair Regrowth 2000. It's a new product that just came out. Last one on the shelf. I thought you might give it a try."

"When... How..." Jeff swallowed. "I don't know what to say."

"Not that I think you're losing your hair, but if it makes you feel better, knock yourself out."

Jeff held the bottle as if it were made of gold. "This is the nicest thing you've done for me since you beat up Mac Williams for taking my lunch back in the second grade."

"He was too big to be picking on a shrimp like you. Are the ad agency people here?"

"Table number five. I sent one of the waitresses over with a plate of ribs so they could taste the product and see what they'll be selling if you decide to go with them."

"You joining us?"

"Tru and I are doing a hot oil scalp massage tonight."

"The Caesar salad thing didn't work?"

"It made me hungry. I gained three pounds. But I bet this stuff'll do the trick. We'll try it right after the massage." He grabbed his briefcase and packed away the treasured bottle. "Don't forget that we're meeting with the accountant on Monday morning, then you're meeting the architect for the new restaurant. Oh, and the lady from Fresh Start, that program to keep kids off the street after school, is coming out to talk to you about jobs for a few of her boys. See you Monday."

Zach said goodbye, then spent the next hour talking with Claire and Doug, two of the ad agency's brightest people, about new advertising ideas for Wild Man Ribs—and doing his damnedest not to think about Delilah James. He'd just about made it when he found himself staring down at a piece of Chocolate Cherry Cha-Cha. With each bite, he thought of her, tasted her, wanted her.

Damn, he had it bad.

Ordinarily that would be good. He could just slip on the old Wild Man determination and go after what he wanted. A few easy grins, a little flirting, and any other woman would be eating out of his hand.

Not Delilah James.

As happy as that made him, it caused an endless amount of frustration. Desperation. Pure stupidity. Zach found himself turning down after-dinner drinks with cute, blonde Claire, who'd been eyeing him over a plate of ribs. Instead, he went home to an empty apartment.

Sitting home alone on a Saturday night with nothing to keep him company but the bottle of Go Away Gray he'd picked up at the pharmacy. He had it real bad, and to make matters worse, he found two more gray hairs.

*Aw, hell.* Make that three.

"YOU'RE HOME." Delilah's voice floated over the line when Zach finally snatched up the ringing phone. "Thank God. Can you come over for dinner? Because since you canceled the fishing trip, my mom thinks you're coming and I tried to tell her you weren't, but then she started talking to my dad about how she was coming soon, and I didn't have the heart. So can you come?"

He stared at the hair-color instructions. "Actually I was kind of busy."

"Auditioning women for the esteemed role of Mrs. Zach baby-on-each-hip-and-one-in-the-oven Tanner?"

"Coloring my hair."

"Right." She laughed. "You're kidding, right?"

"Yeah. The women are forming a line at the door. First up are twins. Mitsy and Tipsy. They bake a mean batch of oatmeal cookies, not to mention they're really stacked—"

"You're not kidding." The laughter died. "Come on, Zach. It was one gray hair."

"Try three."

"Three's even better. Gray hair is sophisticated. It adds character. It says you're a man of experience, intelligence." Her voice dropped a notch. "It's sexy."

"I'll be right over."

*SEXY, SEXY, SEXY.* Why, oh why, had she told him that?

Because it was true. Gray hair was sexy on a man. No, not just any man. *Him.*

She tried to shake away the truth as she sat in the living room across from Zach and her mother, who sat on the sofa dealing with the latest wedding crisis.

The men's tuxedo style. Gladys wanted frilly pink cumberbunds and Zach wanted a leopard print.

"And Delilah? What do you want, dear?"

"I want…" Zach in nothing but a leopard-print G-string and that big sexy, grin…

"Did you say 'grin,' dear?"

"Uh, green, Ma." She took a drink of iced tea to cool her suddenly flaming cheeks. "Green would be nice."

Her mother flipped through the swatch book. "But there isn't any green here. Zach, do you see green?"

"Only in your eyes, Gladys, honey."

"What a sweet talker you are. Now let me see, I suppose we could go with the jungle print if we picked wildflowers…" Her mother's voice faded into several mmm's and ahhh's, while Delilah excused herself to make popcorn.

"You know, dear, all these wedding preparations have really tired me out. I think I'm going to call it a night."

"Me, too." Zach started to get up, but her mother yanked him back down to the sofa.

"Nonsense. There are two wonderful Clint Eastwood videos and a tub of popcorn. You children enjoy yourselves."

"But if Zach has something to do…"

"Nothing that can't wait." His gaze locked with hers.

"But these are your movies, Ma. You picked them out. You should really stay up and watch them."

"If you insist, dear…" The words faded as Gladys touched her chest and winced.

"What is it, Ma?"

"Nothing, dear. I'm just feeling a little pressure right here, but I'm sure it will go away if I just lie down for a little while."

"Let me help you, Ma."

"No, I can find my way on my own and I wouldn't want to spoil your evening. I'll rest easy knowing you and Zach are having a good time without me."

"But Zach could go home and I could make you some soup, give you a back massage, whatever you need—"

"A clear conscience, dear. I would never forgive myself if I stood in the way of true love. What a weight that would be on my poor, frail heart."

"Let me at least tuck you in."

Gladys sighed. "All right, but then you march right back down here and keep your young man company."

THE TREK BACK DOWN the stairs was the longest of Delilah's life. She kept picturing Zach in formal jungle attire. Zach in nothing at all.

Her steps picked up while her brain launched a rebellion. Although Zach might have reached Big Three status, he obviously wasn't the Big Three man she'd been waiting for. He wanted a stay-at-home wife, a woman who would chuck everything to be with him, bear his children and raise a pack of little wild men.

Not an overworked cheesecake caterer, even one who had a major case of lust for him.

Better to keep her distance and resist the call of wild, hot sex because if Delilah gave in to one night, she might want more, and that was a chance she couldn't take. She still had six years left of her business plan. She had potential to reach. Dreams.

Distance, she told herself as she walked back into the living room, and straight into Zach Tanner's waiting arms.

"I..." Her head jerked up and her gaze collided with his. "The movie," she squeaked, her gaze darting to the lifeless TV.

"I thought we could talk."

"We talked enough this afternoon."

"Then we could dance. You've got a nice CD collection.'' He kissed her cheek, then strode toward her entertainment center.

"Zach, don't..." Her words trailed off as he pulled a CD free and started to laugh.

"'Polka Those Pounds Away'? 'Twist That Tush into Shape'? Where did you get these?"

"HEN—the Home Exercise Network. I have an entire collection of instructional dance videos—that's how I got all the dance-related names for my cheesecakes. Anyhow, HEN guaranteed a weight loss of ten pounds or more, so I ordered.''

"And how much did you lose?" he asked, walking back to her.

"Five after six weeks of hell."

"Delilah, you are not fat. You're—"

"Don't say it."

"Say what?"

"Full, voluptuous, rounded. Don't say any of that. Those are just nice words for fat."

"I was going to say perfect."

Her gaze raced up to collide with his. "Perfect?"

He stroked her cheek. "Perfect, as in just right, free of flaws, sleek and sexy and...perfect."

She closed her eyes against the raspy feel of his fingertip stroking, caressing. "Mmm, sleek. I like that."

"Me, too." Her gaze hooked on his mouth as he formed the words.

"And sexy," she reminded him, wetting her lips, wanting to taste him more than she needed to eat or sleep or even breathe.

"That, too." And then he fit his perfect mouth over hers and kissed her.

He nibbled her bottom lip, coaxed her mouth open and plunged his tongue deep. Delilah met him stroke for stroke as she explored his mouth and reveled in the feel and taste and touch of him.

Strong hands skimmed down her back, setting her nerves on fire as they blazed a trail to her waist, then lower, to cup her buttocks. His erection strained through the denim of his jeans, against the cradle of her thighs.

He groaned. She groaned.

Her hands moved with a mind of their own, over his shoulders, down his chest to his waistband, where she tugged at the hem of his T-shirt. With one quick motion, he pulled the material over his head and tossed it aside.

They toppled back down to the couch, Zack on top. He wedged one knee between hers and parted her legs. He stared at her then, blue eyes penetrating while his fingers slid up the inside of her bare leg, pushing the soft material of her skirt higher, higher, until fingertips brushed against her panties.

The air caught in her chest and she closed her eyes against the delicious sensation.

"You're so warm and wet and... I want you. Here. Now."

He kissed her again and her head spun out of control. She came up gasping for air. "I...uh, there are two of you."

"You're delirious with desire."

"No. Really. I don't feel so good."

"I'll make you feel better."

He tried to kiss her again but she dodged his mouth. She blinked frantically and damned herself for not eating anything more than lettuce for dinner that night.

"You're not going to faint, are you?" Concern filled his voice as large hands cradled her face.

"No." The dizziness passed and warmth unfurled inside

her. "I'm just hungry," she murmured, touched by the emotion in his eyes. "Very hungry."

"You're sure you're all right? I'll see what's in the kitchen." He started to move but she stopped him.

"That's not what I'm hungry for." And then she kissed him, and the moment was back.

Their bodies pressed together, their hearts thudded and Delilah lost herself in Zach Tanner's arms.

"I want you, Delilah. I've always wanted you. I knew you were the one. From the first moment I saw you. *You.*"

The word echoed through her head and, in a flash, she saw a little gray-haired woman surrounded by screaming kids and dusty baking equipment. Forgotten mixers and cheesecake pans. Next to the woman stood Zach, as young and handsome as ever. The Wild Man and his little woman. *You.*

"I...we... This can't happen," she blurted, shoving against the hard wall of his chest.

"Are you feeling sick again?"

"No. Yes. Maybe." She bolted out from under him, shoving her skirt down as she rushed into the kitchen, desperate for some air and distance and sanity, because for a minuscule moment, before she'd glimpsed the future, she'd actually thrilled to the idea. *You.*

"Definitely sick," she muttered. "Deranged, distraught, stupid to even think such a thing."

"Think what?"

Delilah whirled at the sound of his voice. "Nothing." She fanned herself dramatically. "I just needed some air. Another dizzy spell."

"Right."

"Whew, it's hot in here." Hotter since he was coming closer. Too close...

"What's wrong? And don't tell me it's dizziness, because you don't have the same glazed look you had a few minutes ago when you really were dizzy.''

"Oh, really? What look do I have?''

"A scared look.''

"Me? Scared?'' She summoned a laugh that faded into a choked cough. "Of what?''

"You tell me. You're the one who ran away.''

"I did not run away. I told you, it was hot in there.''

"And about to get hotter.'' He advanced a step and she retreated. "You're scared, all right.''

She channeled her desperate emotions into a fierce glare. "I am not.''

"Scared and stubborn. You want me as much as I want you and you're too stubborn to admit it. Stubborn and—''

"I am not and never will be stubborn.''

"—and blind—''

"My eyes are wide open, buster.''

"—and so in love with your damned cheesecakes—''

"*Damned* cheesecakes?''

"—that you can't see a good thing when it's standing in front of you.''

"I can see just fine, thank you.'' That was the trouble. She could see him all too well. His broad shoulders, muscular arms, hair-dusted chest. That funnel of dark silk that whirled down over a washboard abdomen to disappear into the waistband of his jeans. Her heart skipped a beat.

Her bravado fled and she sidestepped him, gaining a few feet of blessed distance as she retreated to the far counter. "Look, Zach. I know sex seems like a really good idea right now, but it isn't. There are issues we have to think of, repercussions for the few minutes of pleasure—''

"Hours.''

She swallowed. "Okay, hours.''

"Maybe all night.''

"My point exactly." She busied herself straightening the leftovers from dessert: a half-eaten pecan pie, a bowl of rum sauce, a few pieces of her Luscious Lemon Lambada cheesecake— anything to keep from looking at him. To keep from staring into those blue eyes that made her want to rip off her panties and jump his bones right then and there. "I have to get up early for work, and so do you, not to mention sex completely violates the list. We have a working relationship to think of. A few hours—" she swallowed "—a *night* of pleasure would only complicate things."

"You're frigid, aren't you?"

She whirled. "What?"

"That's it. Hell, Delilah." He shrugged. "It makes perfect sense. Every time we come close to doing anything more serious than a little kissing, you clam up, freak out, run away."

"I am not frigid." She wasn't sure why the concept bothered her so much. If he thought she had some sexual problem, all the better. Maybe he would leave her alone.

The last notion should have brought some measure of relief, but the only thing it did was make her want to prove him wrong. Right here, right now, before she lost her nerve or had another dizzy spell and passed out on the kitchen floor.

"Lots of people have the problem," he went on. "There are counselors who specialize in that area."

"I *am not* frigid."

"I saw a special on *Oprah* one time. This psychologist said it's usually genetic. Your mom seems okay, though, so it was probably your dad."

"Listen to me," she growled, her hands clenching around the bowl of rum sauce. *"I am not frigid!"* A swift throw punctuated the sentence.

The bowl smacked him in the shoulder. Sauce splattered, trickling down his skin in dark rivulets. He wiped at the sticky mixture and glared at her. "What'd you do that for?"

"I don't need you telling me what's wrong with me. The only thing wrong with me is you, mister."

He shook his head like a typical know-it-all male and said, "You're frigid." Just to be sure she heard him, he spelled the word. *"F-R-I-G-I-D."*

"Because I resist the Wild Man? I call that sane. *S-A-N-E.*"

"It's classic denial. You're frigid, as in the ice princess, the deep-freeze diva, the snow queen—"

The half-eaten pecan pie caught him in the chest. Filling smudged his skin, the plate clattered to the floor and Zach's eyes narrowed to dangerous slits.

"You're frigid, as in you couldn't thaw out if you had a blowtorch shoved up your—" The words drowned into a loud "Umph," as he caught a piece of Luscious Lemon Lambada right in the groin.

"You're frigid," he sputtered.

"Yeah?" She grabbed another piece. "As in?"

"As in you couldn't seduce a man if your Chocolate Cherry Cha-Cha depended on it, lady."

"Oh, yeah?"

"Yeah."

"Are you willing to make a little bet on that?"

Challenge gleamed bright and fierce in his eyes. "Name your price."

"I want exclusives to my Chocolate Cherry Cha-Cha back. I prove to you I'm not frigid, and you tear up the contract we signed and finish out your term as indentured fiancé. Is it a deal?"

"I never lose." He smiled and her breath caught. "You're on."

"If there's one thing my mama taught me, Zach," Delilah said as she worked at the buttons on her blouse and pulled the edges apart in one swift motion, "it's that there's a first time for everything, and you, Wild Man, are about to lose. Badly." She unclasped her bra, freed her breasts and worked at the waistband of her skirt.

Clothes puddled at her feet and Delilah, completely nude for the first time in front of a man, fought back every insecurity, focused on the heat in Zach's blazing blue eyes and stepped toward him. "You'll be crying uncle before I'm finished."

# 11

"I NEVER CRY UNCLE," Zach said as Delilah advanced. "Dream on, sweetheart."

"I have been." She dropped to her knees in front of him. "Now I want the real thing." Her tongue darted out as she licked cheesecake from his navel. A shiver ripped through him, muscles contracted and warm skin vibrated against her hungry lips.

"Am I winning yet?"

"Not a chance." Despite his words, another shudder had him trembling against her mouth.

She worked at the button on his jeans. A zipper hissed and his erection sprang thick and pulsing hot toward her. Delilah took him in her mouth and Zach cradled her head. She licked him and loved him, savoring the flavor of warm male and sweet cheesecake. For a few heated moments, she forgot all about winning and reveled in the taste, touch and scent of Zach Tanner.

*Him.*

"I...can't...take...much...more...." He groaned. His fingers tightened and he pushed her away.

"Oh, Zach, I'm sorry," she said. "Did I hurt you? I've never done that before and I didn't know if I was doing it right and—"

"Uncle." The word was little more than a groan, but she heard him loud and clear and a smile split her face. But it wasn't the fact that she'd won. It was the glint in his blue eyes, the anticipation that rippled through her, the knowledge that he wanted her and she wanted him and nothing was going to stop them this time.

"Fair's fair," he murmured, pulling her up into his arms for a deep kiss. Skin met skin. His hair-roughened chest rasped her tender nipples. Then he fastened his jeans over a straining erection and grabbed a nearby dish towel to wipe rum sauce and pecan pie filling from his chest before scooping her into his arms and marching back through the living room toward the stairs.

"Which one?" he asked when they reached the second floor hallway lined with doors.

"That one." She pointed to the one at the far end.

"Where's your mother?"

"Guest room. First floor. Far, far away."

"Good." And with that, he pushed open her door, deposited her on the bed and stripped off his boots, jeans and briefs, until he stood naked in front of her. Perspiration made his muscles gleam despite the air-conditioning blowing from the vents. He was hot. Hard.

"Let's see how long before *you* cry uncle, sweetheart," he said, advancing.

Delilah never did cry uncle. She screamed it when Zach touched his tongue to her moist heat and suckled and tasted and drove her to a mind-blowing orgasm.

She lay limp and panting as he kissed his way back up her belly and paused to lave her sensitive nipples with the tip of his raspy tongue. Her body quivered and heat coiled again in her stomach, pulsing through her, until she thrummed, strung as tight as a violin and ready for more. For him.

She eased her legs up on either side of his thighs. Her hands clutched his buttocks. His hardness probed the moist heat between her legs and she gasped, and then the sensation disappeared. Delilah opened her eyes to see him collapsed beside her, his muscles drawn tight, his erection standing at attention.

"What's wro—" The question died on her lips as she watched him slide on a condom.

Then he reached for her and pulled her on top of him. "This is your victory ride, honey. You take the driver's seat."

As Delilah sank down onto his rigid length, she knew in her heart that everything couldn't have been more right.

*Her. Him. Them.*

For the first time, she embraced the truth, embraced the man, and they cried uncle all night long and a few other choice words that made her burn and blush and admit to herself that Zach, despite his Big Three status, was still a wild man at heart. And she loved him for it.

"Mmmm, that tickles." The sensation started at her belly, a light fluttering, like a butterfly playing against her skin, so soft and warm and tantalizing and...

Ah, the dream. She'd had it so many times, too many since she'd met Zach Tanner. But then it wasn't as if anybody knew. It was her dream. Her own private fantasy...

"Ahhh, touch me just like that." Her voice echoed in her ears, husky and real. "There and there and..."

Her eyes popped open to see tanned fingers playing at her straining nipple. Her gaze followed the hand upward, past a muscled forearm sprinkled with dark hair, bulging biceps and a sinewy shoulder to him.

Not her dream man, but the real thing.

Zach Tanner.

Last night came rushing back in a flood of heated memories. Mouths tasting, bodies touching, sheets tangling, moans filling the air...

Oh, God, they'd done *it,* and she'd liked it. Worse, she'd loved it.

She *loved* him.

Her head snapped back and she stared up at him, his face little more than a dark shadow against the morning sunlight.

Morning? Sunlight?

The grandfather clock chose that moment to chime and Delilah closed her eyes, counting the dreaded gongs and praying for them to stop. They did. Eventually.

"Ohmigod, it's nine o'clock."

"So?" Zach played with her nipple, oblivious to the panic bolting through her body.

"I'm up at five a.m. every day."

"So you sleep in today. It's Sunday."

"You don't understand." She shoved him away and bolted from the bed. "I—I've got work to do." She rushed to the dresser and yanked several drawers open. "I can't believe this. I *overslept.*"

"Everybody oversleeps once in a while."

"Not me. Not through four years of college, four years of running my own business. Not once. I've got this internal clock. If my alarm fails, I wake up anyway. Five a.m. on the dot." She retrieved blue panties and launched a mad search for the matching bra. "Don't you understand what this means? First I started rambling when I never ramble except in front of my mother, then I'm tossing bananas into my Chocolate Fudge Fandango and playing football when I should be working and kissing you on invoice night and sleeping in your T-shirt and now I oversleep."

"You slept in my T-shirt?" His grin widened and she shot him a glare.

"That's beside the point."

"Which is?"

*You. Me. Us. Love...* "Never mind. Just get dressed.

Please.'' She settled for a red and black polka-dot bra, whipped it on and did her best not to look while Zach bent to retrieve his underwear from a tangle of sheets.

Her hands stilled. God, he had such great buns. So tight and firm, and she knew firsthand because she'd touched them, caressed them....

''I thought you were in a hurry.'' His deep voice brought her back to the present and the all-important fact that he was now facing her. He was beautifully erect. Ready.

She swallowed and busied herself yanking a T-shirt and jeans from the closet. When she turned back around, he was just zipping his jeans, leaving only a prominent bulge to tempt her. She forced her gaze upward, to his muscular chest. ''Your shirt,'' she squeaked.

''My shirt's downstairs, in the kitchen.''

''You left your shirt downstairs? In the kitchen? My kitchen? The kitchen where my mother eats breakfast?''

''Right next to your bra and panties.''

''This isn't happening to me. I give to charity. I help old people with their bags at the grocery store. I even stopped to pick up a wounded dog one time and take him to the vet. I donate cakes to several youth centers. This isn't fair.'' She sat down and pulled on her shoes. ''Okay, if we just stay calm, we can figure a way out of this. We have to think of something to tell my mother.''

''Delilah, you're a grown woman. You don't have to tell her anything.''

''But she'll think...'' Mouths tasting, bodies touching, sheets tangling. ''Okay, so that's the only plus of this entire situation.''

He grinned, that lazy, sexy grin that made her want to kiss her business goodbye and drag him back to bed.

But she'd overslept and, Sunday or not, she had work to do.

"Come on." She grabbed his arm, but he didn't budge.

"My boots."

She snatched them from the floor, tugged on his arm and hauled him toward the door.

"You're kicking me out."

"Technically, yes."

"Then I won't ask if it was good for you."

"Please don't ask." She shoved him down the stairs. "Don't ask me anything, just go." Before she did or said something she'd regret.

*It was wonderful.*

*You were wonderful.*

*I'd like to do it again.*

*And again.*

*And again.*

*Him.*

"No!"

"No what?"

"Not that way." She jerked him backward from walking through the living room. "The back door. You can sneak out that way."

"You really want me to go?"

No. "Yes. You have to." She tried to block out the truth, to resist the urge to forget everything and throw herself into his arms.

*Think.* She had to think, and she couldn't do that with Zach Tanner underfoot, making her thoughts ramble, her heart beat faster, her hormones cry out for *more, more, more!*

*No, no, no!*

They made it to the door in record time without being spotted. Her mother's voice carried from the sweet wing, dangerously close, and Delilah shoved Zach out onto the porch.

''I'll see you later.'' She tossed him his boots, slammed the door and leaned back against the cool wood. Gone.

Thankfully.

But Delilah didn't feel so thankful. She felt empty and confused and very, very lonely.

ZACH WAS GETTING way too old for this.

His shoulder, sore after last night's exertion, throbbed as he hopped on one foot and yanked on his boot. The right slid on easily, but the left proved stubborn. He tightened his grip on the leather and jerked.

*He was getting too old for this.*

The full meaning of the words hit him as sharp and cutting as the pain that wrenched down his arm, clear to his fingers.

Too old to be sneaking around like a teenager.

Too old to be lusting after a woman who loved her business more than him. Last night only proved what Zach had already suspected but refused to see. Delilah James loved her cheesecake company, enough to sleep with a man just to win back exclusives on her Chocolate Cherry Cha-Cha.

He'd lost. Nearly two weeks of pretending to be something he wasn't, something he wanted to be, and he'd lost anyway. Forfeited his prize for a few hours—an entire night—of pleasure.

Pure, bone-deep, curl-your-toes and keep-you-coming-back-for-more pleasure.

He smiled as he climbed into his car. He'd lost, yet where was the rush of anger, the sense of helplessness that never failed to piss him off and incite him to fight? Then again, he hadn't lost in a hell of a long time, which could mean he'd forgotten what it felt like.

Or he was too busy remembering what she'd felt, looked, tasted like. Soft and warm and dreamy-eyed and so sweet...

He closed his eyes and leaned his head against the steering wheel. God help him, but he still wanted her, regardless of the reason behind last night. Regardless that she didn't want him.

*She didn't want him.* The truth shook him and he forced his eyes open. He gunned the engine and gathered his determination.

Time to cut his losses and move on. He'd wasted too much time already on one stubborn, beautiful, frantic cheesecake caterer who'd just kicked him out.

*A challenge,* a small voice whispered. *You can do it. You can change her mind.*

Probably. Maybe. Hell, he didn't know anymore. He'd never met a woman like Delilah. A woman immune to the Wild Man, unaffected by his reputation or his money. She was different. She was…*her.*

And Zach wanted her to want him, not for her business's sake or because she was sexually deprived or because he was the Wild Man and she was smitten by his charm. He wanted her for the right reason. For love.

But Delilah didn't love him, and that was that.

DELILAH LOVED him.

The realization hit her as she stood at the living room window and watched Zach's car disappear.

She wanted to run after him, to throw herself into his arms and kiss him until he smiled that smile that did funny things to her heartbeat. She wanted to take him to bed again and taste him and touch him and make babies this time. Lots of babies.

She *did* love him. That was the only explanation. She was alone in the room. No Zach to cloud her thinking. Even her mom was out in the kitchen….

Her mom. That was it! It was her mother making her

think all these crazy thoughts about love and marriage and babies. And with Zach Tanner, of all people, a man who'd made it clear that he wanted a wife minus a career. And Delilah's career was clearly everything to her.

Almost everything.

It *was* her mother. Because no way would Delilah even think such a thing on her own, without some supernatural element—the all-seeing, all-knowing, supermother Gladys James—at work.

"This isn't me. I don't act this way unless provoked or manipulated." A hysterical laugh bubbled on her lips. "She's on to me. She figured out the engagement is a fake and now she's doing something to really make me fall in love with him."

And Delilah had to put a stop to it.

She bolted down the hallway and burst into her mother's bedroom. "Ma, I know what you're trying to do and you can just forget it...." But the room was empty.

She bolted to her mother's dressing table and started a desperate search for evidence. There had to be something going on. No way had she really fallen in love with Wild Man Zach Tanner and had sex with him and overslept with him and—

"Delilah, what's going on?" Her mother appeared in the doorway holding a bowl of strawberries. "Where's Zach?"

"Gone."

"I hope you reminded him about this afternoon. The wedding planner at the department store is expecting you to register today, and Zach really should be there."

"I love you, Ma, you know I do," Delilah rushed on, oblivious to her mother's words. "But you have to stop meddling in my life. When you ran that singles' ad, I went along with it even though I knew it was a disaster. Then there was that grocery store billboard advertising for single men, and I even let your garden club auction me off to Melvin the Mechanic for three hundred dollars.''

"You brought the highest price,'' Gladys pointed out. "I'll call Zach myself and remind him about today as soon as I finish the Strawberry Daiquiri Doo-Wop.''

"But I don't have a Strawberry Daiquiri Doo-Wop.''

"You do now, dear, and the orders are pouring in. Apparently Dale and the other firemen told all their friends about our new flavor. Come out to the kitchen and try some.''

"I don't want to try some.'' She shook her head. "Did I say that? Ohmigod.'' She ripped open the next drawer and rifled through cosmetics. "You've gone too far this time.'' She rummaged through panty hose and bottles of vitamins.

"I have no idea what you're talking about, dear. You and Zach didn't have a fight last night, did you? Because I did hear raised voices. Of course, those sounded like moans.''

"They *were* moans, and now I want to moan some more and it's all your fault.'' Delilah rifled through the next drawer. "You cast some sort of love spell. I knew I shouldn't have let you go to New Orleans with your bridge club. You probably talked to every voodoo queen in the business about your poor, single daughter. What did you do? Slip a potion into my drink? Recite some chant? Dance naked during a full moon or make a voodoo doll with a lock of my hair?''

"I never dance naked, dear. Though there was that time with your father when we—''

"Have a heart, Ma! You're doing this. I know you are. You're making me love Zach and forget the time and think about weddings and babies.'' *And act like a crazy woman.*

"I'd love to take credit, dear, but I'm afraid I haven't done a thing—"

"Aha!" Delilah whirled and held up a plastic sandwich bag filled with gray powder. "What's this? Love dust? Ashes l'amour? Pleasure sprinkles? *What?*"

"Your father, dear."

"Oh, sure." Delilah smirked and gave her mom a get-real look. "Like this is really Dad."

Gladys sighed. "He hated being cooped up in that urn— you know what an outdoorsy man he's always been—so I thought I'd give him a window to the world."

"My *father?*" At her mother's nod, her stomach heaved, her fingers went limp and the bag sailed to the floor.

*Pop!*

Dust whirled, her father scattered. Then Delilah did the one thing she should have done last night, before she'd slept with Zach Tanner, sampled the forbidden fruit and gotten herself into such a mess.

She fainted.

# 12

"...THE LAST TIME, Delilah. Stop apologizing. I'm sure your father didn't feel a thing."

Zach slid into the seat across from Delilah just as Gladys James finished her second plate of ribs. "Sorry I'm late. One of the ovens went down at number ten and I had to supervise the installation of the new one. So what's going on?"

Delilah turned stricken eyes on him and he barely resisted the urge to reach out.

"I spilled my father," she blurted.

"And then you scooped him back up and found a new plastic baggie for him. Relax, dear, and have a chili-cheese fry."

"I shouldn't."

"She also fainted," Gladys told Zach.

His eyes narrowed. "Are you sick?"

"Pregnant?" Gladys asked with hopeful eyes.

"Ma!"

"Excuse a poor old woman for wanting grandchildren."

"You're not old."

"I'm this close to biting the bullet." She clutched her chest and stared heavenward. "Bob, honey, I'll be with you soon."

"Ma, please don't say things like that."

"You being pregnant would sure ease my passage."

*"I am not pregnant!"*

"Why did you faint?" Zach asked.

"She's deprived," Gladys chimed in. "I told her to stop with all the dieting. Don't you think she's perfect the way she is? So soft and round and—"

"You're really trying to kill me, aren't you, Ma?"

"Made to fit in a man's arms just right."

"I'll save you the trouble and do it myself," Delilah said. "Give me the butter knife."

Zach grinned and snatched the knife out of her reach. His fingertips brushed hers, electricity sizzled and his hand stalled. Their eyes met and his heart stopped.

He yanked his hand away and shoved the fries in front of her. "Here, honey. Eat your heart out."

"See, Zach doesn't mind if you have a fry, and if your future husband can't be the judge of whether or not you're too fat, then bury me now. Bob," she said, staring at the overhead light, "I'm on my way."

Delilah threw up her hands. "I'll eat a fry."

Zach tried not to watch, but he couldn't help himself. His mouth went dry when she licked cheese and suckled the potato. He forced his gaze away while she worked at another fry.

"Say, Gladys," he said, turning to her mother. "How would you like a tour of the kitchen?"

"Oh, I'd love it."

"Great, I'll show you—"

"I'd much rather have this handsome young man do the honors." She turned on a surprised busboy, hooked her arm through his and hauled him in the direction of the kitchen.

"She's up to something." Delilah stared after her mother, a thoughtful look on her face.

"What?"

"I don't know. I just get this feeling.… Never mind."

She took a deep breath. "We really need to talk about last night. It was wonderful, but it was still just—"

"Sex."

Her gaze snapped to his. "What did you say?"

"I said last night was just sex. That's what you were going to say, wasn't it? Just sex."

Her eyes twinkled. "Actually, I was thinking great sex."

He nodded. "Fantastic sex."

"Monumental sex."

"But still just sex."

"Yes." She stiffened. "It didn't mean anything. I mean, it did. You wanted me and I wanted—"

"Exclusives back."

"That's right." Her expression went from worried to excited. "I won the bet, didn't I?"

So why did Zach feel like the winner when she smiled at him like that? Her gray eyes twinkling, her full lips curved just so.

He frowned. "I tore up the contract this morning. You won fair and square, and I always honor a bet."

"And that's all last night was," she said, a determined expression on her face. "Just a bet."

He grinned. "And really great sex."

"Wonderful sex."

"Earth-shattering sex."

"Mind-blowing sex."

His grin faded. "And now it's over."

"It has to be."

"We want different things."

"Amen."

"I want a traditional, stay-at-home wife to keep me warm at night, and you want your cheesecakes."

"That's not entirely true. I do want a husband someday,

after my ten-year plan is up. Someone who doesn't mind sharing me.''

"And I don't share." And most of all, Zach didn't have the time to wait for someday. He needed a wife soon. Before his shoulder gave out and his sperm stopped going the distance.

"So we're agreed?" she asked. "No repeat of last night?"

No. "Yes."

Delilah breathed another deep sigh. "You know, this day might not turn out to be so bad after all."

He grinned. "Give it time. We still have to pick out china and crystal with your mom."

Delilah shook her head. "No, we don't. This whole thing has gotten way out of hand. First it was a little lie, then all the preparations and time spent on a wedding that will never take place. I have to tell her."

"It's only four more days."

Delilah stared across at Zach, into his concerned eyes, and her heart beat double time. Four more days with him? Her hormones, not to mention her heart, would never take it after last night. Now she knew what she'd be missing. She knew what she really felt. And it wasn't because of her mother or any spell or potion. It was the real thing, and it was way too soon.

Leave it to her heart to have the most rotten timing, and with the wrong man. The Wild Man, of all people. A man with old-fashioned views of women, and Delilah was way too nineties to fit his ideal.

Even worse, she found herself wanting to be his ideal, to give up everything, especially when he grinned at her the way he was right now.

Temporary insanity. That was it. Just a fleeting thing that would pass if she held out. And she had to. Otherwise, years from now she would find herself regretting the past. Just like her mother.

"Are you sure you want to tell her?"

She gathered her courage and nodded. "I've never been more sure of anything in my life."

"WOULD YOU MAKE UP your mind, Delilah? We've been looking at patterns for more than a half hour. Don't you see anything you like?"

"Not really."

"What about this one, dear? Tea roses and this intricate gold border?"

"I don't know, Ma. It's nice, but..." Just do it, she told herself. Do it, do it, *do it!*

"Zach, what do you think?" Gladys turned to the man who'd followed them patiently for the past half hour.

"Um, Zach." Delilah signaled him with her eyes. "Shouldn't you go over to housewares and pick out power tools?"

"Couples register for that?"

"Of course, dear." Gladys patted his arm. "My Bob and I got a double chain saw and a complete set of socket wrenches when we tied the knot."

Delilah nodded. "When my oldest brother got engaged, rumor had it he was only in it for a fully loaded workbench. But then he called it off and bought his own."

"Thank the Lord Almighty," Gladys said. "He was only twenty-eight. A baby. Much too young to get married."

Zach winked and walked away.

Delilah slid an arm around her mother's shoulder. "I'm glad you said that, Ma, because I really need to talk to you about something."

"I agree wholeheartedly, dear. Let's discuss the merits

of tea roses as opposed to cherubs, then maybe we can make a decision between these two lovely patterns.''

"I'd rather talk weddings.''

"Oh, did I mention SueAnn Merrymore—sea lilies and navy-blue—got married on a raft in the middle of Lake Houston last year. It was dreadful. Started raining right when the minister started, the raft started rocking and the maid of honor ended up going overboard.'' Gladys paused to take a deep breath. "Whew, all this shopping has me a little winded.'' She took another breath. "Anyhow, she— not SueAnn but the maid of honor—met this nice paramedic who gave her mouth-to-mouth and now they're planning a June wedding. Does your friend Melanie know any paramedics?''

"I don't think so, Ma.'' She patted her mother's shoulder and watched the woman gasp for another breath. "I was really talking about my wedding. You see, there isn't going to be—'' Her words faded into the crash of china as the plate her mother had been holding sailed to the ground. Gladys James struggled for another deep breath and held a hand to her chest.

"Ma? What is it?''

"I… I…something's wrong.'' Her mother struggled for another breath. "I…'' she gasped as she sank to the floor between the everyday dinnerware and the really good stuff. "My chest…burning.''

*Chest… Burning…* Oh, no. Oh, no. *Oh, no!*

Delilah yanked out her cellular phone and called for help as her mother's breath came in wheezes. Customers and clerks rushed toward them, and Zach fought his way through the growing crowd.

"Hurry,'' she cried after giving the operator her name and location. "I think my mom's having a heart attack!''

"YOUR MOTHER HAD an attack, all right," Dr. Harvey Tannenbaum, the gray-haired, sixty-something ER doctor said as he walked out of the treatment room where he'd been attending Gladys James.

Delilah bolted from the chair where she'd been praying and crying on Zach's shoulder for the past hour. "I knew it," she sobbed. "I knew I should have paid more attention to the signs. How bad is it, Doctor? Will she make it?"

"Another twenty years if she lays off the greasy foods."

"What?"

"Your mother had an attack of indigestion."

"Indigestion? But she was on the floor, Doctor. She couldn't even talk to me, for heaven's sake, and when she did, it was this faint little croak."

"That was the double order of ribs and the chili-cheese fries she had for lunch doing the croaking. The indigestion gets you right here—" he pointed to his midchest "—and works its way up where it either exits the mouth as a burp, or stalls in the form of this mild burning somewhere in the esophagus. Your mother's lunch was burning instead of exiting."

"But she was so pale."

"That's because she's not getting a balanced diet. She's turning into a pork rind, Miss James, and it's our job to stop her." He handed her several instruction sheets on eating low-fat and low-cholesterol foods while she tried to absorb the truth that her mother wasn't dying.

Not yet anyway, she thought as she stared down at the paper and saw the words no sugar and very little fat. But the moment Gladys James heard about her new heart-smart eating program, she was definitely going to have the Big One.

"Ma?" Delilah poked her head into the examining room

and saw her mother stretched out on the hospital bed, her eyes closed. So quiet and serene and...*dead?* "Ma!"

"Stop all that hollering, dear. I'm just resting my eyes."

"Thank God. She's all right," she told Zach, who followed her in. "Ma, you gave me an awful scare."

"Think of it as training, dear."

"What?"

"We all have to go sometime, and my time is sure to come sooner than later." She touched her chest and winced.

"Is the indigestion lingering?"

"Indigestion?" A smile played at Gladys's lips. "Oh, yes, the indigestion. Just a bit."

"There's something you're not telling me, Ma."

"Of course not, dear. I'm fine. Just fine." She patted Delilah's hand and winced again.

"The doctor said you're free to go home."

"Of course, dear. It's always better to be in familiar surroundings when the old ticker gives out completely."

"Ma, you did not have a heart attack."

"Of course I didn't, dear. Not yet. It was just indigestion. That's what Harvey—er, Dr. Tannenbaum told you. What a nice man. So handsome and clever."

"That is what happened, isn't it, Ma? A simple attack of indigestion? You're not keeping something from me?"

"Certainly not, dear. Now what were you saying about the wedding? I distinctly remember you telling me there wasn't going to be a wedd—"

"A wedding shower," Delilah cut in. "I've done a lot of thinking on this, Ma, and Zach and I don't want to be a financial burden on our guests. They can bring gifts to the wedding, but no prewedding showers. Isn't that right, Zach?"

"You're the boss, honey bunch." He slid his arm around her shoulder and squeezed.

Four more days, she told herself as a strange heat gripped her middle. *Stay strong, girl. Think cheesecakes.*

The trouble was, whenever she thought about cheesecakes, it wasn't baking them. It was licking them off of one dangerously handsome man.

LATER THAT EVENING, Delilah parked the delivery van outside of Wild Man's restaurant number one, the back full of Chocolate Cherry Cha-Cha.

Harold had volunteered to put in some overtime and make the weekly delivery, but after today, Delilah felt she owed Zach a thank-you. He'd jumped right in and played his part when she'd chickened out with her mother, and she owed him.

"It's just indigestion," Delilah told herself for the hundredth time that afternoon.

But what if she was wrong? What if the indigestion was a sign, like the previous chest pains her mother had been having? What if her mother was this close to following in her father's footsteps? Probably not. Maybe not. But it didn't matter. Delilah couldn't take the chance. She couldn't tell Gladys the truth now and possibly crush a dying woman's last dream to see her daughter happily married.

Four more days, she told herself. Then Gladys was leaving for her cruise, even though Delilah had tried to talk the woman out of it. Gladys was stubborn, and still pale. But if she was determined to go, Delilah would do her best to see that her mother left in the best health possible. Complete bed rest for the next four days and plenty of healthy food.

She'd hidden everything remotely fattening or detrimental to the new diet in a locked pantry in the sweet wing, and had left a very cranky Gladys sitting up in bed, eating a low-fat vegetable medley.

Now to talk to Zach and really thank him.

The restaurant was exceptionally busy for a Monday night. Music pumped through the speakers, the loud chatter of voices drifted from the doorway. Delilah made her delivery out back, then started for the main dining room, where one of the busboys had reported seeing Zach mingling with guests.

The minute she reached the archway, she spotted him sitting at a nearby table. He wore the same sexy grin that never failed to scramble her senses. Her heart sped up and she couldn't help herself. She smiled.

Until she saw the woman seated across from him.

The petite blonde with red-tipped nails placed her hand atop Zach's in an all-too familiar gesture that hit Delilah like a punch to the stomach. She winced. While she couldn't see the woman's face, she didn't have to. She could see the woman's features in her mind. Pouty red lips. Dark, bedroom eyes. She knew the type. The big-busted, pinup type that Wild Man Tanner had been photographed with too many times to count.

The trouble was, he wasn't the Wild Man anymore. He was Zach. *Her* Zach.

The woman stood up. Tight jeans outlined a perfect butt and accented a trim waist. Delilah caught her bottom lip to stop it from trembling. She wouldn't cry. Not here, not now.

Zach stared past the woman and his gaze locked with Delilah's. Pleasure chased surprise across his face. He said something to the woman, and then he started toward her.

Delilah did the only thing she could do at that moment. With her eyes burning and her heart breaking, she turned and ran before she did something stupid like scratch Zach's eyes out.

Or worse, throw herself into his arms and tell him she loved him.

DELILAH WAS FLAT on her back, pulling frantically at the zipper of her jeans when the doorbell rang.

She wiped the tears from her eyes, shimmied and wiggled and tugged until her fingers were raw and the zipper finally reached its destination. Another swipe at her face, and she managed to slide the button into place. She drew in a deep breath and wiped at her eyes again. She'd done it.

The doorbell rang again and she struggled to a sitting position. Panting, she stared down at the skintight jeans, and regretted her rash decision to pour her too-big thighs and butt into a size eight when she was clearly a size twelve.

What the hell had she done?

She'd rushed home, straight into her closet, desperate to prove to herself she was enough woman for him and not too much. Stupid. So Zach went for thin, pouty, bedroom-eyed women? It wasn't as if Delilah had any designs on him. Or at least any she was going to act on. She was as threatened by his womanizing reputation, as he was by her career. All the more reason that things would never, ever work between them. They were too different.

The doorbell rang again, yanking her back to reality and she flopped down onto her back. Now to get the blasted things off, stop behaving like a raving lunatic and answer her door...

She tried the waistband, but her fingers were swollen and raw. She couldn't undo the button, much less the zipper. The doorbell rang again and she struggled upright, tears streaming down her face. The jeans cut into her waist, cut off her circulation and she struggled for air.

How had she gotten herself into such a mess?

Her gaze darted frantically around her bedroom for some scissors or a knife or something....

"I've been ringing forever. I was starting to worry about you—" Zach's voice faded away as he came to a staggering halt in her bedroom doorway. "I, um, I didn't realize you weren't dressed." He drank in the sight of her wearing only a bra and a pair of snug jeans. His gaze lingered on the bare curve of her shoulder and need hit him hard and fast and deep. "I, uh, your mom let me in."

"Thanks." Her voice was soft, trembling, and his stomach clenched. "For going along today when I wimped out of telling my mother the truth. You were great, and you deserve exclusives on my Chocolate Cherry Cha-Cha."

"Is that why you showed up at Wild Man's? To tell me the deal is still on?" She nodded, and he said, "But you won the bet fair and square."

"Not really. I mean, I did, but I didn't sleep with you because of the bet. Not entirely. You were right about me."

"You're not frigid."

"No, but I was scared, and I wanted you. I'm still scared, and I still want you." Delilah turned, an anguished look on her face. "What's she got that I haven't got?"

"Who?" His gaze riveted on her breasts heaving and pushing against the lace of her bra. He glimpsed a nipple through the fabric and his mouth went dry as he remembered the feel of the ripe bud against his tongue.

"That woman you were with."

"Woman?" He tried to concentrate on her words instead of the delicate slope of her neck, her rose-tinted cheeks, her deep, liquid eyes.

"The blonde. What does she have that I don't?"

"Nothing, sweetheart." Her bottom lip glistened just so and heat shot to his groin. "You've got it all."

"Too much." She wiped at her face. "I've got too much." She stared down at her jeans. "I bought these last year. They're my wish jeans. I wish I were a size eight. I wish I looked as perfect as that Barbie you were with."

"They're nice." He spared a glance at the jeans. "Take them off."

More tears rolled down her cheeks. "I can't." She sniffled. "They're stuck."

"Stuck?"

She nodded frantically and more tears spilled down her cheeks.

He smiled. "Let's see what we can do about that."

Zach proved to be a master at difficult zippers. The jeans slid off easily enough under his anxious hands. Then he pulled Delilah into his arms and kissed her.

"We shouldn't be doing this," she said as his mouth slid down her neck to nip the curve of her shoulder.

"No," he murmured. "We shouldn't."

"We want different things out of life."

He grinned against her soft, fragrant skin. "Right now I think we want the same thing."

"Okay, so we're attracted to each other," she breathed.

"Damned attracted."

"Desperately attracted." She locked her fingers around his neck. "But this won't change anything."

"Not a thing."

"There's no future for us beyond this bed."

"The buck stops here," he vowed.

"Just so long as we understand each other."

But Zach Tanner understood her all too well. He stroked her just where she ached to be stroked. Kissed her just the way she longed to be kissed. And made her feel as perfect as a Barbie. More perfect, because he touched and tasted and appreciated her exactly the way she was.

An hour later, she snuggled in his arms, her back to his chest, and tried to quiet her pounding heart. "That can't happen again," she said more to convince herself than him. "Because then we'll want to do it again and again."

"And again." His hand cupped her breast and her nipple tingled, throbbed.

"Maybe once more." She arched into his palm.

"Once," he agreed. His hand trailed down her belly to the damp triangle of curls.

"Okay, twice." She sighed as his fingers sought out the wet heat between her legs. "Maybe three times."

His deep laughter filled her ears before he rolled her underneath him and stared down at her. "Three?"

"You're up for it, aren't you?" she asked as her hands trailed down his hair-dusted chest, across his rippled abdomen to his already straining erection. His breath caught.

"With you—" he stared down at her, into her and her heart paused "—I'm up for anything."

True to his word, he was up for anything and everything she wanted that night. Three times and then some...

MORNING CAME all too soon, and reality. Zach left just before daylight after apologizing to the fire department for a false call because he'd mistaken the three alarm clocks Delilah had set for the fire alarm.

She'd actually felt guilty when he'd bolted out of bed and called 911, but then she wasn't about to oversleep again. She had to work, regardless of last night. *Because* of last night. Because Delilah James had fallen even deeper in love with Zach Tanner, and she needed something to occupy her time. They'd had one extra night, no strings attached, and that was it.

Three days, then Zach was out of her life, out of her system, and life would be normal again.

She could keep her distance for three more days.

ZACH WAS KEEPING his distance. One night was one night and it was over. He set his sights on keeping busy, although that didn't include scoping out prospective wife material.

Not that he didn't want to, mind you. He did. But he was a taken man, at least for the next three days, and he felt it was the least he could do to stay faithful even if it wasn't a real engagement. After all, she'd honored their original agreement and given him exclusives to her Chocolate Cherry Cha-Cha and he was damned appreciative.

At least that's what he told himself.

Zach didn't want to think about the real reason that sent him straight home after dinner at Delilah's the next night. To an empty apartment and an even emptier bed. Particularly when Trudy had a nice marriage-minded kindergarten teacher she wanted him to meet.

Hey, a guy had to have his principles.

# 13

DELILAH BURIED herself in her work the next few days. Her mother's Strawberry Daiquiri Doo-Wop had caught fire and the orders, courtesy of Dale's and the other firemen's word of mouth, had proved invaluable.

Professionally, Delilah James was thriving.

And personally? Well, a gal couldn't have everything.

After Sunday's lapse into the land of the sexually desperate, she and Zach had kept their distance. Monday's dinner had been filled with her mother's usual banter, Zach's teasing and Delilah's darting into the kitchen every five minutes. Things appeared the same, but they weren't. She was nervous around him, fidgety, and he was the same old, self-assured Zach. Completely unaffected by what had happened between them.

All the better.

So why didn't she feel better?

Because she'd landed herself an audition for the future Mrs. Wild Man, and she'd obviously failed. Not that she wanted the part, but it was the principle of the thing. Zach could at least look regretful that the situation hadn't worked out between them.

A little moping would be nice, she thought Wednesday morning as she dialed Melanie's number for the sixth time in the past few days and got her answering machine again.

"This is Mel. You know the drill."

"Mel, this is your best friend and this is the last time

I'm leaving a message. I'm starting to worry, so unless you're dead or in the hospital, you better have a damned good reason for avoiding my phone calls.'' Her voice softened. "Call me, okay?" Then she hung up and headed downstairs.

"What's wrong, dear?" Gladys looked up from her cup of decaf and dry whole-wheat toast to give her daughter a thorough once-over when she walked into the kitchen.

"I tried Mel again, but she wasn't home."

"Is that all that's bothering you? Because you look a little preoccupied. Are you getting prewedding jitters?"

"We haven't even set a date, Ma." Delilah poured herself a cup of black coffee, fully caffeinated, and slid into the seat opposite her mother.

"You can still get prewedding jitters. Getting married is like flying to the moon. You've never been there and you don't know what to expect."

"Was getting married everything you expected?"

"Even more, dear. That's why I quit the restaurant."

"I thought you quit the restaurant before you married Dad."

"I wanted to, but your father wouldn't let me."

"*You* wanted to? I thought Dad wanted you to quit."

"Nonsense. Your father was very supportive of my career."

"But what about all that 'I'm your full-time job, Gladys, your future, and don't you forget it'?"

"Oh, that was just your father's insecurity kicking in. When I quit, he was worried I'd get tired of cooking and cleaning and looking after him. I don't know how many times I told your father, 'Bob, I want you to be my full-time job, my future.' He took to saying the words back to me, so I didn't forget them. As if I would. When I said those things to him, I meant them."

"But what about your career? You love to cook."

"And I've spent the past thirty-six years doing just that. What makes you think that cooking for nameless, faceless masses at some restaurant is better than cooking for people you love?"

"I just thought... I mean, you were so happy when you baked for those firemen, and then you came up with a new recipe for me and landed a new account and..."

"I was happy, dear. I adore seeing people smile. I enjoy giving them the same wonderful feeling I get when I sink my teeth into a chili-cheese burrito or coconut fried shrimp or beer-battered chicken-fried steak." Her mother paused to fan herself and lick her lips. "This deprivation is killing me, dear."

"I know the feeling." Delilah thought of Zach and how good he looked sprawled on her bed, his tanned body against her pale sheets. She wanted him so badly, not just his body, his lovemaking, but his grins, his deep, assessing looks, his fingertips brushing aside her tears when she cried, his arms around her, comforting her the way he had when they'd taken her mother to the emergency room. Even that once-irritating drawl, so typical of the Wild Man, had captured a special place in her heart.

"You really loved Dad that much? So much you never had any regrets about what you gave up? No 'what ifs'?"

Her mother smiled. "Well, once in a while I do picture myself in a chef's hat, cooking dinner for the First Lady."

"See, you do have regrets."

"That's a fantasy, dear, not a regret. I've never once wished I had lived my life differently. Of course, every woman's got to have a fantasy every now and then. Your father fulfilled all my, uh, baser desires, so my fantasies involve other emotionally gratifying experiences such as cooking. Let's see, in one fantasy I dished up seafood creole with shrimp au gratin to Jackie Kennedy. Then there was the crème brûlé with Betty Ford. Oh, and my favorite was serving fried oyster po'boys to Barbara Bush. There's a woman who enjoys good food, and that's what I like. I like people to enjoy my food.''

''I like people to enjoy my cheesecakes.''

''But you like the business side a lot more than I ever did. Put me in a kitchen, any kitchen, and I'm as happy as a clam. Not you, Delilah. You have the same competitive streak as your brothers. Landing big contracts, expanding your mail distribution, installing bigger and better equipment—those are the things you really love, dear.''

''I love it all, Ma.''

''And what about Zach? How does he feel about you spending so much time with How Sweet It Is?''

''He's all for it. Some women can have it all, Ma. With a supportive spouse, the sky's the limit.'' Unfortunately, Zach wasn't the supportive spouse in question, and Delilah wouldn't be having it all. At least not with him.

The thought depressed her and she busied herself pouring her second cup of caffeine.

Gladys sipped her coffee and smiled. ''This is nice.''

''What?''

''You and me. Having a heart-to-heart. I like it.''

''So do I. Can I ask you something?'' Gladys nodded, and Delilah added, ''Why are you carrying Daddy around with you? Do you miss him? Is that it?''

''I do miss your father, but he's gone. I know that, dear. I'm taking him on my cruise as a way of saying goodbye. He always loved to fish, so I thought I'd toss him over the side of the ship so he could swim with the big ones. Then I'm on to the buffet and the bar to really enjoy myself.'' At Delilah's glare, she looked sheepish. ''Of course, I'm talking about the fruit buffet and the salad bar. I've got my diet to think of.''

"Good." Delilah reached for a muffin and strawberry glaze.

Her mother frowned. ''Now I know something's wrong.''

Delilah glanced down at the muffin. "Because I'm eating?''

''Without any coercion.''

She slathered her muffin with glaze and took a bite.

No rush of guilt overwhelmed her. No frantic thoughts about fat cells accumulating at her waist, her thighs, everywhere the traitorous things had been known to haunt her. She felt different now. Attractive. Self-confident.

She smiled. "Actually, Ma, things couldn't be more right.''

Sincere words and a night of intense lovemaking had freed her from her lifelong battle with the bulge. A few moments of morning conversation had eased a relationship that had become a constant source of stress.

She frowned. Okay, so *everything* wasn't right. If she could only solve her problem with Zach—namely the all-important fact that there could never be a future between them—her life would be perfect. Fat chance. There were few perfect people in the world and Delilah James had never had the good fortune to be one of them.

Then again, who needed perfection with a mother like Gladys James to lend a hand?

Delilah eyed her mother, who now had a smile plastered on her face. "You're up to something.''

''Me?'' Gladys feigned a hurt look. ''I was just thinking.''

''About me and Zach.''

"About that muffin." Gladys indicated Delilah's plate. "Are you going to eat the rest, dear?"

"Don't even think it." Delilah snatched the plate up and carried the temptation to the garbage. "Ma, just leave things alone, okay?" She dumped the plate into the sink of soapy water. "We're fine. I'm fine. Zach's fine. Everything's fine."

"If you say so, dear."

She wiped her hands, picked up her clipboard and headed for the sweet wing. "I say so. I don't need you meddling."

"We'll see." The words, so soft they could have been her imagination, followed her out the door and she took several deep breaths. Her mother boarded the plane for Miami tomorrow. There was little damage she could do between now and then.

Besides, the damage was already done. Delilah was in love.

"THANK GOD you called," Delilah said to Melanie when she finally reached her later that day. "You're not hurt, are you?"

"More like ashamed."

"What are you talking about?" Delilah finished up an order of Tangerine Tango and turned to start on a mixer of Luscious Lemon Lambada.

"She knows."

"Who knows?"

"Your mother. Saturday at the beauty salon, she grilled me. She was ruthless, Dee. She made me cry right in the middle of my manicure. Pedro had to start over with the base coat. It was terrible. I should have told you sooner, but I couldn't."

"It's all right. I lived with the woman for eighteen years, remember? I know how persuasive she can be."

"She didn't give you hell, did she?"

"No. She's just been acting funny. Come to think of it, it was right after the salon that she started talking to my dad."

"But your dad's dead."

"That's the point, Mel."

"But that's all she's done, right? Talk to your dad?" At Delilah's "yes," she added, "That's a relief."

"No, it's not. It's scary."

"Maybe she's decided to stay out of your life for once and let you and Zach make up your own minds."

"This is my mother, remember? The woman's a walking Love Connection. No, something has to be up."

"You're right. Oh, Dee, I'm sorry. Remember, I always loved you like a sister."

"I'm not dying." Not yet, she thought as she hung up the phone. Then again, this was the last night before her mother left for Miami, and the woman knew the truth. Gladys James *knew*.

That knowledge alone kept Delilah in the kitchen well into the evening, hiding away, working herself into a frenzy and praying for an attack of exhaustion, a freak accident with some of the kitchen equipment, her own heart attack— anything to keep her from walking out of the sweet wing and facing Gladys James.

"Ma," she called out when she finally emerged at half past seven that night. "I know you're probably mad, but you wouldn't harm a defenseless woman, would you? Especially your own daugh—" Her words ground to a halt as she peered into the dining room and spotted Zach. "You're not my mother."

"Not the last time I looked." He wore a black silk shirt tucked into black jeans. The faint smell of after-shave wafted across to her and her traitorous nostrils flared.

"What are you doing here?" she asked. "You're not supposed to be here until eight-thirty."

"Your mom called and said to come right over for dinner."

"But I haven't even cooked."

"Somebody has." He indicated the lavishly set dining room table. Several long white tapers had been lit, the overhead lights toned down to give the room a soft, romantic glow.

Her warning signals went off. *Mother alert! Mother alert!*

"You didn't do this?" Zach asked.

"I've been working."

Something achingly close to disappointment touched his eyes. "I should have known."

"Children, children," Gladys sang from the doorway. "Let's call a truce. I'm responsible for all this lovely food, and the two of you can thank me later after I get back."

"Ma, wait. We need to talk—" A horn cut off the rest of Delilah's words.

"Sorry, dear, no time. There's my ride now. Melanie and I are having dinner together. I love you, dear, but I'm a single, attractive woman and I shouldn't be cooped up here with an old married—make that almost married couple. I need to get out and mingle, and your dear friend Melanie knows this lovely piano bar. Don't wait up. Oh, and, Zach, be sure to try the mushroom sauce. I made it especially for you." Before Delilah could get in a word edgewise, the door closed and she was standing alone with Zach Tanner.

"You look nice," he said, his gaze sweeping her pink overalls.

She touched a few tendrils of hair that had come loose from her ponytail. "I'm a mess. I've been elbow deep in cheesecakes all day." She did look a mess, but she knew when he looked at her, he didn't see it, and the knowledge made her smile. "You look really great, too. There's something different about you." She stepped closer and stared up at him. "It's your hair. You colored it."

He averted his gaze and rubbed his hands together. "The food sure smells great."

"You actually colored it."

He sniffed. "Is that chicken?"

"Zach." She caught his chin and forced his gaze to meet hers. Warm, clean-shaven skin tickled her fingertips, and the uncertainty in his eyes gripped her already aching heart. "You look good, but I thought you looked fine the way you were. Gray hair and all."

"It's just temporary. It'll wash out in a few shampoos. Then maybe I'll let nature take its course."

*Nature.* As in Mother Nature. As in letting things happen, giving in to the natural feelings coursing through her body. The desire to touch him, kiss him, lose herself.

"Uh, nature's overrated," she said and he gave her a sharp look. "But not when it comes to your hair." She swallowed and wished the lights weren't so soft, the tension so thick, the need so fierce and demanding....

"We're being set up," she told him. "My mom knows. Melanie told her days ago."

"You don't think she poisoned the food, do you?"

"She prides herself on her cooking. She would never purposely destroy good food. I think she's past anger. She's determined to turn our lie into reality."

His gaze swept the table and his nostrils flared as he inhaled the aroma drifting from the dining room. "Looks like she went to a lot of trouble."

"Trouble," she said, trying not to notice the way the candle flames reflected in his eyes when he looked at her. "That's definitely what this is."

His gaze caught and held hers. "Are you thinking what I'm thinking?"

*You. Me. Naked and rolling on the floor.*

He licked his lips. She licked her lips.

"Yeah," she croaked, her voice suddenly hoarse. "I am."

"Good." He rubbed his hands together. "Then let's eat."

"Eat?" She shook away the disturbing images dancing in her head. "Oh, yeah, eat. Eating's good."

For the next half hour, Delilah and Zach sat on opposite sides of the table, gazes fixed on their plates as they did their best to concentrate on the eight-course feast Gladys had prepared. Soup and salad. Chicken with mushroom sauce.

"This stuff is wonderful," Zach said around a mouthful. "You should try some."

"I'm allergic to mushrooms."

"They're my favorite."

"No wonder Ma made them. She's trying to win you over."

"It's working. I'm this close to asking her to marry me."

It was a joke, she knew, but the thought of Zach asking anyone to marry him brought tears to her eyes.

She blinked and stabbed at her chicken. "At least all these wedding preparations wouldn't go to waste."

"They don't have to." The words were so soft, she might have imagined them.

She had, she realized when she glanced up and found Zach absorbed in his chicken and mushroom sauce. Wishful thinking.

Wishful?

No way. The last thing she wanted was for Zach to propose. Then she would have to say no and that would make ending their relationship all the harder. They were opposites, and though her mother had never had any regrets, Delilah knew that she would.

She would hate herself later, and then she would hate Zach, and then he would hate her, and it was better to call it quits right now.

If only it felt better.

They ate in silence for the rest of the meal, until they reached dessert. Strawberry Daiquiri Doo-Wop with amaretto sauce.

"So your mom leaves tomorrow," Zach said in between bites.

"Nine a.m."

"That makes this the last supper."

She couldn't help herself. She stared into his dark gaze and saw her own feelings reflected.

Love. Lust. Desperation. Wait a minute. Back up. *Love?* No way, no how. She had to be reading him wrong.

But it was there. Strong and vivid.

She wanted to look away, to stare down at her plate, but she couldn't. This *was* the last supper. Her last night with Zach. "You'll go back to working late," he went on.

"And you'll go back to finding Miss Right."

He stiffened and his expression hardened as he took his last bite of dessert and stared down at his empty plate. "You know what?" His dark gaze locked with hers. "This was all really good, but I'm still hungry."

Before she knew what was happening, he reached for her hand, pulled her from the chair, around the table and into his lap.

"What are you doing?" She stared down as long, tanned fingers worked at the buttons of her blouse.

"Having more dessert, and giving you something to remember me by when you're working late."

She reached for the buttons on his shirt.

"What are you doing?" he asked.

"I'm still hungry, too, and you definitely need something to remember me by when you're looking for Miss Right."

He captured her lips in a deep kiss that took her breath away. He tasted of strawberries and cream and a determination that rocked her senses.

He kissed her again. And again. And before she knew what was happening, she found herself draped over the table, the dishes swept aside and Zach nibbling her neck. Candlelight flickered, casting dancing shadows on the ceiling overhead. Then he came face-to-face with her, blocking out the light, and she reached for him. Her arms slid around his neck and she kissed him with a fierceness that betrayed the feelings inside her.

Love. Lust. Desperation.

He stared into her eyes as he unhooked the clasp of her bra. "I want you, Delilah."

Cool air swept across her sensitive breasts. "I want you, too. So stop talking and do something."

He grinned, his gaze raking her face, then lower, down her body to her bare chest. Her nipples tightened, swelled. He dipped his head and she closed her eyes and waited for heaven.

And waited.

Her eyes snapped open to see Zach stagger backward, a pained look on his face.

"What's wrong?"

"I..." He groaned and doubled over.

Delilah jumped to her feet. "Zach, what's wrong?"

He moaned, loud and heartbreaking. She tugged her clothes together, helped him to a nearby chair and called for an ambulance.

"Hold on, honey. Please, hold on. The paramedics are on the way."

Appendicitis? Heart attack? Cancer? An aneurysm? The possibilities whirled in her brain as she held his hand and waited the longest five minutes of her life. And for the first time, Delilah James realized what it would really be like to say goodbye to Zach Tanner. And it scared her to death.

"Is HE GOING TO BE all right?" she begged as she climbed into the back of the ambulance and sat by helplessly while two paramedics went to work hooking up a precautionary IV and heart monitor.

"His vital signs are stable, but we still don't know what's wrong. The ER doctor will be able to tell you more."

"Zach?" She gripped his hand and stared down at his pale face. "Can you hear me? Please, listen to me, Zach. You can't die because I love you and I want to marry you and have your children and if it means giving up my business, then *c'est la vie*. I don't care. I mean, I do care. I don't want to live with regrets, but if I lose you, that'll be the biggest regret of my life. Please open your eyes. Please, please, ple—"

"I'm here, Delilah." His voice was little more than a groan, but she hadn't heard a more beautiful sound since the whir of her brand-new fifty-gallon mixer.

She smiled and stared down through a veil of tears as he opened his eyes.

"Could you—" Zach swallowed and tried to ignore the pain gripping his middle "—say that...again?"

"Please open your eyes?"

"...before...that."

"If I lose you that'll be the biggest regret of my life?"

"That's...the one." He gasped as a cramp hit him. Delilah's image blurred and he clamped his eyes shut. "Do you, uh," he said with a gasp, "mean it?" He stared up at her.

"Cross my heart and hope to die." She frowned. "I didn't mean to say that. I don't hope to die." Determination lit her eyes. "No one's dying here, mister. We're going to make lots of babies and have years of happiness, do you hear me?"

As her tears hit his face and slid in warm, tickling trickles down his skin, Zach realized the extent of what she was saying. Even more, he realized that it wasn't what he wanted. He didn't just want Delilah James the woman, he wanted Delilah James the cheesecake caterer, the loving daughter, the passionate lover—the whole package. And he didn't want her to resent him because he'd made her give up a piece of herself.

Love wasn't about sacrificing or suffering. It was about sharing and caring and accepting.

"I...you can't...give it up."

"I can do anything I want. If I want to give it up for you, I damn well will. I love you, don't you understand?"

He smiled, the expression dying as pressure gripped his middle. "I—" he gasped "—I...understand. But I...still don't...want you...to."

"Because you don't want me," she said flatly. "I did fail the audition."

"You passed with, ugh, flying colors. What I mean—" he gritted his teeth and fought for the words "—you can have...your cheesecake and...eat it too." He took a deep breath as the spasm passed. "Me," he said, "and the business."

"Really?"

"I love you, I'll be there for you, I'll even help bake

cheesecakes if that's what you want. Anything you want, ugh." He bit back a moan. "B-because I want…you."

"I knew you were *him*." She rained kisses on his cheek.

"And I knew you were *her*."

"It was love at first sight." She beamed, then turned a dark frown on the paramedic attending Zach. "If anything happens to him, I'm cracking some heads."

The paramedic swallowed and rapped on the window. "Step on it, Hal. We've got a wild one."

"They recognize you," she told Zach.

"Not him," the paramedic said. "I was talking about you, ma'am."


"WHERE ARE THEY?" Gladys rushed into the emergency room an hour after Zach and Delilah arrived.

"Mrs. James, I'm Dr. Tannenbaum. Pleased to see you again."

"You're the one responsible for the heart-smart nightmare."

"Guilty, and I must say you look a world better. Your color, that figure…"

"Did you say figure?"

"Hourglass."

"But Doctor," she said with a blush, "it's only been three days."

"Three miraculous days."

"Well, I have been following the diet." She leaned closer and whispered, "I've only cheated once."

"Once is okay. Now about your future son-in-law. I'll have to run some tests because it's the strangest thing.…"

"Doctor, could we speak frankly here?"

"Of course."

"Do you have children?"

"Three daughters."

"Then you can sympathize. You see, Delilah is my only daughter and, well, very stubborn."

"It's the female species," he said. "Since my wife died, I've been severely outnumbered by my girls. When they set their minds on something, there's no changing them."

"Exactly, and my Delilah is a confirmed bachelorette."

"But I thought she was engaged to Mr. Tanner."

"That was just for show, for me. She cooked up this engagement to make me happy." Gladys proceeded to tell him the entire situation and finished with, "So you see, they do love each other. I couldn't simply sit by and let two stubborn young people mess up their entire future, so I made this wonderful dinner and I might have slipped a few 'concrete' pills into the mushroom sauce. Accidentally, of course."

"Concrete pills?"

"The only cure for Montezuma's revenge." Realization dawned in his eyes and Gladys added, "They're over-the-counter, of course."

Dr. Tannenbaum stopped a nearby nurse and gave instructions. "And make sure you have extra bedpans handy. He'll need them."

"He will be all right?"

"After a busy night, yes."

"And we can keep this between the two of us?"

"Well, they were over-the-counter, and there really is no harm done." The doctor looked thoughtful. "You say you only cheated on your diet once?"

"Maybe twice."

"I know this great little Italian restaurant. Maybe we could try the pasta Friday night." He looked thoughtful, then frowned. "Ah, but then you're leaving on your trip tomorrow, aren't you?"

Gladys smiled. "Yes, but the night is young and I have this sudden craving for fettuccine alfredo."

# *Epilogue*

ZACH TANNER BARELY had time to swallow the last of his beer before he saw the giant fist flex in front of his face.

"Come on, Wild Man," Pete Mackey goaded. "How about I give you another chance to convince me that Joe Montana has anything on Terry Bradshaw?"

Zach set aside his beer mug. So much for a nice friendly pregame commentary, his first of the season, and his last. He was trimming back his schedule at Wild Man's now that Jeff had finished the Coping with Stress course Zach had given him this past Christmas, and was back at work full-time.

"Don't do it, Zach," Jeff advised from his place behind the bar. "Mackey's a bully."

"Keep your thoughts to yourself, shorty," Mackey growled.

"He is not short." Trudy, a whopping four-foot-eleven, stepped from behind her five-foot-one husband and glared at the six-foot-plus bruiser. "You're just too tall, mister. And you know what they say. Tall man, short pe—"

"Jeez, Tru, it's getting late," Jeff cut in. "We have to get going." He grabbed his wife by the hand and headed for the kitchen. "We're up early tomorrow for a book signing."

Jeff had finally come to terms with his hair loss, namely that there was none. The admission had come at the advice of a specialist he'd consulted about a transplant. In short,

Jeff's hair was fit and he wasn't a likely candidate. He and Trudy had since turned their hair-renewal efforts into a book called *The Facts and Myths of Hair Loss: Believe It or Weave It*. Now they were local celebrities.

"Come on, Tanner. Your friend ran away, you gonna run, too?"

"I don't run, and I don't arm wrestle, buddy." Zach's thirty-fifth birthday had come and gone, and though he wasn't ready to head out to pasture yet, he was smart enough to keep his right arm and his bum shoulder free and clear of Pete Mackey.

"This is a first, folks." Dan Smith, the sports anchor who hosted the live pregame show, stood near a wide-screen TV, microphone in hand. "Wild Man Tanner walking away from a challenge."

But Zach had all the challenges he needed at the moment. Delilah's garage had proved a hell of a conversion job into a family room big enough for their future family. Not to mention, he still hadn't finished the nursery and Delilah was already in the home stretch for baby number one. True to his word, Zach was helping out with How Sweet It Is, so now they were both making cheesecakes, as well as babies. And the future looked sweet, indeed.

He turned to see his wife seated at a nearby table. She struggled to her feet and he pushed his way through the crowd toward her.

"It appears the Wild Man isn't so wild anymore," the commentator went on as Zach helped Delilah stand.

"Oh, I wouldn't say that." He pulled his wife into his arms as cameras clicked and the crowd hooted. "My woman here thinks I'm still every bit a Wild Man, dontcha, honey?"

"I hate you," she ground out. A wave of giggles and applause erupted. "My feet are swollen, I look like a beached whale, my mother, the future Mrs. Harvey Tannenbaum, is flying here in the morning for a six-week visit, and I *really* hate you.''

He nuzzled her neck. ''Your feet are perfect, your ankles even more perfect, your mother's staying at Harvey's and you don't hate me.''

''I do.''

''That's what you said last night and the night before and the night before that, and then you kissed me.''

''I mean it this time.

''Sure you do.''

He grinned that same, sexy, lazy grin that both infuriated her and melted her insides, and Delilah couldn't help but smile.

Zach was so sweet and sincere and sensitive, and he was hers. Every hunky, gorgeous, Big Three inch of him.

''Looks like Zach Tanner has traded in his Wild Man status for diapers and baby bottles, folks. Never thought I'd see the day, but then we all have to go sometime.'' The sports announcer's voice echoed through the room.

Zach's grin widened. ''And what a way to go.'' Before Delilah could take a breath, he captured her mouth with his.

''Go get 'em, Wild Man!''

''That a boy!''

''Score one for monogamy!''

The crowd hooted and cheered and Delilah did the only thing a woman nine months pregnant, tired and miserable and deeply in love with her husband could do. She kissed him back. Sweetly, tenderly. And *then* she bit him.

''Ouch!'' He pulled away and pouted. ''What'd you do that for?''

''It's time, Zach.'' She grimaced and rubbed her stomach as it contracted again. *''It's time.''*

# EUGENIA RILEY

## Second-Chance Groom

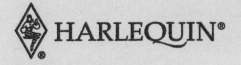

**HARLEQUIN**®

TORONTO • NEW YORK • LONDON
AMSTERDAM • PARIS • SYDNEY • HAMBURG
STOCKHOLM • ATHENS • TOKYO • MILAN • MADRID
PRAGUE • WARSAW • BUDAPEST • AUCKLAND

The wedding of her own daughter inspired bestselling author **Eugenia Riley** to focus her Duets romance on a nuptial theme. Although the bride in Eugenia's story finds her happiness with a "second-chance groom," Eugenia quips that her own daughter was not allowed the luxury of a second-chance wedding, since they're just too expensive! Eugenia does know all about happy endings, having been married to the same man for thirty years.

Eugenia has published numerous contemporary, historical and time-travel romances; she is a winner of the 1998 HOLT Medallion Award in the Southern theme category. She loves to hear from her readers, who may visit her homepage: http://www.brokersys.com/~eugenia or write to: Eugenia Riley, P.O. Box 840526, Houston, TX 77284-0526.

This book is dedicated, with love,
to our newest family member,
my darling niece,
Megan Elizabeth,
born October 23, 1997,
with special congratulations to
her proud parents, Jennifer and Jeff.
Look what blessings beautiful
marriages can bring!

# 1

"Is THE WORST man late?"

Bride-to-be Cassie Brandon was so distracted that she didn't at first hear the fretful question from her five-year-old neice, Emily. Swathed in her fabulous white satin wedding gown and clutching her lush bridal bouquet, Cassie stood in the vestibule of her family's church in Houston. Her make-up was impeccable, dark blond ringlets curling becomingly around her face and a long French braid, interlaced with baby's breath, trailing down her back.

But lost on Cassie were the sweet scent of the flowers, the soft glow of candlelight, the thrum of excited voices. Grinding her jaw and muttering to herself, Cassie stared straight ahead through her wispy veil, hardly even conscious of her six bridesmaids gossiping nearby, and her seven-year-old nephew, Sean, who dozed on a bench, his small blond head resting on the ring cushion, one polished dress shoe dangling half off his foot.

From the sanctuary beyond, Cassie could hear hushed voices, and she knew the wedding guests must be asking themselves the same question that had her almost ready to pop her cork: Where on earth was Brian Drake? The best man was almost forty minutes late for the service, and the organist's incessant choruses of "I've Finally Found Someone" were wearing on everyone's nerves.

To top it all off, Cassie's dad had run off twenty minutes earlier, swearing he would "get the blasted service started" or grab his shotgun—and Bill Brandon still hadn't returned. Cassie didn't know whether to expect a wedding or a Houston-style version of the showdown at the O.K. Corral. Twenty-five years as an independent contractor had definitely turned her dad into a maverick.

But Cassie also had to wonder if she wasn't focusing on the best man's tardiness in order to escape the real issue troubling her—whether *she* should be here at all.

"Is the worst man late?" came the anxious query again.

At last Cassie heard the child's voice and felt a hard tug on her skirts. She gazed past the voluminous folds of brocaded white satin at her little blond niece, adorable in her pink, full-skirted flower-girl dress, with the wreath of miniature tea roses in her hair. At the moment, Emily's round face was pinched with concern, her huge blue eyes focused solemnly on Aunt Cassie. The child strongly resembled Cassie's older brother, Todd, who was Emily and Sean's father.

Cassie smiled and leaned over to touch Emily's cheek. "I'm sorry, sweetie. What did you say?"

Obviously frustrated, the child asked loudly, "I said, *Is the worst man late?*"

Cassie couldn't restrain a laugh at the apt irony, and she heard several of her bridesmaids giggling. "Sweetie, he's called the *best* man," she corrected gently. "And yes, he is late."

The child frowned. "But how can he be the *best* man if he's late?"

"Good question," Cassie agreed dryly.

"Yeah, isn't it?" seconded Lisa, Cassie's maid of honor.

Cassie continued to stew. Brian Drake had missed the rehearsal entirely, and if not for her fiancé Chris's insistence that they hold the wedding until he arrived, surely the service would have concluded by now.

What was Chris's problem, anyway? Usually he was such a stickler for punctuality and propriety. He certainly had *her* life planned out to the nth degree, she added to herself uneasily.

"Why is the worst man late?" Emily pressed.

Cassie flashed her niece a patient smile. "I hear he's off rock climbing in Colorado."

Appearing confused, the child didn't comment. "When the worst man shows up, will he get retention?"

Cassie all but choked out a laugh. "Retention? Don't you mean *detention*, sweetie?"

Emily nodded.

"Don't tell me they have detention in kindergarten?"

Emily shook her head and whispered behind her hand. "No, but they have it in second grade. Sean got retention for three whole hours for wrapping Mrs. Wilson's plant with toilet paper—but don't tell Mama."

"Believe me, I won't," Cassie replied, as again her bridesmaids chuckled.

"Are you going to marry the worst man?" Emily continued.

Unexpectedly, this question gave Cassie pause. *Was* she marrying the worst man? Of course, her fiancé, Mr. Christopher Carlisle, was sane, sensible, and handsome. Other women might look at Chris and consider him a real catch. But he and Cassie did have their differences, and their argument last night had definitely brought those problems into much sharper focus....

"*Are* you?" Emily pressed, breaking into Cassie's thoughts.

"No, honey, I'm going to marry the groom," Cassie explained. "At least I am if the *worst man* ever appears." By now, she was enjoying the game with Emily.

Emily only scowled.

"Hey, Cassie, how long *are* we going to wait for this guy?"

Cassie turned to Lisa, and noted that all six of her attendants were anxiously awaiting her answer, their faces tense and makeup growing moist. She sighed. "I know—I've just about had it with the jerk myself. But Chris seems convinced that Brian *will* show up. Seems he got a call from him late last night, from somewhere in the Rockies. Brian apologized for missing the rehearsal, and said something like, 'Pick up my tux—I *will* make the wedding'—at least I think that was the gist of it.''

Jenny, another attendant, was shaking her head. "It's not like Chris to put up with this kind of nonsense. The Chris I know would never let anyone spoil his wedding. Don't you remember the time when we were all supposed to meet for a movie, and Chris totally freaked because Don and I were two minutes late? And this is his *wedding,* for heaven's sake.''

"I agree," replied Cassie. "But Chris has no brothers, and evidently his mom insisted he make his cousin his best man.''

"You ever met this guy?" asked Molly, a third bridesmaid.

"Nope—and I'm beginning to hope I never will," Cassie replied ruefully. "Brian lives in Denver, and, according to Chris, he's the original carefree bachelor—flying through life by the seat of his pants, traveling on impulse, trying all kinds of risky sports—''

"And breaking feminine hearts in every port?" offered Jenny.

"You've got it," said Cassie with a chuckle.

"Sounds like a real charmer to me," put in Molly, prompting more amusement.

As the women again fell silent, Cassie felt another tug on her skirt. She glanced down at her niece. "Yes, darling?''

Emily's lower lip was trembling. "If the worst man is lost, will I still get to wear my wedding dress?''

Feeling a poignant tug at her heartstrings, Cassie leaned over to give the child a quick hug. "Of course you will, precious.''

Emily beamed.

Cassie straightened, glanced at her watch, and rolled her eyes at Lisa as the organist droned out yet another chorus of the love song. "I can't believe how close we're pushing this, with another wedding scheduled at eight. I'm about ready to send Chris a message insisting we begin—'' she craned her neck and grimaced ''—only I still don't know where the heck Dad is.''

"There he is!'' cried Molly.

Appearing flustered, tall, gray-haired Bill Brandon rushed up in his tux. Cassie was bemused to note that her dad carried a business card and a small bouquet of blue wildflowers—arctic columbine by the look of them.

"Well, thank heaven that numbskull has finally arrived,'' Bill announced.

"You mean Brian Drake has actually graced us with his presence?'' Cassie mocked.

"He sailed into the men's dressing room all of sixty seconds ago,'' answered her dad. ''Would you believe that idiot is late because he lost himself in the joys of rock climbing, then got caught in a ledge in a thunderstorm and missed his flight?''

"You're kidding,'' exclaimed Cassie.

Bill grimly shook his head. ''As if we weren't all cooling our heels waiting for him.''

Meanwhile, Emily was frowning and tugging at Bill's sleeve. ''Grandpa, you're not allowed to be the flower girl.''

At this, all of the women convulsed in laughter.

Bill Brandon grinned at his granddaughter. ''Oh, I know that, honey. The best man gave me these.''

Emily appeared highly suspicious. ''*He* can't be the flower girl, either.''

"I know.'' Amid more giggles, Bill handed Cassie the small bouquet of flowers, their stems wrapped in a damp handkerchief. ''Mr. Wonderful's only real excuse was that he took his last climb to pick these for you at that resort where he was staying—and he asked me to give them to you.''

"He did?'' Caught off guard, Cassie stared down at the tiny, delicate, pale blue flowers edged in deep purple. Brian

Drake was late because he'd climbed a mountain to pick wildflowers for the bride? She felt an unexpected lump in her throat.

Her dad pushed a business card into her hand. "Along with his apologies for being late."

As her father turned away to chat with Lisa, Cassie stared, mystified, at the card, which read, "Brian Drake, Investment Counselor, Noble Rogers, Inc., Denver Colorado." A message was scrawled in dark ink: "Cassie, Sorry to be late. Here's something blue. B."

*Something blue.* Again, Cassie felt touched, disarmed by the sensitivity of a stranger—and this was really odd, since she should be ready to throttle the idiot for almost spoiling her wedding!

Yet all at once, the handpicked blooms Brian Drake had sent her seemed more precious than her own two-hundred-dollar bridal bouquet. Impulsively, Cassie plucked a few blooms from Brian's spray and tucked them into her own arrangement of white roses.

Emily was stretching on tiptoe, intently watching her aunt. "I want some blue flowers, too, Aunt Cassie. All mine are pink."

"Sure, sweetie." Grinning, Cassie tucked the remaining small columbine among the tea roses in her niece's hair. Emily preened like a contented kitten.

As the strains of music poured forth from the sanctuary, Cassie's father heaved a sigh. "Ah, good, I hear the wedding march." Straightening his lapels, he sternly regarded the bridesmaids. "All right, girls. Not long now. In your places."

Lisa saluted Cassie's dad. "Yes, sir."

"Grandpa, Sean's asleep," fretted Emily. "And he's lost his shoe."

"Heavens, you're right. Why didn't you tell us?" Bill asked.

As her father and Emily rushed off to rouse Sean and retrieve his shoe, and her bridesmaids began to line up,

Cassie stood immobile, still staring at the blue flowers in her bouquet. *Something blue.* She couldn't get over the fact that Brian Drake, a man who was a complete stranger to her, had stopped off to pick wildflowers for a woman who was a complete stranger to *him.*

Why had he done this? And would Chris ever do anything so tender or impulsive?

Her dad rushed back to her side, offering his arm. "Chin up, honey. I know it's been a zoo, but everything's back on track now."

"Sure, Dad."

"Are you happy?"

Cassie nodded bravely. "Of course."

But was she?

Anxiously, Cassie watched little Emily head into the sanctuary, dropping rose petals along the way. One by one, Cassie's six attendants followed in their chic burgundy gowns.

Waiting for her own cue, Cassie remained perturbed. She was about to marry a man she had thought she understood, yet her emotions were tantalized by a stranger she'd never even met.

Cassie had always thought of herself as sane and sensible. But she also realized that somewhere deep inside lurked a hidden, impulsive streak. Usually she'd managed to keep her reckless side under rein, but once in a while it took control—like the time she had skipped her high-school prom and gone off with her girlfriends for a college weekend instead. That little escapade had caused her untold grief. Her parents had been worried sick until she'd called, her stood-up boyfriend livid.

Cassie's dear departed grandmother had once told her that pain was the greatest teacher—and Gran had been absolutely right. After a few more such exploits during her college years, Cassie had become convinced that she must never allow her reckless streak to gain control of her life.

Her decision to marry businessman Christopher Carlisle

was definitely a victory over her more impetuous side, since she could not have chosen a man with a more conservative and traditional outlook on life. Chris was also handsome, wealthy, successful—a good partner for her. And she loved him—perhaps not in the most passionate sense, but in a comfortable way. They had their friends, their social life, a commitment to build a world together.

Then why was it, all of a sudden, that Chris didn't *seem* so perfect?

Well, he did have one big flaw, she acknowledged uneasily. He tended to be too controlling, becoming jealous if Cassie spent too much time with family or friends. In fact, three months ago, they'd had a major argument over a stunt he'd pulled, when he'd withheld a telephone message from one of her old college friends who was passing through town; as a result, Cassie had completely missed seeing Stacy and wouldn't get to again for years. When Cassie had later found out and confronted Chris, he'd admitted that he'd deliberately withheld the message because he'd always felt Stacy was a bad influence on her. Cassie had been furious, ready to hand Chris back his ring. But Chris had apologized, promising he'd never do it again. Around this same time, Cassie's dad had suffered huge cost overruns on a construction project, and had been in danger of defaulting at the bank. Chris had generously offered to bail Bill out, *if* there was no more talk of cancelling the wedding. Worried that her dad could face bankruptcy, Cassie had agreed to Chris's terms—something she'd never told her parents, of course. Although Cassie's dad had since landed a lucrative deal that had enabled him to repay Chris, Cassie still felt obligated to honor her own bargain—especially since Chris never hesitated to remind her that she "owed" him now.

Nevertheless, last night had almost been the final straw. Chris had had a bit too much to drink at the rehearsal dinner, and as Cassie had driven him home, he'd begun to lecture her arrogantly on what he'd expect of her as his wife—everything from what friends she would or would not keep, to how she would revamp her wardrobe and re-style her hair. Then he'd started in on her job, declaring that it took up too much of her time, and he'd expect her to resign after they were married. Cassie had felt hurt and betrayed—especially given Chris's previous promise not to try to control her again. But she'd somehow managed to hold back her feelings because he *had* been drinking and might well regret his conduct in the morning.

No such luck. When she'd called Chris this morning and had confronted him with the things he'd said, he'd laughed off the incident and said he wouldn't expect all those miracles to be accomplished on their *first* day of marriage. But he hadn't actually apologized or taken back a word he'd said. Cassie had been devastated, but before she could gather her wits, Chris had shrewdly reminded her that she could *never* cancel their wedding now and humiliate her parents...could she? It had all smacked of, "Hey, I've got you now, so there's no more need to pretend." Even Chris's parting words—"Once we're married, I'm sure it'll all work out"—had come across as shallow and insincere rather than heartfelt. Cassie very much feared that what he'd meant was that their lives would work out according to *his* terms.

Cassie had been terribly upset all day. If the wedding hadn't been about to take place in a couple of hours, she might have backed out. But Chris had been right that she hated the thought of hurting or embarrassing her family, especially when her mom and dad had gone to so much trouble and expense. She was also wary of making a last-minute judgment about Chris, knowing that, as a bride, she might well be a bit on the jittery, vulnerable, or overly emotional side.

Still, Chris's last-minute power play bothered her a lot. It had shattered her trust in him—and what was a marriage without trust? If he didn't hesitate to break his word to her, how seriously would he take his wedding vows?

Abruptly the bridal chorus swelled, and Cassie's stomach took a nosedive.

Her dad squeezed her arm. "Last chance to back out, honey."

Feeling as if her dad were reading her mind, Cassie regarded him in horror. "Don't say that! Isn't it bad luck?"

Her dad chuckled, but appeared misty-eyed. "Honey, remember our conversation a couple of weeks ago?"

She smiled warmly. "Sure, Dad."

"I hope you're not marrying Chris just out of gratitude because he bailed me out. As you know, I've already repaid him, with interest."

Now Cassie, too, felt the sting of tears; if her dad really knew of the subtle blackmail tactics Chris had stooped to, he *would* fetch his shotgun—but it wouldn't be to start the wedding!

Her voice quivered with emotion. "Dad, it's—well, much more complicated than that. Chris does have some fine qualities—and it was generous of him to help you out. Just like it's great of you and Mom to go to all this trouble. I know you've gone into debt over this wedding."

"We just want you to be happy, honey."

She squeezed his hand. "Dad, I'm a big girl and I can take care of myself. You worry about me too much."

"I'm your dad and I always will." He leaned over and kissed her cheek. "You make a beautiful bride, honey. Chris doesn't know how lucky he is."

Cassie sighed. "You may be right."

"Ready to go, then?"

Marshalling her courage, Cassie nodded. She stepped into the church with her dad to face a sea of smiling faces. Their path was lit by candlelight and fragrant with roses. But with each step, the uneasiness that had begun to tug at her recently built to a gnawing anxiety.

She gazed again at her bridal bouquet. *Something blue.* Brian Drake's last-minute, dramatic appearance had definitely rattled her already shaky resolve. Was it his gift of the flowers, the message he had scrawled? Or was it the fact that he had stopped off to pick her the flowers, despite the fact that he kept a bride, a groom, and one hundred and fifty wedding guests waiting for him? The fact that he was just the opposite of her suave but calculating fiancé?

Cassie had tried so hard to put her doubts about Chris to rest, but they kept rising to torment her. All at once, she remembered a time when she and Chris had been on vacation. She'd seen a sign along the roadway in Colorado, and, on an impulse, she'd begged him to stop off at a privately owned canyon to go bungee-jumping. She remembered how Chris had scoffed at her suggestion and insisted they must never do anything so rash and risky. Suddenly, that memory seemed a metaphor for everything that was wrong between her and Chris.

Wrong? What was she thinking? Wasn't she marrying the best possible man, a man who would help her keep her life on track?

But was that what she really wanted—to have every aspect of her life controlled and dictated to her?

Cassie struggled to shake off her anxieties and buck up her courage. She spotted her mom in a front pew, wiping her eyes, and smiled as her own gaze again blurred. Arriving at the front of the church, she watched Chris turn to join her, and a new knot of painful emotion rose up in her. Her fiancé had never looked more handsome than he did in his tux. Then why was it his smile suddenly seemed superficial rather than warm, his blond hair stiff and lifeless rather than thick and lustrous, his brown eyes shrewd and triumphant rather than dark and sexy? Why was it the scent of his cologne, usually so provocative, left her half-nauseated?

Cassie felt clammy. She glanced about in desperation, only to find herself staring at the man standing next to Chris, a man who was staring back at her with equal fascination.

So this was Brian Drake! Heavens, he was so handsome,

with the tanned body of an outdoorsman, the hard-muscled frame of a rock climber, and the hands of a sculptor—strong, with long, beautifully tapered fingers. His hair was dark, crisply curly and closely cropped, his face broad and beautifully sculpted, with high cheekbones, a strong nose, and bright blue eyes filled with mischief. Cassie felt her pulse surging at the sight of him, and her gaze locked with his for an electric moment.

Then his sexy gaze began to slide downward, taking in her veil, her gown, the bouquet in her hands. She saw the grin lighting his face as he spotted his blue columbine tucked among her white roses. Lord, he had dimples! He was too adorable! Then he glanced up and winked at her, and her heart went into a tailspin.

Cassie fought for control. What was happening to her? She couldn't be standing at her own wedding and feeling attracted to the best man, someone she'd never even met before! Yet Cassie was thoroughly intrigued by Brian, his touching gift of the flowers, and especially the passion for life she glimpsed in his eyes. She and Chris had fallen into a sane, predictable rut, but here was a man who relished every moment. These realizations left her feeling unbearably sad and conflicted.

Cassie felt her arm being squeezed, and glanced at Chris, who was scowling at her, as if to ask, "What gives?" She turned to her dad and the gray-haired minister to see both regarding her with equal perplexity. She flashed another pained smile at Chris, and he smiled back tightly.

Reverend Murphy opened his order of service and cleared his throat. "Dearly beloved, we are gathered here…"

Listening, Cassie somehow managed to forestall panic. She was only a bride succumbing to a last-minute case of the jitters. Surely she wouldn't have come this far with Chris if they weren't right for each other. That impulsive demon inside her was rising up, trying to ruin her wedding, and she wouldn't, *couldn't*, allow it to wreak havoc.

"Now I'd like to say a few words to Cassandra and Christopher."

The minister's voice jerked Cassie back to reality, and she turned to Reverend Murphy. Closing his book, the clergyman smiled at the couple. "Cassandra and Christopher, tonight I'd like you both to reflect on the miracle that brought you here to us—the wondrous gift of true love between a man and a woman. There is nothing more precious, more rare, on God's earth." He paused for dramatic effect. "For who can predict that magical moment when one looks across a room, sees a certain face, and falls in love?"

These last words electrified Cassie. Again she found her gaze riveted not to Chris's but to Brian Drake's. Again she glimpsed that sexy, devilish smile, and her insides melted. *Who can predict that magical moment when one looks across a room, sees a certain face, and falls in love?*

This couldn't be happening to her! Surely it was impossible for a handful of blue columbine to change a person's life, or for a stranger's smile to steal a heart.

Yet it all seemed so real. Even now, just looking at Brian Drake, Cassie felt an overwhelming excitement and attraction she'd never known before, and she sensed Brian felt that same, powerful jolt. If one glance into a stranger's eyes could do this to her, then everything about her marriage to Chris *must* be wrong. She didn't really love Chris—not in the passionate sense needed for a lifetime commitment. Her marrying him would be a huge mistake. He would try to premeditate and control every aspect of their lives together and they would *both* end up miserable.

But what on earth could she do about this now?

Cassie felt like a trapped animal. Then she heard the minister's voice again: "Cassie and Chris, I want to congratulate you both on finding that rare, once-in-a-lifetime love."

As *ooohs* and *aaahs* rippled over the congregation, Cassie turned to Chris in desperation.

"Cassie, what is it?" he whispered.

Her voice was thick. "Chris, I'm so sorry. I can't go through with this."

"You *what?*"

"I just can't."

A gasp shook the congregation, followed by dead silence.

"But why?" Chris demanded.

Cassie glanced from her shocked fiancé, to the flabbergasted minister, to her equally stunned father, to Brian Drake—who, strangely, appeared both sympathetic and intrigued. She pulled off Chris's diamond ring and shoved it into his hand. "Because...because you wouldn't go bungee-jumping with me."

Cassie turned and fled the church, leaving utter shock and dismay in her wake.

# 2

SOMEDAY SHE WOULD LAUGH about this...she hoped!

Two hours later, this was the mantra Cassie chanted as she stood alone on the pier fronting the Chateau Lafitte, a condominium hotel built on a wharf jutting into the Gulf of Mexico, on the eastern end of Galveston Island. The hotel loomed behind her, ten stories of concrete and glass, with tables and chairs lining the patio flowing off the restaurant, now closed for the night.

At Cassie's feet was a four-pack of wine coolers, with two missing; the second one, partially consumed, was in her right hand. Beyond her, the tide rolled in, huge glittering waves crashing against the pier, seafoam splashing Cassie's body and the wind tugging at her casual summer dress on this warm and breezy June night.

Her wedding gown was hung up neatly upstairs, in the closet of her maid of honor's condo. Her bridal bouquet, with Brian Drake's blue columbine still intact, was in the refrigerator.

After grabbing her suitcase from the church dressing room, Cassie had fled here, remembering that Lisa had recently given her the key to her beachside condo, saying, "If the pressure of the wedding gets to be too much for you and you need to get away..." Cassie groaned at the irony. The pressure hadn't just gotten to her—she'd totally freaked.

She took another sip of her drink and stared out toward the distant horizon at the large full moon, fringed by silvery clouds. The full moon—perhaps that was the reason for her insanity.

But Cassie knew she had no one to blame but herself for the disaster she'd caused at the church. She'd walked out on the man she'd thought she loved, the man she'd sworn to marry. The ten-thousand-dollar wedding her dad had paid for was down the tube. She felt particularly wretched for disappointing her parents. They had struggled so hard, for so long, and now she had humiliated them publicly— not to mention saddling them with a huge financial loss.

How could she face anyone, ever again? Her friends, her family, her boss…and Chris. Yes, he'd been behaving like a jerk, but he still hadn't deserved to be embarrassed that way. She realized now that she should have cancelled the wedding long ago. Everyone would hate her now!

Why had she chosen tonight to snap?

Well, Chris's last-minute power play was one big reason. And she could think of another: Mr. Brian Drake. A grin, a wink, a few blue wildflowers, and the Incredible Hunk had reduced a sane, sensible woman to a quivering teenager gone ape at her first glimpse of a rock star. More importantly, Brian's appearance had managed to pinpoint for Cassie everything that was missing in her relationship with Chris.

"Cassie? Is that you?" came a deep masculine voice.

Oh, God. It was *him*! Why was it, without ever before hearing his voice, she just *knew* it was him?

Cassie whirled. Just as she'd feared, there he stood, a few feet beyond her. Mr. Brian Drake, In The Flesh. Her heart hammered wildly, then seemed to plunge into her stomach.

For a moment she just stared. He was only a few inches taller than she was, but, oh, he was male perfection in his knitted shirt and dark slacks, especially with the wind ruffling his hair and rippling his clothing against his hard body. She studied the beauty of his bare forearms, the broadness of his shoulders, the flawless contours of his jaw.

Oh, heavens, she couldn't bear it—she felt that treacherous twinge of excitement again, just as she had at the church, and could have sunk through the pier. She had no business feeling this way so soon after she'd run out of her own wedding!

"Cassie?" he repeated, stepping closer.

She waved her bottle. "Please, go away."

"Hey, don't be frightened," he cajoled. "I'm Brian Drake, and I was at your—"

"I know who you are," she cut in, brushing a wisp of hair from her eyes. "It's just that I can't face you—or anyone—not now."

But he merely grinned and continued toward her. "You're not being very hospitable, Cassie."

"I'm not *feeling* very hospitable," she replied ruefully.

He arrived at her side and gazed at her with concern. Cassie felt as if she were dying by inches. The man was too sexy. Moonlight gleamed in his hair, and the spicy scent of his cologne teased her senses. He was so vibrant and real, his smile so disarming, his eyes so gorgeous, deepset, fringed by long, dark lashes. Not to mention, those adorable dimples.

Heavens, what was she thinking—doing? Two hours ago, she'd walked out on her fiancé. Now she was once again salivating over the best man!

"Cassie, are you okay?" he inquired in that same voice of rich, deep silk.

"Of course I'm not okay," she replied tightly. "Brides who stage a fifty-yard dash out of their own weddings are definitely *not* okay. What are you doing here, anyway?"

He sighed. "I've come on a mission of mercy, to beg you to reconsider and come back to the church with me."

"Gee, a regular nice guy," she muttered. "Who appointed you Mr. Fix-it?"

"Well, after you ran out, we were all so worried, and I—well, volunteered to come after you."

Her gaze narrowed. "How'd you know where to find me, anyway?"

"I spoke to Lisa, and she told me about the condo."

Cassie's voice was trembling badly. "Ah, so you're a master detective, too. Why don't you be even more clever and leave me alone?"

"Why?"

"Why?" Drawing a shaky breath, she gazed out at the ocean. "I thought that would be obvious. I want—*need*—to be alone."

He nodded toward the Gulf. "You're not going to throw yourself in the drink, are you?"

She harrumphed and sipped her cooler. "I intend to drown my sorrows—not my person."

He stared down at the four-pack at her feet, then pulled a face and touched her arm. "You sure you can handle two of those?"

She flinched as if burned by his touch. "Watch me." She took another sip and grinned at him crookedly. "Want one?"

"I don't think so," he replied.

Cassie took note of his worried scowl. "You know, for someone who's supposed to be Mr. Spontaneous, you're not being very spontaneous at the moment. You should be suggesting we hang glide off the seawall or something."

He chuckled. "Who told you I'm Mr. Spontaneous?"

"Come, now," she chided. "Losing track of time while rock climbing? Bringing the bride blue columbine? Besides, Chris told me all about you—or, should I say, he warned me. The original free-spirited bachelor." She paused. "But I must say you're not doing your cavalier image justice."

His laugh was deep, edged with self-deprecation. "Well, perhaps it's not too often that I get upstaged."

"I stole the show tonight, all right," she lamented.

His voice took on a husky note. "Every bride steals the show. But you definitely added a new spin."

Cassie groaned and raised her wine cooler again. "Sure you don't want one?"

He shook his head. "One of us had better stay sober if we're going to get you back to Houston tonight."

"*We're* not going to get me back anywhere," she replied sharply.

He was quiet for a long moment, appearing perplexed. At last, he asked gently, "Cassie, do you have any idea of the chaos you caused when you fled the wedding?"

Cassie shut her eyes, and felt tears burning. "Do you have to remind me? You think I don't know what I did? Running out on my parents, my friends, not to mention Chris. Everyone must think I'm terrible—plus, a nutcase. Now you want me to go back and face the disaster I caused?"

"Cassie, why did you run out on Chris?"

Panic clutched at Cassie's throat, and she glanced away. "I—I can't tell you."

"Well, I think I know."

Wide-eyed, she turned to him. "You—you do?"

He nodded. "I should have remembered how jittery brides are. But no, I had to act like a self-absorbed jerk and be late for your wedding. I ruined your perfect day, and that's why you got so upset, right? I mean, I'm the real reason, aren't I?"

She laughed dryly. "Oh, yes, Mr. Brian Drake. You're the *real* reason, all right. But you'd never guess why."

He frowned. "Look, Cassie, I want to apologize for disrupting your wedding. But it's not fair to take this out on Chris. It's not his fault I acted so rudely."

She sighed. "How *is* Chris?"

"Well, I'm not so sure. The last time I saw him, he was drowning his sorrows in the champagne fountain."

Her mouth fell open. "You mean my folks went ahead with the reception?"

Amusement glinted in his eyes. "Your dad was bellowing something about not letting five thousand dollars' worth of perfectly good food and booze go to waste. As for your mom—well, she was worried about you and very relieved to hear I was coming after you."

Again guilt stabbed Cassie. "Oh, heavens. That sounds just like my folks. How can I ever face them again?"

He extended a hand in entreaty. "Cassie, go back. It's not too late. Reverend Murphy is at the reception, and if we hurry, you guys can still tie the knot. Just tell Chris this was all a bad joke."

Cassie shuddered. "I can't—not now. Come to think of it, Chris is likely better off without a kook like me." She gave an ironic laugh. "Look, it was good of you to come down here, but you've said your piece. And I really do need to be alone. So if you don't mind…"

HER VOICE TRAILING OFF meaningfully, Cassie turned away to stare moodily at the ocean, and Brian Drake stood watching her with a feeling of helpless frustration. He remembered the moment when he'd first spotted Cassie gliding down the aisle, remembered thinking how he'd never seen a more beautiful bride. How lovely she'd been, and still was, with her wide, round face, delicate nose and nicely sculpted cheekbones, the pointed chin that hinted of inner fortitude, the large green eyes that sparkled with vitality, the thick, dark-blond hair that crowned her vibrant beauty. He remembered thinking his cousin Chris was the luckiest guy alive.

Then when Cassie had arrived at the altar, she had looked at him with such frank interest, and he'd been utterly charmed to note that she'd tucked a few of his blue columbine into her bouquet. But when he'd grinned at her, some sort of panic had seized her. As the service had begun, he'd watched her struggle for control, then lose it and appear on the verge of tears. Giving Chris his ring back and muttering something bizarre about bungee-jumping, she'd fled the church.

Such strange behavior, especially since Chris had

claimed his fiancée was so together. What had happened to the girl? Now she refused to even discuss her reasons for fleeing the wedding, refused to budge off this pier. What was he to do?

Surely he'd caused this mess by being so late. Until this morning, he'd been having one of his best climbing trips ever at a resort in the Rockies just north of Denver, and as always he'd pushed the experience to the limit, deciding it wouldn't be that terrible to miss Chris's wedding rehearsal as long as he made it to Houston in time for the wedding itself. Then this morning, sunrise over the Rockies had been so glorious that he'd taken a final dawn climb in order to pick Cassie some wildflowers—his way of apologizing for being late. He hadn't counted on the thunderstorm that had trapped him on a ledge and made him miss his late-morning flight back in Denver.

Now he realized that, although his motives may have been good, his lateness was entirely his own fault, and it was his responsibility to get the wedding back on track. He couldn't go back to Houston empty handed. Nor was he convinced it would be wise to leave Cassie alone, when she'd been drinking and seemed to be in such a weird mood.

She turned to stare at him, raising an eyebrow as if to inquire, *Well?*

He smiled. "Mind if I hang around for a while and watch the ocean with you? It really is a lovely night."

She shrugged. "Suit yourself. Still afraid I'll cast my fate to the tide, eh?"

"Well, the thought has crossed my mind."

Cassie sipped her wine cooler, then set it on the railing. "Don't worry, I'm not planning any swan dives into the Gulf. Not for Mr. Christopher Carlisle." She wrinkled her nose at him. "Maybe for you, but definitely not for Chris Carlisle."

Brian appeared mystified. "You're kidding."

She laughed. "Brian, of course I'm kidding. You know,

for a free spirit, you take things much too seriously. I'm the one who's supposed to be in sackcloth and ashes right now.''

Ruefully, he replied, ''Cassie, if you don't mind my honesty, you make a guy take you seriously.''

Cassie turned away to hide an expression of secret amusement.

For a moment both watched the waves roll against the pier and listened to the roar of the surf. ''I never realized the Gulf was so beautiful,'' he murmured after a moment.

''You've not seen it before?''

''Not here in Galveston. I've been to New Orleans. This stretch reminds me of a section of Baja California where I used to surf.''

She glanced at him. ''You look like a surfer. You've got the tan.''

''You ever tried it?''

''Oh, once or twice, when I was younger. After being tossed around like a rag doll and drinking in half the Gulf, I pretty much gave up.''

''It does take perseverance.''

''And a great deal of daring.'' She chuckled. ''Chris has told me about you—the rock climbing, scuba diving, helicopter skiing.''

He scratched his jaw. ''There's some perverse demon inside me that loves extreme sports. My mother has often accused me of having a death wish. She should know. I got my first broken arm at seven.''

''Your *first* broken arm?''

He held up a forearm. ''Skateboarding accident. That was my right arm. Years later I broke my left arm in two places while playing ice hockey in college.'' He flashed her a grin. ''Now I play the market—it makes some of my colleagues pop antacids, but I thrive on the risk.''

Cassie laughed, thinking of Chris, who sat at a computer all day long, estimating costs for drilling projects and moving heavy equipment around. ''My, you are a daredevil.

How did you and Chris end up in the same family, anyway?"

"Beats me. I remember when I was ten and our families rented cabins together in New Mexico. I wanted to climb a rock formation, and Chris sat at the bottom of the trail and refused to budge."

"Sounds like Chris. He's so conservative."

A teasing light glinted in his eyes. "And what about Chris's fiancée? Are you conservative, Cassie?"

She sighed. "Usually. I mean, Chris and I have a lot in common. We have this group we run around with—to plays, movies, out to dinner, that sort of thing. I thought we had our life settled, all mapped out. Then—"

"Then what, Cassie?" he asked.

She fell silent. "There's—well, another side of me. Guess you'd call it an impulsive streak. Usually, I can keep it under control, but once in a while, I'll get this wild hair and—"

"I've noticed," he put in dryly.

She stared beseechingly at the sky as memories of her behavior tonight again lanced her brain. "Oh, Lord, what have I done? *What* have I done?"

Brian took her by the shoulders and gently turned her toward him. "Why did you leave tonight, Cassie?"

She chewed her bottom lip. "I can't tell you."

"But you must tell someone, or this thing will eat you up."

She was silent, emotion churning inside her.

He flashed her an encouraging look. "Help me with this, Cassie. At this point, all I know is Chris wouldn't let you go bungee-jumping."

Cassie shook her head. "Lord, how could I have said anything so inane? Ever had one of those moments when you just freeze up and can't think of anything else to say?"

He nodded. "Sometimes it's the story of my life."

Cassie had to laugh.

More seriously, he asked, "Have you and Chris had any problems lately, any arguments?"

"You're very perceptive," she muttered.

"So you did have a fight?"

"Well, yes. Chris is on the possessive and controlling side. We had a major fight about it three months ago, but I thought we had that resolved. You see, an old, very special friend came through town, and Chris didn't give me the message that she had called."

"Maybe he forgot."

"Nope," she replied bitterly. "I didn't find out until a week later, when Stacy sent me a note saying she was so disappointed that I'd never called her hotel, and didn't Chris give me her message?"

Brian whistled.

"When I confronted Chris, he admitted he'd deliberately withheld the message because he felt Stacy was a bad influence."

Brian was flabbergasted. "A bad... You've got to be kidding!"

"Well, Stacy and I did get into some scrapes together in college," she admitted. "One time, we were almost expelled after we got caught parking the housemother's car in the hallway of the dormitory."

He laughed, then grew more sober. "That still doesn't give Chris the right to choose your friends."

"I agree. The hardest part for me was that Stacy couldn't get back for the wedding, so we missed our only chance to be together for years. But Chris did apologize, promising it would never happen again. Then he generously helped my dad out of a financial bind—but with the understanding that I wouldn't cancel the wedding."

Brian appeared perturbed. "That was very manipulative of him—but maybe he was just scared of losing you."

"If so, he wasn't about to let up on the reins." She sighed. "Last night as we drove home from the rehearsal dinner, Chris started in on me again—telling me how he intended to totally reshape me into his perfect little wife, how I would quit my job, give up my friends, you name it.''

"Oh, brother," Brian groaned. "The guy doesn't know when he has it good, huh? So that's why you ran out?"

"Yes. Chris broke his word to me. Guess I finally realized I was trying to play honorably with a man who—well, just isn't honorable.''

He touched her hand. "Why do I get the feeling there's more?''

"There is.''

"Tell me, Cassie.''

She pulled her fingers away. "I can't. Not you.''

"Why not me?''

"Because, well, *you're* the reason—''

"You mean, my rudeness was the reason—like the straw that broke the camel's back?''

"No. Well, not entirely.''

"Tell me, Cassie.''

She slowly shook her head. "This is going to sound so crazy.''

He grinned. "I'm a little crazy. *Un poco loco.* Isn't that how you say it here in Texas?''

She chuckled. "You really think you can handle this?''

"I can handle anything," he declared confidently.

She faced him boldly. "Okay, Mr. Brian Drake. It was your blue columbine.''

"My what?''

"The wildflowers you sent out. That, and the message you scribbled on your business card: 'Here's something blue.' It was all so sweet, so spontaneous.''

He appeared confused. "You mean you walked out of your own wedding because of a handful of wildflowers?''

"You don't get it. It was like a sign. It shook me up, made me realize everything I was missing, everything that was wrong between me and Chris.''

"I see. I think. And that was it?''

"No. There's more."

"Go on."

She twisted her fingers together. "You don't want to hear this...."

"Cassie, I do."

"Very well." Taking a deep, bracing breath, she blurted, "I also ran out because something crazy happened, something totally unexpected. An impulse. I looked across the church, saw a certain face, and fell in love."

Now he appeared totally baffled. "Fell in love? You mean with Chris?"

"No." A second of explosive silence ticked by. "I mean with you."

For a moment, Brian just stared, his expression utterly stunned. Then he turned away, gripping the railing with trembling fingers. "You were right, Cassie. I can't handle this."

Cassie laughed. Brian appeared so helpless and mystified that he was downright comical. "Don't worry, I'm sure it's not really true," she reassured him. "I mean, I only succumbed to a momentary insanity, but it woke me up and made me realize I'll never really love Chris. Chris is—well, just too premeditated and controlling. About everything. He'd never lose himself in the joys of rock climbing, or be late because he stopped off to pick me wildflowers on an impulse. Suddenly, I just couldn't face a lifetime of such sane predictability. As for my feelings for you, I think Fate just brought you here to help me realize something was terribly wrong. I'm sure in reality, people never fall in love that quickly." She stopped to catch a ragged breath. "Do they?"

Now they both stared, the tension between them thick and palpable. "Yes, that would be impossible," he agreed, his voice cracking.

At first, Cassie wasn't even conscious of the fact that she and Brian were moving closer together. In the next instant, Cassie was in his arms, their lips were passionately meeting, and suddenly, she was no longer so certain of her claim that love at first sight was impossible. Brian's kiss was breathtaking and sweet, his mouth warm and firm over her own quivering lips. His hard body molded perfectly to her own soft curves. Cassie felt shaken and deeply thrilled, heat streaking through her from head to toe. As their tongues sought and tasted, she curled her arms around his neck and moaned ecstatically. A tremor shook him and he nestled her closer. His hand at the small of her back felt so strong and reassuring. His fingertips stroking her bare arm washed her with shivers. They stood with lips and bodies tightly locked as the waves pounded out a romantic cacophony.

At last they broke apart, staring at each other breathlessly.

Appearing shaken, Brian pulled his fingers through his hair and regarded her contritely. "I—I'm sorry. I can't believe this is happening. I can't be kissing Chris's fiancée."

Cassie smiled back tremulously. "I can't be feeling what I'm feeling for you. This is crazy, Brian. But, oh, I like it."

But, as she would have moved closer, he held up a hand. "Cassie, I... You've been drinking, and I think we need to quit while we're ahead here."

Disappointed, she reached out to touch his bare arm, felt him flinch and saw his eyes darken. "You sure, Brian?"

"Uh—yeah," he replied tightly. "Otherwise, we'll both regret this in the morning—I mean, won't we?"

"I suppose you're right."

"It's late, and I think we'd best get you upstairs."

"Okay," she murmured. "But—what about you?"

He swallowed hard. "Um—perhaps you shouldn't be alone."

She raised an eyebrow.

"I mean—does Lisa's condo have a couch?" he hastily added.

"Sure. Three of them, as I recall."

"Would you mind if I—"

"No, not at all."

"All right, then." He wrapped an arm around her shoulders and they started off.

"Know what?" she asked softly.

"What?"

"I'm glad you're here, Mr. Brian Drake."

Brian was almost glad Cassie stumbled then, relieving him of the necessity to respond. He clutched her more tightly. "Hey, steady on your feet, mate."

Cassie rested her head on Brian's shoulder. A contented sigh escaped him.

BRIAN HELPED CASSIE navigate her way through the tables at the edge of the patio and enter the lobby through the back door. As they crossed toward the elevator—Cassie slightly dazed, half staggering, her head still resting on Brian's shoulder—he noted the curious look on the desk clerk's face. He tossed the man a glare and tightened his grip on Cassie. Lord, she smelled so good and felt so warm and curvy next to him. With her head snuggled on his shoulder, he was so tempted to turn his face toward hers and kiss those delectable lips again. She had been so sweet, so vulnerable, in his arms just now. The memory made him starved for her.

*Get a grip,* he scolded himself.

Once they were safely inside the car, just the two of them with the piped-in music, Cassie awakened with a gasp and pulled a face. "Oh, no, not that song again!" she wailed.

Brian listened. "'I've Finally Found Someone'? I think it's kind of nice."

"It's Chris's favorite song."

"Ah. But not yours?"

In slurred tones, she replied, "Not after I listened to *fifteen* choruses of it while waiting for the worst man to show up."

"The worst man?" Brian was fighting laughter.

She eyed him haughtily. "That's what my niece, Emily the flower girl, calls you."

"Can't blame her," he ruefully agreed.

Cassie listened another moment, then her expression turned morose and she sniffed. "No wonder this didn't work. I was going to marry a man who likes elevator music."

Brian chuckled.

"I bet Barbra Streisand and Brian Adams never had these problems."

"I suppose not—especially since they're not married to each other."

"Good point."

The elevator jerked to a halt and the doors popped open. As they emerged in the softly lit corridor, Cassie pulled a key from the pocket of her dress and handed it to Brian. She was humming the Streisand/Adams love song as she led him to the door, prompting him to glance at her in perplexity. He unlocked the door, reaching inside to switch on the lights. She wobbled in ahead of him, and he glanced at the luxurious expanse of three white sofas grouped about glass windows and balcony doors, of pricey art and handsome accessories.

He whistled. "I take it Lisa is loaded?"

"Something like that." Cassie was staggering toward the bedroom door. "Oil leases."

"Ah."

"'Herited them." She said it with a hiccup.

Watching her totter, Brian rushed after her, catching her about the waist. "Here, let me help you to bed."

"My, aren't you a prince?"

Rolling his eyes, Brian opened the bedroom door and whipped on another light. Assisting Cassie inside, he helped her ease herself down onto the bed. She was still humming the love song as he leaned down to unbuckle her sandals. He noted how lovely her feet were, the skin slightly tanned and smooth, the toenails painted pink. Tugging his mind out of dangerous territory, he dropped her shoes onto the floor and pulled a quilt over her. Then he looked up at her.

Finished with her humming, she was gazing at him dreamily. Lord, she was too tempting! Those large green eyes of hers were simply breathtaking. Heart thumping, Brian again felt hard-pressed not to kiss her. "You okay now?"

"Yep." She grinned crookedly. "You know, you're awfully cute, Mr. Brian Drake."

He raised an eyebrow. "You know what, Cassie Brandon?"

"What?"

"You're a tease. No wonder Chris wants you."

Solemnly, she trailed a fingertip along his jaw. "But I don't tease Chris."

Brian drew a sharp breath. "Then what changed?"

She smiled.

He backed away. "Lady, you're dangerous. I'm out of here."

"Shucks." Giggling, she pointed toward the bathroom. "Pillows and blankets are in the linen closet."

"Thanks." Brian rushed over, flung open the closet door, grabbed a pillow and blanket and all but bolted from the room. As he turned off the light and closed the door, he caught a last glimpse of Cassie, already fast asleep, a dreamy expression on her lovely face.

MOMENTS LATER, Brian was tossing and turning on a couch in Lisa's darkened living room. He could hear the mantel clock ticking, the surf pounding outside.

His heart was keeping pace. What a mess he was in now. And to think that only yesterday, he'd dreaded coming to this wedding. Another boring family occasion.

Boring, indeed. Cassie Brandon had proven to be anything but dull. Usually, Brian was the crazy one, the wild one, the nut everyone else had to worry about. But this woman—not only was she more beautiful than any law should allow, but she was exciting, unpredictable—not to mention sweet, helpless and adorable. She'd already led him, the original free spirit, on a merry chase. Had she no idea what she did to a guy when she talked about falling for him at first sight? When she pressed that lush, sexy body into his and opened her lips to his kiss?

He rolled violently, pounding down his pillow with a fist. Where had his cousin found her, anyway? Chris for damn sure didn't deserve her.

But did he? The question hit Brian like a fist in the gut.

What was happening to him? This woman was doing a number on him, making him forget why he was really here.

He was here to help Chris, to retrieve Cassie and rescue the wedding. Granted, Chris had caused much of this mess by acting like such a jerk. Still, he was Brian's cousin and deserved a measure of loyalty. Besides, surely tonight Cassie had given Chris enough of a reality shock that he'd be more than willing to shape up. He'd certainly appeared shaken enough when Brian had left him at the church.

As for Cassie—surely she had only experienced a last-minute panic, a really bad case of the jitters. Most likely she'd come to her senses in the morning and be mortified about what had happened between her and Brian tonight. Thank heaven he'd at least had the presence of mind not to take advantage of her in her confused, tipsy state. Otherwise, he'd have two lifelong enemies tomorrow—Cassie *and* Chris. Make that three—himself included.

Cassie would surely pull out of this, and he must, as well. Yes, he'd been very turned on by her helplessness tonight. But none of that was any excuse for kissing his cousin's girl. He had come here tonight to retrieve Chris's fiancée, *not* to seduce her. And he'd best not forget it again!

# 3

CASSIE AWOKE with a gasp and sat up, only to wince as her head pounded with the force of a rifle recoil. Grimacing at the full light of morning, she glanced about to see that she was in Lisa's bedroom. She looked down and saw she was still in her dress, though a quilt was draped over her.

Then she remembered, and moaned in agony. She had fled her own wedding and run off here.... Brian had showed up, charming her, and she had poured her heart out to him. Then—oh, heavens!—the two of them had shared the most incredible kiss. What must he think of her now? Perhaps that she was a hopeless flake, and also couldn't wait to jump into his bed? How could she face him, much less Chris and everyone else she had disappointed at the wedding?

Gingerly, she got up, trudged to the bathroom, grimaced at her reflection in the mirror, splashed water on her face, and brushed her teeth. Rummaging through the medicine cabinet, she found a bottle of aspirin and downed a couple.

Soon afterward she emerged in the sun-splashed living room. Glancing toward the sofas, she spotted a crumpled blanket and mussed pillow, a bag that Brian must have retrieved from his car—but no sign of him.

The hiss of the cappuccino maker, along with the smell of the rich brew, enticed her on toward the kitchen. She wobbled into the alcove...and came face-to-face with Brian Drake.

He stood next to the counter, wearing shorts, a T-shirt, and athletic shoes. Irresistibly her gaze moved from his tanned, hard-muscled legs with their covering of coarse masculine hair, to his sinewy arms. Her heart thudding with a mixture of excitement and anxiety, she dared a look at his face. He was grinning at her.

Oh, damn, those incredible dimples, and those blue, blue eyes! She was going to melt on the spot—if she didn't pass out from the jackhammers pounding inside her skull.

He extended a small cup toward her. "Good morning. Cappuccino?"

She took the cup with trembling fingers. "My, aren't you perky and efficient? Bet you've been up since dawn, bench-pressing the sofas, eh?"

He chuckled. "If I'd been so lively, wouldn't you have heard me?"

She took a gulp and shuddered. "A man of your finesse? Never."

"How's the head?"

"Don't ask."

"Need some aspirin?"

"I found some in the bathroom cabinet. Now if it will only find my headache."

He nodded toward the breakfast nook. "Think some nourishment could help?"

"How thoughtful of you." Taking a step toward the table, she staggered. "Guess I'm not much of a drinker."

He took her arm. "I've noticed. Two wine coolers pretty much did you in."

The heat of his fingers on her flesh seared her. As he seated her, she caught a whiff of his scent, a glimpse of the sexy stubble along his jaw. A new wave of dizziness washed over her.

Watching him straighten, she flashed him a brave smile. "Thanks. Wow, orange juice and English muffins. So, you can cook, too."

He sat down across from her. "You mean I can take a can of juice and a package of muffins out of the freezer. And use a toaster and a cappuccino machine."

She took a gulp of orange juice. "To your health."

"To yours."

For a few moments they ate in strained silence. At last Cassie cleared her throat. "Brian, about last night…"

He held up a hand. "You don't have to explain."

"I don't?"

"I understand all about what happened. You had a bad case of the jitters, and Chris didn't help at all by acting like such a jerk. Then I showed up late and pretty much jinxed your wedding. So you freaked, right? It's perfectly understandable under the circumstances. But that doesn't mean things can't still work out between you and Chris. I'm sure he already regrets the arrogant way he's been acting. You just need to call him, now that you've had a chance to calm down and see things clearly. Right?"

She sighed. "Wrong."

"Wrong?"

She stared at him in terrible confusion. "Brian, you're right that I see things more clearly now. But unfortunately, what that really means is that I'm more convinced than ever that Chris is the wrong man for me. Maybe it's because he's too controlling, and I've finally realized he's not going to change. Maybe I really did need to break free. On the other hand…"

"Yes?"

She took a deep, steadying breath. "Don't you remember what I said last night? That I… I think I'm in love with you now?"

Swallowing hard, he nodded.

She waved a hand. "Here I was, convinced that I'm the world's most sane, sensible person. But if I can jump off the deep end like that on a whim, then I'm not ready to marry Chris…or anyone. Am I?"

For a moment, Brian appeared perplexed. Then he frowned, got up, and began to pace.

"Cassie, please don't be so hasty. I know Chris has really tried your patience, but he has a lot going for him—"

"Don't you think I know that? He's just not right for me."

"He seemed perfect until last night—"

"Yeah, and we both know exactly what happened then," she finished dryly.

For a moment, they just looked at each other, stark uncertainty in their gazes, the atmosphere between them charged, electric. Then he coughed and glanced away. "I'm sure if you've fixated on me, it's only due to some last-minute panic over committing to Chris. I'm sure if you'll just give this some more time, you'll come to your senses—"

"Brian, I already have."

He could only gaze at her helplessly.

She stood and crossed to his side. "Look, you've done your good deed. You've tried to solve this, but you can't."

"But this is my fault—"

"No, it's not you. It's me. After last night, I'm dealing with a major identity crisis." She waved a hand. "Heck, I'm beginning to feel like Dudley Moore."

"Dudley Moore?" he asked, laughing. "I think you're a bit young—not to mention the wrong sex."

"Don't you remember that old movie *Ten?*"

"Well, yes," he replied cynically. "Bo Derrick is rather hard to forget."

She slanted him a look of amused indulgence. "My mom really loved that movie, and we used to watch it together. Here, old Dudley thought he had his life all settled, then he totally flips out over some sweet young thing—"

"Can't recall when I've been called a sweet young thing before," he put in.

"Well, you're definitely a ten," she quipped back.

He grinned—but, to his credit, sheepishly.

Now Cassie began to pace about. "To tell you the truth, after last night, I'm feeling pretty disgusted with myself, and need some time to regroup. I've got to get my head on straight, figure out what kind of person I really am. Deep down, am I really sane and sensible? Should I spend my life with someone steady like Chris? Or, should I just give up and become a beach bum?''

He snapped his fingers. ''Now there's a thought.''

''Maybe I'm afraid of commitment. Or fickle as hell.'' She sighed. ''You see, something similar to this happened back when I was in high school. I ran off for a college weekend rather than attend my high-school prom.''

''And why was that?''

''Well, my best friend warned me that my boyfriend was planning to propose that night—for about the third time. Of course I had already said no to marriage at least twice. I knew I wasn't ready for such a big step. But, according to my friend, Tommy was convinced I'd relent if he just presented me with that huge 'rock' in front of everyone.''

Brian whistled. ''Talk about twisting your arm.''

She nodded. ''I pretty much decided on the spot that I wanted to pursue a higher education, so I went with some girlfriends to investigate Baylor instead. My point is, the thought of marriage made me freak—just like last night.''

''Ah, but there's a big difference. Last night, you had already said 'yes' before you freaked.''

She rolled her eyes. ''Thanks so much for reminding me.''

He fell silent, scratching his jaw. ''Maybe you are afraid of commitment. We could even be two of a kind.'' He glanced up eagerly. ''Perhaps I could help you with this.''

''You mean perhaps you could convince me to go running back to Chris? It won't work, Brian. No matter what comes out of this, I just don't think there's a future for me and Chris.''

He appeared crestfallen. ''Your mind's made up?''

''Yes.''

''So, what are you going to do, Cassie?''

She shrugged. ''I don't know. I've got the week off. Stay here and think, maybe. I know I've got to call some people and majorly apologize, but otherwise I'm just not ready to face the music back in Houston."

He touched her arm. "Please let me stay and help you."

She cast him a chiding glance. "Brian..."

"Yes?"

"After last night, who do you think you're kidding?"

He actually colored.

She looked him over with an expression of regret. "You're a real charmer, all right, Brian Drake. But my grandmother always said a woman on the rebound is a dangerous creature...and bound to make a big mistake."

"So you're saying our spending time together would be a mistake?"

"The timing is wrong," she said gently. "I know you want to help, but believe me, you'd only complicate things."

He touched her arm, then sighed. "Okay, I get the message."

Tossing Cassie a last, anguished glance, Brian turned away to pour them both more coffee.

MOMENTS LATER, riding down in the elevator, Brian was scowling, his fingers tense as they gripped his bag. He and Cassie had parted with awkward words and a last, chaste kiss. Still, it had been the right thing to do, he told himself. For the best.

He needed to be far, far away from her. For Cassie Brandon was one potent feminine package and she was making him crazy as hell. He'd never before met anyone like her. So far, she'd proven to be as refreshing and unpredictable as he liked to think he was. If she was in the midst of some kind of life crisis, she wore her vulnerability with more allure and sex appeal than anything Victoria's Secret had to offer.

Everything she did and said fascinated him. And she was smart—too smart. She'd seen through him as if he was some giant picture window. She'd known the real reason he'd offered to stay and help—and it was far from totally altruistic.

Hell, it would have been suicidal to stick around, expose himself to constant temptation, hear her laughter and her teasing, possibly even watch her cavort in the surf in a bikini! All under the guise of helping Chris? Crazy!

Too bad. He'd really wanted to be Cassie's friend during this crisis, but as always, that old demon of physical chemistry had gotten in the way. He may have come here for Chris, but if he'd stayed...he very much feared it would have been for himself.

The elevator doors opened, and Brian felt strangely empty inside as he crossed the lobby. At the front doors, he hesitated, his fingers on the handle.

He shouldn't. He couldn't. This was no time to do something crazy. To give in to an impulse.

No, it just wasn't the time at all.

IT WAS ALMOST NOON by the time Cassie came down in the elevator. First, she'd kicked herself for sending Brian away, even though she'd known that letting him stay would have confused the issues even more. Afterward, she'd dozed awhile, then she'd bathed and dressed in a cotton shirt and slacks. Finally she'd gotten up the nerve to call her folks and Chris and apologize for last night. Yes, she was okay, she'd told her folks, she just needed some time to think. She was so sorry about the wedding. When her dad had said, "Honey, it's okay. Like I told you last night, we just want you to be happy," Cassie had felt like bawling.

Next, she'd called Lisa and, after playing twenty questions with her friend, had asked if it was okay to stay at the condo for a week. "Sure, take your time," Lisa had said.

Afterward, her conversation with Chris had been terribly awkward. She'd apologized for embarrassing him and not cancelling the wedding sooner; despite their differences, he'd deserved better than that. Why had she done it? he'd asked. Was it because of their fight before the wedding? That and too much else, she'd told him. Wouldn't she reconsider? he'd asked. Please, he mustn't hold out hope, she'd replied.

Now she was feeling really low. And at loose ends, to boot.

Cassie stepped out into the lobby. A businessman and a couple were checking in. Two elderly gentlemen were playing chess near the front windows.

The smells of food lured her toward the restaurant. She walked out onto the patio, where several guests were eating lunch at umbrella-shaded tables. The sound system was playing "You've Got a Friend." She continued onto the pier and did a double-take, then a triple take.

It couldn't be! That man sitting at the small table placed at the edge of the pier *couldn't* be Brian Drake.

But it was him, wearing white slacks, a green tropical shirt and designer sunglasses. He was sipping a margarita at a table set for two, with taco salads and a second margarita already deposited!

"May I help you, miss?"

Flustered, Cassie turned to the waiter. "No, thanks. I— um, think I see my party."

"Ah, yes." The waiter gestured toward Brian. "The gentleman said you wish to have lunch at the edge of the pier."

"Yeah, he likes to live his life on the edge, all right," she muttered back.

Heart pounding, Cassie started across the pier toward Brian. He spotted her, grinned, set down his drink and stood.

"Brian, what in heck—"

He dashed about the table to pull out her chair. "You know, Cassie, one thing I really love about Texas is the Mexican food."

Her mouth fell open. "Brian, *what* are you doing here?"

"You do have to eat, Cassie." He indicated her chair. "Have a seat, won't you?"

Flabbergasted, she sank into her chair. "Now explain what you're doing here!"

He resumed his seat and removed his sunglasses. His blue eyes gleamed with mischief. "Try the margarita. It's excellent."

"You expect me to drink after last night?"

"Good old hair of the dog," he replied cheerily.

Cassie was mystified. "*What* are you doing here, Brian?"

"Oh, being spontaneous."

"What?"

"You didn't think I'd really leave without showing you my impulsive side?"

For a moment, Cassie couldn't speak. "How did you know I'd come down here, anyway?"

He scratched his jaw. "What is it they say about the criminal always revisiting the scene of the crime?"

Cassie threw a napkin at him. Chuckling, he tossed it back.

"All right," she said sternly. "'Fess up. What are you up to, Brian Drake?"

He took an elaborate moment to unfold his own napkin. "Well, I've just rented myself a room at a delightful establishment called the Beach Shack."

"You've what?"

At last turning serious, he said, "Cassie, I have the week off, too. I just don't feel right about leaving you alone with this. I think I need to stay and help you through it."

She took a minute to calm her raging heart, then raised an eyebrow. "Don't you remember what I said upstairs?"

"I do—and I still think you need me here."

She slanted him an admonishing glance. "That's the kind of thing a guy usually says to a girl right before he tries to put the moves on her."

He stared, hard. "Cassie, I don't think I *can* leave."

Her toes curled.

"There's more."

"Oh, Lord."

Intently, he leaned toward her. "Do you think you're the only one who has been forced to do some self-examination here? You know, I tend to be a pretty self-absorbed guy. Always thinking of myself first. Last night really brought that home for me."

"So?"

"So for once in my life I'd like to try to do the right thing. And maybe I *can* help you with this."

For a moment she was speechless again. At last she whispered, "*How*, Brian?"

"Last night, you got sidetracked over some feelings for me. Now you're afraid your impulsive side could take over your life, right?"

"Well, I suppose…"

"And you're trying to decide what kind of person you really are—Ms. Sensible or Ms. Flake."

Her lips twitched. "Something like that."

"Then you need to spend some time with me."

"What?" she laughed.

He leaned closer. "Cassie, I'm the most impulsive guy in the world. Spend some time with me, and you'll see that you could never be happy living as recklessly as I do—or spending your life with someone like me."

"You've got to be joking."

"No, not at all. Maybe you do need to explore your forbidden side and see where it leads you." A husky note entered his voice. "I mean, in a sense, aren't you really saying that you can't marry Chris until you get me out of your system?"

That comment brought Cassie surging to her feet with a clang of dishware. She stood with hands trembling on the railing, staring at out the green, sun-splashed gulf, at a colorful sailboat gliding by in the distance. She felt the wind caressing her face and tugging at her clothing.

Brian also stood. Seeing how shaken Cassie appeared, he suddenly had second thoughts about his impetuous ac-

tions in returning to the hotel. He had wanted to come back
here to help her, but was he only complicating her life even
more? Still, he felt so drawn toward her—and compelled
to set things straight.

Gently, he asked, "Cassie, did I say something wrong?"

She turned to eye him sharply. "Are you suggesting we
have a love affair, Brian Drake?"

He colored. "No, not at all. I'm saying I got you into
this mess and I intend to get you out of it."

"Brian, you didn't get me into this mess."

He appeared utterly sincere. "I want to stay, anyway.
Are you really going to force me to leave?"

"Well, you are cute," she conceded with a touch of humor.

"Then you'll relent?"

He appeared so helpless and eager that a rueful smile
hovered on her lips. "Brian, try to see this from my per-
spective. I just don't trust my feelings right now. Last night,
I walked out on Chris, and now I could be—well, falling
for you on the rebound."

He grew thoughtful. "Cassie, that's a good point. I was
about to say pretty much the same thing. Don't you think
that so often when there's an instantaneous attraction, it
tends to fizzle quickly?"

"Are you speaking from experience?" she asked.

His sheepish expression gave away that he was. "Just
think about good old Dudley and Bo."

"Them again?"

"Something that hot tends to burn itself out, don't you
think?"

She frowned. "So you're saying—"

"If what you feel for me is an impulse, then won't this
fade? And there's one surefire way to find out. Why don't
we spend a week together—separate cabins, of course—
and get to know each other better?"

She shook her head. "What would that solve? Your life

is in Denver, and I don't recall your saying you want to become involved with me.''

"But that's the beauty of my plan. I've dated girls like you before, and I always drive them crazy. A week with me, and I swear you'll be perfectly happy to spend the rest of your life with a dependable guy like Chris. You'll see all my faults—''

"Such as?'' she asked.

He began to count on his fingers. "I'm rash and a thrill-seeker. I have a short attention span. I'm sloppy. I can never stay with one woman for long. I'm a sports buff, and there's no prying me away from the World Series—''

By now, Cassie was breaking up with laughter.

"What's so funny?''

"You!''

"It's all true. To top it all off, I'm not a marrying man. One week with me, and you'll be ready to shoot me, for sure.''

Cassie regarded him with amusement in her eyes. "And what if this doesn't work?''

"What do you mean?''

She edged closer. She gazed into his eyes—so blue. And for once, so vulnerable. "I mean this could backfire, Brian,'' she whispered. "Big time.''

His voice grew rough. "Cassie, what do you think you're doing?''

"I'm not *doing* anything, Brian.'' She sighed heavily. "But how can either of us forget about last night?''

He was silent, looking half ready to run, half prepared to devour her on the spot.

Cassie spoke with the force of her own mixed emotions. "What if your little scheme doesn't work, Mr. Fix-it? What if you can't convince me to go running back to Chris? What if we should fall in love—for real?''

He gulped. "Fall in love?''

"You heard me.''

"And you heard me say I'm not a marrying man?''

"Yes."

"Then—well, if we fall in love, I'll just have to go back to Denver with a broken heart. And you…" He broke into a crooked grin. "You'll commit yourself to a convent, of course."

Caught off guard, Cassie chortled. "You know what, Brian Drake? You're a nut!"

"I'm a nut?" he asked, incredulous. "You've got me so rattled that now *I'm* acting sensibly."

She gestured toward the table. "This is sensible?"

Seeming to regain control of himself, Brian took Cassie's arm and firmly steered her back to her chair. "Do we have a deal, Cassie?"

Rolling her eyes heavenward, she sat down. "Why is it I get the feeling *we* have a deal whether *I* like it or not?"

He joined her. "Well, you don't have to be a martyr about it."

She cast him a scolding look, then noted him waiting for her answer with such touching expectation that she began to relent. "Okay, perhaps we do need to spend a little time together here in the tropics—*separate cabins, of course.*"

With a relieved sigh, he lifted his glass. "Then let's toast to it."

Smiling wryly, Cassie lifted her glass. "To Dudley and Bo."

"And to being spontaneous."

Even as Cassie dutifully clicked her glass against Brian's, she wondered what on earth she was getting herself into. *Why* hadn't she been able to summon the force of will—or the heart—to send him away again? That would have been the most sensible thing to do.

Yet, ever since last night, Cassie wasn't being very sensible. Perhaps she did need a friend right now, and clearly Brian had come back out of a sincere desire to help her. But given her current vulnerable state, he might well be helping them *both* into much deeper emotional trouble!

# 4

"BRIAN, this is fun. This is... *Eeeeeeeeeek!*"

Hours later, Cassie was skating down the seawall with Brian, both of them decked out in Lycra bodysuits and armored in helmets and numerous protective pads, when they swerved to avoid a bicycle-built-for-four, and all but collided with a snow-cone stand just off the promenade. Even as Cassie squealed in fear and struggled to brake, Brian skidded to a halt ahead of her, whirled his body about, and caught her neatly. Nonetheless, her forward momentum slammed them both into the side of the stand, though Brian's back took the brunt of the impact.

The sensual impact of having their bodies collide was even more breathtaking.

"You okay?" Brian asked.

Cassie panted to catch her breath. Feeling Brian's strength surrounding her, looking up into his gorgeous blue eyes, she reflected rucfully that she *wasn't* okay. She needed her head examined for allowing this sexy man to stay here on the island with her. What was it they were supposed to be doing now—exploring her more impulsive side? At the moment, her rattled impulses were urging her to grab this delicious hunk and kiss him senseless. Even the sweat breaking out on Brian's handsome male brow seemed incredibly sensual.

Outwardly, she managed to flash him a brave smile. "Sure, I'm okay. How 'bout you?"

"I'm fine."

Recovering her equilibrium at bit, she laughed. "I still

say we're both nuts for skating down the seawall.'' She nodded toward the Gulf. ''Just look at the sheer drop going down to the beach. I wouldn't want to tumble down *that* treacherous incline.''

''With me here to protect you? No way!'' he scoffed.

''Ah, so you're not only brave, but humble,'' she teased.

''Of course.'' With a playful gleam in his eyes, he looked her over. ''Besides, we've got to be very careful with all this, um, equipment we've rented.''

''Right,'' she murmured. ''Heaven forbid we come out of this with any of our, um, *equipment* damaged.''

The two gazed at each other with tender amusement, then Brian glanced around. ''Hey, how 'bout a snow cone?''

''Sounds good.''

After Brian bought them both snow cones, they glided over to a small table and sat down together, then took turns holding the cups as each removed helmet and wrist pads.

At last, Cassie took a slurp of her drink. ''Mmm, this is excellent.''

''Sure hits the spot in this heat.'' Brian gazed down at the beach. ''Wow, look at those whitecaps. Wouldn't mind catching a few waves this afternoon.''

Following his gaze toward the billowy Gulf, Cassie shook her head. ''You're not going to suggest we go surfing right after skating? Talk about going from the frying pan into the fire.''

He winked. ''Actually, I was going to suggest we try surfing *on* skates.''

She threw a chip of ice at him. ''You would!''

He glowered. ''Hey, cut that out or I'll retaliate!''

''With what, a slap of your wrist pad?''

He leaned closer. ''Actually, I'd prefer to dunk you. If you don't want to surf, why don't we go for a dip in the Gulf?''

''Now?'' she asked, taken aback.

''Aren't you hot?'' he teased.

Not certain just what he meant, she stammered, "Well, I—"

Brian's expression was pure mischief as he reached out to pat her hand and spoke as if to reassure an overanxious child. "I realize an invitation to go swimming is a huge shock for conservative old you, but I promise you can handle it."

"Stop it, Brian," she scolded, while fighting a smile.

"We'll just have to change first," he continued patiently. "Okay?"

Cassie frowned, uneasy at the thought of herself and Brian frolicking about in skimpy swimwear, when she was already far too affected by the sight of his hard-muscled, Lycra-clad body. "Haven't you had enough excitement for one afternoon?"

"Excitement?" he repeated, wiggling his eyebrows over the rim of his snow cone.

"Brian, you're asking for it," she warned.

"Meaning you don't want to go swimming with me?" he pressed.

"Well..." She stared at her drink.

"Something wrong, Cassie?"

Glancing at his face, she sighed. "The problem is—well, my bikini."

He grinned in delight. "Your bikini? Now you've got me fascinated." He leaned closer, until she could smell his exciting scent and feel his heat. "You don't want me to see you in your bikini, Cassie? Then I think I must insist."

Heart suddenly hammering and cheeks burning, Cassie pulled back. "Brian, that's not what I meant. I'm hardly *that* modest."

"Then what?"

She chewed on her lower lip. "Well, I just bought that bikini for Chris, and you know, all the memories..."

"A brand-new bikini has memories?" he mused, scratching his jaw. "There's a new one."

She tossed him a forbearing look. "Think about it for a moment. I bought that bikini for—well, the honeymoon."

"Ah. The dreaded honeymoon."

"Brian!"

He grinned sheepishly.

"And I just—well, *can't* wear my honeymoon bikini to go swimming with you."

He turned solemn. "Cassie, are you having second thoughts about us being here together?"

She gestured helplessly. "No. Yes. Well, I guess I am feeling a little sad."

"Sad?"

She nodded. "I didn't mention it earlier, but after you left this morning, I called my folks and Chris."

"Ah. How did it go?"

"It was pretty much awkward all the way around. My folks were too sweet. As for Chris—well, he begged me to reconsider, but I just couldn't."

Carefully, he asked, "Are you still feeling that way—as if you can't reconsider?"

"Yes," she admitted with a sigh. Watching him blanch, she added, "That's not the answer you wanted to hear, is it?"

He considered her words with a frown. "For Chris's sake, no. For mine..." He took a slow sip. "Well, guess I'll have to take the fifth."

Cassie fought the treacherous thrill his last words stirred. "It's always hard when a relationship doesn't work, especially since Chris and I did have a lot of history together. That makes me blue. We both put so much time and heart into a something that was never meant to be."

"You're certain it was never meant to be?"

"Yes."

He sighed. "So what does a girl do when she's blue?"

All at once, Cassie brightened. "Go shopping."

"What?" He laughed.

Secret amusement shone in her eyes. "Well, you want

me to indulge my more impulsive side, don't you? And it's the perfect solution. We're going to be here a week, and it's silly for us not to swim at all. So I'll just buy myself a new bikini. You know, there are some wonderful outlet stores over on the Strand.''

''So I get to watch you model bikinis?'' he asked eagerly.

''No way!'' she retorted. ''But if you want to go swimming with me, you do get to sit and wait *patiently* while I choose one.''

'''Patiently,''' he repeated with a scowl. ''I'm not sure that word is in my vocabulary.''

She shrugged and slurped her drink. ''I'll be happy to go shopping by myself, while you skate off into the sunset.''

''No way!'' came his indignant response. ''What red-blooded American male can resist an opportunity to go bikini shopping with a pretty lady?''

She rolled her eyes.

Chuckling, he stood and offered his hand. ''As they say here in Texas, let's mosey on over to the Strand, partner.''

She accepted his assistance and stood. ''Brian, you're about as Texan as a snowmobile.''

He snapped his fingers. ''Want to take one to the Strand?''

''Get out of here!''

''That's what we're trying to do, Cassie.''

Laughing, they skated off down the seawall together.

TWO HOURS LATER, in a small, trendy boutique on the historic Galveston Strand, Brian sat on a stool scowling at his watch. Behind him was a three-way mirror. At his feet were planted two huge shopping bags, stuffed with all the goodies Cassie had purchased during her spur-of-the-moment shopping spree, including the new bikini she had, unfortunately, refused to model for him.

Not far from Brian, two young mothers were browsing

through the racks, one of them pushing a baby stroller, the other leading along a cute little daughter. Cassie was in the dressing room, where she'd been ensconced for a least twenty minutes, and Brian was on the verge of popping his cork.

Yes, he had to admit patience was not his long suit. On the other hand, why was it *every* shopping expedition with a female turned into an ordeal? As for the male of the species, guys tended to be quick, decisive, in and out. In fact, Brian knew his own sizes and brand preferences well enough that he seldom wasted time trying on clothing. His suits did have to be tailored, but on casual stuff, he'd just waltz into his favorite men's shop in Denver, grab slacks in assorted colors, coordinating shirts and socks, and that was that.

What was the big deal, anyway? Why couldn't a woman even buy a bathing suit without graduating into major investments? For a bikini was never enough. Then she needed some sort of wrapper to go over it, then sandals for the beach, then she moved on to shorts and tops, and finally, to a brand-new wardrobe.

Hell, before it was all over, Cassie would most likely insist on a Givenchy gown and a fur coat. All due to an impulse to buy a bikini.

And Brian hadn't even seen her in the darn thing, had only caught a glimpse of it as she'd taken it to the cash register sandwiched between other goodies. Craning his neck to check the entrance to the dressing room, and viewing no signs of life, he found he was unable to resist temptation any longer. Much as he knew he was being terribly naughty, he leaned over, poked around in her bags, then pulled out the diminutive swimsuit with its huge tag.

Brian whistled. Forty bucks for those little scraps of fabric? Cassie had a thing for color, all right. Passion flowers in exotic shades of pink and fuchsia beguiled his eyes. The top was composed of nicely round cups—the bottom, hot strips of sheer temptation—all held together by spaghetti straps.

Damn, the fragile thing was little more than a wish—and his fervent wish at the moment was that he could see Cassie in it! Yes, he was being a very bad boy, and he had no business succumbing to such decadent thoughts. Yet all he could do was to envision her in it—those lovely legs of hers, her arms, her flat belly, and...

"Mister, that's the lady's, and you're not 'posed to be peeking at it," scolded an indignant young voice.

Brian glanced up to see the little girl, a ponytailed moppet in shorts and T-shirt, standing nearby, frowning solemnly and shaking a finger at him.

Feigning an expression of horror, Brian dropped the bikini and pressed a hand to his heart. "You're right, ma'am. Caught me in the act. Please don't turn me in!"

The minx squealed with delight and dashed off to rejoin her mother.

Brian chuckled, welcoming the distraction. He liked kids. Liked them too much, in fact. Whenever he was at a social gathering where children were present, he was forever the one to teach the boys how to play softball, or to read stories to the girls. He even had a knack for quieting irritable babies. His friends often teased him that he was so good around children because he was basically an overgrown child himself.

But on a deeper level, Brian knew better. He had a secret yearning to become a father himself one day.

Of course, the fact that all of this would entail finding a bride, settling down and getting married made him very uneasy. Being around Cassie shook him up even more. Surely that was the main reason his thoughts were straying in the uncomfortable direction of home and hearth, a direction diametrically opposed to his purpose here.

He stifled a groan as he recalled her soft curves colliding against him outside the snow-cone stand. Oh, being so close to her had been exquisite torture—the scent of her, the way the wind had pulled wisps of hair free from her helmet, the slightly dazed, expectant look in her eyes.

Was he only kidding himself? He'd wanted to stay here out of guilt over the botched wedding, and to convince Cassie to go back to Chris. He'd been certain Cassie belonged with a steady guy like his cousin, a man who could offer her the lifetime commitment Brian doubted he could ever provide. And he'd been sure that as soon as Cassie discovered what a pain he really was, she'd be delighted to go running back to Chris.

Only the master plan wasn't working out quite as neatly as he had envisioned. From her earlier comments, Cassie had no intention of getting back together with Chris, and knowing how his cousin had treated her, Brian was having difficulty blaming her. So where did that leave them?

On the horns of a real dilemma. With her splurging on a new wardrobe, and him wickedly peeking at her new swimsuit.

"Brian? What do you think?"

Brian all but jumped at the sound of Cassie's soft voice. He glanced up to watch her stroll out of the dressing room in a wispy, form-hugging white cotton dress, a smooth, sleeveless sheath with a scooped neck and short skirt that barely covered her to midthigh. Damn, she had gorgeous legs, just as lovely as his errant thoughts had envisioned. And the dress was the perfect showcase for her beauty— in its demure way, sexy as hell, revealing smooth expanses of gleaming feminine flesh and outlining flawless womanly curves.

Brian gulped. "Um—so we've graduated to dresses now? What's next? Ski suits?"

She giggled. "Brian, be serious. The dress is awfully nice, and the price is irresistible."

*You're irresistible.* Brian almost said it aloud, then caught himself in time. "I've yet to find a woman who can resist a bargain."

Her vibrant green eyes met his, and she appeared touchingly hesitant. "Do you like it?"

Brian's heart was pounding like a kettledrum. "Um—yeah. Sure."

"I thought it might be nice for..."

"Dinner tonight?" he suggested.

"Sure. Why not? We do have to eat."

"Yeah." Brian fought an instinct to squirm. "Cassie, are you finished yet?"

She laughed. "You don't like shopping, do you?"

"I don't like making a career out of it."

"Career? We've only been here for—"

Brian raised his wrist. "Two hours, fourteen minutes, and thirty-seven seconds."

She laughed. "Wow, you really *don't* like shopping."

A roguish smile pulled at his mouth. "Well, maybe I'm just disappointed that I never got to see you in that bikini."

She made a sound of outrage. "Brian, I couldn't just walk out into the middle of the store in a bikini."

"Why not? I can't think of anyone else who could have pulled it off better."

"Well, it would have been scandalous," she declared primly.

"That the real reason, Cassie?"

She smiled. "We women like our secrets."

"Do you ever. You especially like keeping the male of the species in suspense."

"We do."

He slanted her a chiding look, then scowled again at his watch. "And it's getting so late that we may have to wait till tomorrow for our swim."

"Agreed. Anyway, I'm famished."

"After all that shopping, I'm not surprised. Ready to go?"

Cassie was frowning at the tag on her dress. "Just let me change and pay for this."

"Fine. Now you're talking."

Cassie turned and started back toward the dressing room, then stopped to peruse a rack of sundresses, holding out a jade-colored one. "Brian, do you think—"

He jumped to his feet and wagged a finger at her. "Not on your life! I forbid you to buy so much as a bow for your hair. We're out of here, lady."

Grinning with secret pleasure, Cassie moved away.

BRIAN DROVE them back in the small, snazzy green sports car he'd rented in Houston. The radio was playing an apropos Beach Boys tune, and the sunroof was open as they glided down palm-tree-lined Broadway with its historic Victorian mansions.

Inclining his head toward all the bags filling the back seat, Brian winked at Cassie. "Think you did enough damage?"

She groaned. "I'll worry about the bills when I get back."

"That's the spirit."

"Impulsive, right?" she quipped.

"I'm not so sure. Every woman may be impulsive when it comes to shopping."

"Well, at least I did buy a bikini to replace the other one."

He chuckled. "You know, I spotted a Goodwill store as we drove up to the Strand. If you like, we can drop off your entire trousseau there."

"Trousseau," she murmured. "You know, I hadn't thought of it quite that way, but I guess I did pretty much replace my trousseau today."

"All those memories," he reminded. "Want to give it all away, Cassie?"

"No, I think just my old bikini."

"You mean your old, new bikini."

"Right." She laughed.

"Well, we could burn it in a bonfire on the beach, then roast marshmallows afterward."

"Why not?" she declared. "Out with the old and—"

"In with the new?" he suggested.

He gazed intently at her, and she at him, then they both glanced away uneasily.

Guilt stabbed Brian. Why had he hinted he should become the "new" in Cassie's life? His errant libido, that was why! Memories of her in that sexy white dress. Fantasies of her clad in the skimpy new bikini.

Dangerous images all, stirring up feelings he couldn't afford to indulge, and leading him further away from his goal in being here. He was supposed to be here helping Chris, not helping himself to Chris's fiancée.

# 5

"SO, BRIAN, do you miss your job?"

That evening, Cassie sat with Brian at a seafood restaurant at the harbor. Both of them were eating breaded shrimp, cole slaw, and hush puppies. Their table was near a large window, with a nice view of the harbor at sunset, where shorebirds were swarming about docked shrimp boats.

Brian had been unusually reticent during the meal, and Cassie felt it was time to comment on his mood. He also appeared altogether too appealing in his green polo shirt and khaki slacks, especially with the golden light outlining his handsome features and tanned, muscular forearms. The five-o'clock shadow along his strong jaw only added to his masculine allure.

He tossed her a perplexed look and sipped his beer. "What makes you think I miss my job?"

"Well, you've hardly even looked at me during dinner, and you keep rapping your fingertips on the tabletop. Don't you like the food?"

He grinned sheepishly. "Oh, it's wonderful, very fresh."

"But you can't sit still."

He chuckled. "Cassie, I can *never* sit still. That's one aspect I do love about my job—things are constantly changing, new challenges, new decisions to make. There's the pressure of constantly striving to make the best investment choices for my clients. But I love the thrill-ride part, too, relying on my gut as well as on research. Will semiconductors go up today and transportation stocks go down?

Will the upheavals in world markets depress the Dow? That sort of thing.''

"And you miss it?"

He shrugged. "I don't mind working, but I'm not a workaholic, if that's what you're suggesting."

"But you're bored right now."

An unexpected dash of mischief brightened his eyes. "I never said I was bored, Cassie. Tense maybe, but hardly bored."

They gazed at each other in the charged silence.

"And why are you tense?" she dared to ask.

He raised his beer. "I'll take the fifth again."

She chuckled. "What do you do to relieve tension?"

He lifted an eyebrow meaningfully.

"The G-rated version, please," she directed primly.

Appearing amused, he leaned back in his chair. "Oh, there's my rock climbing. Sometimes I'll leave the office early, pop into my Jeep, pick up one of my climbing buddies, and drive straight up into the Rockies, watching the sunset from a mountain pass."

"Sounds spectacular. But isn't it dangerous?"

Surprising her with his vehemence, he replied, "It damn well can be, if you're poorly trained, or overconfident."

"Or impatient?" she suggested.

He solemnly shook his head. "Not when I climb, Cassie. Climbing is one sport at which you literally can't be too cautious. In fact, that was why I was late for your wedding. Got trapped on a ledge in a thunderstorm."

"Ah," she murmured demurely. "I suppose under those circumstances, I might forgive you."

"You'd better," came his indignant response. "I made the climb to pick those flowers for you."

"Yes, those sweet little flowers," she repeated, remembering how those very blooms had created such havoc in her life and set all these crazy events into motion.

"Anyway, I was fortunate to have as my mentor one of the best climbers in Denver," Brian went on. "I know how tricky the sport can be, how long it can take to develop the right judgment, and how the tiniest mistake can result in death. But for the average yo-yo who thinks he can just buy some equipment and try rappelling as a one-shot, fun excursion, the consequences can be lethal." He took a sip of his beer. "My climbing buddies and I have had to rescue a few idiots over the years."

She smiled. "Sounds like you don't get too many opportunities to rap your fingernails."

"Cassie, that's just nervous energy."

"So what else do you do to release it?"

"Why am I sensing another loaded question here?"

Cassie felt her cheeks warming. "Brian, you're doing the loading."

"Am I?"

She waved a hand in defeat. "Okay. Guilty as charged. Do you have girlfriends, Brian?"

"I've been known to," he replied modestly.

"Anyone right now?"

His expression darkened. "Actually, my latest flame dumped me a couple of weeks ago. We spent a weekend together in the mountains, and at ninety-five hundred feet, she wasn't exactly a happy camper."

Cassie chortled. "Probably some minor nuisance like not being able to breathe."

"She mentioned that," he admitted dryly. "She also didn't care for the too-friendly chipmunks that kept trying to join us at meals, and when the temperature dipped into the teens and our drinking water froze over, that was pretty much the last straw. It was your basic camping trip from hell."

Cassie was shaking her head. "What do you find so appealing about roughing it that way?"

He leaned closer and spoke soulfully. "Watching the sunrise over the Rockies. Hearing the quaking of the aspens. Taking a drink from a pristine stream. It's about as close to heaven as a guy can come."

Sensing a hidden meaning in his words, his expression, she pulled back. "I believe you."

Slowly, he leaned back in his chair. "What about you, Cassie?"

"What about me?"

"You've played twenty questions with me. Now it's your turn. What do you do for fun?"

Her smile was self-deprecatory. "Well, I'm not a big outdoorsman—er, *woman*—if that's what you're asking. I kind of got over that in the Girl Scouts."

"Hey, I was a Boy Scout."

"You probably still belong to a troop, eh?" she teased.

He shot her a chiding glance.

Cassie frowned thoughtfully. "Let's see, what are my hobbies? Well, I like to read, shop. I dabble in sewing. Also like going to movies, the theater, the symphony, that sort of thing."

He groaned. "A born city girl."

"Sewing *isn't* city," she protested.

He slapped his forehead. "Right. I stand corrected."

"Furthermore, I like the country life-style as well as anyone else," she continued defensively. "In fact, my mom is really big on antiques, and I used to love it when Dad was tied up and the two of us would take off together. We'd drive through the back roads of Texas and the South, visiting antique stores, sometimes touring old mansions. I've managed to acquire a few nice pieces myself."

Brian rolled his eyes. "Oh, Lord. A born shopper and tourist. I should have known from this afternoon."

"Brian, you're asking for it!" she warned.

He chuckled. "Okay, no more about hobbies. So, do you miss your work?"

"Brian, you're exasperating."

"Answer the question, please," he directed.

She did, albeit through gritted teeth. "Not really. An ad agency can be a real pressure cooker. Like you, I get satisfaction from keeping my clients happy. I'm pretty organized and detail-oriented.''

"Yes. Sewing demands that.''

"Brian!''

"Cool it, Cassie.'' He flashed her a grin. "I actually like the sewing part. And you were saying?''

For a moment, she glowered at him, too flustered by his teasing to speak. Then she snapped her fingers. "Yes, I was saying. About work.''

"Right.''

"Well, at least I don't have to come up with the actual ad campaigns, since we have copywriters and creative people for that. I think that must be the greatest challenge of all.''

"You seem pretty creative to me,'' he commented generously.

She laughed, then turned serious. "Well, it *was* pretty imaginative, the way I broke up with my fiancé. That took real genius.''

An awkward silence descended, then Brian cleared his throat. "You finished?''

"Sure.''

"Dessert?''

"Are you kidding? I'm stuffed.''

"How 'bout a walk along the harbor?''

"Sounds nice.''

Brian tried not to stare at Cassie as they left the restaurant and strolled along the wide promenade that lined the harbor to the east. Music and laughter drifted off an open oyster bar to their left, while additional shrimp boats and tankers floated down the wide channel to their right. The sea breeze was crisp and slightly cooler, and the gilded light of the fading day was lovely.

Lovelier still was the breathtakingly beautiful woman walking beside him in that soft, sexy light.

Unable to resist any longer, Brian turned to look at her. Cassie's sexy white dress hugged her feminine body, revealing her creamy throat and highlighting her nicely rounded breasts, slender waist and shapely hips. The motions and curves of her bare legs enthralled him; his hungry eyes drank in every delicious contour from her smooth thighs to her shapely, sandaled feet. Glancing up at her face, he watched her lick her full lower lip even as the wind pulled sexy wisps of dark blond hair free from her braid.

Brian felt as if a hard fist had slammed into his gut, a fist of desire. The urge to kiss Cassie was overpowering. She looked young, carefree, all too irresistible—though, he noted with satisfaction, there was a bit of tenseness about the way she held her jaw. Was she feeling the same doubts he was feeling—wondering why the two of them were here together, when they were so attracted to each other, but knew a romantic relationship could prove disastrous?

"Penny for your thoughts," he ventured.

She flashed him a smile. "It's so nice here—watching the sun gleam on the water, feeling the wind on my face."

He nodded.

A small frown knitted her brow. "Know what I really don't miss?"

"Tell me."

She sighed, glancing off to watch a sailboat glide down the channel. "Chris. I should, but I don't."

Brian was perturbed. "But you're feeling something, aren't you, Cassie?"

She sighed. "Well, there's guilt."

He glanced away uneasily. "I know."

"And it's like there's something still unfinished between me and Chris," she went on with a perplexed expression. "He's not here, but in a sense he *is* here. Do you know what I mean?"

"Oh, yes," Brian admitted heavily. "Don't you think you need to talk with him again?"

She hesitated over the question. "I don't know. Sooner

or later I suppose I'll have to. But for now, I'd just as soon it's later.''

They strolled along in silence for a few more moments. ''Know what else I was thinking?'' she ventured.

''Yes?''

She paused to smile at him. ''That I should thank you.''

''Thank me?''

Her expression was sweetly luminous. ''Yes, for being here today. It's been great—fun, low-key, just the two of us together, talking, being friends. I need this break before—well, tackling reality again.''

He avoided her eye.

''Did I say something wrong?''

With an uncomfortable expression, Brian gazed at a cargo ship off-loading in the distance. ''You're making me out as too noble.''

''Am I?''

He nodded, daring a glance at her. ''Want to know the real reason I was so quiet—so *tense*—during dinner?''

''Dare I ask?''

His gaze slowly drank her in again, devouring all the seductive curves hidden beneath that virginal white sheath. ''That dress, Cassie.''

She gazed downward. ''My dress?''

He placed his hands on her shoulders. ''Any idea what you do to a guy when you wear a sexy number like that?''

High color bloomed in her cheeks. ''I wasn't trying to be provocative, Brian. The dress just looked so comfortable.''

''Uh-huh.'' Releasing her, he continued walking.

''I bought it for me,'' she insisted, falling into step beside him. ''Besides, this dress is—well, like my emancipation proclamation from Chris.''

''Emancipation?''

Her expression tightened with resentment. ''Chris never would have approved of a dress like this. He's so conservative.''

"Ah." For a moment Brian was perplexed. Then, irresistibly, he grinned. "What a shame. Chris doesn't know what he's missing."

"Brian!"

Earnestly, he explained, "What I mean is, yes, that dress is beguiling, but it's hardly in the streetwalker league. I'd think Chris would be proud to have you wear it." *As I am to have you walking beside me,* he added to himself.

"Well, you're very nice to say that, but Chris would have pitched a fit," Cassie related grimly. "He always wanted me to look like the upwardly mobile, junior-executive wife."

"So you're rebelling against that?"

She shrugged. "I'm supposed to be exploring my more impulsive side, aren't I? Maybe this dress is the real me."

"It certainly *reveals* the real you," he put in dryly.

She blushed deeply. "Brian, stop it before you make me self-conscious."

He held up both hands. "Heaven forbid."

She fought a smile. "You know, this reminds me of the time when I was thirteen, and had to have my tonsils removed. I had the surgery during my Christmas break from school, and the minute I could get up out of bed, I made my mom take me to the mall to buy a party dress."

He laughed. "A party dress? Wasn't that a rather unusual way to celebrate, post-surgically?"

"No, not at all," she explained. "You see, I had missed so many cool Christmas parties due to nonstop bouts of tonsillitis. So once the little boogers were out, I decided there was no way I was going to miss the New Year's Eve dance at Lisa's house." She smiled. "Guess I felt the same way after walking out on Chris."

Brian grimaced. "Oh, Lord. Chris would love to know he's in the same league with a pair of inflamed tonsils."

She snickered. "Brian, really, you're missing the point."

"Which is...?" He snapped his fingers. "Let me guess. You love to shop."

"No," she replied, exasperated. "The point is, I was declaring my freedom. Freedom from my tonsils then, and from Chris now."

"Freeing you for what, Cassie?" he asked carefully.

For a moment the question just hung between them, charging the air.

"I don't know," she admitted at last. "Freeing me just to live my life, I suppose. Isn't that what you believe in, Brian? Freedom, no ties?"

Abruptly he swung around, gazed into her eyes and spoke huskily. "Cassie, at the moment, I'm feeling pretty tied."

She stared up at him helplessly. "Brian, I—I thought we weren't going to start this again."

Cassie's sweet, lost expression tore Brian's control to shreds. He doubted he could survive for the next ten seconds if he didn't kiss her. Would one little kiss be so terrible?

Terrible or not, Brian was beyond resisting. As he leaned closer, he watched Cassie's eyelids flutter shut and knew she was feeling the same turmoil as he was. Lord, she was irresistible. He caught her lips in a lingering, tender kiss. Her mouth was incredibly soft and warm. He could taste the slight saltiness of her lips and could smell the freshness of her breath. Desire stabbed him with painful intensity.

Her eyelids fluttered open and she gazed up at him in uncertainty. Brian died a thousand, slow deaths.

He managed to smile. "*That's* for wearing that dress."

She laughed nervously. "Well, now that I've been chastised—"

"Have you?"

Her gaze darkened, and her voice faltered on her reply. "No."

For a moment Cassie just stared at Brian in that same lost, vulnerable way. The sexual tension was palpable between them, excruciating in its intensity. Then she began stretching toward him, a dreamy expression on her face—

The unconscious gesture of surrender made Brian wild. But just as he was on the verge of crushing her close, a gull swooped low over their heads, cawing raucously. The two broke apart, both breathless and laughing.

"What did we do to offend him?" Brian asked.

"Maybe that's what we get for misbehaving," she teased back.

At once Brian turned sober, not certain whether he was relieved or disappointed over the bird's intrusion. He gazed at Cassie questioningly, watched her awkwardly glance away.

"Maybe," he agreed.

He took Cassie's hand, and they continued down the docks in silence.

# 6

"HI. Ready for our swim?"

These were the first words out of Brian's mouth when Cassie opened the door for him the following morning. He stood in the hallway wearing shorts and a partially unbuttoned tropical shirt, and held a small nylon bag in one hand.

Cassie, wearing a crisp cotton short set she'd bought yesterday, was still sipping her orange juice. Drinking in the sexy man standing across from her, the enticing scents of fresh soap and cologne wafting over her as memories of their sweet kiss bombarded her senses, she wasn't sure she was ready for *anything* with Brian.

She managed a tremulous smile. "My, you're an early bird. Come on in."

He stepped inside. "Well, we need to get outside before the sun gets too hot. And besides, when a guy's been promised he'll at last get to see *the* bikini, believe me, he's on time."

She cast him a chiding look. "You want some orange juice?"

"No, thanks. Already tanked up at the motel restaurant."

She nodded toward the glass doors to the balcony. "You know, when I stepped outside earlier, it seemed awfully windy."

"Still is. Storm flags out, as a matter of fact. That's why I was going to suggest we swim here at your hotel. The pool is shielded on two sides from the Gulf breezes."

She was taken aback. "You mean you already checked?"

He chuckled. "I'm a resourceful fellow."

Eyeing that meaningful glint in his eyes, Cassie said, "Brian..."

"Yes?"

"Let's swim later."

"Later?" He appeared disappointed.

"Perhaps the wind will have died down by then. And I thought—well, why don't we do the tourist thing first?"

He groaned. "The tourist thing. You mean stuffy old museums and galleries?"

"Not exactly. Galveston has a fascinating history—Jean Lafitte, the Moody family, the great 1900 storm. You could learn a lot."

Brian rolled his eyes. "Know what I'd learn, Cassie? Every time I do the 'tourist thing' with a date, we waste half the day in some overpriced gift shop while she spends a small fortune on stationery, potpourri and meaningless knickknacks."

Cassie shook her head. "Brian, you're such a cynic. Besides, I'm not your date."

A flicker of some darker emotion crossed his eyes. "Right, you're not my date. So, what are you, then, Cass? An acquaintance?"

For a moment Cassie was too unsettled to speak. She liked the way "Cass" rolled off Brian's tongue, liked even better his giving her a pet name. Of course she couldn't afford to express those sentiments to him now.

Gently, she replied, "I'd like to think I'm your friend, Brian."

He lifted an eyebrow meaningfully. "My friend. Aren't we dodging the real issue here?"

"Which is?"

"Come on, Cassie, you're not that dense."

"Humor me."

"All right." His passionate gaze held her riveted. "You. Me. Our kiss last night."

Cassie felt her face heating. "I've not forgotten, Brian. That's why I feel we need to lighten up a bit."

"So you're avoiding me."

She laughed. "Avoiding you? Who do you think I'll be with on the tours?"

"You know what I mean," he continued solemnly. "You're avoiding being *alone* with me."

"Are you saying I shouldn't?" she challenged.

He stared at her intently for a moment, then sighed. "No, Cassie. Of course not. Very well—bring on the moldy mansions."

BRIAN TRIED his best to be a good sport as he and Cassie did the tourist thing. He dutifully trooped with her through the three best-known historic houses on Broadway—the Bishop's Palace, Ashton Villa, and the Moody Mansion. He struggled to retain his patience as they strolled through several museums in town.

But it was hard, when his thoughts were consumed by memories of her in his arms last night, and fantasies of what she would look like when she finally donned that sexy bikini—

When all he could do was *want* her.

He felt so torn. He had come here to help Chris, but was straying further and further away from his objective. He was ready to kick himself for coming on to Cassie, yet he couldn't seem to resist her. She was like no woman he'd ever known before—full of fun and humor, with enough imagination to surprise even him, yet also sensible and levelheaded in her own way. Not to mention more demurely sexy than any woman had a right to be. His body hungered for her, when his mind knew he had nothing lasting to offer her, except more heartache.

CASSIE, TOO felt preoccupied, her thoughts still focused on her exciting moments with Brian last night. Intellectually, she was glad they'd been interrupted before they'd gotten in too deep, at a time when she didn't trust her own judgment, when she was still so vulnerable and must practice caution. Yet emotionally and physically, she just wanted to finish what their bodies had begun. Being with Brian was so much fun, such an adventure, and even though he could try her patience, he was a complete doll at heart, without a mean bone in his body. Every time she drew close to him, the urge to give in to her feelings became overpowering, despite the fact that there was no future in it. She was playing with fire, yet she couldn't seem to force herself to back away.

And, from the way Brian was reacting with such impatience to their "tour," she judged he was feeling equally tense and conflicted. At the Center for Transportation and Commerce, he frowned at all the old train cars lined up out in the yard. "What, we don't get to ride them?" he asked Cassie.

Cassie laughed. "You would say that. But you can walk through all the cars."

He shook his head. "It's not the same. Give me a train that moves."

"Well, there's a huge train layout back inside," she suggested.

"Really?"

"But I'm afraid it's not interactive."

His face fell. "Shucks. They won't let me run it?"

"Nope. Sorry."

Brian crossed his arms over his chest and feigned a childlike pout. Cassie broke up laughing.

They had a quick lunch downtown then headed toward the western end of the island. Cassie noted to her relief that Brian seemed to loosen up a bit when they toured the Rainforest Pyramid at Moody Gardens. She felt equally captivated. She found the huge, gleaming glass enclosure enchanting, with its lush tropical foliage and musical sounds of birdsongs. Brian clasped her hand as they strolled among the lily ponds and banyan trees, watching colorful finches and tropical butterflies swoop about, studying macaws and exquisite scarlet ibises. The setting was exotic and very romantic.

When an animal handler walked by with a gorgeous green-and-red parrot perched on his shoulder, Brian held out his arm and asked, "May I?"

The young man appeared flustered. "Sir, we're not supposed to—"

But he stopped in midsentence as the parrot squawked loudly, then flew off his shoulder and landed on Brian's arm, from there quickly climbing to his shoulder and peering about proudly.

"Sorry," Brian muttered, though he appeared pleased as punch.

"Sorry," squawked the parrot, and all three humans laughed.

The boy held out his arm. "Come on, Captain Joe, get on back here."

"Get on back here," echoed the bird.

Cassie studied the parrot's powerful beak and talons. "Brian, are you sure you should be—"

"As a teenager, I worked part-time in a pet store," he assured her, while letting the parrot chew on one of his fingers. "Don't worry, Cassie."

"Don't worry, Cassie," repeated the bird.

Cassie shook her head. "You're certainly full of surprises."

By now, the trainer had removed several grapes from a pouch at his waist and was trying to tempt the bird back. "Here you go, Captain Joe. Mealtime."

"Mealtime!" squawked the bird, sailing off to land on the boy's shoulder.

Watching the trainer and bird move away, Brian grinned. "I'd forgotten how much fun it can be to handle a bird."

"Well, I'm glad we've finally found *something* that interests you."

He eyed her mischievously. "We already did that."

"Behave yourself."

He winked. "You don't want to hear about how good I am at handling women?"

She coughed. "I think I already have an idea."

He squeezed her hand. "Come on, let's go see the fruit bats."

"Fruit bats?" She pulled a face. "Yuck!"

He raised an eyebrow at her. "Yuck? Now you know how I feel about rotting old mansions."

"Brian, they were *not* rotting!"

She playfully punched him in the arm, and he tugged her off with him.


"YOU EVER BEEN tested for attention deficit disorder?" Cassie asked as Brian drove them back toward the condo hotel.

Brian laughed. "I don't need to be tested. I'm sure I'm a hopeless case. But what makes you ask?"

"Oh, when we were touring the Moody mansion, you wouldn't let me stop to read the plaque on the first Mrs. Moody—"

"Borrrrrrring," he echoed. "Can you blame me?"

"Then, in town, you refused to go see the film on the great hurricane—"

"Destruction and desolation made me antsy."

"At the transportation museum, you wouldn't stop and listen to the phone conversations from long ago."

"Maybe I'm more interested in right now."

"That's my point."

He fell thoughtfully quiet a moment. "You know, Cassie, when I see exhibits like that, it makes me sad."

"Sad?"

He nodded. "So many of those people died so young, due to hurricanes, epidemics, you name it. Where are their lives, their hopes, their dreams, now? That's why I like to stay focused on the present and get everything I can out of life.''

"Sounds kind of fatalistic to me."

"To enjoy life moment by moment?" he challenged. "I don't think so. And so many people live their lives for the future, not now. Like my dad."

"Yes?" she prompted, intrigued.

He frowned thoughtfully. "My father owns a small trucking business, and my mom is his bookkeeper as well as a homemaker. Dad slaved all his life to put me and my two sisters through college. Now he's in his fifties, and still working like mad to save for his and Mom's retirement. My point is, he's not enjoying his life."

"And that bothers you? Do you think people with families can't enjoy themselves?"

"All the responsibilities sure can hamper enjoyment. I know this was true for my folks." His brow grew deeply furrowed. "And tell you what—if I make a killing in the market, things are going to change for them."

She gazed at him tenderly. "You're a good son."

He chuckled. "A good son? Don't believe it for a minute. Growing up, I was more trouble than triplets. Just ask my mom."

"Ah, so it's your guilt speaking now?"

"Smart girl," he quipped back. "And if I can help out my folks in the future, believe me, I will."

She nodded.

"What about your family, Cassie?" he went on.

"My folks have struggled, too," she admitted, "but things are a little better for them, now that my brother Todd and I are on our own." She sighed. "Just wish I didn't disappoint them like I did with the wedding. They were great about it, but I know my actions hurt them both emotionally and financially. In fact, if Chris hadn't acted like such a jerk after the rehearsal dinner, well, I'm sure I'd be married to him now."

Brian appeared perturbed. "Are you certain he hasn't reconsidered things?"

She gestured passionately. "So what if he has? He's reversed himself too many times, on too many issues. He lacks character, and I just can't trust him. At least with you—"

"Yes, Cassie?" he asked tensely.

She flashed him a sincere, grateful smile. "You haven't tried to deceive me, Brian. You haven't represented yourself as anything but what you are."

"Yeah, what I am," he repeated grimly. "A wolf in sheep's clothing, perhaps?"

"Brian, that's not what I said."

"But it's about what I feel," he admitted. "You're giving me too much credit again. I'm not very proud of myself right now."

"And why not?"

"You know I came down here to help Chris."

"I know."

His agitation was evident in his voice. "But the more I learn about him, the less sympathy I have for him."

"I know."

"He had everything going for him, and he threw it away."

"Guess he did."

Brian's hands tightly gripped the steering wheel. "And the more I'm around you…"

"I know," she acknowledged.

Braking to a stop for a red light, he turned and gazed into her eyes. "Then you know what a hard time I'm having keeping my hands off you?"

"Yes." Her voice trembled. "But we can't do anything about it, Brian."

"We can't?"

She met his gaze soberly. "It's just too soon for me. I'm still too confused, and this might not be real. And besides, Chris is somehow still there between us."

"In what sense?"

A wistful smile curved her lips. "Well, it's just like back in high school. One time, my best girlfriend broke up with her steady, and I had a huge crush on him. But I never would have dreamed of dating him."

"Why not?"

"Because it's an unwritten rule. You don't go out with your best friend's ex. Translated to this situation, the rule reads, 'You don't go out with your ex-fiancé's cousin.' "

Brian laughed and accelerated the car again.

"What's so funny?"

"Well, I'm afraid I never was much for high-school rules."

"Oh," she muttered. "Then we could be in trouble."

"Yeah," he agreed.

They turned onto the seawall, and Brian rolled down his window, causing a wave of heat to roll in. He whistled. "Lord, the air is like steam."

"I know. Galveston can be a real pressure cooker in the summer."

"You hot?"

She glowered. "Brian, why do you keep asking me if I'm hot?"

He flashed his dimples. "Cassie, you're the one who keeps sensing a double entendre in my words."

"Just sensing?"

He chuckled. "Okay, guilty as charged. But I was wondering if you're ready for our swim yet."

Peering out at the billowy Gulf, Cassie pulled a face. "In that? Looks like the wind hasn't died down at all."

"Then we'll stick with plan two—the pool back at your hotel. Okay?"

Cassie hesitated, still reluctant to place herself in Brian's intimate company while practically unclothed. Then she realized how silly she was being. This was Galveston, and sooner or later they would have to go swimming together.

Besides, she loved the water, and perhaps the physical activity might take the edge off for them both.

Yeah, sure.

"Yes, I could stand to cool off," she told Brian.

"Me, too," he added dryly.

She cast him a scolding glance. "Brian, don't go getting ideas."

His laugh was self-deprecatory. "Cassie, I already *have* ideas."

"TIME FOR the unveiling."

Twenty minutes later, after they'd both changed at Lisa's condo, Cassie stood in the deserted pool area with Brian. The pool itself was a pleasing kidney shape, its gleaming white apron lined with chaises; just as Brian had promised, the hotel's exterior walls shielded the expanse from southerly and western winds, though the air was definitely hot and buoyant.

Brian's typically impatient remark was little distraction from the provocative reality that he now wore only a navy swim brief, and carried nothing more than a towel that covered one muscular forearm. Cassie was painfully conscious of the beauties of his physique—the splendidly muscled chest and arms, the flat belly, the sinewy legs with their covering of coarse masculine hair, the bulge between his thighs that his form-hugging brief only enhanced. She was beginning to regret her bravado in the car, and felt very vulnerable alone with him in her bikini, even though she wore a thick terry cover-up—which she would soon have to remove.

Setting down his towel, Brian rubbed his hands together. "Well, Cassie?"

Cassie blushed. "Brian, really. It's only a bikini."

"So, let's see it."

Casting him an admonishing look, she removed her wrapper to reveal the pink-and-fuchsia-printed suit with its skimpy top and equally brief bottom. She glanced up to see Brian devouring her with his eyes.

Brian's gaze was, indeed, riveted to the enchanting creature standing before him. Why was it that the sight of a woman in a bikini was sexier even than the sight of her naked? It was the titillation, the promise of even greater delights. The way her bikini top barely cupped her ripe breasts, teasing him with the enticing valley of cleavage open to his view. And when she turned to lay her wrapper on a chair, it was the way the bottom rode high over her buttocks, tantalizing him with a glimpse of a firm bottom he ached to sink his fingers into. And those legs. So creamy, long and smooth.

Lord, he had better get a grip. Ever since he'd first taken a peek at Cassie's new bikini yesterday, he'd been dying to see her *in* it. Now he'd gotten his wish, and was landing himself in the deep end before they'd even started swimming.

Turning back around, Cassie felt herself breaking out in gooseflesh at Brian's hot perusal. Feeling more self-conscious by the moment, she cleared her throat. "You like it?"

His voice came out husky. "It's perfect. The only way it could be more perfect is if—"

"Yes?" she asked breathlessly.

"You weren't wearing it at all."

"Brian, really!"

He stared at her, and she stared back in the charged silence.

Then he stepped closer. "Tell me something."

"Yes?"

"Did you buy it for me, Cassie?"

She guiltily glanced away. "I—I bought to feel free from Chris—"

"Free *with* me?" he suggested.

She slowly shook her head. "My Lord, you're cocky, to assume you'd have that much influence over me."

He grinned. "Then I don't?"

Cassie wasn't about to answer such a provocative question, nor could she bear any more of the excruciating tension. Desperate to lighten things up, she grabbed a child's duck-shaped life preserver from a nearby chaise and threw it at Brian. "There. Go play with your rubber ducky."

"That does it!" Laughing, Brian tossed the toy aside and started toward her with a meaningful glint in his eyes. "Now you're going to get it."

"No, I'm not."

Cassie raced for the deep and dived in, squealing as the coolness hit her near-naked body full-force. She heard Brian splash in after her, but the promised retribution did not come right away. He began swimming laps as if training for the Olympics. Cassie paddled about and played, swimming on her back and gazing up at the beautiful, clear skies.

Long moments later, she was working her way toward the shallow end when she felt him catching her hand and pulling her upright to face him. He looked gorgeous, water gleaming on his beautiful body, droplets glistening on his hair, face and eyelids.

He stared at her, smiling as he brushed moisture from her cheek. "I didn't have the heart to dunk you," he admitted. "Though you did deserve it."

"Thank you," she replied primly.

Abruptly, his expression grew dark, purposeful. "Don't thank me, because I'm not finished."

Brian pulled Cassie close and passionately kissed her, and all the tension and hard-fought attraction between them seemed to burst in that moment. For Cassie, the sensation was incredible, Brian's smooth wet flesh surrounding her and his warm tongue seeking the sanctuary of her mouth. She reeled, her body thrilling to conflicting yet overwhelmingly pleasurable sensations. How could she be so cold from the water yet so warm in Brian's embrace, so hot deep inside herself where she longed to feel his body claiming hers? Whatever the logic, the effect on her senses was devastating. As if she'd been robbed of all will, she surrendered to his kiss, her mouth opening wide, her hands caressing the strong slick muscles of his shoulders, his arms, his back. Gently she pushed her tongue past Brian's teeth, and heard his tortured moan as he crushed her closer.

When at last they broke apart breathlessly, his fingers were teasing the back clasp on her bikini top, and his gaze was fixed on her breasts, on the taut nipples prominent even through the cloth of her suit. She heard him catch a raspy breath, saw a muscle work in his jaw.

His gaze slid up her throat to her eyes, and burned with fire when it met hers. "Why don't we lie out awhile? I'd like to coat you with cocoa butter, then—"

She pulled back, shivering. "Brian, if you don't mind, I'm a little cold."

"That can be fixed." He moved to embrace her, but she backed away again.

"The—the pool is in a shadow and the water is colder than I expected."

"All the more reason to lie out in the sun."

"But—I'm hungry," she blurted.

"What?" He appeared stunned. "We've only gotten started swimming."

"Yes, but I'm *really* hungry," she hastily added. "Think I could eat a T-bone steak. That wasn't much of a lunch we had, you know. And all this—well, this *swimming,* is really making me—"

All at once, he laughed.

"Did I say something funny?" she asked, frowning.

Brian was shaking his head. "Cassie, you delight me. I must admit I'm fascinated to learn of your various passions. Let's see…" He began to count on his fingers. "There's shopping. Touring. Eating. And…" Lecherously, he wiggled his eyebrows. "Is there a fourth?"

Outraged, Cassie splashed him but good.

Laughing, Brian caught her wrists. "All right. When

you're hungry, I'll feed you.'' He leaned over and barely touched her lips with his own.

Cassie moaned, then wiggled away, climbing out of the pool while she could still summon the will to do so. She dared not look back at Brian. She was hungry now—no, starved—but it wasn't for food.

Brian stood watching her, his gaze riveted to her sleek, dripping, delectable body, his fists clenched at his sides. He hadn't intended to kiss Cassie again just now—but, once more, *not* kissing her had become impossible. God, she had been an angel in his arms, wet, curvy, and slick. The feel of her skimpily clad breasts pressing into his chest had been agonizingly sweet. And the taste of her tongue in his mouth—Lord, the memory alone made him tremble.

Damn, damn, damn! He was getting them both in trouble again, his desires for Cassie overwhelming his better judgment. What was he going to do?

Brian turned and began vigorously swimming laps until he was almost too exhausted to move.

# 7

THE NEXT MORNING, Brian was supposed to pick Cassie up early. When he didn't arrive, she went down to the lobby to wait for him.

Entering the sunny expanse, she was surprised to hear the sounds of male laughter, then bemused to see Brian at a table playing poker with three elderly gentlemen. Moving closer, she noted that a large jar stuffed with pennies evidently served as the official cache for the game. By now, all four men were scowling over the cards just dealt them by a white-haired gentleman who served as dealer, and Cassie smiled at the sight of the earnest frown on Brian's face.

Then he spotted her, glanced at his watch, and popped to his feet. "Cassie, goodness, I'm sorry. I was early, and got involved in this game—"

She waved him off. "Finish your hand."

By now the three elderly gentlemen were all staring at Cassie with interest. "That your girlfriend?" one of them asked Brian.

"Yep," he acknowledged proudly.

Cassie felt herself blushing at Brian's brazen acknowledgment, but didn't have the heart to correct him. Another man gestured toward a nearby chair. "Have a seat, young lady. But no spying."

"Oh, I wouldn't dream of it," Cassie declared primly, seating herself.

As Brian also sat down, the last gentleman spoke up. "Actually, miss, why don't you just take him away? He's robbing us blind."

Ignoring chuckles from the others, Brian glowered and arranged his cards. "Sore loser."

Cassie watched in amusement as the men requested new cards, though Brian, expression smug, held on to all of his.

The first man pushed forward a stack of pennies. "I'll open the bidding at ten."

"I'll see your ten and raise you five," declared next man.

"I'll see your five and raise you fifty," drawled Brian.

*"Fifty?"* gasped the fourth man. "You're bluffing!"

"Then call my bluff," he suggested.

"Ah, heck," grumbled the man, throwing in his cards.

Another man also folded, then the last holdout met Brian's bet. "All right, sonny, I'm calling you." Grinning, he held up his hand. "How are you planning to beat a full house?"

Brian held up four tens. "How 'bout with four of a kind?"

Amid much groaning and grumbling, the man threw in his cards. Brian stood. "Well, gents, it's been fun."

"Sure, fun for *you*," declared the loser.

"You want to collect your pennies, sonny?" another man inquired.

Brian was helping Cassie to her feet. "Naw, use my share to stoke the pump."

All three oldsters grinned.

Cassie and Brian said their goodbyes and left. Outside, she burst out laughing. "Remind me never to gamble with *you*."

His expression was one of secret amusement. "You mean you *aren't* gambling with me, Cassie?"

Her look was reproachful. "Evidently you must think so, since you called me your girlfriend back there."

He held up both hands. "Hey, it was the other guy who said it. I was only playing along."

"Uh-huh. States the artful dodger."

He flashed her a guilty grin. "What can I say? I was with three other guys. It was a male-pride issue."

"Male pride, eh?"

He wrapped an arm around her waist. "Yeah, and I'm *very* proud to be with you."

Privately charmed, Cassie didn't comment as they strolled toward the car. "So, I hadn't realized you were into poker, Brian. Do you visit casinos in Colorado?"

"Oh, I've been known to take dates to Central City or Cripple Creek."

"Guess all those lights and noises must keep you well occupied, huh?"

"Cassie," he scolded, opening her door.

She was still chuckling as he got in the car beside her. "I never would have pictured you with a bunch of older guys like that."

"Why not? I'll have you know I enjoy people of all ages. I've always played chess with my grandfather."

"Have you? That speaks well of you, Brian."

"Good. I'm managing to charm you." He started the engine. "So, what will we do today?"

"Gee, I hadn't really thought."

"Well, my poker buddies suggested we go over to Bolivar Peninsula."

"Oh, yeah. Riding the ferry is always fun."

"There's evidently some interesting mudflats, as well as a park there. We could pick up a bucket of chicken and have a picnic."

"Sounds good."

"They said the park even has some armaments and bunkers left over from World War II."

"Ah. This from the man who scoffs at history?"

"I merely scoff at moldy old mansions," he explained. "My grandfather was a Navy man, stationed in the Pacific."

Cassie snapped her fingers. "Right, war. Big boats, guns, tanks. Classic guy stuff. This is the grandfather you play chess with?"

"Yeah—my mom's dad. My other grandfather died

when I was young, but Granddad really made up for that. He's the best.''

"Wish I could meet him," she said without thinking.

Instead of retreating from her words, Brian merely grinned. "Then we'll just have to arrange that, won't we?''

Cassie was thoughtfully silent as he backed the car then drove out of the parking lot. Brian had so many endearing qualities—his charm, his consideration toward others—and all of them made her want more than friendship with him, even though she shouldn't. It was still too soon for her.

They drove through a fast-food restaurant, buying a bucket of chicken and fixings, then stopped at a convenience store, where Brian purchased a cheap Styrofoam cooler and filled it with sodas and ice. They continued to the Bolivar ferry and followed the other cars onto one of the large boats.

As the ferry glided away from the dock, they got out of the car and moved toward the bow of the ship. The morning was warm and sunny, the air smelling of the sea and fish. Cassie enjoyed feeling the wind in her face, watching the gulls swoop about, and the barges plod down the channel. She relished having Brian by her side, especially when he slipped his arm about her waist. The two laughed over the antics of some dolphins diving about close to the vessel.

"Now there's something I don't see in Colorado," he murmured.

"Not many ferries or dolphins there, eh?''

For once appearing serious, he stared down into her face. "There's a *lot* that isn't there, Cassie."

She glanced away, cheeks hot and pulse thrumming.

Soon they reached the other side and followed the long string of cars onto the narrow, barren peninsula. They drove along the main road, passing a convenience store and an old, abandoned lighthouse. Soon after they passed a sub-division of beach homes, Brian turned at a sign that read Bolivar Flats. He drove them down a dirt road to the beach.

They parked and strolled along the sandy flats, which

were teeming with thousands of shorebirds—sandpipers digging in the mud, herons diving for fish just offshore, gulls swooping about overhead. They laughed at the sight of two seagulls trying to steal a fish from a smaller bird.

"This is the life," said Brian, stretching his arms with a happy sigh. "Perhaps in my next life, I'll be a shorebird."

"Yes, all that wing-flapping should keep you busy," she agreed drolly.

Brian was throwing her a mock scowl when both noticed an elderly couple, wearing khakis and brandishing binoculars, moving toward them from a sand dune. "Hello there," called the man in a clipped British accent. "Have you folks ever seen so many godwits and dowitchers about? Not to mention the red knots and terns south of here. Why, this even surpasses Padre Island—Rose and I were down there just last week."

"Were you?" Brian asked, smiling at the two. "You know to me, it just looks like a bunch of birds digging in the mud."

The duo laughed. "I don't suppose you folks have heard of the whereabouts of the parasitic jaeger that's been spotted along the coast here?" the woman inquired anxiously. "It's such a rare species, and Horace and I were hoping to add it to our life lists before our group departs for the Rio Grande Valley."

"The parasitic jaeger?" Brian repeated, rubbing his jaw.

"We're dying to catch a glimpse of him," put in the man.

Brian snapped his fingers. "I know. He's been spotted out on the east end of Galveston Island."

"You're sure?" asked the woman.

"Positive."

The woman clapped her hands. "Oh, Horace, this is splendid. We must go over there straightaway!"

"Indeed," agreed the man. "Thank you, young man."

"Oh, it's nothing," Brian assured them.

Cassie watched the duo rush off with her mouth hanging open. "Brian!"

"Yes?" he inquired innocently.

Irate, she balled her hands on her hips. "I can't believe you just lied to those nice people."

He shrugged, though his expression was full of mischief. "Well, it was good to get rid of them. I could tell the lecture on ornithology was on its way, any second now."

Cassie made a sound of disbelief. "How dare you! You sent them off on a wild-goose chase!"

He grinned. "I thought bird-watchers *liked* wild-goose chases."

"Brian!"

"Cassie, Brits are fanatical about bird-watching."

"Of course I know that," she retorted. "A lot of them visit the Texas coast because our bird-watching here is so spectacular."

"They visit Colorado, too," he informed her cynically. "Lord knows I've run into enough of those nuts in the Rockies. And besides, I didn't lie to those Brits."

She shook a finger at him. "Oh, yes, you did! Come, now. Admit you know nothing about the parasitic wagger."

"Jaeger," he corrected. "And darn straight I know about it. I can't believe how poorly informed you are. That rare bird's arrival on the island is the talk of the town right now. One of my poker buddies mentioned it this morning."

She waved a hand. "I give up. I never would have pegged you for a liar."

Now he appeared stern. "Cassie, I was an Eagle Scout, and Eagle Scouts *never* lie."

She rolled her eyes.

"Tell you what," he went on. "If I'm lying, I'll spring for dinner, anywhere you like. And if I'm telling the truth..." His eyes twinkled. "I get a very sweet, very contrite kiss."

Though Cassie was more thrilled by his titillating offer than she cared to admit, she affected a shrug. "Sure.

Since's there's no way to prove you're right or wrong, why not?''

After they finished exploring the flats, they drove over to the adjoining Fort Travis Seashore Park, parked and strolled about the grassy grounds, examining old gun armaments and abandoned bunkers. They even stepped down into a tiny lookout bunker not far from the Gulf. The inside was lined with concrete and hardly larger than a phone booth.

"One of the old gents said lookouts were stationed here during Word War II," Brian explained.

"Yuck, kind of a cramped place to spend much time watching for enemy ships or planes," Cassie commented.

Brian was peering out the slitlike window toward the Gulf. "Especially since the enemy never showed up. Now, if a soldier had *you* for company—"

"Yes?" she asked.

He winked. "Then heaven help this island if it had ever really gotten attacked."

She shot him a chiding glance. "Clearly it's time for us to move on."

Brian chuckled.

They continued to make their rounds through the park, strolling around the camping area, where a few families were staying in RVs, trailers, or shelters. Not far from the playground, Cassie spotted three boys, all of whom appeared to be around ten or twelve, skateboarding on a large abandoned concrete foundation.

Watching one of the boys attempt an airborne stunt, then fall on his rump as his skateboard went careening off, Cassie winced. "Brian, did you see that?"

"Yeah," he answered, and ran off toward the boys.

Intrigued, she raced after him. By the time she joined the others, Brian had already helped the fallen boy to his feet and was dusting him off.

"You okay?" he asked.

The boy, a cute redhead with freckles, nodded. "Yes, sir. Thanks. But I feel pretty dumb."

"You shouldn't," Brian answered. "Mastering an ollie isn't easy."

All the boys appeared intrigued, gathering about Brian. "You know about ollies, sir?" asked a second.

Brian drew himself up proudly. "You're looking at the former Midwest Skateboarding champ."

"Wow," declared the boy.

"Cool!" said a third.

"You know, an ollie requires just the right popping maneuver to get off the ground, as well as some very tricky footwork and balance," Brian told the boys.

"Would you show us, sir?" asked the boy who had fallen.

"Sure."

Cassie watched in amazement as Brian demonstrated some skateboarding basics for the enthralled boys, showing them the ollie, the ollie flip, and even a heelflip. The boys clapped and cheered as he made the skateboard dance with all the skill of a master. Even Cassie became enthralled, watching him maneuver, spin and flip the board. It was so ironic. Brian was behaving like an overgrown child, but he excited her so as a man. Perhaps because he didn't hesitate to meet these children on their own terms, because he gave no thought to his own dignity—and especially because he was so kind to help them. Chris Carlisle wouldn't have been caught dead giving skateboarding lessons to a group of juveniles.

As for Brian, he was too perfect—as she well knew from her own unsettled emotions.

Soon, a bearded man in jeans and western shirt strode up to join them, and one of the boys rushed up to him. "Dad, this man is helping Pete," he declared. "He's a skateboard champ."

"Good," replied the father, grinning at Cassie. "I'm

glad you boys found some help. I was afraid y'all were going to end up in the hospital.''

As everyone else watched, Brian guided Pete through the steps of the ollie, until he mastered the short flight through the air on his own. Afterward, the small group cheered as the boy stood grinning and holding his board aloft like a trophy.

Brian ended with a safety lecture. "Now I want all of you guys to promise me you'll get helmets and pads, and that you'll master all the basic moves before you even try any complex tricks, much less wallriding."

The boys eagerly gave their word, and the father stepped forward to shake Brian's hand. "Thanks for coaching the boys."

"My pleasure."

After he exchanged high fives with the boys, Brian and Cassie strolled off. Moments later, sitting at a picnic table with Brian and nibbling at chicken, Cassie was shaking her head. "You were great with those kids."

"I love kids," he admitted.

"You do?"

"Oh, yes. I'm a big brother back in Denver."

She was taken aback. "You're referring to the Big Brother/Big Sister program?"

He nodded. "My kid is named Otis Cleburne. He's eleven, from one of the worst projects in Denver. Otis's father is in prison, and his mother was killed in a drive-by shooting."

"How terrible."

"I know. But the kid has a wonderful grandmother who makes him go to church every Sunday." He chuckled. "Lois and I are determined to keep him on the straight-and-narrow path."

"Are you succeeding?"

"Oh, yes. I've already promised Otis I'm going to see him through college, even if I have to pay for it myself."

"Brian! That's quite a responsibility you've taken on."

He regarded her earnestly. "I'm serious, Cassie. But the kid is also shaping up to be a great basketball player. We shoot baskets together often. I'm sure he'll win a scholarship, especially if he keeps up his grades."

She shook her head. "You're amazing."

"But not so amazing that you don't still think I'm a liar?" he teased.

"You definitely lied to the bird-watchers."

He chuckled.

She thoughtfully nibbled at her chicken. "You know it's odd, Brian. You like kids, but you don't want any."

"What makes you think I don't want any? I have Otis."

"You know what I mean—your own kids, a family of your own."

He nodded. "Ah—marriage."

"You say that as if it's a prison sentence."

"I do not."

"Brian!"

He smiled sheepishly. "Well, perhaps it is a bit daunting to someone who's not quite ready."

"Aha."

Brian propped his chin in his hand and gazed at her. "Come to think of it, my attitude is odd, as much as I do like kids."

Now Cassie was becoming uncomfortable. She pretended to be fascinated with selecting her next piece of chicken.

"I love babies, too," he remarked.

Rattled, she dropped a drumstick. "You do?"

"I'm in big demand with my sisters."

"Tell me about that."

He chuckled. "I have twin older sisters, Sidney and Shelley."

"Ah. So twins run in your family?"

"They do. Anyway, four years ago, the twins got married in a double service."

"What fun."

"Then, two years later, within days of each other, they both delivered."

"Delivered—babies?"

"Yeah. I'm an uncle thrice over."

"Thrice?" She laughed.

"Shell had a little girl, and Sid had twin boys."

"Wow! You really *are* an uncle."

"And I'm a very popular guy—well, baby-sitter. When all else fails, I'm the only one who can stop my niece and nephews from crying. In fact, my mom brags that I'm the only man she's ever known who can stop any baby from crying."

Cassie shot him an incredulous look. "Now wait just a minute! No man can stop *any* baby from crying."

Brian appeared supremely pleased with himself. "Honey, you're looking at him."

"And you're lying again."

He threw a wishbone at her.

She tossed it back. "Hey, stop that, right now."

He leaned toward her. "Cassie, I *can* stop any baby from crying. I think maybe it's because babies fascinate me. Have you ever watched one?"

"Well, sure. I watched my niece and nephew when they were tiny."

Brian's expression was awed. "An infant is always in motion, waving his hands or chewing on his toes. Always looking around, cooing, gurgling, laughing."

"Yes, all that activity. No wonder you're fascinated."

He frowned. "You still think I'm lying."

"Yep. Let's see—birds and babies. Do you lie about bees, as well?"

He snapped his fingers. "Actually, I have an uncle who's a beekeeper."

"And you can calm any bee," she provided cynically.

"Nope," he replied. "Bees freak me out. It's babies I love."

Cassie was breaking up with laughter. "Liar!"

Brian shook a finger at her. "Enough, woman. We're really going to sweeten the pot now. When I prove I'm *not* lying, I get two kisses."

"And when I prove you *are*, I get two dinners."

"Fine. You got a deal."

She feigned a yawn. "Whatever. It's all useless speculation, anyway. You'll never be able to prove you're right, just as I'll never be able to prove you're wrong."

"Never?" He smiled with secret pleasure. "We'll see."

THE LINE of cars returning to the ferry was unexpectedly long, and the wind was brisk, the water bumpy as they rode back across the channel. After they finally recrossed and drove off the boat, they stopped to visit the picnic and restroom facility on the other side.

Exiting the ladies' room, Cassie found Brian pouring soft drinks for them at a picnic table near the water. "Thirsty?" he called.

"Yes." She took the cup he extended and drank heartily. "Um, that's good."

He gestured toward the choppy bay. "Just look at those whitecaps. Looks like it's going to shape up as a perfect evening to go sailing. How 'bout we rent a boat tonight?"

"After this long excursion, you still want more?" she asked.

Lifting his cup, he said wickedly, "I always want more."

Cassie groaned. She had asked for that one.

"You don't have to go," he added casually. "Why don't you just turn in early?"

She wrinkled her nose at him. "I ain't a granny yet."

They were smiling at each other when both tensed at the loud sounds of a baby wailing. Brian glanced at a table in the distance. "Well, would you look at that?"

Cassie turned to see two women in casual clothes with a shrieking baby girl in a yellow dress. The younger woman, obviously the child's mother, was trying to get the baby to take a bottle even as she wailed and shoved it away.

The older woman, who appeared to be the grandmother, looked on fretfully and offered suggestions.

"Oh, the poor thing. She must be late for her nap," Cassie murmured.

Brian grinned. "Yeah, and this is my perfect opportunity to convince you I wasn't lying."

She was flabbergasted. "You're not going to quiet *that* baby."

"Oh, I'm not? You just watch," he stated confidently, striding off.

"This I've got to see," Cassie muttered, starting after him.

They arrived at the other table, only to have the two women eye them with perplexity and some suspicion.

Brian smiled. "Hello, ladies. My friend and I were wondering if you needed some help."

Before the mother could respond, the older woman said crossly, "No, thanks. Can't you see we've got our hands full here?"

"Well, that's just it," Brian continued, undaunted. "I was bragging earlier to my friend that I can quiet any baby, and she refused to believe me. So, you ladies could settle a bet for us."

Now the grandmother scowled. "I think you'd better leave."

But the mother was eyeing Brian with interest as she struggled to pacify the squalling infant, who was sobbing and squirming against her shoulder. "You really can quiet any baby?" she asked doubtfully.

"I'm the Houdini of babies. Want me to demonstrate?"

Before either woman could respond, Cassie stepped in. "I know you must think my friend is nuts, but I promise you he's an okay guy. He's helped his sisters raise three babies, and he's also a big brother for a ghetto child."

"Well..." The mother seemed to be wavering, but the grandmother was still frowning.

Even as the women hesitated, the most amazing thing

happened. First, the bawling baby twisted about in her mother's arms. Cassie noticed how adorable she was, with her full cheeks so flushed and her mouth screwed up in a pout. Then she spotted Brian. Brian grinned and made a face. The baby whimpered and stared, her lower lip trembling. Brian stuck his thumbs in his ears and wiggled his fingers. The baby frowned and hiccuped, then stuffed a thumb in her mouth and began to suck. Finally, as Brian rolled his eyes and pulled another goofy face, the baby giggled and cooed at him.

The mother and grandmother regarded each other in amazement. "Good grief! I've never seen nothing like this," declared the grandmother.

"Me neither," said the mother.

Brian held out his hands and smiled. "May I?"

Everyone was further astounded when the baby waved her plump arms and legs at Brian and squealed, obviously imploring him to pick her up!

"Be my guest," said the mother, handing over her child.

In Brian's arms, the child chortled and made eyes at him, tugging at the collar of his polo shirt, and gleefully grabbing handfuls of his curly hair.

With a superior air, Brian turned to Cassie. "Well?"

"I give up. You *can* quiet any baby in the world."

"You sure can," said the mother, popping up. "Say, do you want a job? We've been looking for a good nanny. Of course you'd have to have the best references, and—"

Laughing, Brian shook his head. "Wish I could." Gently, he transferred the baby back to her mother's arms. When she began to pout, he wagged a finger at her. "Now you be good for Mama."

The baby gurgled again, and both women shook their heads in mystification. "Thanks, mister," said the mom.

"Thank *you*," said Brian.

As Brian and Cassie walked away, she heard not another peep out of the child. When she glanced at him, he raised an eyebrow in triumph. "Well?"

Cassie remained stunned. "If I hadn't seen it with my own two eyes, I never would have believed it."

"Right." At the table, Brian grabbed the cooler and they walked back to the car. He quickly stowed the cooler, then turned to her, his expression devilish. "Now you owe me a kiss."

"You rascal."

He was leaning toward her when they both jumped at the sounds of a horn blaring, and a loud, British-accented voice called, "Sonny! Oh, sonny!"

They turned to view the British couple in a subcompact car waiting in line for the ferry. Brian grabbed Cassie's hand and tugged her over to the car. "Well, imagine seeing you two again," he greeted cheerily.

"We just wanted to thank you," the woman gushed. "The parasitic jaeger was exactly where you said it would be."

"You're welcome," Brian said, flashing Cassie a smug grin.

Cassie groaned.

"Now we're on our way back to Bolivar to inform the rest of our group," added the man.

"Good luck to you, then," said Brian.

Walking back toward the car with Brian, Cassie could feel his gaze boring into her.

"Well, Cassie?" he demanded at last.

She turned to him, struggling not to laugh. "You planned all this, didn't you?"

"*What?*"

"You hired those bird-watchers, and the women with the baby, to make a fool out of me."

"Cassie, really." He crossed his arms over his chest and glowered. "You did that all by yourself."

"Oh!" Outraged, she began pummeling him playfully.

He caught her wrists. "Well, Cassie?"

She sighed. "Okay, so you didn't lie."

"Either time."

"*Either* time."

"I'm an Eagle Scout, and Eagle Scouts never lie."

She rolled her eyes.

"Say it, Cassie."

"Okay! You're an Eagle Scout, and Eagle Scouts never lie. There. So tell me, are you perfect, too?"

He flashed his devastating dimples. "What do you think? And by the way, now you owe me *two* kisses."

Cassie snapped her fingers. "Shucks. There go two great dinners."

In the next instant, Brian pulled her close, and she was gazing up into his vibrant, challenging eyes. Oh, this man was irresistible, and she was falling for him—hard.

"So you prefer food to my kisses?" he demanded.

Cassie snickered. "I take the fifth."

At first Brian appeared ready to call her bluff. Then, even as she waited in delicious anticipation, he took a deep, bracing breath of sea air and slowly released it.

"You know, this is going to be a simply grand evening for sailing," he murmured.

"What?" she asked, taken aback.

"Later, Cassie," he said meaningfully.

As he helped her into the car, Cassie found the "later" more provocative than any kiss could have been....

THAT NIGHT, Cassie sat next to Brian in a small sailboat out in the moonlit bay. The two were huddled close together on the narrow bench near the stern of the craft as Brian expertly worked the rudder and trimmed the sail. Armed with running lights, the mainsail fully catching the brisk breeze, the craft skidded smoothly over the waves. The night was cool and glorious, the swells edged in silvery foam, the large yellow moon framed by pale wisps of clouds.

The setting couldn't possibly be more romantic, especially with the dreamy man sitting beside Cassie, and especially since she was all too aware that she still owed him two kisses. Kisses she'd been shamelessly anticipating for hours now.

What was she going to do? She hadn't meant to fall for Brian so quickly. But he was such a sweetheart—kind, if mischievous, but always so much fun to be with. And he was honest, so unlike the hypocritical Chris. He didn't try to con her with promises or lies. That she found most endearing of all. She *trusted* him.

It was her own feelings she didn't trust. Not now.

As he navigated them over a tall, rolling wave, the craft hiked windward. Cassie gasped and instinctively leaned closer to him to help counterbalance the boat. "Are you sure this isn't dangerous?" she asked tremulously.

"Naw," he reassured her, guiding the craft across an even larger swell.

"It's so beautiful, Brian—so special," she whispered.

"*You're* special," he whispered back.

His tender words set her heart to racing. "Brian, please," she pleaded.

"No, it's true," he insisted, then solemnly winked. "Just look out at those waves, Cassie. I doubt we can find a sea nymph or mermaid who can hold a candle to you."

She laughed. "Now there's a compliment I can accept with complete modesty."

"What did I tell you? You're humble, too."

Cassie was chuckling, only to squeal and squeeze Brian's arm as the craft hiked over a monster wave, then crashed into a gleaming valley of sea foam. "You really like the thrill ride, don't you, Brian?" she asked breathlessly.

"Yes," he replied, his voice slightly rough as he leaned toward her.

The fact that his kiss came so unexpectedly made it all the more sexy and special to Cassie. Brian's lips caught hers half-parted, and his warm tongue drowned her soft whimper of pleasure. The effect was exhilarating. She delighted to the taste of his lips, slightly salty from the spray, the exciting sound of the surf in her ears, the wind blowing across their bodies. Her senses exulted in the sensual feast, and she clung to him giddily.

All too soon, he pulled away, evidently sensing the motion of the boat as it climbed a new swell. They soared over the rise, sea foam splashing them both, and Cassie laughed exuberantly. This was so much fun, a thrilling roller-coaster ride, a romantic adventure such as she'd never known before. All because of Brian.

Suddenly she felt close to the edge in too many ways...

LATER, he walked her to her door.

"Hey, thanks again for a great day," she murmured, avoiding his eye.

He touched her cheek. "Want me to come in?"

She dared to meet his intent gaze. "I don't think so, Brian."

"You still owe me another kiss, you know," he teased.

She raised an eyebrow.

"Or, we could just talk," he hastily added.

"Talk?" She laughed nervously. "Somehow I doubt that."

He stared at his feet. "You're probably right."

She took a deep, bracing breath, then regarded him soberly. "Brian, where do you see this leading?"

His gaze shot up to hers. "What do you mean? Is this a reference to our kiss in the boat?"

"Yes. And to a few others we've been stealing."

"Cassie, those kisses were very spontaneous, very special."

"Of course they were. But we're both more than aware that spontaneity can lead one into big trouble."

He grinned sheepishly. "I know."

"Do you? In a few days, you're going back to Denver, to your life of confirmed bachelorhood, and I'm going—"

"Yes?"

"Back to my own life, one with very different aspirations."

"Meaning?"

Cassie chose her next words carefully. "Brian, being here with you has helped me start rethinking my life. I know now that I could never marry Chris, because I can't live with a man who would smother me that way and premeditate our entire lives together. I'm not completely sure as yet just how I'll want to redefine my life. But I do sense that eventually, I'll want the rest of the package—home, family, all of that. I have a feeling that when all is said and done, I'll come home to some pretty traditional values." She glanced at him meaningfully. "In other words, a fling isn't right for me."

"Did I ever suggest one?" he asked tensely.

"No, of course not. I'm talking about what our *bodies* keep suggesting."

"I know," he said ruefully.

"Do you?"

He spoke passionately. "Cassie, my mind keeps telling me we shouldn't proceed with this. But every time I'm with you, all I can think of is how exciting it is to be with you, how much fun we're having, how great we are together, and…" He swallowed hard. "How I want more."

"I know," she commiserated. "I'm having the same problem."

"Should I go back to Denver, Cassie?"

Taking in his torn expression, she felt equally confused. At last, she slowly shook her head. "No. I should probably tell you to go, but I just can't."

He sighed. "So we should try to remain friends?"

"Yes, we should try." Eyeing his disheartened expression, she stretched on tiptoe, just pecking his lips with her own. Then she brightened. "There. Second kiss. Signed, sealed, and delivered."

He stroked her cheek and spoke sadly. "But is it enough, Cassie?"

As he turned to leave, his eyes told Cassie what she already knew—that their kisses were only making them both starved for more, and that remaining friends was becoming more difficult with each passing day.

# 8

THE NEXT DAY dawned stormy, with the wind and rain so intense that, after Brian arrived at the condo half-soaked, Cassie suggested they stay in for the morning. As he dried himself off in the bathroom, she managed to hunt up a game of checkers and set it out on the game table in the living room.

They played most of the morning, with the rain slashing against the glass windows and doors. Cassie found it difficult to focus on the game with Brian so close, and the sounds of the storm so romantic. Her gaze kept straying to his damp hair, which was so sexy curling about his handsome face. And his intent expression as he considered strategies was so endearing. She thought of how he poured himself into everything he did—a game, a sport, a conversation.

*A kiss.* It was no wonder, with her thinking so unsettled, that she lost five games to him in a row.

As he was winning the fifth game he grabbed up the last of her checkers and shoved them aside with uncharacteristic impatience. "Cassie, you aren't concentrating."

Cassie offered a guilty smile. She was concentrating, all right, but not on the game. "Sorry."

Brian got up, strode over to the patio doors and slid them open. A gust of warm air blew in off the balcony. "Looks like the rain has finally let up."

Cassie came over to join him. "Yeah, but the wind hasn't died down. Why don't you shut those doors and come back in?"

His expression tense, Brian turned to stare at Cassie. She looked very feminine today, in a pink-and-white-striped cotton shirt and white shorts; her hair was in a bouncy ponytail, with becoming wisps trailing about her lovely face. She appeared young, breezy, unconsciously sexy, like someone's adorable wife.

*That* image brought up possibilities he couldn't afford to consider.

Being here in this domestic setting was getting the better of him—seeing Cassie's smiles, hearing her laughter when she fumbled at checkers. She was a wretched player, but even that perversely delighted him, making his thoughts stray in the decadent direction of suggesting they try a few hands of strip poker.

Especially with the bedroom only a few, tempting yards away. His thoughts now made his bargaining for kisses yesterday pale by comparison.

Lord, he needed to get out of here, before her nearness, and memories of their exciting kisses, made him snap. Again he lamented his own rashness in staying in Galveston in the first place. How often had he gotten himself into a big mess through his own impulsiveness?

And what in heck had the plan been, anyway?

Ah, yes. He'd just stick around, straighten out Cassie, get her back with Chris, then all would be hunky-dory. Yeah, sure. Now his entire scheme was in chaos—as were his emotions.

He cleared his throat. "Cassie, I think I need to go out for a while."

She gestured at the opened door. "In that?"

He closed the doors. "It's a perfect day for surfing."

"You're joking."

"I need to blow off some steam."

"May I ask why?"

He lifted an eyebrow. "Do you really want me to answer? This time I can't promise a G-rated version."

"Oh." She blushed. "Are you sure it'll be safe?"

"I'll be okay."

She rolled her eyes. "I'm coming, too."

"Cassie, this is no day for a beginner to be out."

She crossed her arms over her chest. "I'm not going along to surf, but to summon the coast guard after you're swept out to sea."

Chuckling, Brian tweaked her beneath the chin. "How you overdramatize."

"Brian, you need a keeper."

Brian didn't comment, for he was far too tempted to suggest Cassie take on that role...permanently.

"BRIAN, ARE YOU SURE you should be doing this?"

Cassie felt very concerned as she and Brian struggled to navigate their way down the wet, windy beach. Brian, carrying a rented surfboard, had changed into swim trunks; Cassie still wore shorts, shirt and sandals. Beyond them, the waves of the Gulf billowed and roared; powerful gusts buffeted their bodies and blew sand into their faces and eyes.

"Yes, I know what I'm doing," he replied patiently. "I've surfed Redondo Beach and the bonsai pipeline. This is nothing."

She gestured toward a nearby jetty. "Those storm flags mean nothing?"

"I've surfed in worse."

"But there's no one else even out," she protested. "Doesn't that tell you something?"

"I wish you would go back to the hotel. Like I told you, these waves are too good to miss. But I don't want you here endangering yourself."

Incredulous, she asked, "It's fine for you to risk your neck in those monstrous currents, but too dangerous for me to remain on the shore watching you?"

"Yes."

"Damn it, Brian, do you realize how little sense you're making?" she demanded.

"It makes perfect sense to me."

"You've been just itching to try this stunt, haven't you? No wonder you became so antsy back at the condo."

He grinned guiltily. "Cassie, you're wrong on why I'm antsy. Now just go. I'll be fine."

"Will you? And who's going to summon help when you get into trouble?"

"I'm not going to get into trouble."

"Famous last words."

He touched her arm. "For the last time, will you please go back to the condo?"

Stubbornly she lifted her chin. "No."

He ground his teeth. "Then you stay right here on the beach, do you hear me? You get anywhere near that surf, and I swear, I'll wring your neck."

"If you're dead, you won't be able to," she informed him sarcastically.

A grudging smile pulled at his mouth. "I mean it, Cassie. Under no circumstances are you to come after me."

"Believe me, I wouldn't dream of it."

"Good girl."

His last, smug words made Cassie mad enough to kick him. But her annoyance was soon replaced by anxiety as she watched him wade into the billowy waves, then begin paddling out on his surfboard. For a moment he disappeared over a rolling mound of water, then she spotted him wending his way toward the horizon again. Heavens, he was going out so far! She glanced around nervously, wondering what she'd do if she needed help, but spotted not a soul in sight.

Just as her uneasiness reached a crescendo, Brian appeared, rising up on his surfboard as he caught the crest of a wave. A breaking shaft of sunlight made her gasp as his gorgeous body was outlined in golden light. Even as she mused that he had never appeared more magnificent, she was equally certain she was about to watch him die before her very eyes in the raging surf, and this realization brought home how much she'd come to care for him in such a short period of time.

Her heart hammered with fear and concern. She gasped again as he sailed over the top of the wave and glided down its face, a wicked wall of water curling over his head and threatening to tow him under. Yet, somehow, he just managed to elude the clutches of the water monster. Captivated and appalled, she watched him make his surfboard dance, performing a wicked roller-coaster maneuver and a 360, raising dazzling sprays of water in his wake. She wanted to kill him for his recklessness, yet never had he fascinated her more.

"Lady, is your boyfriend nuts?"

Cassie turned to watch a young man in lifeguard's suit approach her. "Guess he shouldn't be out, huh?"

The frowning man jerked a thumb toward the jetty. "You know what those flags mean?"

Still anxiously watching Brian, Cassie nodded. "Yes, I know, but unfortunately, my friend doesn't. I think a good storm only gets his blood going."

"Let's hope he doesn't break his neck. The undertow could get him, or the currents could propel him straight into the rocks."

Grimacing, Cassie glanced at the pilings, a long line of granite boulders, and imagined Brian's beautiful body being smashed there. She stared back at him, watching with her heart in her eyes as he successfully rode the wave to the shore. Then at last, watching him drop into waist-deep water, she heaved a huge sigh of relief.

The lifeguard was shaking his head. "Your boyfriend's one lucky psychotic."

"I know," Cassie agreed ruefully.

Drenched and exuberant, Brian ran up with his surfboard. "Wow, what a ride!"

The lifeguard glowered. "Sir, are you aware you aren't supposed to be out there?"

"Yes, sorry," Brian said.

"I'm going to have to ask you both to leave the area," the lifeguard continued sternly.

"Sure," Brian readily agreed. "We're out of here. And thanks."

As they walked away, Cassie glanced over her shoulder to see the lifeguard still watching them and shaking his head. She and Brian stopped to turn in the surfboard at the stand where he'd rented it. As they started off again her expression was grim.

"Okay, what's wrong?" he asked.

"What's wrong?" she repeated, waving a hand in frustration. "Why should anything be wrong?"

"Come on, Cassie."

Furious, she swung about and stepped into his path. "Very well. If you ever again try anything so stupid, I'll kill you."

He whistled. "Wow. That's direct."

She stormed off again. "Thanks for taking me seriously."

He sprang into step beside her. "Cassie, I do."

"Baloney," she retorted. "I may as well have been screaming into the wind for all you've listened to me. Does everything have to be a thrill ride with you, Brian?"

"Is there something wrong with having fun?"

"When you risk your life? Absolutely."

Heatedly, he replied, "Cassie, that may have seemed risky to you, but it wasn't to someone who's successfully caught seven-footers at Oahu."

She gave an incredulous laugh. "Then you know more than the authorities who put out the storm flags, or the lifeguard who said you could have gotten smashed up on the rocks?"

Brian's mouth tightened. "Cassie, you're making too much of this. Why is it every time I get involved with a girl, she wants to control me?"

"*Involved?*" she repeated. "Who says we're involved, Brian? I thought you were here to help me solve my identity crisis, and to get me back with Chris. Furthermore, if I'm trying to control you, then you damn well need some control."

He gave a groan. "You know what I mean. We *are* involved, as much as we're both trying to fight it."

She was silent, unable to refute his argument.

"As for being controlled, be fair, Cassie," he continued. "You don't like being dictated to either, do you? Isn't that a big reason you walked out on Chris?"

"Well, yes," she admitted. "But we're discussing apples and oranges here—"

"Are we?"

She dug in her heels. "Brian, there's a big difference between walking out of a wedding and the kind of psycho stunt you just pulled. You're a thrill junkie, and I want to know why."

He was silent, scowling.

"Is it because you feel your parents never enjoyed life enough? Now you have to make up for it by being a danger addict?"

"Well, maybe in part," he admitted.

"What's the rest? Do you have a death wish, Brian?"

The question hung in the air as they started off again. "No, of course not," he answered after a moment. "But I'm not afraid of death, if that's what you're asking."

"That's pretty obvious from your actions just now. Why aren't you afraid?"

He turned serious. "Maybe I don't see much point in being cautious."

"Why not?"

He sighed, frowning into the distance before he spoke. "In high school, I had a best friend, Jason. The two of us were like brothers. We were on the football team together, and we spent many weekends rock climbing or parasailing."

"Sounds like fun."

He nodded. "But Jason did have one flaw—or, so I

thought. He was a fanatically safe driver—too safe, really. You see, he and his dad spent an entire summer, not to mention a small fortune, restoring Jason's '63 Corvette. Jason was terrified he'd get a scratch on his 'Vette, and I used to tease him, call him an old lady, every time we went out in his car together." Brian drew a ragged breath and pulled his fingers through his hair. "Then a drunk driver killed Jason and totalled his car."

Gasping in dismay, Cassie touched his arm. "Oh, Brian, I'm so sorry. Bet that was hard on you."

"I was devastated," he admitted, his eyes revealing his inner anguish. "But my point is, what good did being cautious do for Jason? He was the most careful driver in the world, and got killed, anyway. That experience taught me how unpredictable fate is—and that life is short and should be lived to the fullest."

Cassie carefully thought over his words. "Brian, I hear you," she said feelingly. "But losing someone special is still no excuse for taking unacceptable risks."

He glanced off toward the stormy surf. "Perhaps I don't think they're unacceptable."

"You're impossible," she declared.

He offered her a contrite smile. "Cassie, sometimes when I'm out in nature this way, it helps me focus."

"A thrill ride helps you focus?"

"Sometimes when you're close to the edge, things just become so much clearer."

"What becomes clearer?"

He paused, turning to touch her face and gaze searchingly into her eyes. "That the ride itself was not nearly as important as you waiting for me on the shore."

Cassie's anger dissolved at his tender words. "Oh, Brian."

For a moment they regarded each other poignantly, then they continued back to the hotel in silence. Finally, after they crossed the lobby and entered the elevator, Brian said heavily, "I should probably go."

Taken aback, Cassie asked, "Go? You mean, leave Galveston?"

Grimly, he nodded. "You were right that this whole escapade is a mistake. I'm not fixing things, but only making matters worse for you."

"Brian..." Her emotional gaze sought his. "No, that isn't true. I don't want you to leave. You've helped me, really you have."

"Are you sure?" he pressed.

She touched his arm. "Please stay."

The two were gazing into each other's eyes when the elevator stopped and the doors popped open. Then they sprang apart as both became conscious of a glowering man who stood but a few feet beyond them.

It was Christopher Carlisle.

# 9

"WELL, ISN'T THIS a cozy sight," Chris said cynically.

Just as Cassie was trying to absorb the shock of seeing her ex-fiancé again, he made the nasty crack. Stepping out of the elevator with Brian to face their glowering visitor, Cassie could feel the color moving up her face—as if she and Brian were guilty of something, when they weren't. And, taking in the cold stranger standing across from them, his hair and clothing impeccable, his handsome features gripped in a cold sneer, she found it impossible to believe she'd ever *thought* she loved this remote, judgmental man.

"Chris, what are you doing here?" she asked.

He laughed. "Oh, paying you two a little visit. And it's funny, I was about to ask the same question of Brian." He turned to his cousin. "So tell me, coz, what are you doing here with my fiancée, both of you half-clothed?"

Hearing Brian's sharp intake of breath, Cassie struggled not to flinch. "She's your *ex*-fiancée, we're hardly half-clothed, and we've been at the beach," Brian answered tersely.

"The beach, eh?" Chris taunted. "And what sport were you two planning to indulge in next?"

Spotting thunderclouds in Brian's eyes, Cassie retorted, "Chris! What a rotten thing to say."

"Yes, you well know Cassie doesn't deserve that kind of ugly insinuation," Brian added furiously.

"She doesn't?" Chris countered, feigning bewilderment. "Well, what do you expect me to say when the two of you appear in this risqué state outside your little love nest?"

Cassie grabbed Brian's arm to restrain him. "Risqué? Love nest?" she exclaimed. "How dare you! I'll have you know Brian is *not* staying with me. He only came back here to change."

Chris smiled nastily. "How convenient for you both."

By now, Brian was white-faced. "Chris, I think you'd better knock it off—now—and state your business."

Chris glowered back. "And I think you'd better tell me what *you're* doing here, Brian."

Again, Cassie jumped in. "He came here to help me."

"Did he?" Chris scoffed. "Looks to me like he came here to help himself."

"Stop it, Chris." Blinking rapidly, Brian protectively placed himself between Cassie and the other man. "You know, I always wondered why I didn't like you. Lord knows, I tried, but something about you always put me off. Now I know for sure. You're a real horse's ass, *coz*. And I want to hear you apologize to Cassie—*now*."

"Apologize?" Chris scoffed. "If anyone is owed an apology, it's me."

"Not on your life."

Brian was moving toward Chris again when Cassie shook her head. Relieved when Brian managed to restrain himself—though his expression was murderous—she turned to Chris. "Why don't you just tell me why you're here."

He laughed cynically. "Actually, I came down here to find out for certain if it's over between us. I was even hoping you might have had second thoughts. That's a real joke, isn't it? You sure didn't waste any time, did you, Cassie?"

Now Brian shook a finger at Chris. "I'm warning you. One more crack like that, and you're going to be picking your butt up off the floor."

As the two men glared at each other, Cassie pleaded, "Chris, leave Brian out of this."

"You're the one who brought him into it, Cassie."

Cassie gritted her teeth. "Why don't I just answer your question?"

Chris glanced scornfully at Brian. "I think you already have."

"Damn it, Chris, that's enough," Brian ordered hoarsely. "If you want to take this out on me, fine, but I won't hear any more insults to Cassie."

For a moment, his fists clenched at his sides, Chris appeared on the verge of swinging at Brian. Then he glanced at his watch, and gave a contemptuous shrug. "Actually, who cares? I'm running late, anyway. Ever since the wedding debacle, Mother's been urging me to date the daughter of one of her bridge partners. In fact, I'm due to meet her tonight, so guess I'll leave you two to..." Voice trailing off meaningfully, he finished, "Whatever you two were doing."

Arrogantly he strode off, leaving Brian and Cassie to glare after him.

"Lord, how I'd love to punch that idiot's lights out," Brian muttered. "I've half a mind to go after him and teach him some manners."

Distraught, Cassie implored, "Brian, no. I need you here."

He glanced at her with concern. "You okay?"

She managed a nod.

"Let's get you inside."

Inside, Cassie strode off toward the windows, fighting the hard lump of anger and pain in her throat. Damn Chris for coming down here and acting like such an ass! She felt humiliated, mad enough to scream, or cry. Then she felt Brian's warm hand on her shoulder; the tender gesture all but tore her apart.

"Cassie, what is it?" he asked.

Cassie could no longer contain herself, and a sob burst forth from her. She felt herself being turned about and pulled into Brian's strong arms, and she wept against his bare chest. She was so overwrought that she no longer cared about his scandalous proximity.

"Cassie, please don't cry," he implored, kissing her hair. "Damn it, I am going to go find that braying jackass, and—"

"No, please don't," she begged, sniffing. "You'll only make matters worse. Besides, you're too good a person to lower yourself to Chris's level."

Brian's expression was miserably torn. "Then why are you crying? Do you still love him?"

Her voice came muffled. "No, but I *thought* I loved him. And he's such a jerk."

"Sweetheart, I know." Brian cuddled her close, caressing her hair with his hand. "And to think I came down here for him."

She pulled back to gaze starkly up into his eyes. "Is he the reason you stayed?"

"Oh, Cassie."

For a long, heartrending moment, the two simply stared at each other. Then Brian hauled Cassie close and passionately kissed her.

A flood tide of repressed emotion seemed to break free between them as Cassie kissed Brian back and clung to him. Being in his arms just felt so wonderful. She realized they'd both fought this for so long, and neither could resist any longer. Brian's death-defying stunt, followed by Chris's gut-wrenching visit, had brought their feelings into sharp focus.

Without even realizing it, they backed toward the sofa then fell across the soft cushions together. Brian cuddled Cassie close and kissed her soft throat. His voice shook with turmoil. "Cassie...it's okay, darling. I want you to forget him."

Taken aback, she asked, "You do?"

He nodded solemnly into her eyes. "He's a stupid jerk who didn't deserve you and had no idea how good he had it. And I was a fool ever to feel any sympathy for him, much less try to get the two of you back together. You were right when you said Chris has no character. He likely would have cheated on you, to boot.''

''I think you're right.'' Intensely conscious of how solid, warm, and hard Brian felt lying beside her, Cassie regarded him tremulously. ''So where does that leave us?''

Swallowing hard, Brian caressed Cassie's flushed cheek. His voice came roughly. ''Do you have any idea how much I want you?''

''Yes.''

''Do you?'' His expression was anguished. ''I *want* you, Cassie. I love your company, love being with you. And now I want to be with you all the way. But that makes me feel guilty as hell, because you're on the rebound and I don't know if I can offer you anything beyond these brief days we have together.''

''I know,'' she whispered, her emotional gaze meeting his.

''But what I feel for you is so strong—and I keep thinking, that could be special in its own way. Couldn't it?''

Smiling through her tears, she hugged him tight and spoke ecstatically. ''Oh, yes, Brian. Yes.''

With a moan of tormented pleasure, Brian caught her lips in another heartfelt kiss. Cassie eagerly opened her mouth to him. She felt the tremor of emotion jolting his body, felt his tongue plunging inside her mouth in a primal demonstration of his need. She sensed he was feeling just what she felt. Neither could resist this overwhelming attraction any longer.

Abruptly he pulled back to stare dazedly into her eyes. ''Cassie, are you sure?''

''Yes,'' she whispered back, leaning over to plant kisses on his bare, smooth chest. ''I just know this feels good, so right, that I need you, Brian.''

''I need you, too,'' he whispered hoarsely.

''Even if our time together is only brief.''

His gaze was tortured. "Oh, Cassie. Aren't you afraid we could be going—"

"From the frying pan into the fire?" she finished. "Take me there, Brian."

"Eagerly." He mouth possessed hers in a deep, searing kiss, and then fiery need took over for them both.

Cassie sank her fingers into Brian's hair. He unbuttoned her blouse, then undid the clasp on her bra. She gasped in ecstasy as he leaned over and touched his lips to her nipple. Then she felt the tiny peak tautening beneath the skilled caress of his tongue. Her back arched deliciously. The pleasure was almost too intense.

"I've dreamed of this for so long," he murmured.

"Me, too," she admitted. "But I never dreamed it would be like this."

"Oh, Cassie."

Brian sucked her nipple into his mouth, and she reeled in torment and delight. She nibbled at his ear, stroking him with her tongue as he planted lingering kisses on her breasts, and in the valley between. Soon her hands slid down his warm body, her fingers slipping inside his swim brief, closing over his erection. His groan of pleasure excited her deeply. He was so warm, so hard and ready! Her body ached in anticipation. She heard his ragged breathing, then his burning gaze met hers.

"Hold on just a minute, darling."

Cassie watched, unabashed, as Brian stood, removed his swim brief, then all but lunged for the small bag with his clothing. Watching him straighten and rip open a condom, she couldn't believe how gorgeous he was—the beautiful lines of his muscled back and hard buttocks, the chiseled contours of his tanned chest, the sensual splendor of his arousal, and the breathtaking expression on his face, so fierce with desire.

Within seconds he came back to her side, covered her with his body, and drowned her senses with a hot kiss. Cassie purred like a contented cat as his hands moved to her shorts, tugging them down with her panties. Within seconds, her clothing hit the floor, and the sensation of being completely naked beneath him, and open to him, left her delirious with desire.

Then Brian rolled and brought Cassie on top of him. She felt the hard heat of him probing against her feminine folds and thought she might die of bliss.

His strong hands caught and kneaded her breasts. "You're so damn beautiful," he whispered. "Are you forgetting him, Cassie?"

"Oh, yes," she whispered back.

He smiled then, his fingers moving between her thighs, his touch burning her with ecstasy. And then, in a single, smooth stroke, he filled her completely, filled her with *him.* A cry of pleasure rent her, then Brian pulled her close, tenderly kissing her. The sensation of her bare breasts rubbing against his warm chest was enthralling.

His hands gripped her hips and, slowly, he began to move. "That good for you?"

"Heaven," she whispered hoarsely, drowning him with a French kiss that drove him mad, from the provocative thrust she received in response.

He pulled his lips from hers and nibbled at her ear. "Easy. I want this to be right for you, too."

"It is."

"Show me."

He pushed her back and helped her set the rhythm, observing her face, gauging her reactions as she bobbed to and fro, allowing the tension to build for them both. He moved in counterpoint to enhance her pleasure, gripping her hips and rocking her closer. Soon harsh cries escaped her as fervor built to frenzy for them both. Brian straightened, claiming Cassie's lips in an aching kiss as he climaxed in a torrent of strokes that pulled a contented moan from her.

THEY FOUND THEIR WAY to the bedroom. After they settled in, Brian went to the kitchen to get them both a glass of wine. Returning to the bedroom, he caught Cassie's tremulous smile and winked at her. She looked incredibly sexy sitting up in bed in the soft light, her hair tousled, her shoulders bare, the sheet draped about her provocative curves, her eyes luminous as she took him in. Her cheeks were still rosy from the rub of his whiskers, and her lips were bright.

Her body bore his imprint, just as he felt hers.

Such heaven she'd brought him! He couldn't believe he had actually made love to this glorious creature, and he was still walking on cloud nine.

He crossed the room, handed her one of the glasses and got into bed beside her. "You okay?"

"I'm great."

"You know, that was incredible," he whispered, nibbling on her shoulder.

"Yes, it was."

"You're something else, Cassie."

Sipping her wine, she murmured, "It was very intense—kind of like those waves you like to ride, eh?"

"They can't compare with you."

"You're very gallant." Her expression turned serious. "You know, about Chris—"

"Yes?" he inquired tensely.

"He—well, he never cared whether I—um...whether it was good for me."

Tenderness surged within Brian, as well as new anger toward Chris, and deep pride that Cassie had shared with him on such an intimate level. "Ah. And was it good for you just now?"

Cassie grinned. "You betcha. Several times."

Brian smiled back, then a darker expression filtered in. "There's yet another reason not to defend that jerk."

She nodded. "So you're through with the guilt?"

"Absolutely." He lifted his glass. "Here's to no more guilt."

She clicked her glass against his. "Hear, hear."

Brian regarded Cassie almost helplessly. "You've made me so happy, Cassie."

"Me, too."

He frowned pensively. "And you know, we never did burn your bikini."

She burst out laughing. "What brought that up?"

"Chris's visit. Actually, I was thinking it wouldn't hurt to burn *him* in effigy."

She chortled.

"I don't suppose you brought along a reasonable facsimile we can charbroil?"

She shook her head and regarded him tenderly. "Wow, you really are on his case now."

"I've seen him for what he really is," Brian acknowledged grimly. He patted her thigh. "So how 'bout that bonfire?"

"No, I don't think so," she answered gently. "In fact, I think I'd really prefer to give my old bikini to Goodwill."

"Really?" He took her glass and set it, with his, on the nightstand. "What brought about this change of heart?"

"Chris doesn't matter to me anymore," she admitted happily. "Not after the way he acted. Why should I even care enough to burn a swimsuit that someone else might have use for?"

"That's the spirit," Brian encouraged. "As far as I'm concerned, you can give away every stitch you own."

"Brian!" Laughing, she playfully punched him in the arm. "Come on, now. You have to admit you'd grow tired of just lying in bed naked with me."

He was incredulous. "Wanna bet?"

They cuddled and kissed for several happy moments. Sighing dreamily, he said, "I can't believe how good this feels."

"I know. Me neither."

His lips nuzzled her brow. "There's something I want to tell you."

"Oh?"

"About getting tired of being naked in bed with you."

Cassie raised an eyebrow playfully. "Yes?"

Turning very serious, Brain rolled Cassie beneath him on the mattress and gazed ardently into her bright eyes. "Cassie, you're right that I'm an antsy guy, and easily distracted. But I just want you to know that I have a *long* attention span when it comes to loving you."

And he proceeded to demonstrate this, to Cassie's complete satisfaction.

# 10

AT SUNSET, Cassie and Brian strolled the beach, both bare-foot, holding hands. She noted that the wind had died down now, much like the storm of passion that had peaked so powerfully between them, then ebbed so tenderly. Beyond them, the waves flowed smoothly, a silvery landscape of water rolling toward them from the spectacular pink-gold horizon. A few surfers and swimmers were braving the calmer seas, while a group of children tossed Frisbees along the shoreline. Gulls swooped about and cawed as the sea breeze blew its fresh essence across their bodies.

"Do you want to talk about it?" Brian asked.

"Talk about it?" Cassie repeated. "You mean us?"

"Us," he murmured as if savoring the word. "Interesting how things have changed so quickly."

"It's kind of like what we predicted, though, isn't it?" she asked. "Instantaneous attraction, spontaneous combustion. Perhaps I—we—needed to get this out of our systems."

"That's all it is then, just some chemistry thing?" he asked with a hurt expression.

"Of course not," she reassured him, squeezing his hand. "We have something very special, Brian, a really strong rapport. We have loads of fun together. But we shouldn't delude ourselves about what it means."

"And what does it mean?" he asked, voice crackling with tension.

Cassie carefully considered her answer. "Two people coming together because they need each other. Something that, inevitably, probably can't last. How did you put it before, soon after we met? Something hot, quickly burning itself out?''

"Ouch," he said, grimacing. "My own words come back to haunt me."

"Words with an element of truth, don't you think?"

He pulled her close, running a hand over her back. "What makes you think this will burn itself out?"

Gazing up at Brian, Cassie could see the sincerity and passion in his expression. She sorely wished the reality between them could be different.

"Is there really any other way?" she asked with regret. "Soon you'll go back to Denver, and where can this realistically lead? As you've already informed me, you're not a marrying man. And I'm not ready for another big commitment, not while I'm on the rebound from what I *thought* I wanted for a lifetime."

"Is that all?" he teased. "So what *really* makes you think this won't last?"

"Your short attention span?" she suggested.

He leaned over and tenderly kissed her. "Cassie, all I know is, ever since we met, all I think about is you."

Her heart melted at his words. "Oh, Brian, me too. Let's just enjoy it for what it is—a beautiful experience—and not expect more right now, okay?"

"Fine, Cassie," he replied tightly. "The only problem is, I already *want* more."

Cassie knew just what Brian meant. She, too, wanted more. Making love with him had only enhanced her already deep feelings, and she shuddered to think of the pain she would experience when they parted. But she had to remind herself that the very aspects of his character that made him so special—his spontaneity, his sense of humor and love of adventure—also made him the free-spirited soul who likely would never be happy with one woman for long. She had to remind herself to enjoy what they had for what it was—special and meaningful, if fleeting—and not wish for more. All the while, she suspected she was asking too much of herself.

Brian, too, felt consumed with turmoil as he strolled along with Cassie. Making love with her had been so very special, not just the sating of a physical craving, but the fulfillment of emotional and spiritual needs. Never had he felt a rapport with a woman such as he did with Cassie. Just the fact that she was insisting on no lasting ties between them made him yearn for ties, though he also suspected a future between them would be very difficult. He'd just never thought of himself as being ready to commit an entire lifetime to one woman, when he'd never before possessed that level of singlemindedness and dedication. Yet the other possibility—letting Cassie go—was worse torture. After making love with her, the thought of another man holding her, touching her, loving her, was repugnant to him.

What could he do? He couldn't have her, yet he couldn't let her go...

CASSIE THRILLED to her next days with Brian. They went for long swims and walked the beach. They rode the antique trolley and rented an all-terrain vehicle for an afternoon of fun out on the dunes. They lingered over lunches in town. They talked endlessly, comparing experiences and perspectives. They made glorious love.

On the Sunday afternoon before they were scheduled to leave Galveston, they decided to sunbathe on the chaises on Lisa's balcony. Brian brought out some cocoa butter to rub on Cassie's back. He sat down beside her, and she flashed him a smile before turning over on her stomach. She absorbed his warmth, inhaled his scent, and gloried in the closeness, running a hand over his male thigh.

"Mmm," he murmured, moving aside her hair to rub oil on her shoulders. "I've been wanting to do this ever since I first saw you."

"Your hands feel good," she said contentedly.

"Your skin is glorious," he whispered. "So smooth,

fresh, and glowing. You don't get out in the sun much, do you?''

"My mom managed to convince me it would ruin my skin.''

"Good for your mom.'' He undid the clasp on her bikini, leaning over to kiss her smooth flesh. "I've been wanting to do this, too.''

Cassie felt delicious gooseflesh breaking out on her spine. "Don't get too fresh, now.''

His hand glided sensually down her body, pausing on her bottom. "Why? Who is going to see us?''

"Someone might.''

"And you don't like to live dangerously?''

She laughed. "Something tells me I'm already doing just that.''

But her laughter faded into a purr of pleasure as Brian's slick fingers slid beneath her and he began kneading her breasts, his touch unbearably erotic. When his fingertips lingered on her nipples she almost lost all control, desire twisting pleasurably inside her. She was beyond speech, panting, riveted to his skilled strokes as his hands moved down her belly. Cassie never realized torture could be so sweet. Then he moved around to her lower back, pulling down her bikini bottom and rubbing the oil on her hips.

Cassie groaned. "Oh, Brian. You're getting us in trouble. We're going to have to go in.''

He leaned over to nibble at her nape. "No, we're not, darling. Just hold on for a moment.''

He left her briefly. Cassie was in no condition to move as she lay there still burning from his massage, the sun warm on her back. Then he rejoined her, lying down beside her and pulling a cotton afghan over their bodies.

"Now turn over, darling.''

Cassie did, and felt Brian's warm, naked body sliding over hers. The sensation was glorious, both of them so warm and slippery. She gasped in delight, then looked up into his gorgeous blue eyes, saw his handsome, fiercely passionate features outlined against the crystal-clear skies.

"You're so slick," he whispered, kissing her chin.

"So are you," she murmured.

He began stroking her between her thighs. "I've been dreaming of doing this."

"Making love on a chaise?" she teased, then wincing as he touched her in just the right place.

"Making love in the sunshine," he whispered ardently. "Watching the pleasure build and peak in your eyes. You're a sunshine kind of girl. You sure brighten up my life."

"Oh, Brian." Tenderly she kissed him. "You brighten up mine." She felt his hard arousal moving against her pelvis and arched against him pleasurably.

"How 'bout we go dancing tonight?" he asked.

She caught a sharp breath. "An odd time to bring up dancing."

"But isn't this a dance?" he asked huskily, then joined their bodies with a deep, powerful stroke. "The movement, the rhythm, the way our bodies fit together so perfectly?"

Cassie arched against him in ecstasy, enhancing her own bliss. "Yes, it's a dance," she whispered, moving with him. "A dance of love."

THAT EVENING, Cassie and Brian had a seafood dinner, then drove along East Beach, watching the sunset with the windows down and the sunroof open. Cassie rested her head on his shoulder, looking out at the lovely pink-gold horizon and enjoying the caress of the sea breeze on her face. The mood was so romantic.

After night fell, they stopped at a little cantina with a patio strung with colorful lights. Cassie waited at their small table, gazing at the beauties of the moonlit Gulf, as Brian went inside, soon emerging with beers for them both.

As the band inside launched into a Selena song, "I Could

Fall in Love,'' playing the popular melody to a calypso beat, Cassie sighed. "I just love that song."

He grinned. "Wonder why?"

*Because I'm falling in love with you,* she thought, but dared not voice her feelings aloud.

He extended his hand. "Want to dance?"

"Sure."

They got up and he pulled her into his arms. Cassie savored the moment, knowing it might have to last her forever, committing to her memory the smell of Brian, his warmth, the rhythms of his body moving with hers, the sensual music of the band, the sound of the surf.

She tried to tell herself that this moment was so wonderful, heaven couldn't surpass it. She tried to tell herself this night would last her forever—yet still she wanted more.

Brian, too, savored the moment. Cassie felt so wonderful in his arms, her warm curves brushing against him, the enticing scent of her perfume filling his senses. His brief time with her was almost over, and he didn't want to give her up. How he wished he could hold her like this forever. But he still feared he couldn't go the distance for her, and become the kind of responsible husband she truly deserved.

"What are you thinking, Cass?" he asked.

She smiled up at him. "That this setting is so romantic. The moonlight, the beach, the sound and scent of the surf."

"The beautiful woman in my arms," he finished.

"The wonderful man in mine."

"Cassie..." With a groan, he hugged her tight. "I'm going to miss you so much."

"Me, too."

"How I wish I didn't have to go back tomorrow. What if I call my boss—"

"But wouldn't that only make it harder later on?"

"I don't know," he muttered. "We just haven't had enough time together."

She pulled back to gaze up at him searchingly. "Yes, but in a sense, isn't it better that we part now, when our feelings are still strong, rather than just wait for this to die a natural death?''

Brian felt wounded by that. ''Why do you keep insisting this will end?''

''Is there any other way, as different as we are?''

''Are we so different, Cassie?'' he challenged. ''Seems to me we've gotten along pretty well.''

''Here in this dream world,'' she replied with obvious turmoil. ''But now it's time to come back down to earth, to face reality and all the difficulties we'd encounter if we really tried to keep this together.''

He sighed and clutched her closer. ''We'll never know unless we try.''

''True, I suppose.''

''When can you come to Denver?''

Taken aback, she said, ''Well, I don't know.''

''Next weekend?''

''Brian, really.''

''Have you thought of moving there?'' he continued earnestly.

''What, so I can be your flavor of the month rather than of the week?''

Brian winced. ''Cassie, that's not fair.''

''You're right,'' she said, flashing him a penitent smile. ''I'm sorry, I don't know why I said that. This is just so hard.''

''I know. So when *can* you come to Denver?''

She laughed. ''Brian, there you go again.''

''There's so much I want to show you—the mountains, my favorite places to climb and ski.''

''That's great, though I'm not quite the outdoors fanatic you are.''

''That's cool. Denver has great restaurants, shopping, theater, you name it.''

She raised an eyebrow. ''You mean you'd actually go shopping with me? This must be desperation.''

He swallowed hard, gazing at her starkly. "I don't think shopping will ever again be the same without you."

Cassie sighed poignantly. "Oh, Brian. I think that's the sweetest thing you've ever said to me."

"I just hate the thought of going back without you. How 'bout I pack you up in my suitcase?"

She chuckled. "Have you thought of moving to Houston?"

Brian glanced about. "Well, it's nice having the Gulf so close, but otherwise, it's awfully flat."

She stiffened. "Meaning, if this were to continue, I'm the one who would have to give up my family, pull up stakes, and make all the compromises? When you haven't even offered anything beyond—well, the status quo?"

"Not necessarily," he hedged.

"Then what? A long-distance relationship? I think we both know that would be doomed."

"Yes, I know." Brian felt as if he might burst with frustration. "But, damn it, Cassie, we haven't had enough time. I just don't want to give you up."

"You don't want to give me up, but you aren't really offering anything, either, are you?" she asked.

He hesitated. "If I did, would you be ready?"

"No," she admitted with a regretful smile.

He pulled her closer. "I can't let you go."

"You're going to have to, Brian," she whispered sadly. "You're going to have to."

# *11*

THE NEXT MORNING, Cassie stood outside with Brian. They embraced between their two cars, in the parking lot of the condo hotel. He was gazing at her with tenderness and anguish.

"Lord, I wish I didn't have to leave on that plane today," he muttered.

"I wish you didn't, either," she said feelingly.

He frowned anxiously. "I've got both your phone numbers in Houston, your work address, your home address, your e-mail—now if only I had you. Sure you don't want to be a stowaway, Cass?"

She laughed. "You'll have me in your thoughts."

"And in my dreams. So, we'll get together Labor Day weekend if not sooner?"

Taking in his expectant expression, Cassie hated to dash his hopes. "Brian…well, sure. But, realistically speaking, I just don't think there'll be a Labor Day weekend for us."

"Why not?" he asked with an irate scowl.

"For one thing, are you going to be a monk until then?"

An expression of hurt crossed his features. "My God, that's only two months away. Don't you trust me, Cassie?"

"It's not just a matter of trust," she replied, regarding him contritely. "I know your intentions are good. But I also think you'll get lonely and find someone else before long, and that one of these nights I'll get an awkward phone call saying maybe we shouldn't get together, after all."

"Well, you're wrong," he said vehemently.

"It's asking a lot, Brian."

"You mean for you?" he chided.

"No, I don't mean that. But I think…" She sighed. "Well, maybe this all just happened too soon."

"Then you're sorry?"

"No," she reassured him. "I have no regrets at all about being with you. But some time apart could help me—help us *both*—discover if this is truly lasting."

He cuddled her close. "It feels pretty lasting to me." He leaned over and tenderly kissed her lips. "Damn it, I wish we didn't have to leave."

"I know."

"How 'bout I follow you back to the city?"

Cassie felt intensely conflicted. "Brian, we're going to have to go in different directions once we reach the outskirts—"

"I know. I just want to savor every possible second. And I'll call you tonight from Denver, okay?"

"Okay." Taking in his tense, vulnerable expression, she smiled bravely. "I just want you to know, you really have helped me. You showed me everything I was missing with Chris. No matter what happens between us in the future, I feel I have a much better grasp on what I want out of life."

"And what is that, Cassie?" he asked quietly.

*Someone like you.* Cassie had to stop herself from blurting out the heartfelt words, knowing to do so would only cause them both more pain. Bravely, she replied, "Oh, how to live my life in a less structured way, how life can be more fun when I'm not so rigid about everything, how I don't have to be so afraid to let go a bit. You certainly demonstrated all of that to me."

"I'm glad, Cassie," he answered sincerely, stroking her cheek. "But I feel as if I came away with a lot more than I gave."

She nodded. "That makes two of us."

After a last, emotional hug, a kiss and a longing glance, they went to their separate cars.

Cassie tried her best to keep a stiff upper lip as they

drove back to Houston, Brian's car behind hers a constant reminder that she was losing him. When they finally reached the loop and her turnoff toward the west side of town, she bravely waved, and caught a poignant image of him blowing her a kiss in her rearview mirror. Then their cars went their separate ways, just as their lives seemed to be splitting asunder, and Cassie headed home with tears streaming down her face.

BRIAN WAS FEELING equally torn as he drove north on the interstate toward the airport. From the moment he and Cassie had parted in Galveston, he'd been sorely tempted to honk his horn, signal her to pull over, tell her their saying goodbye had been a big mistake, that they *had* to have more time together. Then when she had turned off, he'd felt a sick, aching regret such as he'd never known before.

Why was he feeling so desperate? Simple. Because, despite all his bravado to Cassie, she'd spoken the truth; realistically speaking, their parting today would mean an end to their relationship. And Brian hadn't realized until this moment how devastated and empty that would make him feel.

Why was he leaving, when in his heart, all he wanted was to be with her? Was he still afraid he'd disappoint her in the long run? Or was he afraid to commit, afraid he might again risk being deeply hurt as he'd been when he'd lost Jason in high school?

But wasn't he hurting now? Cassie was alive. She was going back to her own world—alone. But he doubted she'd remain single for much longer. Surely some other guy who wasn't nearly the dope he was would realize what a fabulous prize she was and snap her up. Someone else would hold her, kiss her, *love* her.

God, the very prospect was unbearable. What was he to do?

THE MINUTE CASSIE walked through the front door of her Memorial-area apartment, the silence and emptiness hit her like a stunning blow. After setting her bags down, the first thing she spotted was stacks of unopened wedding gifts on the sofa and coffee table. She groaned. The last thing she needed was to see such painful reminders right now. Plus, she was sure her mom must have taken home a truckload more of gifts from the actual wedding, assuming the guests hadn't reclaimed them. Of course everything would have to be returned, along with notes of apology, but she couldn't handle that right now. Fighting back new tears, she grabbed stacks of boxes and began shoving them into a closet.

Finishing up, she was just catching her breath when she spied Chris's picture on an end table, his visage grinning at her, seeming to mock her. She rushed across the room to lay the photo facedown.

Then she collapsed on the couch, shutting her eyes to hold back the pain she was feeling. She fought a riot of conflicting emotions, and literally couldn't believe how much her life had changed in such a short time.

A week ago, she'd been ready to start a new life with the man she'd thought she loved. Then she'd walked out on him, only to find the man she *really* loved, then lose him as well.

Yes, she did love Brian. She must, for nothing else could hurt this badly. The realization of her feelings, coupled with the depth of her loss, was devastating.

She got up and tried to busy herself. She started unpacking, then began to sob again as she pulled out the bikini she'd bought in Galveston, the one she'd worn only yesterday when Brian had made love to her. She toyed with her mail, thought of calling her mom or Lisa, but didn't have the heart to.

Then the doorbell rang. Cassie felt filled with dread, wondering if the visitor would be Chris. When she opened the door, her astonished gaze was immediately drawn upward to a gaggle of mylar balloons emblazoned with confetti and Welcome Home banners. Glancing downward, she found herself staring into the face of a familiar stranger who was grinning back like a Cheshire cat.

"Brian!"

He thrust the balloons into her hands. "Welcome home, Cassie. You look like you've just seen a ghost."

Overwhelming joy filled Cassie. "I have. When the doorbell rang, I thought you might be Chris."

He was looking at her as if he might devour her alive. "Happy it's me instead?"

"Am I?" With a delighted laugh, Cassie released the balloons and fell into his arms. "Oh, Brian, I'm so glad to see you."

"Me, too, darling."

"But—what about your flight?"

Cassie was touched to see that Brian was actually misty-eyed, and hear his voice tremble when he spoke. "I—I just couldn't get on the plane, Cassie. So I missed my flight."

"My Lord. And your job?"

"I called my boss and insisted on a reprieve. If he doesn't like it, he can fire me."

"But—why did you come back?"

"Why? Isn't that obvious?" He eased her inside and shut the door after him. "I haven't gotten *you* out of my system yet."

"Oh, Brian."

Blissfully they clung together, hugging and kissing.

"So, Brian, do you want to stay here?" Cassie called.

Brian smiled as he heard her query. Cassie was out in her impeccably neat kitchen, making frozen margaritas in a blender, while he roamed her adjoining living room. He was so glad he'd come after her, so thrilled to be here with her in her home. For this room was all Cassie—warm and bright, with its blue traditional couches and the framed prints of old-fashioned family scenes on the walls.

She was a neatnik, and her decorating was frou-frou and ultrafeminine—the polished-glass-and-walnut coffee table seeming to beg for a pair of muddy male hiking boots to add a dash of rugged individualism—but the atmosphere was also cozy and so *welcoming*. Brian lifted a crocheted throw pillow and was certain he caught the lingering scent of Cassie's hair, her perfume. Tenderness filled him. He admired her antique Singer sewing machine on its unique stand—a restored, old-fashioned child's school desk, and could just picture her sitting there, efficiently putting the finishing touches on a dress. He paused before an étagère crammed with absurdly frilly knickknacks, including a lady's gloved hand, fashioned of china, and porcelain cachepots. Cassie certainly loved antiques, and had a passion for frivolous gewgaws. If they ever traveled together, she'd doubtless drag him through every antiques shop they passed. Yet somehow this image, instead of daunting him, only endeared her to him more.

He studied her portraits of family members, in frames ranging from fussy china to handsome brass, then grinned with pride when he discovered that Chris's picture had been laid face-down. Just what the numbskull deserved.

Beyond him, the whir of the blender stopped, and Cassie called out, "Well, Brian?"

He sauntered over to her patio doors, gazing out at a tree-lined ravine, watching smoky rays of light filter through the foliage to the forest floor. "You do have a nice view."

With a drink in each hand, Cassie joined him. "Lots of trees for you to swing from, Tarzan."

"Yeah," he agreed, taking his drink and lifting it to lick the salt from the rim. With a grin, he clicked his glass against hers. "To us."

"To us," she agreed, smiling. "So, do you need a place to stay or not?"

He regarded her tenderly. "Actually, I've already booked myself a room at one of those hotels near the Galleria."

"Oh." She sounded disappointed.

He clucked her beneath her chin. "I appreciate the invitation, darling, but think about it a moment. It might not look too cool if your mom pops in and sees my shoes under your coffee table, eh?"

She brightened. "How gallant you are, to consider my reputation. And you're right—I've given my family enough shocks for now, haven't I?"

He chuckled and pulled her over to the couch with him. "Don't worry, we'll be spending plenty of time together."

"I'm counting on it. How much longer do you have?"

He sighed. "I talked my boss into another week—though he's hardly happy about it."

Her bright smile quickly faded. "Brian, I don't want you to lose your job."

He leaned over and solemnly kissed her. "Cassie, I don't want to lose *you.*"

She gazed at him dreamily. "You know something? You're a real sweetheart, Brian."

"So you're only now figuring that out?" he asked indignantly.

Cassie was about to answer him when the phone rang. Feeling a bit anxious, she picked up the receiver. "Hello?"

"Cassie, you're back."

Cassie heaved a sigh. "Hi, Lisa."

"Boy, you sound relieved. Were you thinking I might be Chris?"

A guilty cackle escaped Cassie. "You know me so well."

"So you're okay?"

Cassie wrinkled her nose at Brian, who sat sipping his drink and watching her. "Never better."

"And you're still satisfied with your decision to dump Chris?"

"Absolutely."

"Well, I don't blame you," Lisa remarked vehemently.

"Really?"

"Yeah. You know, I ran into that jerk the other night, and boy is he ticked off at you."

"So what's new?"

"Said he went down to Galveston, and you were already shacked up with his cousin down there."

Cassie was livid. "Oh! What a rotten thing to say!"

"Then you weren't?" Lisa sounded disappointed. "You know, I thought Chris's cousin was awfully cute."

Lips twitching, Cassie glanced at Brian. "He is."

Brian grinned and saluted her with his drink.

Lisa gasped. "Don't tell me he's there with you now?"

Cassie struggled not to burst out laughing. "Okay. I won't tell you."

"Cassie. Come on!"

"So what else is new, Lisa?" she smoothly hedged.

"Oh, you're driving me crazy," Lisa declared. "So you're not going to tell me about your great time in Galveston?"

"Nope."

"I get it. You refuse to speak in front of Romeo."

"Lisa, stop it."

Lisa cackled. "Well, I did want to tell you not to concern yourself about crummy old Chris."

"Believe me, I won't."

"When I ran into him, he was with some girl his mom introduced him to—and this chick was all over him. She looked barely twenty-one, and acted *mucho* stuck-up."

"Sounds like they'll make a wonderful couple," Cassie commented drolly.

Lisa laughed. "So you're really okay about all of this?"

"Lisa, quit fretting about me. I'm great."

Lisa chuckled wryly. "Then guess I'll leave you to make margaritas for Chris's dreamy cousin."

"Lisa!"

"I can still read your mind, eh?"

"You sure can."

When the two women hung up, Cassie was still laughing. "So what's so funny?" Brian asked.

"Lisa. She's a hoot. She knew you were here, and I was making you margaritas."

Brian raised an eyebrow. "Ah. So this is the way you normally stage your seductions?"

She playfully punched his arm. "You turkey!"

"Well?"

She slanted him a chiding glance. "Lisa just knows margaritas are my favorite drink."

"Uh-huh."

Cassie leaned closer to him. "You knew it, too. Remember what you ordered at our first lunch?"

He grinned and wrapped an arm around her shoulders. "You're a margarita kind of girl."

"Thought I was a sunshine girl," she teased back.

"That, too." He nuzzled her chin with his lips. "Umm. Margaritas and sunshine. Nothing better."

She sipped her drink. "I'll drink to that."

"So what else did Lisa say?"

"What do you mean?"

His expression turned serious. "Something she said made you mad, right?"

Frowning, Cassie set down her drink. "Lisa ran into Chris, who informed her you and I are 'shacking up.'"

Brian slammed a fist against a cushion. "That jerk! I ought to punch his lights out."

"Don't bother." Cassie waved a hand. "Besides, it's the nineties and to be perfectly accurate, we *are* shacking up—at least, in a manner of speaking—aren't we?"

Brian scowled massively. "I don't like his cheap way of putting it, and besides, when he came down there and acted like such a horse's patoot, we hadn't as yet made love."

"Isn't that splitting hairs at this point?"

He sighed. "You may be right."

She patted his hand. "Let's just forget him, Brian. According to Lisa, he's already painting the town with his latest flame."

"Is he? And how do you feel about that?"

Grinning, Cassie used her fingers to mimic a bird in flight. "Like the last vestiges of my guilt just flew out the window."

Brian laughed. "Mine, too."

He caught Cassie close and kissed her.

CASSIE CALLED her mom, letting her know she was back and okay. She was relieved to hear that both of her parents were doing fine, and had begun to settle down from the wedding disaster.

She decided to wait a while before telling her folks about Brian, since she had indeed jolted them enough for now. She was actually relieved to hear that her parents were about to leave for two weeks at Padre Island. She wished them well, and promised to stop by the house while they were away to pick up more wedding gifts that needed returning.

She and Brian had a late lunch at an Italian restaurant at the Galleria, then went ice-skating on the lower level. Cassie loved the rink, with its three-storied view of lights and shops and the glass dome above. She was a bit rusty on her skates, wobbling when she and Brian first ventured out on the ice. Of course, he promptly began dancing circles around her, wearing a smug grin.

Once Cassie gained her bearings a bit, they glided about the rink together, hand in hand. They were approaching a turn when Cassie felt herself beginning to slip. Before she could even squeal or otherwise react, Brian caught her about the waist and pulled her against him, saving her from a fall as they smoothly made the turn.

Cassie smiled up at him tremulously, and he dimpled back. Never had she felt happier. It was as if they were one mind, one body. He'd sensed her beginning to stumble, had known she'd needed him, and he'd protected her. Was that why he'd come back? Had he sensed she'd needed him then, too? Did he need her, as well? Oh, she hoped so. She felt so special, so cherished. How could there *not* be a future for two people so deeply attuned?

Brian too was so thrilled to be skating the rink with Cassie by his side. She looked incredible with the flush of excitement on her cheeks, the happiness shining in her eyes. Lord, he was so glad he'd come back for her. And when she'd begun to stumble, how proud he'd been to help her. She *needed* him. How could he even have considered not being there for her? He still wasn't sure where their future might lead, but never had he felt happier.

Afterward, they rode the elevator to the observation deck on the 51st floor of the Transco Tower. Only a couple of other people were present as they stepped up to the chrome railing, with the solid glass wall only a few feet beyond. In Brian's arms, Cassie gazed out at the spectacular Houston skyline, the splendor of the waning day gilding the tall buildings and treetops. She felt deeply thrilled to be sharing such a special moment with him.

"Wow, what a view," he murmured.

"Yes, indeed." Cassie hugged him tight. "So, are you going to be okay without me tomorrow?"

He feigned a scowl. "I'll manage, though it won't be easy."

"How are you going to entertain yourself?"

He nodded toward the panorama beyond them. "Oh, maybe I'll just come on back here and bungee-jump off the tower."

"Brian! Be serious."

He touched the tip of her nose with his finger. "You just get your work done quickly so we can be together again."

Cassie nestled her head beneath his chin. "I'll try to, sweetie."

They gazed out at the sunset together, tightly embraced.

# 12

CASSIE WAS SHOCKED at her own high energy level when she returned to work the next morning, especially since she and Brian had been up half the night making love, and he hadn't departed for his hotel until after 2:00 a.m. The memory made her smile. Even though he'd gallantly insisted on separate quarters for the sake of appearances, she had a feeling he'd be sticking to her like glue. She welcomed the intimacy, and was ready to attack her duties with vigor so she could get back to him.

But she found that, after her absence, she was snowed under, dozens of phone calls to return, projects that were overdue, and a major client to placate because her assistant had forgotten to mail off a publicity campaign proposal while she was gone.

Plus, everyone at the office was intensely curious about why she had walked out of her own wedding. With her assistant, Jen, it was mainly curious glances and sympathetic comments. Her boss was more direct, ducking his head inside her office early that morning.

"So, Cassie, are you okay?"

Cassie glanced at the short, heavyset man with his beard and twinkling eyes. "Just peachy, Mark."

"How was the honeymoon for one?"

"Actually, quite an adventure."

Grinning sheepishly, he stepped inside. "You know we had a betting pool going, with three-to-one odds that you would cancel your honeymoon and come back to work early."

"You rascals." Cassie leaned toward him and smiled. "So you lost?"

"Sure did," he admitted with a chuckle. Then he frowned. "Hey, you look kind of tense. You sure you're ready to come back to work?"

She harrumphed. "In an ad agency, 'tense' goes with the territory. The work has stacked up on me and there have been a few glitches. Hank over at Gulf Coast Digital is miffed because his project is late, but I'm managing to get things smoothed over. Usual stuff. And yes, I am ready to come back."

He nodded. "I'm sure you know best, Cassie. And—er—if you ever want to talk about what happened at the wedding—"

"You'll be the first one to know," she finished dryly.

He chuckled. "Right. Gotcha."

As the morning passed, other co-workers stopped by on various pretexts, everyone attempting, subtly and not so subtly, to grill her on why she'd become a runaway bride. Cassie managed to evade everyone. Meanwhile, the phone rang and rang.

By 11:00 a.m., Cassie was feeling harried, and that was when it rang for at least the twentieth time. "Hello?" she answered impatiently.

She heard a low whistle. "Ouch, you sound fried. How about some lunch?"

She laughed. "Brian, where are you?"

"Oh, I think just a few blocks from your office. I've already jogged through Hermann Park and toured the zoo, and I'm bored."

"Boy, I wish *I* were."

"You can't break away?"

Hearing the disappointment in his voice, Cassie felt torn. "Brian, I'm sorry, but I'm snowed under. Plus I have a critical meeting to prepare for after lunch. A major energy client I've been trying to sign up for two years now—and I'm so close."

"Okay. I get the picture. Think I'll go eat worms."

"Brian! Lay some guilt on me, why don't you?"

"Sure you can't break away?"

Cassie sighed. "I'd love to, doll, but I just can't."

"And I found this cool Mexican place I was going to take you to."

"May I have a rain check?"

"Sure. So we're still on for dinner at your place?"

"Of course."

"Hurry up and come back to me. Kisses, Cassie."

"Kisses."

She set down the phone, halfway tempted to run out of the office, abandon her job and just go find Brian. She smiled. That would be typical Brian Drake style. Act on impulse, to hell with the consequences. Brian had changed her, but not *that* much. For, to Cassie Brandon, actions did have consequences, and responsibilities still mattered. Unfortunately.

Thirty minutes later, Cassie was in the conference room, feverishly going over the notes for her meeting, when she heard a commotion out in the hallway. Then Jen, her assistant, stepped inside. The short, pretty, dark-haired young woman appeared quite perplexed.

"What's going on out there?" she asked distractedly.

Jen shook her head. "Cassie, you're not going to believe this."

"Believe what?"

"Your lunch has arrived."

"My lunch?"

Jen opened the door, and Cassie watched, flabbergasted, as a caravan of five men proceeded inside. First, came a white-coated waiter with a large take-out bag; he was followed by four grinning, mustachioed mariachi players, two guitarists and two trumpeters, in glittery Mexican costumes and sombreros. Even as Cassie gazed in amazement at the entourage, the players formed a line and started up a snappy rendition of *"Cuando Caliente el Sol,"* while the waiter stepped forward to place his large bag on the conference table.

"May I help you?" Cassie asked confusedly.

The grinning man began taking containers out of the bag. "*Señorita,* a certain gentleman who is your admirer has sent over your lunch."

"You're kidding." Cassie glanced at Jen, who was giggling by the door. She turned back to the waiter. "Where are you guys from?"

"Casa Fajita."

Now Cassie was laughing. "Are you certain you're not from Western Onion?"

The man only smiled as he opened up containers of fajitas, beans, tortillas, chips and various condiments and placed them before Cassie. Then he uncapped a plastic goblet filled with a margarita. She took the drink with an amazed smile.

"Cassie, who sent all this?" asked Jen. "It couldn't have been Chris."

"No, it couldn't have been Chris," she replied, laughing. "He never possessed this level of imagination."

Jen chortled.

Cassie waved a hand. "All right, come over here and help me eat all this stuff."

"You betcha!"

As the waiter served her and Jen, and the players continued their jaunty concert, Cassie felt so charmed and touched. She had no doubt as to who had treated her to lunch. Count on Brian to come up with a truly original way to surprise her.

Soon, practically everyone in the office dropped in to hear the music and steal tortilla chips, and Cassie alternated between embarrassment and joy at all the curious looks she got. When the players began a soulful rendition of "I Could Fall in Love," Cassie remembered her glorious moments dancing with Brian at the cantina in Galveston, and wiped away a bittersweet tear. Brian Drake had turned her life into such an adventure.

"HI, HON. How was work? Did you have a good lunch?"

These devilish words were the first out of Brian's mouth when Cassie admitted him to her apartment that evening. The second he was inside, she gleefully grabbed him, pushed him down on the couch and kissed him senseless.

"Wow," he said afterward, his huge grin lighting even his eyes as he roved a hand over her backside. "I'll have to send you lunch more often."

Cassie attempted a stern glance, though the smile pulling at her mouth gave her away. "You know everyone at my office is insatiably curious now, and gossiping about me like crazy. First there was the disaster at my wedding. Then your little surprise today. Before it's all over, no one will ever take me seriously again."

"You mean at an ad agency, they don't value creativity?"

"You're certainly creative," she agreed. "Perhaps you should have my job."

He chuckled. "How was the meeting?"

"Actually, very productive."

"So the lunch did help?"

She kissed his chin. "Yep. It helped. And I must admit, you were a doll to think of me."

"You're welcome, ma'am."

Mussing his hair, she sat up. "And how was the rest of your day?"

He sat up beside her. "Well, I toured the Battleship Texas and the Astrodome. And got us tickets for an Astros game tonight. They're playing Pittsburgh."

Cassie was crestfallen. "A *baseball* game? Brian, I'm beat!"

"You'll be fine after dinner, I'm sure."

She groaned. "You're going to have me dropping of exhaustion."

He chuckled. "After I got the tickets, I remembered that one of my old frat brothers, Chuck Reinhardt, supposedly settled here. So I managed to look him up. Would you believe he has a wife and three kids already?"

"No kidding."

"Well, he was an upperclassman, so he had a head start. But it's odd, since he was quite a party animal in college."

"Uh-huh."

"Anyway, Chuck loves to jet-ski at a local lake, and invited us to join him later this week. So what do you think? Could you get off work early one day?"

Cassie groaned. "Brian, I think you're not only a thrill junkie, but you're *really* high maintenance."

He caught her close. "All I want is your undivided attention."

"I've noticed. I'm just so pooped. And I have a jillion wedding gifts to return."

"Come on, girl, you can make it." He snapped his fingers. "I know, how 'bout a nice shower before dinner?"

Her ears perked up. "A shower for two?"

Brian grinned. "Now you're talking."

OVER THE REMAINDER of her work week, Cassie found her relationship with Brian falling into a pattern. He was busy with nonstop activities, and constantly called her at work wanting her to drop everything to go horseback riding in west Houston, or to tour the Space Center. Although Cassie did manage to leave work early on Wednesday to go see an IMAX film on the Grand Canyon with him, she had to decline the other invitations, much as she wanted to be with him. And she was dismayed that he couldn't seem to understand how swamped she was, that she couldn't just stand up clients for meetings or miss any more deadlines.

Their lovemaking remained fantastic, and they had some beautiful moments together. But the atmosphere between them was growing increasingly strained. Cassie had been afraid of this all along—that Brian's adventurous nature would not mesh well with the demands of her own day-to-day world.

As Brian drove them home from the film, he remarked, "Spoke with Chuck earlier today, and we're going jet-skiing at four-thirty tomorrow. Can you get off early and join us?"

Cassie shook her head. "Brian, my boss left town today, and I already promised him I'd lead the weekly staff meeting in his absence. It's at four tomorrow."

His frustration was evident from his tone. "We keep missing connections, don't we?"

"Brian, I have a job."

"So do I."

"I know."

"Know what else I did today?" he added rather defensively.

"Tell me."

Braking for a light, he shot her a heated glance. "I called my boss in Denver and told him I won't be back Monday."

"What? You rescheduled your flight again?"

"Sure did."

"What did your boss say?"

Brain shrugged. "Well, he was plenty ticked off this time."

"Can't blame him."

"He said to be back by next Thursday morning or I won't have a job."

"And what did you say?"

He grinned. "That I'd be back bright and early next Thursday morning."

Cassie could only shake her head.

"My point is, I put our relationship first."

"Oh, Brian! That's not fair," she protested.

"Why not? Because I *do* put us first?"

"No!" she said vehemently. "Because we're *different*, Brian. And life is more than just one gigantic vacation. I like to have fun as much as the next girl, but I also need to have my life organized and honor my responsibilities. It's the only way I can live and be comfortable with myself. You, on the other hand, are the daredevil, constantly acting according to your whims. You have to push everything to the limit.''

He scowled. "I don't think I do that.''

"Oh, Brian, yes, you do! Even with your boss, it's like you're playing cat and mouse. You provoke him until he gets really mad, then you manage to escape by the seat of your pants. Maybe you get off on that kind of recklessness, but I can't live that way.''

As Cassie turned away to stare out the window, Brian, too fell moodily silent. Did he live life strictly according to his whims as she was arguing? Had he treated his boss badly?

He sighed. Yes, he had behaved thoughtlessly toward his employer; Cassie had been right there. He'd have a lot of apologizing to do when he returned to Denver, and he'd need to put in some extra effort and overtime to set things right.

But Cassie had been dead wrong when she'd insisted he was acting strictly on impulse. He was a desperate man who'd taken desperate measures, staying here and risking his job, because he was scared to death that he was losing Cassie. Things just hadn't been the same between them ever since they'd come to Houston—"back to reality,'' as she'd put it. They spent too much time apart, and this scared him.

Yes, he knew Cassie had a job to do, and he recognized that she was more conservative, and less of a risk-taker, than he was. But he still found himself wanting more from their relationship than she seemed willing to give. Maybe he was being selfish, but he was miserable every second he was away from her. And, despite all her logical protestations, he couldn't help but feel he was willing to put a lot more on the line for them than she was.

Yet, was it fair to make such demands of her, when he

still wasn't ready to offer a lifetime commitment? Lord, he felt so torn and confused. If she was slipping through his fingers, then it was likely his own damn fault. Perhaps that was what bothered him most of all.

THE NEXT EVENING, Cassie was already home, at the kitchen table packing up wedding gifts, when Brian returned from his jet-skiing excursion. She answered the doorbell to find him standing outside, slightly sunburned and wearing rumpled shorts and T-shirt. "Hi, come on in," she greeted.

He stepped inside, closed the door, and quickly kissed her. "Hi, darling."

Looking him over, Cassie gasped at the sight of a thin cut along one of his calves. "What happened to you?"

"That?" Glancing at the cut, Brian shrugged. "Just a scratch, ma'am. I had to swerve to avoid another jet-skier out at the lake, and I nicked my leg on a dead tree limb protruding from the water."

Cassie was horrified. "You had to swerve? You mean you almost had a collision?"

"Cassie, you're making too much of this."

"I am not! I watched a program on TV where they showed the dangers of jet-skiing. People have been paralyzed in accidents, even killed."

He rolled his eyes. "Yes, Mother. But not if you know what you're doing."

She balled her hands on her hips. "It's the other guy who didn't know what he was doing, right?"

"Well, yes," Brian conceded.

She waved a hand. "Oh, I give up. You're so darned cavalier about everything. You haven't even cleaned that cut."

"Cassie, it's nothing."

"Well, *nothing* can get badly infected if you don't clean it properly." She grabbed his hand.

"You mean you're going to play nurse?" he asked eagerly, wiggling his eyebrows.

"Oh, hush."

She led him into the bathroom and made him sit down on the edge of the tub. As she stretched on tiptoe to find peroxide in the medicine cabinet, she could feel his gaze boring into her. She glanced over her shoulder to spy him unabashedly admiring the curves of her bottom as her skirt rode up over her hips. She stuck out her tongue at him, and he winked. She was mad enough to shake him, but he was just so adorable.

Armed with peroxide and cotton balls, she started toward him. "You bad boy."

"*Now* what have I done?"

"You were ogling me."

"Ogling?" He repeated the word as if savoring it. "Yeah. Ogling. I like that."

She cast him a scolding look and knelt on the plush rug, trying not to concentrate on the rugged beauty of his tanned legs as she opened the peroxide. He smelled of the outdoors and male sweat, a combination she found quite potent and pleasing.

She soaked a cotton ball with peroxide, then began to dab.

"Youch!" he yelled.

"Hold still so I can get this done," she admonished. "You know, you're slightly sunburned, too. Didn't your mother warn you to limit your exposure to the sun?"

He nodded. "She'd be thrilled to know you're nagging me in her place."

"Nagging? Mister, you're asking for it."

Brian whistled. "Wow, do you have a bee in your bonnet."

"Well, I have cause," she snapped back, dabbing away.

He grimaced. "Damn, that smarts. Guess I shouldn't provoke a woman with a loaded cotton ball, huh?"

Cassie fought a smile. "No, you shouldn't." She

grabbed several clean balls. "So how was your friend? Did he survive the water combat without any battle scars?"

Brian expelled a frustrated sigh. "How you exaggerate, woman. As for Chuck, he's fine. In fact, he invited us to have dinner with his family at their home on Sunday. Said I'd check with you first."

"Sounds like fun."

There was a moment of silence, then he said softly, "I missed you today, Cassie."

She glanced up to find his gaze unexpectedly tender and intense. Her pulse automatically quickened. "Yeah. Me, too."

"I *always* miss you."

"That's sweet."

He reached down and toyed with the top button on her silk blouse. "I like your blouse."

"You like unbuttoning it."

"Yeah." His voice was husky. "Hurry up and finish, will you?"

Glancing up at him again and seeing his rapt expression, Cassie felt her mouth going dry. There was no doubt as to what Brian wanted. She did, too. Even as angry as she was, she was still starved for him. She finished dabbing off the peroxide, and tossed the soiled cotton balls into the waste-basket. "There, I'm done. That looks better. I suppose we should just let it air."

"Yeah." Abruptly Brian caught Cassie beneath both arms and pulled her up onto his lap. His gaze was dark with ardor as he slid his hand inside her skirt and up one nylon-clad thigh.

"What's this?" she teased.

He nibbled at the tip of her nose. "You know, when I watched you dig in that medicine cabinet, all I could think of was getting this skirt and blouse off you."

"I noticed."

"Well, you're the one who said I like to push everything to the limit," he teased.

"Is that why you stayed, Brian?"

He regarded her solemnly. "You're the reason I stayed, Cassie."

"I know, sweetie," she said, embracing him. "I know."

Brian stood and pulled Cassie with him into the bedroom. At the bed, he pulled back the covers. Both removed their shoes, then they fell across the sheets together.

As Brian nibbled at her ear, Cassie moaned contentedly and ran her fingertips across his stubbly jaw. "You know something, fella? You're insatiable."

Brian's deft fingers were making quick work of the rest of her buttons. "But I haven't made love to you in sixteen whole hours."

She chuckled. "You're counting, eh? Or, did almost getting killed today make you hot?"

His words were vehement. "I didn't almost get killed. And *you* make me hot, lady." Removing her blouse, he lowered the straps on her lacy camisole, opened the front clasp on her bra, then kissed her breast. "That, and your work clothing."

Cassie panted ecstatically. "My—work clothing?"

Even as his mouth found her aching nipple, his fingers were pulling down the side zipper on her skirt. "Yeah, so demure and professional. Makes me wild to unmask that hot little vixen inside."

By now, Cassie was arching her back and feeling very vixenish. She pulled off Brian's T-shirt and trailed her fingertips over the smooth muscles of his chest. His response was immediate as he slid upward and captured her lips in a drowning kiss, the roughness of his slight beard abrading her face. Meanwhile, he tugged off the rest of her clothing.

Cassie groaned as Brian's lips slid down her body, kissing every inch of her until he reached her thighs, then parting her. Taking of her. And giving even more. Cassie reeled, arching into his skilled, tormenting lips. She went hurtling over the edge of incredible pleasure, crying out hoarsely.

He smiled, sliding upward to claim her. Gazing into Brian's bright eyes, Cassie reached another shattering peak. His mouth smothered her ragged cry. Bittersweet tears filled her eyes. It didn't get any better than this.

AFTER THEY made love, Brian announced he would return to his hotel to clean up and change. Since Cassie was exhausted, she gave him a key in case he wanted to return later.

He didn't rejoin her for most of the night, and she slept soundly. Then, long before morning, she was stunned and rather irritated when he appeared in the bedroom, whipping on the lights. "Rise and shine, sleepyhead!"

Cassie sat up in bed and groggily rubbed her eyes. Brian stood by the door, grinning, dressed in casual slacks and a sports shirt. She glanced at the clock. "What's this? It's 5:00 a.m. I don't have to be at work until nine."

He rushed over and kissed her, then pulled her out of bed. "Come on. I have a surprise for you."

"Brian!"

Refusing to tell her what he was up to, Brian insisted she get dressed immediately, then left the room. Moments later, she was walking into the kitchen, scowling and buttoning her jacket, when she spied him closing a picnic basket. Bemused, she watched him fill two car mugs with coffee, then hand them to her. Picking up the basket, he smiled smugly.

"No need to stop for breakfast. I've packed us a picnic."

"So I see."

Sipping coffee with Brian in the car, Cassie was perplexed when he drove them toward the far west side of Houston, away from her office. But her questions and protests fell on deaf ears.

Thirty minutes later, she was stunned to find herself aloft with him in a colorful hot-air balloon, drinking champagne and nibbling on a croissant, admiring the sunrise skies as the operator stood behind them working the cord to keep the balloon afloat. The atmosphere was awesomely quiet except for the hiss of the flames.

"So, how's this for a surprise?" Brian asked.

Cassie felt as if dreaming, soaring on a cloud. She gazed below at the beautiful landscape, cloaked in morning mists. Sleepy neighborhoods flowed off lush forests and tree-lined bayous. The morning air smelled fresh and very sweet.

All thanks to Brian. The world was perpetually new, filled with magic, seen through his eyes. She doubted she could ever adequately express what she felt at this moment.

She smiled at him tremulously. "I must hand it to you, Brian, you've topped everything this time."

Brian chuckled, then nodded toward the operator. "George here wouldn't let me take up his balloon alone, even though I assured him I've operated them before."

Cassie glanced at the man, who was grinning. "Can't blame George. Is there any sport you haven't tried, Brian?"

He scowled. "Let's see. We could parachute off the gondola." He turned to George. "What do you say?"

"I say you're certifiable," declared George.

"Me, too," added Cassie, laughing.

Brian leaned toward Cassie and whispered, "Hope this makes up for yesterday."

She eyed him mischievously and whispered back, "You did that last night."

He grinned, then snapped his fingers. "I almost forgot." Leaning over, he took a small tape player from the picnic basket then punched a button. The soulful strains of a familiar song spilled forth.

Cassie felt deeply touched. "Oh, Brian. You remembered."

"'I Could Fall in Love,'" he replied soulfully. "Think that's our song, don't you, darling?"

"Oh, yes."

Trembling, Cassie slipped inside Brian's arms. Never had their kiss seemed more heartfelt.

BY THE TIME they disembarked from the balloon, it was after eight. Since Cassie was running a bit late, Brian insisted he would drive her to her office, then pick her up later. "Besides, I want to spend every second I can with you," he declared.

"Even being a chauffeur?" she asked.

"Even being a chauffeur."

Cassie walked into her office whistling, "I Could Fall in Love." She propped her feet on her desk, whipped out a nail file, and began to shape her nails. She even ignored her blaring phone.

What was wrong with her? she wondered in awe. She was changing. Brian's love was changing her. Her feelings were strong, and showed no signs of fading.

Jen burst in with a phone-message slip in hand, only to do a double take. "Cassie!"

"Hi." Cassie neither removed her feet from her desk nor stopped her nail-filing.

Obviously flustered, Jen stammered, "I—I wasn't even sure you were here, since you didn't answer your phone."

"I'm here."

"Well, since you are, I'll just tell you who called. It was Sid Halliday and it's bad, Cassie."

"Um?" she murmured, only half listening.

"Yes, he said he hates the new slogan for his home-security systems, and if our 'knucklehead' copywriters can't come up with something snappier, he's switching his account to Whitney Haines."

"Okay," Cassie murmured with a bored air. "I'll take care of it." She began whistling the love song again.

Jen appeared confused. "Cassie, what gives? I thought you'd go ballistic."

"What's the point?" Cassie inquired pleasantly.

Jen could only shake her head. "What are you so cheery about this morning? Is it that guy?"

"What guy?"

"Don't be coy, boss. The cool guy with the fajitas."

"Yeah, fajitas and a lot more," Cassie muttered wickedly.

"I beg your pardon?"

"Never mind. And yeah, it's the guy with the fajitas."

Grinning smugly, Jen slipped out of the office.

After she left, Cassie continued to smile. Why was she so cheery? Then she listened carefully to what she was humming.

Of course. She *was* falling in love. With Brian.

# 13

On Sunday afternoon, Cassie and Brian pulled up to the curb of a prosperous-looking, two-story brick Tudor home in the posh Kingwood subdivision. The house was surrounded by tall pines, and a large sport-utility vehicle was parked in the driveway beneath a shady silver maple.

Gazing at the beautifully landscaped, manicured lawn, Cassie whistled. "Wow. Nice house. What's your friend Chuck do?"

"He's a mechanical engineer for an oil-tool manufacturer," Brian explained. "I know he and Sally struggled early in their marriage, when the oil industry wasn't hiring much. But he managed to land with a strong company that has held on to its employees through the various cycles of boom and bust."

"Good."

Brian got out of the car and came around to open Cassie's door. After she got out, he reached into the back seat to retrieve the tote bag containing their swimsuits and a bottle of wine they'd bought on the way. As they strolled the curving walkway toward the door, Cassie smoothed down her sundress and thought of how handsome Brian looked in his casual white slacks and green shirt.

Their knock was answered by a tall, blond man accompanied by two tow-headed boys who appeared about five and six, and a large golden retriever that rushed up to Cassie and wagged its tail. As she petted it, the man shook hands with Brian.

"Brian, good to see you again. And this delightful creature must be Cassie?"

"Yes," answered Brian. "Cassie Brandon, I'd like you to meet my old pal, Chuck Reinhardt."

"A pleasure," said Cassie, shaking his hand, then laughing as the dog tried to climb up her skirt.

"Down, Aggie," scolded Chuck.

"Yeah, down, Aggie," seconded the older boy.

Grinning, Cassie petted the dog. "Actually, I like dogs. And only in Texas would you find one called 'Aggie.'"

"I named him," exclaimed the younger child proudly.

"Did you?" asked Cassie. "Well, you did a great job."

As the boy shyly smiled, Chuck said, "These are my sons, Chuck Jr. and Trey."

"How do you do?" Cassie asked, offering her hand to each boy in turn. She noted how cute they were, both sporting crew cuts, and wearing shorts, cartoon character T-shirts and sneakers.

Brian grinned at the boys. "Hey, men, give me five."

The two laughed and eagerly smacked Brian's hand. Cassie shook her head in grudging admiration. He always knew how to break the ice.

"Come on out to the kitchen, guys, and I'll introduce you to Sally," Chuck was saying.

Out in the huge, sparkling, country kitchen, a pretty blond woman in shorts and a cotton shirt was chopping vegetables at the sink. Wiping her hands, she turned to them. "Hi, you guys must be Brian and Cassie."

Crossing the room, Chuck proudly wrapped an arm around the woman's shoulders. "Meet the love of my life, Sarah Ann Reinhardt."

"*Sally,*" corrected the woman, extending her hand.

Cassie eagerly shook hands with the other woman as Chuck completed the introductions. She at once liked Sally, who had a vivacious, friendly manner.

Soon the older boy was tugging at Chuck's shirt. "Dad, you promised us we could swim."

Chuck snapped his fingers. "Hey, that's right." He glanced at Brian. "You guys remember your suits?"

"Sure did." Brian held up the tote bag. "Oh, I almost forgot." He pulled out the bottle of wine and handed it to Sally. "For the chef."

"Thanks," said Sally, setting the wine on the counter.

"You girls want to join us outside?" Chuck asked.

Sally shook her head. "I still have cooking to do."

"I'll keep you company," Cassie offered.

Sally protested, "Cassie, if you'd rather—"

Cassie touched her arm. "No, I'm delighted to stay here with you."

Sally smiled.

Chuck clapped his hands together. "Okay, then. We guys will watch the boys and start up the grill. Send out the steaks when they're ready."

The men grabbed beers and left with the boys. Cassie smiled at Sally. "You have a wonderful family."

"I'm very blessed," she agreed.

"It's great you have two sons so close to the same age. They can keep each other company."

"We have a daughter, too."

"You do?"

Sally beamed with pleasure. "Gretchen. She's nine months old, and sound asleep at the moment."

"I can't wait to see her." Cassie glanced around the kitchen. "In the meantime, what can I do to help?"

"Actually, you could go check on the baby for me."

"I'd love to!"

"Just go back through the living room, then down the hallway, third door on the left."

Cassie made her way to the nursery and creaked open the door. She sighed in delight at the lovely setting—the walls and ceilings painted with clouds, the yellow and white furniture, the various stuffed animals and mobiles.

Tiptoeing over to the Jenny Lind crib, she spotted plump little Gretchen sound asleep, her blond head peeking out over a precious teddy-bear quilt, her cherub face exquisitely beautiful. Cassie reached down and stroked the baby's incredibly soft cheek and listened to the soft sounds of her breathing. Pain and tenderness clutched at her heart. Never had she so wanted a baby—Brian's baby. How she wished the two of them could build a beautiful home together as Chuck and Sally had done.

Was she feeling this way because Brian was leaving soon?

No, she was feeling this way because she *loved* him. *And* because he was leaving soon.

Returning to the kitchen, she pronounced, "She's an angel—and sound asleep."

Sally stood at the stove stirring a pot of beans. "Thanks, Cassie."

Crossing the room, Cassie was bemused to watch Sally wiping away a tear. "Sally, are you okay?"

Sally nodded and braved a smile. "Oh, I'm just a little misty-eyed. You see, I've been weaning Gretchen to the bottle, and since she's likely our last, it's kind of hard."

"Oh." Cassie smiled sympathetically, then winked. "She needn't necessarily be your last."

"Well, I guess one never knows," Sally conceded with a laugh. "Anyway, I'm thrilled she's still asleep. She's been having a rough time lately—teething, you know."

"Oh, yeah. I went through that with my niece and nephew."

As Cassie spoke, she moved toward the window. The backyard was beautiful and green, shaded by large pine trees. The boys were swimming in the shallow end of the pool, throwing a colorful beach ball around, while Brian and Chuck stood on the sidelines drinking beers and starting up the fire.

"Looks like the guys are having lots of fun," she called to Sally.

"Yes. Brian's a real doll."

Cassie turned. "I know."

Sally raised an eyebrow. "Things serious between you two?"

"Well, we're pretty crazy about each other, but it's hard," Cassie admitted with a sigh. "He's from Denver, while my roots are here. And, well, he's not the marrying kind."

Sally smirked. "That's what Chuck said until I convinced him otherwise."

"Good for you," Cassie declared.

The group dined in the Reinhardts' large dining room, the adults eating steak, salad and baked potatoes, while the boys gobbled down hamburgers and baked beans. The atmosphere was lively and fun, especially as the guys retold escapades from their frat days at college, recounting how they'd once painted all the windows black at a rival fraternity house, and had serenaded their sister sorority house at 4:00 a.m. Cassie had to laugh at some of the antics they described, and even the boys listened in fascination.

Then a tense moment ensued when Brian said to his host, "So, Chuck, don't forget to give me the phone number of that pilot you know, and draw a map to the private field he flies out of. I really do want to go skydiving on Tuesday."

"Skydiving?" Cassie cried. "Is there any extreme sport you don't indulge in?"

Brian turned to her with a shrug. "Actually, I'm dying to try sky-surfing, but haven't been able to as yet."

"Sky-surfing? What is that?" Sally inquired.

"It's when you parachute out of a plane with a small surfboard attached to your feet, and surf the air baffles going down," Brain explained.

Cassie waved a hand. "My Lord. You *are* certifiable."

"Agreed," put in Sally.

Brian flashed them both a chiding glance. "Come now, ladies. None of this is dangerous if you know what you're doing."

"Famous last words," pronounced Cassie.

Chuck was laughing and shaking his head. "Do you

know that back in college, this guy used to do skateboarding stunts—flips and 360s—on the front steps of the administration building?''

"I'd believe it," said Cassie.

"Me, too," said Sally.

"Did you really?" asked Chuck Jr., expression rapt.

Brian solemnly nodded. "Yes, but that's not for you guys to try, you understand?''

"Yes, Chuck, don't you and Brian be giving the boys ideas," scolded Sally. "They're into enough mischief already.''

"Sorry," Chuck told his wife. To Brian, he added, "You always did have a death wish, Drake.''

Brian glowered at his friend. "Now you're all ganging up on me. Tell me, Chuck, who went jet-skiing with me the other day?''

Chuck shook out his napkin. "Okay, so I like to indulge in an occasional sport just like the next guy. But you're the fanatic.''

"You tell him, Chuck," Cassie encouraged.

Brian wagged a finger at her. "You just wait. You're in big trouble now.''

After the meal, the men tried to help with the dishes, but the boys grew rowdy, and Sally shooed all the males outside to play baseball. Then the baby woke up, and Cassie finished up in the kitchen while Sally went to change her.

Afterward, since Sally still hadn't returned, Cassie wandered out onto the deck and sat down on one of several homey, slat-back rockers. The scent of honeysuckle was thick in the air, and again she admired the backyard, with its gleaming pool on one side and gorgeous thick grass on the other. Brian stood with Chuck Jr. beneath a tree, coaching the boy on how to swing a bat, as Chuck Sr. gently threw a softball. As the child successfully hit the ball, a cheer went up from Trey and the men.

Brian was so good with kids, she thought. And he was

such a pain. Now he was going skydiving. Another stunt to worry her sick. What next?

"Oh, there you are," Sally called, emerging from the house with the baby and a bottle.

Cassie smiled at the sight of Gretchen in her little pink dress embroidered with periwinkles. The baby cooed at her, and her heart again melted. "May I feed her?"

"Sure. I'd love to put my feet up for a while."

Cassie took the child and bottle, and nudged the nipple inside her mouth. Gretchen drank slowly, while staring up at Cassie solemnly and twining a strand of Cassie's long hair around one chubby finger.

Leaning over to kiss the baby's downy head, and inhaling her sweet scent of baby powder, Cassie sighed in pure ecstasy. "She's too adorable," she told Sally.

"Thanks." Sally was happily rocking, her feet propped on a stool. "But watch out, she can yank your hair like the very devil."

"Oh, I don't care."

Chuckling, Sally glanced out at the men. "Brian is great with the boys. Looks like he'd make a wonderful family man."

"Yeah—if he ever grows up himself," Cassie replied dryly.

The women were sharing a conspiratorial laugh when suddenly, Gretchen pushed the bottle away and began to squall, her precious features screwing up mutinously. Wondering what she might have done to upset the child, Cassie put down the bottle, then sat the baby up and tried to comfort her, gently patting her back. To Sally, she said, "What happened? Did I do something wrong?"

"No, not at all," Sally reassured her. "But like I said, she's teething. And she'll do that—just be drinking along, then hit a sore spot and start screaming, apparently for no reason at all. Want to give her back?"

Still trying to comfort the wailing child, Cassie was struck by inspiration. "No, I've got a better idea. Brian!"

At once the men and the boys came rushing over. "What's wrong?" Brian asked, staring with concern at the baby.

"We've got a fretful, teething baby here," Cassie explained.

Chuck was scratching his jaw. "You know, my dad used to put whiskey on my gums."

"Chuck!" scolded Sally. "Over my dead body!"

"Yeah, Chuck, this is the nineties," seconded Brian. "Get with the program."

Even as the men grinned, Cassie announced smugly, "We don't need folk remedies. We have Brian."

He stared at Cassie questioningly.

"Well?" she prodded.

As if on cue, he hunkered down, gazed at the baby's face, then began making goofy faces. Observing him, the boys howled with laughter. Chuck and Sally exchanged mystified glances. As for the baby, she continued to sob for a moment, then whimpered, then merely stared at Brian, obviously fascinated. He held out his arms and she gurgled. Cassie handed her over.

As Brian stood with the happy child, both parents still appeared dumbfounded. "What gives with this guy?" Chuck asked Cassie, while shaking his head. "He's great with the boys, too. Kind of like the pied piper."

"I wouldn't have believed it unless I saw it myself," Sally added in awe.

Cassie stood and handed Brian the bottle. "Tell you what. You guys can tend the baby. Think Sally and I will play catch with the boys."

"Yippee," shouted Chuck Jr., jumping up and down.

"Mommy's gonna play catch!" added Trey, clapping his hands.

"Yes, Cassie, that's a great idea," agreed Sally with an eager nod. Watching Brian sit with the child, she winked at Cassie. "You know, this guy is amazing. You really are going to have to marry him, Cassie."

Cassie felt her cheeks heating. She glanced at Brian, and he grinned back.

Lord, he was too adorable. Yet as Cassie moved away with Sally and the boys, she found her thoughts were bittersweet. Yes, Brian was wonderful around kids, but wouldn't his daredevil approach to life still prevent him from becoming a responsible father and the kind of husband she needed? He might welcome the fun and distraction of entertaining the Reinhardt children, but would he really be there for long nights with a sick baby, or tense conferences at the school principal's office? Spontaneity and instant gratification might be Brian's long suits, but he still seemed woefully lacking in the patience and tenacity needed for a successful marriage. As much as she loved him, these realizations made her very sad.

As HE DROVE them home, Brian kept glancing at Cassie. How proud he'd been to have her with him today at his friend's house. Both Chuck and Sally loved her, as had all of the children.

Being with her in such a family setting had brought powerful emotions welling within him. He was feeling more torn with each passing day, his heart aching at the prospect of leaving her on Wednesday. He was beginning to entertain all kinds of wild thoughts, like kidnapping her, begging her to marry him.

But even if he could persuade her, would he still disappoint her in the long run?

The minute they were inside her apartment, he caught her close for a passionate kiss, savoring the feel of her curves in his arms, inhaling her scent, devouring her mouth with his tongue.

When at last their lips parted, she appeared slightly dazed. "Wow. What brought that on?"

He stroked her cheek and regarded her soulfully. "I guess because today was so special. Seeing everything

Sally and Chuck have together. Their lovely home. Three wonderful children.''

She smiled. "I know. It meant a lot to me, too."

"It showed me how much fun having a home can be," he continued thoughtfully, "even for someone like me. You know, Chuck was as wild and unruly as I was in college, but he's totally settled down now, content to be with Sally and the kids."

"So it's not all just responsibility, eh?" she teased.

The tenderness Brian was feeling made his chest ache. "How I loved being with those kids. Playing ball with Chuck and his sons. And when I held that baby, I looked down at her cute little blond head and thought about you. Your pretty blond hair. Your green eyes. If you could give me half a dozen baby girls that looked like you, I'd be the happiest guy alive."

Appearing both thrilled and somewhat skeptical, she asked, "Brian, what are you saying?"

His arms trembled about her. "I'm saying it was so special—and here I am walking away from it all on Wednesday." He gazed at her in torment. "Come with me, Cassie."

Cassie felt equally torn. "Brian, we've been over this. You're a wonderful guy—fun, spontaneous, very romantic. And I know you've made sacrifices for our relationship, trying to make this work, and sticking around when you shouldn't. But we both know you're not ready to commit for the long haul—and I probably shouldn't, either, given the fact that I walked out of my own wedding just two weeks ago. As for today—although it may have been fun for you, it's a far cry from all the responsibilities of 'till death do us part.'"

He sighed heavily. "We just need more time."

"Meaning, you want the full package, but you're not willing to make any of the sacrifices required to get it?"

He was silent.

She flashed him a sad smile. "Brian, I don't want to be

with you if it's going to stifle your spirit and make us both miserable. Besides, if you were really ready to settle down, would you still be running from one extreme thrill to another?''

He frowned. ''What does my love of sports have to do with this?''

''It shows me where you are as a person,'' she said soberly. ''Hardly ready to sit in your rocker by the fire. For that matter, what we have could be just another thrill ride that won't stand the test of time, right?''

''Cassie, really.''

Her voice caught on a tremor of emotion. ''Besides, jumping out of planes is a lot more important right now, isn't it?''

''More important? But you'll be working—''

''Ah. So if I don't entertain you every second, you have to punish me by trying some crazy stunt?''

He appeared bewildered. ''Punish you? I'm not trying to punish you, Cassie.''

''Sometimes it feels that way.''

He groaned. ''Cassie, all I know is I *want* you. More than anything else in the world.''

She hugged him tight. ''Me, too, Brian.''

But Brian well knew both of their worlds would change forever come Wednesday.

FOR BRIAN, the next days before he was scheduled to leave passed too quickly, especially with the new tensions between him and Cassie regarding his departure. *It could all be resolved if you'd just ask her to marry you, chump,* he would often scold himself. But Brian still had doubts about taking such a big step so soon. He and Cassie had only known each other for two weeks. What if their feelings weren't truly lasting?

More importantly, just as their argument had reflected, could he go the distance for her, become the kind of husband she deserved? Someone ready to settle down. Someone who could commit himself to her alone for a lifetime, someone who would make all the sacrifices that commitment entailed. Much as he cared for Cassie, he wasn't sure he was ready for such a huge step.

He hoped his skydiving excursion on Tuesday would help him clear his head. For on Wednesday, he might well lose her.

YET WHEN Brian trudged up the steps toward Cassie's apartment on Tuesday evening, he was hardly feeling the sense of liberation he'd hoped to gain from skydiving. He was exhausted, tense, most dispirited. For he'd lived through a nightmare today, a scary near miss, and he still felt unsettled about it, especially when he considered that he could have lost Cassie forever.

He might lose her tomorrow anyway, he mused dismally. Part of him wanted to call his boss and tell him to shove the job, but that would be rude and unprincipled, especially when his boss had already given him two extensions on his vacation. It wasn't the man's fault that his life was a mess. Besides, if he just walked away from his life, his responsibilities, in Denver, he would only convince Cassie that he was a reckless flake.

Reaching her door, he sighed. Whatever he did, he'd best not let on to her about how shaken he really was over today's misadventure. He rang the doorbell and tried to force a cheery expression.

The door creaked open, and Cassie appeared before him in a pool of light. Still dressed in her professional clothing, she wore an apron, and sexy little tendrils of hair spilled around her face. She held a large, spattered spoon in her hand, and he could smell tomato sauce in the air.

Tenderness rent his heart. Cassie. Home. Lord, he loved her. He really did love her. The realization set him reeling and was almost too much for him to absorb in his current, emotional state. He didn't know what to say to her, how to react. His feelings were too new, too raw.

She regarded him curiously. "Hi, Brian. You okay?"

"Sure, darling." He stepped inside and hugged her tight his arms trembling about her softness. He tipped her face up to his. "Lord, you're a welcome sight."

Brian crushed Cassie close and ravenously kissed her Thank God he was here, safe in her arms again. Her soft warmth comforted him and the taste of her set him on fire He wanted to be in bed with her now—naked and very intimate.

But she pressed him away and regarded him with concern. "Brian, what's this?"

"What do you mean, what's this?" He flashed her a hungry grin. "I missed you. I want you. Come here, darling. Let's make love."

Yet she held up a hand. "No."

"No?" Hurt lanced him.

"Brian, what's wrong?"

He spoke defensively. "What makes you think something is wrong?"

"Well, for one thing, you're white as a ghost. Then you walk in here and all but jump me—"

His voice turned cold. "Jump you? I take it you mind?"

"That's not the point."

"Then what's the point?"

"The point is, you're hiding something," she shot back

Lord, she could read him like a book! "Cassie, you're exaggerating."

"No, I'm not. What happened to you today?"

"Nothing happened."

Her eyes snapped with anger. "Damn it, Brian, don't lie to me!"

Now she was PO'd, and Brian knew he might as well fess up. "It was nothing," he muttered. "Just a little glitch skydiving."

She went pale, gasping as if she'd been stabbed. "A glitch? Brian, a *glitch* skydiving could get you killed!"

He threw up his hands. "No wonder I don't tell you things. You overdramatize terribly."

She spoke through gritted teeth. "I do not. Now tell me what happened."

He groaned. "Very well. For some reason, my main chute didn't open—"

"*What?*"

He stepped toward her, speaking almost frantically. "Cassie, please, don't panic. It was no big deal. I just had to use my reserve chute."

She just stared at him. Her face looked frightful—white, drawn. Her eyes were filled with fear and anguish, and he hated himself for causing her such distress. Lord, there was no way he could *ever* tell how scared he'd really been.

At last she spoke, her words deadly quiet. "Brian, you could have been killed."

He clutched her shoulders. "Cassie, it's okay. Really."

She shoved him away, tears shining in her eyes. "You stop lying to me. When are you going to face the truth and grow up?"

"I know what I'm doing."

"I'm tired of hearing that, Brian. Furthermore, you *don't* know what you're doing."

"So what are you saying?"

"That you're risking your life on surfboards, jet-skis, and jumping out of planes. It's time for you to quit being an overgrown child and give it up."

He was stunned. "You mean give it *all* up?"

She hesitated a moment, then nodded. "Yes, I think I do."

"You can't be serious."

She set her mouth stubbornly. "Damn it, I am."

"Cassie, be reasonable," he pleaded. "You're trying to control me again."

Her voice trembled with outrage. "Brian, I'm trying to keep you alive."

"That's ridiculous."

''What, keeping you alive?'' she half shouted. ''Or try
ing to control you?''

He sighed. ''I know that sooner or later, I'm going to
have to become more conservative on the sports I pursue.
I just don't think your extreme approach is the answer.''

''Why not?'' A tear trickled down her cheek. ''You're
extreme about everything. Why can't I be extreme, too?''

Feeling miserable and aching to comfort her, Brian tried
to touch her, but she flinched again. Helplessly, he dropped
his hand. ''Cassie, you're just upset because I'm leaving.''

She took a step closer, blinking rapidly in her anger.
''Brian, if you think our only problem is that you're leav
ing, then you really are clueless.''

She turned on her heel, stormed back to the kitchen, and
began banging pots. With a groan, Brian collapsed onto the
couch.

# 14

THE NEXT MORNING, Cassie's expression was grim as she sat at her desk. She felt tired and overwrought, and was in no frame of mind to tackle a very full schedule today.

She and Brian had continued to argue last night, but they hadn't settled anything, not even kissing goodbye when he'd left for his hotel. The feelings of distance and alienation between them had been keenly painful.

Although he'd called early this morning, their conversation had been terribly awkward. Brian had wanted to meet for lunch, but Cassie was booked solid. Sounding disappointed, he'd promised to call again before he left for the airport.

Nothing was settled. Cassie remained furious at him for being so cavalier about his own life and safety. Perhaps she had gone too far by insisting he give up all his sports, but he sorely needed to make some changes and grow up.

She wasn't sure just what the answer was for him, for them, or even whether their relationship would have a future. But she did know she was miserable without him.

The phone rang and she jumped, grabbing the receiver. "Yes?"

"Hi, Cassie." Brian sounded as tense as she felt.

"Hi, Brian."

"Look, we need to talk."

She sighed. "We tried that last night and got nowhere."

"Yes, and I'm flying back to Denver at eight tonight. Do you really want to part like this?"

Cassie felt intensely conflicted. "By the time I get out of here, it'll be too late."

"I've thought of that, too. When I was downtown before, I really fell in love with Tranquility Park, and it's not far from your office. Meet me there at four-thirty. I'll even bring dinner. Then we can talk things out for a couple of hours, and I can still make my flight."

She laughed dryly. "Talk about a photo finish."

"Please, Cassie?"

Cassie shut her eyes as turmoil welled. "I'd love to, but I can't. I've got a four-o'clock meeting with our biggest corporate client, and I wouldn't be surprised if it runs through dinner."

"But you knew I was leaving tonight," he said defensively.

She groaned. "I *thought* you were leaving on Monday, but you switched things again. This meeting has been set up for over a week, and I can't cancel now."

"Looks like you can't put our relationship first, either."

"Brian, that's not fair!"

"You're shutting me out, Cassie."

"And you're being your usual cavalier self, expecting me to drop everything on an impulse."

His voice tightened. "Look, I'm going to be at the park whether you're there or not."

"Fine."

"Fine."

After they hung up, Cassie sat in her office, staring out at the skyline, feeling terrible about their fight. She hated to see Brian leave with their relationship still unresolved, but she just didn't know how to fix things. She also wished she had made more of an effort to meet him halfway, though her pride bristled at his expecting her just to abandon her responsibilities.

She remembered his accusing her of trying to control him. Was it true? If so, didn't he deserve this, given his own reckless conduct? And wasn't he trying to dictate to her, as well, by expecting her to be at his beck and call?

Drawing a hand through her hair, she got up and began to pace. In Galveston, Brian had once contended that she didn't like being controlled either, that this was the main reason she'd run out on Chris.

He'd been right, of course. Chris had always tried to smother her, telling her precisely how to live her life.

And wasn't this just what she was doing with Brian now, by expecting him to give up all his sports for her?

Cassie groaned. She'd never intended to strangle Brian's spirit as hers had been strangled by Chris. Brian's risk-taking just scared her so! But then, wasn't living itself a risk? Wasn't loving? Was she always going to be afraid, or could she become willing to make that leap of faith and believe her and Brian's love could work? Hadn't Brian taught her that she didn't have to be so afraid of her own impetuous side, or keep her life under such rigid rein—that, indeed, life could be a real adventure when lived more spontaneously?

She felt so torn. And she didn't know what to do!

FEELING AT LOOSE ENDS, Brian went to the park early, strolling about with a large take-out bag labeled "Casa Fajita." He roamed about the beautifully landscaped grounds—the man-made knolls, the spectacular central fountain with water running down its tall columns, the interesting modern sculptures displayed around the park. He watched pigeons forage about for crumbs and cars whiz past in the street.

Would Cassie come meet him? He rather doubted it. He had himself to blame for being such an ass and issuing ultimatums. He was scared to death she was shutting him out, that he was losing her. But he didn't know how to make things right.

He spotted an old gentleman hobbling with his cane to-

ward a park bench. When the man stumbled slightly, Bria
rushed over to offer a hand. "Here, please let me help."

The old guy, wearing casual clothes and a golf ha
clutched Brian's arm and smiled at him out of a deepl
wrinkled face. "Thanks, sonny."

Brian assisted the man to the shady bench, and helpe
him cautiously lower himself onto the seat. After Brian als
sat down, the man pulled off his hat, revealing a head c
thinning white hair, and waved the cap over his face. "Su
is hot today."

"Yeah, sure is."

The man gestured toward the sack at Brian's feet. "Yo
waiting for someone?"

"Yes. My girlfriend. I'm hoping we can have a sunse
picnic."

"How romantic."

Brian nodded. "And you? Just out catching some rays?"

"Yes, it seems to help these arthritic old bones."

"A long way to come for some sun," Brian remarked

"Oh, I live down here."

"You do?"

He pointed to a glamorous-looking, pinkish gray sk
scraper several blocks away. "See that building?"

"Yes. Very impressive."

"I have a condo on the thirtieth floor."

Brian was intrigued. "But why would you want to liv
downtown?"

"Oh, I like the concerts, the theater, and my church i
here." A weary sigh escaped him. "Don't have much fan
ily left anymore. And at my age, there's no sense living i
the suburbs. I can't exactly go jogging through Memori
Park or zip through the malls—time has done too muc
damage to this old body for that."

Brian nodded. "Were you injured in the war or some
thing?"

Chuckling, the old guy shook his head. "No. I wa
drafted into the army close to the end of World War II, b

was still in the States in basic training when Japan surrendered. Nope, I have no one to blame but myself for the
wretched state I'm in.''

Brian frowned. ''You're making me intensely curious,
you know.''

The man grinned. ''Well, I've lived quite a life. I was
an oil wildcatter, you see. And one helluva thrill-seeker. I
won and lost several fortunes, traveled the world, skied the
Alps and scuba dived at the Great Barrier Reef.''

''Wow. I'm impressed.''

''I had a ball,'' the man went on. ''Loved many women.
Of course, I also almost broke my neck in a skiing accident
in Switzerland, and I ruined my knees running marathons.
Sometimes I think I wouldn't trade my life for anything,
and other times...'' He paused, a melancholy, faraway look
in his eyes.

''Yes?'' Brian prodded.

The old guy waved him off. ''Ah, you don't want to hear
this nonsense.''

''Yes, I do,'' Brian insisted. ''I find this quite interesting.''

The man's expression was wistful. ''Well, sometimes I
think I lost out on the things in life that matter the most—
like the home, wife and children I walked out on over thirty
years ago.''

''Ah.''

The man gave an ironic laugh. ''My wife kept trying to
run my life, or so I thought. I thought nothing mattered but
what *I* wanted.'' A self-deprecatory laugh escaped him. ''It
never occurred to me what a selfish SOB I was really being.''

The man paused, and Brian was thoughtfully quiet.

The man sighed heavily. ''Now I'm an old man alone
with my regrets, a man whose adult children barely speak
to him, a man sitting on a park bench hoping the sun will
heal these crippled old bones.'' Shifting his weight slightly,

he grimaced. "My doctor warned me thirty years ago that I would have to change my life-style, but I never listened."

As the old man paused to rub an obviously aching knee, Brian sat in stunned silence. The stranger's account had hit home with a vengeance.

Was he looking at himself forty years from now—alone, possibly crippled, with nothing but a few meaningless memories of so-called good times? No, he wanted much more than that from life. He wanted and needed Cassie's love, and he was willing to make whatever sacrifices it took to win her over. What an idiot he'd been to think otherwise, to childishly insist he must have everything his way, even taking stupid risks. Cassie had been right last night—and he must tell her so, now. He'd go to her office and camp out there, waiting for her until her meeting was over. Then he'd beg for her forgiveness.

"Anyhow, didn't mean to dump my troubles on you," the old gent continued, breaking into Brian's thoughts.

Brian flashed him a grin. "No problem. Really."

"Where do you suppose your young lady is?" the man asked, glancing about.

"Not sure, but think I'll go find her." Brian retrieved his take-out bag and stood. "Hey, how 'bout a Mexican supper?"

"You're joking."

"Nope." Brian set the bag on the bench. "Enjoy yourself and take care."

"Thanks."

"Thank *you*."

Brian shook the old man's hand and raced off, running out of the park, then tearing down the skyscraper-lined street. He was racing around a corner when he stopped in his tracks at the sight ahead of him. He couldn't believe what he was seeing—a dream come true!

"Cassie!" he called jubilantly.

DOWN THE BLOCK, Cassie spotted Brian racing toward her. Never had she seen a dearer sight. She ran forward, her heart singing with joy. They met under an awning and embraced eagerly.

"Forgive me for being such a jerk—I was just so scared of losing you," he said breathlessly, clutching her close.

Catching her own breath, Cassie melted at the look of vulnerability on Brian's face. "It's okay," she reassured him. "I was wrong, too. And I think you just met me halfway."

"Oh, darling. More than halfway." Cupping her face in his hands, Brian stared tenderly into Cassie's eyes. "Cassie, I want you to know I love you and I can't live without you. And I know now that you're good for me, that I need your levelheadedness to help me ground my life. I'm willing to give up all my sports if that's what it takes for us to be together."

Tears filled Cassie's eyes at Brian's touching admission. "You really mean it?"

"Oh, yes."

"Brian, I love you, too," she replied tremulously. "Knowing you has made me more willing to live life more spontaneously. But I'd never want to change you that drastically. Today, I've done some serious thinking, and I realize now that I was wrong to insist you give up all your sports."

"But, Cassie—"

She pressed her fingers to his mouth. "Please, hear me out. That was my fear talking, and I realize our relationship will never work if it's ruled by fear. Chris made the mistake of trying to control my life, and it strangled our relationship. I'm not going to make the same mistake with you."

"Oh, Cassie." He hugged her tight.

She pressed him away slightly. "Still, if we're going to have a future together, you must set some reasonable limits and stop taking really foolish risks as you did on the surfboard."

"I agree, darling," Brian admitted at once. "I think my

taking those chances was my way of running away, avoiding commitment so I wouldn't have to risk being hurt again. After I lost Jason, I think I convinced myself that risks don't matter." He smiled into her eyes. "Well, they *do* matter, Cassie. They matter because I want to be here to love you for the rest of our lives together."

"Oh, Brian." She clung to him, blissful tears spilling from her eyes.

His voice was breaking. "And from now on, I'm not taking any risk that could take me away from you."

Cassie couldn't believe she was at last hearing the words she had prayed for for so long. "Oh, Brian, I'm so glad."

"And I'll be delighted to move to Houston," he added. "I just can't lose you."

Wiping a tear, she laughed. "But Houston is so flat, and it wouldn't be fair to ask you to give up your rock climbing, when you love that activity so much."

"Then what, Cassie?"

She shook her head. "I don't know, maybe I'm ready for a change. Since we got back from Galveston, my job just hasn't felt right. Think I'd like to try something more creative for a change instead of just managing accounts. And having to move would be the perfect excuse to resign."

Joy lit his eyes. "Are you saying—"

"I'm saying, why don't we try Denver for a year? Then maybe we can flip a coin regarding where we might live next."

Brian laughed. "Now you're sounding like me."

She chuckled, too. "I'm not suggesting we become vagabonds, but maybe I am a lot more like you than I ever knew. I think we're two people who were both afraid of being controlled, and we've found a special kind of freedom in each other. Yes, knowing you has made me a little more crazy, willing to indulge my impulsive side. But I hope knowing me has made you a little more sane."

Solemnly he replied, "A *lot* more sane, Cassie. I want

you to marry me, and I promise you this is *not* an impulse. This is forever, darling. I'm going to do everything in my power to build a safe, secure future for you and our children. I know we can work out everything in time.''

"Do you really mean it? Scout's honor?" she asked raptly.

He held up three fingers. "Scout's honor. So what do you say?"

"Yes!" cried Cassie ecstatically.

Cassie threw her arms around Brian's neck and passionately kissed him. She sensed their hearts and minds meeting in that moment, and knew both of them were confident in the strength of their love, and that together, they would find their happy medium.

# Epilogue

"IS THE WORST MAN late *again?*"

A month later, standing for the second time in the vestibule of her family's church in Houston, and wearing her new bridal gown and veil, Cassie laughed at five-year-old Emily's question. All of her attendants were again gathered about her as everyone waited for the service to begin. History was repeating itself tonight—but with a wonderful new spin.

She leaned over toward Emily, so beautiful in her flower-girl dress. "No, darling, the worst man isn't late at all. And he's no longer the worst man, he's the *groom.*"

Emily frowned. "Then why do we have to wait, Aunt Cassie?"

Cassie smiled whimsically as she listened to the lilting melody on the air. "So the organist can play Brian's and my favorite song. Can't you hear it now? It's called 'I Could Fall in Love.' But don't worry. Soon she'll be playing the bridal chorus."

Emily's gaze was reproachful. "You know I've been waiting a *long* time for this wedding, Aunt Cassie."

"Oh, I know, sweetie. Me, too."

The child's expression grew suspicious. "You aren't going to run away again, are you?"

Cassie giggled. "No way."

Emily shook a finger and grinned. "Well, if you do, I'll make Teacher give *you* retention."

Cassie feigned a horrified look. "Don't worry, I promise to behave."

Evidently satisfied, Emily twirled about in a rustle of petticoats and silk organza. "At least I got to wear my wedding dress again."

"You sure did. And you're just beautiful, darling."

Emily reached out to finger a fold of her aunt's silk skirt. "You're pretty, too. But why are you wearing a different dress this time?"

Cassie stared down at her luscious gown of cream-colored silk, with its embroidered, full skirt and lavish train. "Because I had to have 'something new.'"

Emily chortled and bounced on her heels. "But you already have something new, Aunt Cassie. You have a new *groom!*"

"I sure do, minx." Cassie leaned over and tickled her niece, who squealed with joy.

Straightening, she saw Lisa smiling at her. "Happy, Cassie?"

"Never happier."

"That's the spirit."

Giving Cassie a thumbs-up, Lisa leaned over to straighten a bow on Emily's dress. Cassie smiled to herself. She thought over the last month. It had been frantic, yet so delightful. Quitting her job. Going to Denver and meeting Brian's wonderful family. Arranging for the move.

Brian had persuaded her not to go job-hunting yet, arguing that she could always do so after their honeymoon. He also kept hinting he'd like to have a baby soon. She smiled and shook her head. He was taking on the responsibilities of married life with a zeal that matched everything else he did.

It was so ironic. Six weeks ago, she'd balked at Chris's insisting she quit her job. Yet now she'd cheerfully walked away from it, and she even found the prospect of waiting a while before she returned to work, so she could have Brian's children, absolutely lovely. Especially as she stared at her darling niece.

Her dad and Sean now stepped into the vestibule, both

looking handsome and polished, grinning when they spotted her. She was bemused to note that her dad held one hand behind his back.

"Cassie, I've never seen you looking so beautiful," her father said, kissing her cheek.

"Thanks, Dad."

"Yeah, Aunt Cassie, you look really cool," added Sean, prompting everyone to laugh.

Cassie gave her nephew a quick hug. "Thanks, sweetie. That's the nicest compliment I've had all night. And you look awfully cool yourself in that handsome suit."

The boy beamed.

Bill Brandon produced his hidden hand. "Oh, I almost forgot."

Cassie gasped in delight at the sight of the small bouquet of blue wildflowers wrapped in a handkerchief. "Blue columbine! Brian remembered. But how did he get them?"

Her dad placed the tiny bouquet in Cassie's hands. "He had one of his climbing buddies pick them this morning before he left Colorado to attend the wedding. Brian said to tell you they're for good luck."

"Oh, how sweet," said Cassie, wiping a tear. "I'll put some in my bridal bouquet."

"I get some, too, Aunt Cassie," insisted Emily.

"Of course, darling."

As Cassie placed several flowers in her bouquet and others in Emily's wreath, her dad was clapping his hands. "All right, troops. Heads up."

Lisa saluted. "Aye, aye, sir."

As everyone began lining up, Bill smiled proudly at his daughter and squeezed her hand. "Are you really happy honey?"

"Dad, I'm ecstatic."

He extended his arm. "Ready, then?"

She placed her hand on his arm. "I can't wait."

Bill turned to wink conspiratorially at the bridesmaids. "Of course I was tempted to bring along handcuffs this time, to shackle Cassie to the altar, just in case she might try to bolt again. But her mom wouldn't hear of it.''

The girls chuckled, and Cassie playfully punched her dad in the arm. ''Stop it. You know I'm not going anywhere. Except to Paris with Brian.''

''That's the spirit.'' Pausing to look her over, her dad appeared misty-eyed. ''In truth, honey, I knew you weren't going to run again. As soon as your mom and I met Brian and saw the two of you together, we knew he was the one for you.''

''He sure is,'' Cassie agreed rather hoarsely.

The bridal chorus swelled. Emily giggled, waved at her aunt, then started into the church. Sean and the bridesmaids followed.

''Well, honey, this is it,'' her dad said.

Cassie smiled at him through blissful tears. ''I'm ready.''

Cassie stepped with her dad into the church, nodding toward the many happy faces they passed, smiling lovingly at her mom. It was so ironic, she mused. Only six weeks ago, she'd dreaded walking up this very aisle. Now she was tempted to run joyously to the man she loved.

There Brian was, waiting for her before the altar. Never had he looked more handsome than he did in his black tux, his face lit up with love and pride as he watched her approach, his gaze unutterably tender as he spotted the blue columbine in her bouquet. Cassie's heart felt so full.

Then she had to grin as she spotted Brian's best man standing next to him—his very own, eighty-two-year-old grandfather! The tall, distinguished, silver-haired gentleman appeared pleased as punch as he watched his grandson's bride approach.

Cassie had been flabbergasted to learn of Brian's choice of best man at the rehearsal last night. After meeting his gracious grandad, she'd taken Brian aside. ''Your grandfather is wonderful—but he's your best man? Isn't that a bit unusual?''

Brian's eyes had gleamed with mischief. ''Actually, no.

Although Grandad is a widower, he's promised me he's never going to marry again. And given your tendency to go to the altar and fall in love with someone else…well, I just wasn't taking any chances, darling.''

Cassie's heart felt warmed by the memory. Her wonderful, spontaneous Brian. Life was going to be such an adventure, and so filled with love, with him by her side. She hoped she would never change him too much.

Moving closer to the altar, Cassie melted at the sight of her groom's adorable dimples, his huge grin. As she arrived by his side and took his arm, her glowing eyes told Brian just what she'd already said to him last night—that he was the *only* best man for her!

If you enjoyed what you just read,
then we've got an offer you can't resist!

# Take 2 bestselling love stories FREE!

# Plus get a FREE surprise gift!

 **HARLEQUIN®**
*Makes any time special ™*

# In celebration of Harlequin®'s golden anniversary

Enter to win a *dream!* You could win:

- A luxurious trip for two to *The Renaissance Cottonwoods Resort* in Scottsdale, Arizona, or

- A bouquet of flowers once a week for a year from **FTD**, or

- A $500 shopping spree, or

- A fabulous bath & body gift basket, including **K-tel's** *Candlelight and Romance* 5-CD set.

Look for **WIN A DREAM** flash on specially marked Harlequin® titles by Penny Jordan, Dallas Schulze, Anne Stuart and Kristine Rolofson in October 1999*.

**FTD**

**R**
**RENAISSANCE.**
**COTTONWOODS RESORT**
SCOTTSDALE, ARIZONA

**K-TEL**

*No purchase necessary—for contest details send a self-addressed envelope to Harlequin Makes Any Time Special Contest, P.O. Box 9069, Buffalo, NY, 14269-9069 (include contest name on self-addressed envelope). Contest ends December 31, 1999. Open to U.S. and Canadian residents who are 18 or over. Void where prohibited.

PHMATS-GR

"This book is DYNAMITE!"
—Kristine Rolofson

"A riveting page turner..."
—Joan Elliott Pickart

"Enough twists and turns to keep everyone guessing... What a ride!"
—Jule McBride

See what all your favorite authors are talking about.

*Coming October 1999 to a retail store near you.*

# HARLEQUIN WIN A NEW BEETLE® CONTEST
## OFFICIAL RULES
### NO PURCHASE NECESSARY TO ENTER

1. To enter, access the Harlequin romance web site (http://www.romance.net) and follow the on-screen instructions: Enter your name, address (including zip code), e-mail address (optional), and in 200 words or fewer your own original story concept—which has not won a previous prize/award nor has previously been reproduced/published—for a Harlequin Duets romantic comedy novel that features a Volkswagon® New Beetle®. OR hand-print or type the same requested information for on-line entry on an Official Entry Form or 8 1/2" x 11" plain piece of paper and mail it (limit: one entry per person per outer mailing envelope) via first-class mail to: Harlequin Win A New Beetle® Contest. In the U.S.: P.O. Box 9069, Buffalo, NY 14269-9069. In Canada: P.O. Box 637, Fort Erie, Ontario, Canada L2A 5X3.

   For eligibility, entries must be submitted through a completed Internet transmission—or if mailed, postmarked—no later than November 30, 1999. Mail-in entries must be received by December 7, 1999.

2. Story concepts will be judged by a panel of members of the Harlequin editorial and marketing staff based on the following criteria:
   - Originality and Creativity—40%
   - Appropriateness to Subject Matter—35%
   - Romantic Comedy/Humor—25%

   Decision of the judges is final.

3. All entries become the property of Torstar Corp., will not be returned, and may be published. No responsibility is assumed for incomplete, lost, late, damaged, illegible or misdirected e-mail, for technical, hardware or software failures of any kind, lost or unavailable network connections, or failed, incomplete, garbled or delayed computer transmission which may limit user's ability to participate in the contest, or for non- or illegibly postmarked, lost, late nondelivered or misdirected mail. Rules are subject to any requirements/limitations imposed by the FCC. Winners will be determined no later than January 31, 2000, and will be notified by mail. Winners will be required to sign and return an Affidavit of Eligibility, and a Release of Royalty/Ownership of submitted story concept within 15 days after receipt of same certifying his/her eligibility, that entry is his/her own original work, has not won a previous prize/award nor previously been reproduced/published. Noncompliance within that time period may result in disqualification and an alternate winner may be selected. All federal, state and local laws and regulations apply. Contest open only to residents of the U.S. and Canada who are 18 years of age or older, and is void wherever prohibited by law. Any litigation within the Province of Quebec respecting the conduct and awarding of a prize may be submitted to the Régie des alcools, des courses et des jeux. Employees of Torstar Corp., their affiliates, agents and members of their immediate families are not eligible. Taxes on prizes are the sole responsibility of winners. Entry and acceptance of any prize offered constitutes permission to use winner's name, photograph or other likeness for the purposes of advertising, trade and promotion on behalf of Torstar Corp. without further compensation to the winner, unless prohibited by law.

4. Prizes: Grand Prize—a brand-new Volkswagon yellow New Beetle® (approx. value: $17,000 U.S.) and a Harlequin Duets novel (approx. value: $6 U.S.). Taxes, licensing and registration fees are the sole responsibility of the winner; 2 Runner-Up Prizes—a Harlequin Duets novel (approx. value: $6 U.S. each).

5. For a list of winners (available after March 31, 2000), send a self-addressed, stamped envelope to Harlequin Win A Beetle® Contest 8219 Winners, P.O. Box 4200 Blair, NE 68009-4200.

Sweepstakes sponsored by Torstar Corp., P.O. Box 9042, Buffalo, NY 14269-9042

Volkswagon and New Beetle registered trademarks are used with permission of Volkswagon of America, Inc.

# Duets™ Win a New Beetle® Contest!

Starting September 1999, Harlequin Duets is offering you the chance to drive away in a Volkswagen® New Beetle®!

In addition to our grand prize winner, two more lucky entrants will also have their winning stories published in Harlequin Duets™ series and on our web site!

To enter our "WIN A NEW BEETLE®" contest, fill out this entry form and in 200 words or less write a romantic comedy short story for Harlequin Duets that features a New Beetle®.

See previous page for contest rules.
Contest ends November 30, 1999.

## Be witty, be romantic, have fun!

Name _____

Address _____

City _____  State/Province _____

Zip/Postal Code _____

**Mail to Harlequin Books: In the U.S.:** P.O. Box 9069, Buffalo, NY 14269-9069; **In Canada,** P.O. Box 637, Fort Erie, Ontario, L4A 5X3

\* No purchase necessary. To receive official contest rules and entry form, send a self-addressed stamped envelope to "Harlequin Duets Win A New Beetle® Contest Rules." In the U.S.: P.O. Box 9069, Buffalo, NY 14269-9069 (residents of Washington or Vermont may omit return postage); In Canada: P.O. Box 637, Fort Erie, ON, L4A 5X3. Or visit our web site for official contest rules and entry forms at www.romance.net/beetle.html. Open to U.S. and Canadian residents who are 18 or over. Void where prohibited.

Volkswagen and New Beetle are registered trademarks and used with permission of Volkswagen of America, Inc.

HARLEQUIN®
*Makes any time special*™

HDBUG-E